CONQUEST III

The Anarchy

CONQUEST III

The Anarchy

Tracey Warr

First Published 2020 by Impress Books

Impress Books, 13-14 Crook Business Centre, New Road, Crook, County
Durham, DL15 8QX

British Library Cataloguing in Publication Data

A catalogue record for this book is available from the British Library.

ISBN: 978-1-911293-43-9

In loving memory of Arthur Burton

CONTENTS

Cast of Characters

THE WELSH

The Royal House of Deheubarth

Nest ferch Rhys, daughter of the last Welsh king of Deheubarth, Rhys ap Tewdwr, who was killed and displaced by the invading Normans; former mistress of the Norman king Henry; widow of Gerald FitzWalter, steward of Pembroke Castle; former lover of Haith de Bruges; now married to Stephen de Marais, constable of Cardigan Castle

Gruffudd ap Rhys, claimant to the kingdom of Deheubarth; Nest's brother

Gwenllian ferch Gruffudd ap Cynan, wife of Gruffudd ap Rhys; daughter of King Gruffudd ap Cynan of Gwynedd; sister of Cadwallon, Owain and Cadwaladr ap Gruffudd ap Cynan

Anarawd ap Gruffudd ap Rhys, son of Gruffudd ap Rhys

Cadell ap Gruffudd ap Rhys, son of Gruffudd ap Rhys

The Royal House of Gwynedd

Cadwallon ap Gruffudd ap Cynan, eldest son of Gruffudd ap Cynan, the aging king of Gwynedd

Owain ap Gruffudd ap Cynan, second son of Gruffudd ap Cynan

Cadwaladr ap Gruffudd ap Cynan, third son of Gruffudd ap Cynan and

Ida, Flemish companion to Nest; sister of Haith; renegade nun known as Sister Benedicta in *Conquest I* and *II*; former lover of Amaury de Montfort

Amelina, Nest's Breton maid

Robert, unacknowledged, illegitimate son of Nest and Haith

Breri, a travelling Welsh bard and spy

THE NORMANS

The Royal Family

Henry I, king of England, duke of Normandy

Adelisa de Louvain, queen of England, duchess of Normandy; wife of King Henry

Maud, Holy Roman empress; daughter of King Henry and his first queen, Matilda of Scotland; wife of Henry V, Holy Roman emperor

Henry FitzEmpress, son of Empress Maud; future King Henry II

Other Normans and Flemings

Alice of Chester, daughter of the earl of Chester; sister of Ranulf de Gernon; wife of Richard de Clare, lord of Cardigan Castle

Amaury de Montfort, count of Evreux; rebel leader supporting William *Clito*

Berold, a butcher who survived the wreck of The White Ship

Gilbert de Clare, lord of Pembroke Castle; married to Isabel de Beaumont

Haith, sheriff of Pembroke; former lover of Nest

Henry FitzRoy, lord of Arberth; illegitimate son of Nest and King Henry

Isabel de Beaumont, wife of Gilbert de Clare; former mistress of King Henry; sister of Waleran de Meulan

Luc de La Barre, minor Norman nobleman and poet; supporter of William *Clito*

Mabel FitzRobert, countess of Gloucester; wife of Robert, earl of Gloucester; Nest's foster-sister

Maurice FitzGerald, castellan of Llansteffan Castle in Wales; son of Nest and Gerald FitzWalter

Maurice de Londres, castellan of Ogmore Castle in Wales

Miles of Gloucester, sheriff of Gloucester, lord of Brecknock

Morin du Pin, steward to Count Waleran de Meulan

Ranulf de Gernon, son of the earl of Chester; brother of Alice of Chester, lady of Cardigan Castle; half-brother of William de Roumare

Richard de Clare, lord of Cardigan Castle; married to Alice of Chester

Robert FitzRoy, earl of Gloucester; illegitimate son of King Henry; married to Mabel, Nest's foster-sister

Robert FitzStephen, son of Nest and Stephen de Marais

Stephen de Blois, count of Mortain; nephew of King Henry (named Etienne de Blois in *Conquest I* and *II*)

Stephen de Marais, constable of Cardigan Castle; husband of Nest ferch Rhys

Waleran de Meulan, count of Meulan; rebel leader supporting

William *Clito*

William *Clito* de Normandy, nephew of King Henry; claimant to the duchy of Normandy through his father, Robert Curthose, King Henry's oldest brother who is imprisoned in England

William de Pirou, minor Norman nobleman; dapifer or steward to the king

William FitzGerald, lord of Carew Castle and steward of Pembroke Castle; son of Nest and Gerald FitzWalter

and others.

Genealogies appear at the end of the book.

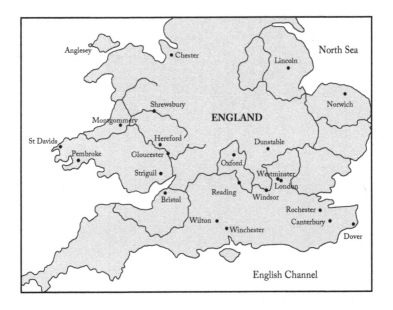

Map of Wales and England

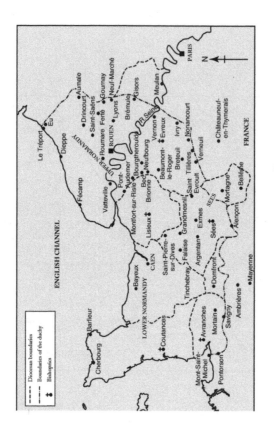

Map of Normandy and northern France

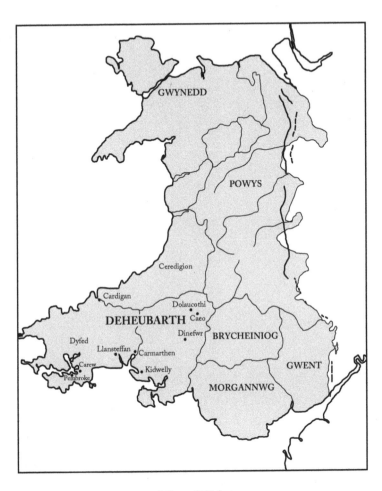

Map of Wales

Part One

1121–1123

Yr wylan deg ar lanw, dioer
Unlliw ag eiry neu wenlloer,
Dilwch yw dy degwch di,
Darn fal haul, dyrnfol heli.

O sea-bird, beautiful upon the tides,
White as the moon is when the night abides,
Or snow untouched, whose dustless splendour glows
Bright as a sunbeam and whose white wing throws
A glove of challenge on the salt sea-flood.

1

Lost Upon the Tide

June 1121, Cardigan Castle, Wales

'Stephen de Marais and Nest ferch Rhys.' The sound of my name
had barely ceased to resonate around the courtyard walls of Cardigan Castle when Haith shouldered his way through the crowd
to gape at me.

The prior pronounced a blessing on my unwanted marriage.
The coupling of my name with de Marais's sounded like a death
knell to my ears. I stared at Haith. It really was him. Alive. Not
drowned. I gazed at him, bewildered, holding my breath for
what became an uncomfortably long time. I breathed out and in.
With the intake of new air, I swung from numbness to panic as
I realised the full import of what was happening. Five minutes
ago, we all thought Haith was long dead, drowned with the other
three hundred souls who had gone down in the English Channel
with *The White Ship* before Christmas. Five minutes ago, Haith
was pushing his way through the crowd, hoping to find me,
hoping to delight us all with his unexpected resurrection. Five
minutes ago, I was unmarried.

Numb, I glanced back at the grey-haired prior. He stood on a
platform raised above the heads of the crowd who were gathered
before the chapel doors to witness my marriage and two other

weddings. In his heavy robes, the prior perspired under the June sun. A rivulet of sweat made its way down from the end of his eyebrow, rolled forward a little along his cheek bone, meandered around the pockmarks of his cheek, and fingered at the edge of his mouth. He had pronounced me married to Stephen de Marais and it could not be unsaid. He mopped at his upper lip with the broad, brown sleeve of his habit and began to intone the next blessing. I returned my gaze to Haith as the prior blessed the marriages of Isabel de Beaumont and Gilbert de Clare, and Sybil de Neufmarché and Miles of Gloucester. Isabel was the king's current mistress and was very conspicuously carrying his child. If the prior did not hurry up he might find himself with a christening to perform as well as three marriages.

The muscles in Haith's face clenched as he looked at me and worked to keep his expression bland. This marriage gaped raw between us, like the sudden slash in flesh at the thud of a butcher's blade. A memory of my first encounter with Haith flickered in my mind's eye. I was on a ferryboat on the Thames, eighteen, a wide-eyed girl attending court at Westminster for the first time. The boatman was about to push off from the pier when Haith yelled to wait for him. I had smiled at his funny Flemish accent. Haith was late rising from bed, as was his habit, and was a little dishevelled. He leaped into the boat and had to steady me, with a hand to my elbow, as the vessel rocked from his impact. I remembered the impression he made upon me: his height; his broad shoulders and long arms; his straight, butter-gold hair, cut in Flemish fashion at chin-level; his friendly, apologetic smile. Now, I am confronted with the man again, when I thought I had only memories left. He is not much changed. There are a few new grooves running the length of his cheeks where he has smiled too often and a few more silver strands in his yellow hair.

King Henry momentarily tore Haith's attention from me. The king grabbed Haith's shoulder and pulled him round to face him, enfolded him in a laughing embrace, pushed him out to arm's length again, shook his head in disbelief. The king repeatedly gripped and squeezed Haith's biceps, as if to check that he was no apparition. Looking at the two friends reunited, I was torn between sharing in Henry's delight at Haith's return, and my feelings of sour resentment towards the king.

With the three forced weddings performed today, King Henry renewed the Norman stranglehold on the south west kingdom of Wales that had formerly belonged to my father. He ensured that I, the daughter of the last Welsh king of this region, would continue disempowered. King Henry did not want to run the risk that I could be used again as a symbol of right to the land by a Welsh or Norman challenger to the king's own rule. The king's 'disposals' of noblewomen, including me, were his 'knitting' of strategic marriages and alliances. Most kings rule through the sword and the law, but Henry has added the bed to *his* repertoire, and makes exhaustive work of it.

At last, the king realised that I was staring at him and at Haith. Henry gave me a shamefaced grin, somewhere between smile and grimace. He felt guilty because he had forced me to this unwelcome marriage to de Marais. He knew he should have allowed me to marry Haith when we asked for that favour last year. He owed me that but, now, it is too late. Haith, the king's best friend, is returned from the dead, and I am married to the wrong man. The king's guilt can do us no good.

I dropped my new husband's hand and hitched the skirts of my fine red gown above my boots to squelch across the mud of the bailey towards them. Growing nearer, I slowed my pace. Like a sleepwalker, I arrived, unsure how I had come there, blank as to what I might say or do. The king and Haith turned to face me. I dropped the embroidered flounces of my skirts to settle over my muddy boots and longed to touch my finger to the smile line on Haith's cheek as I had used to. I clenched my fists at my sides.

'Lady Nest.' Haith's voice was level and stirred more recent memories of the time when he had been my lover.

'I am so glad that you live,' I said, struggling to find my voice. My resolution evaporated and I could not resist reaching for his hand. The king relinquished him to me.

'I am so glad that you live,' I said again, more slowly. I could think of nothing else to say.

Haith was also at a loss for words. Expressions of distress flickered across his face and in his eyes, and he struggled to suppress them.

With a false brightness I adapted the words of a poem he once gave to me: 'O, sea-bird, lost upon the tide. You return to us!' I turned my head aside, pretending to glance around the crowd, to conceal my blurring tears and muffle the break in my voice.

'What happened?' King Henry asked. 'How did you survive the wreck? We heard there was only one survivor—a butcher.'

I glanced back to Haith, quickly touching the tears from the corners of my eyes. He pulled his gaze from mine to answer the king. 'I went onboard *White Ship* at harbour but decided to disembark.' So many years in the king's employ, so many years at the Norman court, and he still speaks a garbled Norman French with a Flemish accent. He looked at me again and in that look is everything we cannot say now. Love. Regret. His pain that I am suddenly married to another man. Mine, that I am struggling with the shock that he lives after all, that I have found him, and, yet, I have so utterly lost him.

Haith and the king looked over my shoulder and I guessed that my new husband was hovering behind me, wanting to claim me. 'Lady Nest?' de Marais's voice was hesitant. I gave no response and did not turn to him. I failed to prevent the contempt that I felt at the sound of de Marais's voice from glinting in my eyes as I stared at the king. Reluctantly, I let go of Haith's hand.

I took a deliberate breath again, and my voice was barely a whisper: 'I am glad.' I dipped my head to them and moved away, looking for my maid, Amelina, aghast to think that I must find a way to live with this de Marais and without Haith. I was aware that de Marais was dogging my footsteps, but I paid him no heed. 'Lady Nest?' he said again behind me. My son Henry tried to step into my path and speak with me. He, too, felt guilty that he and his younger brothers had concurred with the king's decision to marry me to de Marais. I could not speak of anything to anyone, with my heart and head so full of Haith and my eyes brimming to betray my grief to all the gawpers gathered here for the weddings. 'Later,' I breathed to Henry, as I brushed past him. From the corner of my eye, I saw de Marais staring at me with his mouth open, wondering where I meant to go and why I was ignoring him. I did not meet his eyes.

I headed with determination towards the hall where Amelina confronted me. 'He's alive then,' she said.

I sat on the bench next to her and tried to gather my wits, to recover from the shock of Haith's return. Her hands moved towards me. She was thinking to give me comfort. I saw her read my face and stance and think better of her intention. If she held me I would weep uncontrollably. She crossed her arms instead. 'What now?' she asked.

I twisted the ring on my finger that de Marais had just given to me. It was a fine ring: a thick gold filigree band with a broad, complex knot on its face. I took the ring off and placed it, with deliberation, on the table. I pushed it away from me, further across the table.

Amelina watched and pursed her lips. 'We have to prepare you for the wedding feast,' she said firmly, ignoring the implication of my action. 'And the bedding,' she added, in a quieter voice that was less sure of itself.

'I cannot engage in this marriage now. Yet. I have to leave.'

Amelina pulled a face. 'You can't do that! De Marais will be incandescent if you leave. The king will be furious.'

'I can't go to Pembroke.' I continued thinking aloud. 'It is not mine anymore.' The king had transferred Pembroke Castle, which had been my home for the last fifteen years, to Isabel and

Gilbert. By marrying me to a mere constable, enmeshing me again in Norman intermarriage, and taking Pembroke away from me, the king sought to further subsume the claims of my royal Welsh lineage. 'I can't go to Carew. It is steeped in memories of Gerald.' Gerald FitzWalter had been my first husband and the father of most of my children, apart from my oldest son who was the king's, and my youngest, who was Haith's.

'Your sons would be shamed …' Amelina attempted.

'I can't do it right now!'

'The marriage should be consummated, Nest,' she whispered gently. 'In time ….'

I interrupted the platitude that she was forming. 'No.'

Her eyes were liquid with sympathy. She took my hand and tried to unfurl my fist but I curled it again. I started to shake and she could no longer resist pulling me into a hard embrace, squashing me against her breasts. I smelt the camomile scent of her light brown hair, was enveloped by her warmth, and felt my own cold tears wet against her ear. I allowed myself a couple of gasping sobs and a few moments of comfort and then forced her from me. I stood, pulling her to her feet. 'I will go to Llansteffan.' Ida, my companion and friend and Haith's sister, was at Llansteffan and she could give me counsel. 'Perhaps if I do not allow a consummation of the marriage, if I escape now, I can find a way out of it.'

'You're married. In front of witnesses. There's no way out,' Amelina stated. Seeing that the resolution on my face did not change, she tried a more feeble protest: 'The renovations at Llansteffan are not finished. It is not fit for you.'

I ignored her words. 'Ida needs to hear the news. She will be heart-glad that her brother is alive, after all.'

'Does he know about her?' Amelina asked, meaning did Haith know that Ida had escaped her former life in a convent as the nun Benedicta and was living with me.

I shook my head. 'I doubt he knows yet. I will go to Llansteffan,'

I repeated.

Amelina studied the set of my face. She had been my maid since we were both children and she could read me well. 'We'd best go, then,' she said, 'before they realise what we are about.'

I acknowledged her grim smile with my own. 'Yes, Amelina!'

'I'll meet you in the stables with your riding clothes.'

I watched her move hastily to climb the stairs to the upper bedchamber. If I lingered for any more time in the hall, de Marais would come looking for me. I took a deep breath, glanced at the discarded wedding ring on the table, and moved into the servant's passageway, striding past the buttery and the pantry, stepping through a side door, and taking the back route to avoid being seen.

In the stables, I saddled our horses. Amelina was soon back. She stripped off my wedding finery and crammed the red gown, neck first, unceremoniously, into a saddle bag. It was odd to see her treat the gown in that way, when I was so used to seeing her carefully folding and husbanding all my possessions. The upended, squashed flounces of the red dress spilled from the top of the dusty saddle bag like a sea anemone pinched between brute fingers. 'We must be quick. De Marais is asking where you are.' She dropped my riding tunic over my head and had me swiftly booted and cloaked for the journey. Twilight was falling. 'Will we ride through the night, then, without an escort?' she asked, her eyes wide and anxious.

'Yes. It's the surest way for us to reach Llansteffan unhindered. I have a knife.' I drew the blade from the scabbard at my waist to show her its long gleam in the dim, brown light of the stables. It screeched as I let it slide back into its sheath.

'What then? When we reach Llansteffan.'

'I will consider that when I get there. I want to stand on my own ground.'

2

Three More Weddings

August 1122, Pont Audemer, Normandy

Haith opened his eyes on the prince's lividly pale face inches from his own in the water. Bubbles streamed frantically upwards from Haith's mouth, but nothing came from the boy. He gathered the prince's tunic in his fist and kicked, trying to raise them both to the surface but the boy was a dead weight on Haith's oxygen-starved limbs. The scissoring of his legs grew feeble and ineffective and his chest was paralysed with pain. He raised his face hoping for light but the dark water stretched on and on above their heads. The bubbles from his own mouth slowed and stopped. Haith's grasp on the prince failed, and he floated helpless against the boy's unmoving chest, all power draining from his long, muscled limbs. Haith's big hands floated aimlessly, like the slick fronds of seaweed in the current. The dead eyes of the prince opened, gelatinous, inky black and deep as the sea that would let neither of them go.

Haith sat up in the bed gulping for air, cold sweat pooling on his chest and the back of his neck. 'By the Lord's death!' He looked around, disoriented by the strange room. The inn in Normandy, he told himself. He was here, and not in the cold, grey swell of the suffocating sea that was still so vivid from his dream. He reached for the beaker on the floor beside the creaking bed but it was empty. Could he have saved Prince William from drowning if he had boarded *The White Ship*, instead of disembarking to follow Stephen de Blois? He swung his long legs from the bed and sat on the edge for a moment, pressing his fingertips to his eyelids, trying to dispel the horrid images of the drowned prince. Most likely, he could not have saved him. If Haith had been onboard that night when the ship foundered, he probably would have drowned with all the rest, all three hundred of those souls, including two of King Henry's illegitimate children and his only, legitimate, male heir. The least Haith could do was lay his suspicions about the wreck to rest.

After stumbling upon Nest's wedding at Cardigan, Haith had returned with the king to London to make his first appearance as sheriff of Pembroke at the Michaelmas Court of the Exchequer. He should have returned to his post in Wales as soon as the business of the court was concluded, but instead he travelled to Normandy. He wanted to be away from where Nest was. Pembroke was too close for comfort to Cardigan where she lived with her new husband.

Haith turned his thoughts away from the painful memories of Nest and focused again on the sinking of the ship. With the king's son dead, his nephews Thibaut and Stephen de Blois stood next in line to Henry's throne. Haith had no suspicions of Thibaut who was an honourable man and had been nowhere near Barfleur on the fateful night of the sinking. But Stephen had been on the ship and left it minutes before it sailed carrying all its passengers to their deaths. Had Stephen conspired to cause the sinking and make himself heir to the king?

Haith could not get the suspicion from his mind and must pursue it. He had a few threads to pull on: a butcher named Berold who was the sole survivor of the shipwreck; William de Pirou, the king's dapifer, who had been listed on the rollcall of victims, but then blithely appeared back at court without explanation; the two monks from Tiron whom Haith had witnessed following Count Stephen from the ship. He doubted that he would get anywhere probing amongst Stephen's servants and that was far too risky. Stephen de Blois was powerful at court. The king's friendship with Haith would not weigh enough if he, a mere sheriff, raised the ire of the king's nephew. Haith frowned. It irked him that Stephen, who had formerly been known to all as Etienne de Blois, had lately styled himself Stephen—the English version of his name. It spoke of pretensions to be Henry's successor that had received no warrant from the king.

Haith could not return Henry's drowned children and young nobles to him but, if there had been foul play, he could prove it and protect Henry from its intent. This self-imposed mission in Normandy kept him away from having to encounter the sight of Nest forced to another man. There was nothing he could do for her either. She was wed to de Marais and there was an end to their hopes. Surely, his presence nearby could only make things worse for her. He shook his head, trying now, reluctantly, to empty it of visions of Nest—the long, gleaming curls of her black hair on the pillow beside him, her blue eyes laughing with him. His memory lingered on the curve of her wide mouth. He lurched to his feet, looking for escape from the images in his mind, and narrowly avoided a collision with a ceiling beam. He had to get water. He lent to grip the beaker again, briefly considered that he was only wearing a loin cloth, but no one else would be about at this hour. Haith padded out barefoot to the inn courtyard, enjoying the cool night air on his naked skin and the scent of jasmine that was twining around a low wall. The stone basin of the spigot was cold against his palm as he lent against it to pump cold water into his beaker. Hundreds of crickets chirped on the riverbank as Haith closed his eyes and swallowed down the water.

'Sir Haith de Bruges,' he shouted up to the guards' query at the gate of Pont Audemer Castle. The drawbridge began to lower and he kicked his horse on. He had tracked the Rouen butcher named Berold to the lands of Count Waleran de Meulan. Pont Audemer was one of Waleran's main strongholds. This Berold, the survivor of the wreck of *The White Ship*, had no business being on the ship. That was a mystery that Haith intended to prod at. When the butcher had been located and interrogated, Haith could speed on to Fontevraud Abbey and visit his sister Benedicta. She had not replied to his letters and was, perhaps, still unaware that he had survived the wreck. Or maybe she had immersed herself in illuminating a new manuscript and was merely neglecting her correspondence. Haith was unconvinced by his own guess, but suppressed his anxiety. He had to tackle one problem at a time. Worrying would not get him to Fontevraud and to the reassuring sight of his sister's face any quicker.

Once inside the courtyard, Haith was forced to immediately dismount because of the great crowd of people and rushing servants before him. He grabbed the arm of a passing maid. 'What's going on here? Why so many people?'

She grinned at him. 'Three weddings, sir! That's bound to require a lot of people, no?' She stood on tiptoe to get somewhere near his ear and pulled him down nearer to her whispering mouth. 'I might be interested in trying out for a fourth if you find yourself free later.'

Haith laughed and shook his head. 'Let me get my foot in the door won't you? Which way to the stables?'

Seated in the hall, Haith watched the servants' frantic preparations. Tabletops were hauled in and set up. Delicate glassware teetered dangerously on trestles and shivered with the passing of heavy boots. Six maids, ranged in a straight line across the breadth of the hall, advanced upon Haith, strewing sweet-smelling rushes from baskets held in the crook of their elbows.

One of the maids was the forward girl he had encountered in the courtyard. She smiled flirtatiously at him and he sighed at the dimple in her cheek that reminded him of Nest.

Haith ascertained in casual conversation with other guests that the brides were Count Waleran's sisters: Adeline, Aubree, and Matilda, and they were marrying Hugh de Montfort-sur-Risle, Hugh de Châteauneuf-Thimerais, and William Lovel. The king's permission was required for all noble marriages, but Henry was certainly unaware that these three daughters of an earl were preparing to marry here, within the hour. The other business in Normandy must be hurried and Haith needed to return to England as soon as he could with the news. King Henry would be furious at this flouting of his authority, and wary. A bread board covered in flour had not yet been cleared away and sat on the table next to Haith. He smoothed the flour flat with the palm of his hand and dotted his finger into the white surface, plotting the locations of the bridegrooms' castles. He added this castle of Pont Audemer and Waleran's other holdings. Yes, that would make a very good frontline if everyone here were planning another rebellion against Henry's rule in Normandy. Haith suddenly felt conscious of being alone, a supporter of the king, in a nest of rebels. Was he imagining it or were people looking askance at him? He swiped his palm across the flour, erasing the map.

A maid nudged Haith's foot with her broom and he lifted up both his legs so that she could swipe beneath him and the bench he sat on. Haith's enormous hound stayed immobile beside him, ignoring increasingly irritated prods from the broom and exclamations from the maid until Haith roused from his distraction and commanded the dog to shift.

The brides' brother, the instigator of this triple wedding, Count Waleran de Meulan, was standing near the hearth talking with the three bridegrooms and his steward, Morin du Pin. Waleran's presence here was a surprise. Haith had merely stopped at Pont

Audemer looking for a short respite for his horse and had not expected to encounter either Waleran or these surreptitious marriages. Haith had known his host and his twin brother, Robert, since their early childhood and often seen them at court when they were the king's wards. He had never liked Waleran, viewing him as an arrogant stripling who garnered over-indulgence from the king.

Waleran looked up at the maid's grumbling and noticed Haith. The count headed across the hall, frowning at this uninvited guest. Waleran's wedding outfit was a gold-embroidered purple tunic that suited his dark colouring and emphasised the newfound breadth of his shoulders. The young man moving purposefully towards Haith had recently inherited vast swathes of land in Normandy and France and become one of the most important Norman barons.

'Haith! I did not know you were in Normandy. Welcome.' Waleran's expression contradicted his words. His face showed the perplexed annoyance that he was likely feeling at finding one of the king's compatriots observing this unlicensed event.

'Thank you. It is your sisters who are marrying today?'

'Yes. Will you join the feast?' Hospitality could not be what Waleran really wanted to offer to Haith. The twins had been frustrated when King Henry delayed granting their inheritances to them beyond their minorities, preferring to keep their English and Norman lands safely, and profitably, in his own hands for a few more years. Perhaps Waleran also felt some resentment at the king's treatment of his eldest sister, Isabel, who had been the most recent of Henry's many mistresses. Isabel had first been betrothed to Amaury de Montfort but the betrothal had been quietly dropped when the king took Waleran's sister to his bed. Perhaps she and her brothers had expected that she would be the next queen and were bitterly disappointed when the king married Adelisa de Louvain instead. Isabel, in turn, found herself married off to the lord of Pembroke in the far reaches of Wales.

Haith was as surprised to find himself witnessing this defiance of the king's law, as Waleran was to find Haith sitting in his hall. The servant who had greeted Haith and sent him straight in had assumed he was one of the wedding guests and did not announce his name, else Haith would surely have been turned away.

Since, in courtesy, there was no choice to it, Haith indicated his acceptance of Waleran's offer of hospitality and Waleran smiled insincerely in return. 'What brings you to Normandy, Haith? You are a long way from the savage outposts of Wales!'

Haith ignored the slight to his office as sheriff of Pembroke. 'Yes. The king sends me on his business,' he lied. King Henry had no more idea that Haith was in Normandy, than he knew that Count Waleran was giving his sisters away in marriage to three castellans with lands and castles that were strategically well-placed for brewing a new rebellion in Normandy.

Waleran waited to be further enlightened on Haith's business. When no further information was offered, the count frowned and moved away to greet other guests.

Standing before their brother and a priest, the three Beaumont sisters placed their hands into the grasp of each of their respective husbands. Haith tried to suppress the echo of the three other weddings that he witnessed in Cardigan last year: Gilbert de Clare marrying Isabel de Beaumont, the oldest sister of Count Waleran and these three girls, and visibly carrying the king's child in her womb; Miles of Gloucester marrying Sybil de Neufmarché. Haith closed his eyes, reluctant to remind himself of the third marriage, but, like a battle wound, it would not heal by ignoring it. And Stephen de Marais, constable of Cardigan Castle, marrying the Lady Nest ferch Rhys. Haith could only look on at the devastation of his happiness and hers, keeping the grief from his face for her sake. The king's command could not be contested. Haith took a long draught of the wine set before him, blinked again momentarily, as if this feeble gesture might wipe the memory burnt into his eyeballs.

'Sir Haith de Bruges, is it?'

Haith opened his eyes on a strikingly handsome man. 'Aye, my lord.' The man's clothes and bearing set him out as a person of importance. He was not young; around Haith's own age of 50. His thick blond hair, like Haith's, was mixed with grey and white strands, and there the resemblance ended. This man had expressive, deep brown eyes and his face had the symmetry and colours of a fresh bloomed peach. He looked like the hero of a troubadour's *roman*.

'Amaury de Montfort, count of Evreux.' Amaury bowed.

Haith returned the courtesy. 'Haith de Bruges, sheriff of Pembroke.'

'And a member of the duke's *familia regis*, I believe?'

Here, in Normandy, Henry was known as the duke, whilst in England, he was called king. Haith bowed his head modestly in agreement with de Montfort's description. Haith had been a member of Henry's military household since their shared childhood. He studied the man before him. This was the king's greatest enemy in Normandy, and he was brazenly introducing himself to one of the king's greatest friends. De Montfort bore out everything Haith had heard about his charm and his effrontery, but his next words were a surprise: 'How is your sister?'

'Benedicta?' Haith swallowed astonishment with a mouthful of wine.

'I met her at Fontevraud, and in Reims too.'

Haith hesitated, searching for reasons why his sister's name should be on the lips of this man. 'She is well, I believe. I haven't heard from her in some time and plan to visit her in Fontevraud next week.'

'Ah! I wonder if you might do me a kindness, then?'

'I will endeavour to, my lord.'

'I have a gift I would like to give to Benedicta, to Sister Benedicta. Would you convey it to her?'

Haith's confusion grew, and he struggled to conceal it. Why was the count of Evreux giving a gift to a nun? Haith knew that Benedicta had spied on Amaury's sister, Bertrade de Montfort, the former queen of France, whilst Bertrade was in the cloister at Fontevraud Abbey, but he could think of no respectable reason for a gift from de Montfort to Benedicta.

'It's nothing,' Amaury's tone was urbane. 'A trifle. Just a small book of Ovid's poems that I came across and knew she would like, from some conversation I had with her.' Reading the confusion on Haith's face, he added, 'For the abbey library.'

'Yes, of course.' What subterfuge was here, beneath the words? A gift for the abbey library would be sent to the abbess. Why send it, in particular, to Benedicta? The library was his sister's sphere of responsibility, but even so, it was odd. She used Ovid's poems as a cipher to communicate with Haith sometimes. Was de Montfort making a veiled threat? Haith held his gaze. De Montfort's expression did not appear threatening.

'Excellent,' said de Montfort, 'One moment, I have it to hand, in my baggage.' He beckoned a servant and gave him instructions. The man returned to them a few minutes later carrying a small parcel wrapped in fine black wool. 'Ah!' Amaury took the package and handed it to Haith. 'I am very grateful to you.'

Haith nodded, still at a loss for words. Amaury bowed and withdrew to converse with other guests while Haith looked anxiously at de Montfort's elegant, retreating back. Had harm come to Benedicta? From him? She had played a part in the downfall of Robert de Bellême, de Montfort's compatriot in the previous rebellion, and Amaury must know that. The sooner Haith concluded his business with the butcher, the sooner he could get to the abbey and be reassured about his sister.

There was a sudden hushing of the babble of voices and a palpable shift in the crowd standing about the hall as they parted to allow entry to a new guest. A richly dressed young man stepped into the space created for him. His dark blue cloak swept the floor at his heels and was held in place with a magnificent ruby clasp. Waleran de Meulan hurried to welcome the newcomer and knelt to him. The whispered rumour: 'The *Clito*' slid around the edges of the hall. The *Clito* was the Norman name given to the heir of the duke of Normandy. Here he was, in person, then: William *Clito*, the son of Henry's older brother, the pretender to the throne of Normandy, and the king's nemesis.

The last time Haith had seen William he was four years old. Henry defeated his own brother Robert Curthose in battle, imprisoned him and took his position as duke of Normandy. Robert Curthose, this young man's father, was still in prison in England, some twenty-four years later. Despite the years that had passed, Haith would have easily guessed at the young man's identity. He had the same stocky build, the same dark eyes as Henry and was evidently his kinsman. Henry had not imprisoned the boy and had come to rue that kind decision in recent years. William *Clito* had been in arms against Henry, trying to reclaim the duchy since he came of age, and he was the rallying point for rebellion. Since King Henry's only legitimate son had drowned, William *Clito* was, for many, the obvious male heir to Normandy. His cause was supported by the French king Louis and by many lords, such as Amaury de Montfort and Waleran de Meulan, who desired the separate rule of England and Normandy. Haith could see how a young man, this William *Clito*, would appear a more glamorous option to the inflexible grip of King Henry for the likes of young Waleran. Haith became aware of eyes upon him and looked away from William *Clito* to meet Waleran's glare. His host could hardly be pleased that Haith's unexpected presence had revealed this nascent rebellion too early. The gaze of Waleran's steward and veteran warrior, Morin du Pin, was also focused on Haith in nothing resembling a friendly manner.

Morin had been entrusted with the guardianship of Waleran

and his twin brothers as teenagers when their father died and he was a fierce guard dog. Morin's grey hair was cropped close to his large head and his beard was plaited, Viking-style. One of his ears had been shorn away in combat, and he made no effort to conceal the ugly scar on the side of his head. He had berserker eyes that had terrified many an opponent on the battlefield. Haith noted that Morin was wearing a short chain mail tunic, quite unnecessarily for a wedding. The chainmail was a symptom of Morin's resolute attitude, which was also evinced by his ramrod stance. Haith knew that Morin did the dirty work for the urbane Count Waleran so that he could keep his hands lily-clean.

Haith sat through the feast, thinking how best to withdraw from the castle before his host decided to take action against him. He smiled and conversed and waited. The drinking dragged on long into the night and Haith sat it out. When the last drunk rolled from the bench to the floor, Haith made an appearance of settling down, wrapped in his cloak. His hound warmed his right side, and a drunken, heavily snoring wedding guest stretched against his other. The crowded hall reverberated with the wheezing of men and dogs and smelt of evaporating sweat and alcohol. Every now and then, the scaffold of logs in the hearth collapsed further in on itself and the night chill in the vast hall dropped a few more degrees. Waleran and Amaury knew that Haith would tell tales to the king of these marriages, of brewing rebellion, and of the appearance of William *Clito* in Waleran's hall. It was likely that an assassin was moving through the sleeping hall, inching towards Haith, intending to slip a knife between his ribs and stop his story.

3

The Inky Clerk

August 1122, Cardigan Castle, Wales

Time passes, and things happen. The view from my window casement at Cardigan Castle was doing nothing to improve my disconsolate mood. I, Princess Nest of Deheubarth, was married to *him*. And that was that. A thick, grey fret swirled and shifted above the river, mirroring the lowering grey of the sky. I had tried to shake my depressed feelings for several days but this morning, I resolved to indulge them for one whole day and then rise tomorrow and put them behind me. It could be worse. He was not bad-natured or violent. On occasion, he was, in fact, quite kind. Nevertheless, Stephen de Marais was an idiot. Two months after my flight from Cardigan to Llansteffan, my sons William and Maurice had remonstrated with me to return to this unwanted marriage. My behaviour was detrimental to their standing in the Norman community they told me. Never mind my feelings and my standing. My argument with my sons still resounded in my memory. William and Maurice had come to Llansteffan and pleaded with me to cease shaming them in the matter of my marriage. 'We are already slighted by our peers, Mother,' William complained, 'for our part-Welsh heritage.'

'And why would I have sympathy with that,' I said angrily,

'being entirely Welsh!'

Now that I had calmed down, I tried to understand their position. They were trying to be Norman but were regarded as half-Welsh mongrels by their fellows. William had just been appointed steward at Pembroke Castle by Gilbert de Clare, a position that his father had held before him, and I was glad for him, proud of him. Since there was no out from my marriage, it seemed that I should do my best to protect my sons from the contempt of the Norman lords in Wales, to maintain their positions.

My face and my body betrayed me. My hair gleamed, my dratted dimples came and went and there were no outward signs of my grief and frustration. The ends of my two long, black plaits lay curled in my lap. I picked up first one, and then the other, squeezing them hard as if it were my hair's fault that it showed no signs of my distress, as if I would wish it to turn white in protest at finding myself married in my forties to a man in his twenties who I could not care for and whose station was far below my own. Richard de Clare, the lord of Cardigan Castle, had complete faith in de Marais as his constable. I could see that de Marais's management of the garrison was more than competent, but in matters of conversation.... I closed my eyes and threw my hands up in despair, in pantomime conversation with myself.

Embarrassed, I looked around the chamber quickly to see if anyone had witnessed me talking to myself. Amelina had just retrieved the bed canopy from the laundress and was standing on a stool refixing it above the bed to ward off spiders and flies. Would that it could ward off my husband too. I looked at my companion, Ida, who had been a nun and known then as Benedicta. She was Haith's sister and resembled him, so that I was reminded of my loss of him every time I looked at her. She was bareheaded. She always flung her headveil off the moment she entered the privacy of my chambers, a practice she told me she had acquired as a nun. She was absorbed in the book held open on her lap, her fair head bent over it, her hair the exact same colour as Haith's. My small son, Robert, was playing on the floor with his wooden horse. He did not notice my odd behaviour. I smiled. At him, at myself, but then my mouth curved down again at the return of thoughts on my husband. The man was a nitwit. He had no interest whatsoever in literature or music. He had no sense of humour. There was no malice in him, but, often, I found that I could hardly hold my seat and keep my face in a semblance of politeness, when he spoke such drivel.

I watched Amelina humming her way around my chamber. She stopped suddenly in her track and sniffed dramatically at the scents rising from the kitchen. 'Cabbage! If thou desirest to die, eat cabbage in August! We'll have none of it.' Ida and I exchanged an amused glance. Amelina's head was stuffed with adages that she insisted were all true and we must abide by them. She set out my hairbrush in front of the burnished mirror. I looked on sourly as she splayed out a handful of long blue ribbons. 'I'll brush your hair now, Nest?'

I moved to sit before the mirror. Around the patchy burnishments of the mirror, if I shifted my head to and fro, I could find my dark blue eyes staring gloomily back at me. 'Tch! Keep your head still, my lady!' Amelina first loosed and unwove my plaits, and then began her rhythmic brushing. My face was not greatly lined but it was the face of a woman, not a girl. Amelina reached for a ribbon to weave through my hair.

I caught her arm. 'No ribbons.'

'But they can cover up the grey threads, my lady.'

She was skilled at weaving the ribbons so that the grey in my hair was near-invisible. 'I am not a girl to be trinketed out.'

'For your boy-husband?' she wheedled.

'The boy can please himself. I have no cause to do so.'

She clucked her tongue but dropped a hand briefly to caress my shoulder in sympathy, holding my gaze in the mirror.

De Marais had driven away my children. None of them liked him and rarely visited because of it. My daughter Angharad had gone early to live in the household of her betrothed husband at Manorbier. She could have stayed with me a while longer, but she begged to go, unhappy to see me unhappy and grieved at the changes in our lives. My eldest son, Henry, told me he could not stand de Marais's company and that I must visit him in Arberth in the future. 'Mother, come and live with me. He might not even notice!' he declared on his last visit, which had been some six months ago.

I missed my eldest son, but unfortunately de Marais *would* notice. If I were gone, he would notice that he could not boast to anyone that would listen that his wife was a royal princess. He would notice that I was not in my bed for his weekly visits to get himself an heir. Since I am a Welsh woman, he believes me primitive and uncultured. He had made it clear that Prince Owain ap Cadwgan's rape of me makes me tainted in his eyes. 'I was rather surprised that Gerald FitzWalter took you back as his wife after that sordid episode,' he told me, his small mouth pursed in distaste. On the other hand, he is proud of my former association with the king and the fact that my eldest son is the king's son. My royalty and the king's stroke his snobbery.

Robert moved to sit at my feet, dragging with him a heavy book that Ida had found in the castle library. She looked up and grinned at him as he turned the pages of the bestiary, which was filled with exotic, colourful images. I reached my hand to Robert's fair head. 'What have you there, Robert?'

My son turned enthusiastic, pale blue eyes—Haith's eyes—to me to tell me all about the fabulous animals in the book.

'Have you written to your brother yet, Ida?' I asked, when Robert returned to his quiet study of the book. I found it difficult to say Haith's name out loud, although I voiced it over and over in my head whenever I had a private moment to myself.

Ida was shamefaced. 'I can't find the words to tell him.' She had not yet told Haith that she had left her nunnery in Anjou and was hiding in plain sight in my household. Very few people in Wales or England would recognise her and she should be safe from exposure in my service.

I frowned. 'You *must* tell him. Perhaps it would be easier in person? I could invite Haith to visit us here.' I heard the reluctance in my own voice. I would have to face him sooner or later. It was a wonder with his work as sheriff of Pembroke that we had not encountered each other before now. I struggled not to remember him, not to remember his hands on my body, his mouth on mine.

There is no joy in my coupling with my husband. I am fifteen years his senior and know he has a young mistress in the town. Sixteen and buxom, Amelina says. Our sexual congress is solely about getting an heir for him. I made a fool of him by abandoning him on the day of our wedding and he has not forgiven me for it. He makes no attempt to make me feel that he finds me beautiful or irresistible. Why should he when I am near old enough to be his mother and have a body that has undergone pregnancy and childbirth seven times. I am no nubile virgin for him. And I make no pretence that the marriage is palatable to me. He is all business-like in his visits to my bedchamber. He arrives, plants his seed, thanks me and leaves. The first few times, I wept bitterly, thinking of the men who had loved me, who had touched me in love and passion: King Henry; then my first husband, Gerald; and then Haith, Robert's father. But now, I am simply grateful that de Marais's visits are quick, infrequent and he does not stay or ask me for words of love that would be wormwood on my tongue. And, I remind myself, since this is my day of wallowing in misery, this marriage is nowhere near as bad as my time as the hostage of Prince Owain.

'Ida, would you help me lay the cloth in the hall below?' Amelina asked.

'Of course.' Ida marked the place in her book and rose to

accompany Amelina from the room.

When they were gone, I reached inside my small casket for my journal and stylus. I ran my hands over the dark crimson leather of the journal's cover and traced its decorations with my finger. Interlacing patterns in bright yellow, pale yellow and blue-grey twisted inside two narrow, rectangular frames at the top and bottom of the cover. In the middle of the cover, there was a drawing of a chalice with projecting stems that sprouted leaves and fruits. I turned the book over and traced the bright yellow and blue-grey crosses that decorated its back. King Henry had given the book to me years ago, calling me his 'inky clerk' because I liked to scribble down the occasional note on the events of my life. I felt that I had reached such a plateau, after the initial trauma of my forced marriage last year, it was time to commune with myself. Sometimes, I found that I did not truly know what I felt until I had committed it to writing.

I have been displaced at Pembroke Castle by Isabel de Beaumont and Gilbert de Clare. Richard de Clare and his young wife, Alice of Chester, command Cardigan Castle, which is now my home. The de Clare family are preeminent in my father's former kingdom, and their uncle Walter holds Striguil on the Gower. Through their wives, Gilbert and Richard de Clare are connected to the two strongest earldoms in England: to Robert de Beaumont, Earl of Warwick, who is Isabel's brother and to Ranulf Le Meschin, Earl of Chester, who is Alice's father. When Isabel was delivered of the king's child, a daughter, I visited her, and it was harsh for me to see her mistress in Pembroke, in the hall that had belonged to Gerald and me, and before that, to my father.

Richard de Clare and Alice of Chester are frequently away from Cardigan. Richard attends on the king or travels to oversee his estates in England, and Alice always travels with him. At those times, de Clare works through written instructions to my husband and it has been some mercy to me that de Marais has been kept very busy managing the castle and estate. Here, I am merely the wife of the castle's constable. The fact that I am a princess of the Welsh royal house of Deheubarth is no longer of any significance in these days of Norman rule. In my father's former kingdom, I am the only Welsh landowner remaining and what I own is little enough. In mid and north Wales, the Welsh rulers continue to stand their ground against Norman incursions, with Madog king in Powys and the aging Gruffudd ap Cynan king in Gwynedd, but here, in Deheubarth, my brother, who should be king, is reduced to poverty and lives under threat of execution.

I remind myself that my miserable marriage to de Marais does not compare with the time when my father and brothers were massacred and I was first taken into a Norman household at Cardiff Castle. Yet, I have loathed the stifling of myself that I have had to exercise to survive this first year with de Marais.

I looked up abruptly from my scribbling at the unmistakeable sound of glass shattering on the stone floor of the hall below. Robert held his toy horse in mid-air and gaped at me. 'Broken?' he said. 'Need mended?'

'Yes, sweet. Something is broken. Let's go and see.' I took his little hand and helped him, laboriously, one step at a time, down the big steps and bends of the stone staircase.

In the hall, de Marais was standing, hands on hips, hovering over Amelina as she crouched to sweep up shards of pale glass. I saw a fragment of incised griffin tail. 'My goblet from Sybil?' I tried to keep the tone of my voice neutral, but it sounded somewhere between whine and wail, nonetheless.

Amelina glanced up. I looked from her rueful face to de Marais's flushed features. 'You broke it, husband?'

'Yes. I apologise dear. I believe you have another, no?'

'They were a pair. A gift from my foster-mother, Sybil de Montgommery. I have had them since I was a child.'

'I do apologise, dear. But it is simply a goblet after all. I will get you a new pair at the next market.'

I turned my face from him and moved towards the fire with Robert still clinging to my hand, but now more to give me comfort than for me to aid him. When I sat by the fire to make that the new object of my gaze, Robert climbed into my lap and put his arms about my neck, sensing my dismay. I did not glance at Ida who took a seat opposite me but I felt her sympathetic eyes upon me.

There was no point in telling the fool that I had carried the goblets with me through all the tribulations of my life for so many years without so much as a slight crack; that I had first used them to drink with King Henry, my first love; that they carried my heart. And as for his offer of buying new ones next market day; he would not find such fine work anywhere. Sybil had sent for them from Normandy. He would not spend the silver that such fine craftsmanship required. Whatever he did buy would be cheap and shoddy and no replacement. And he would forget his promise in a blink of an eye, in any case. My emotions, I, I mean nothing to him. Nothing, except the unlikely promise of an heir. I am likely past childbearing and do not quicken. Perhaps a child can only come in love, not in such loathing.

Amelina straightened up from her task and moved towards the doorway where she encountered Lady Alice. 'Did I hear something break?' Alice glared at Amelina. I swivelled in my chair readying to defend my maid, but Amelina needed no defence.

'The constable clumsily broke one of his wife's precious goblets, Lady Alice,' she told her.

'Ah.' It was of no further interest to Alice. It was not one of her possessions that had been shattered. 'Take your child with you, Amelina,' she commanded. 'The boy should not be about Lady Nest's skirts all the time like this.'

'Yes, my lady.' Amelina reached out a hand to Robert who reluctantly let go his embrace of my neck. Amelina and I exchanged a covert look. Everyone believed Robert to be Amelina's son and not mine. Since Haith and I had not wed, Amelina was the cover for our child. I wondered what Robert himself thought. Was he confused? Perhaps he just thought he had two mothers, or three even, since Ida was Haith's sister, Robert's aunt, and loved him to distraction too. He had no shortage of love.

'Constable, Lady Nest,' Alice said in a declarative tone, intending that her voice should ring command, but she was an inexperienced teenager, without a great deal of wit about her, and her voice quavered rather than rang. 'My husband and I leave for court tomorrow and all here is left in your custody. We trust that you will serve us well in our absence.'

'Indeed, we shall, my lady,' declared de Marais loudly, performing an unctuous bow, to compensate for the fact that I made no response. It was near impossible for me to accept that my status was less than this chit of a girl. I, a royal princess was subordinate to this Norman child-bride in Cardigan Castle, which had once been another of the strongholds belonging to my father and a long line of my ancestors stretching back into the mists of memory and legends.

'Godspeed on your journey, Lady Alice,' I murmured, at last, reaching for something to say.

'Perhaps, you would like to send your good wishes to the king,' de Marais remarked.

I looked away to conceal my furious expression from them both. My husband loved to bruit how I was the king's former mistress. This was too much. It was in poor taste. I did not trade on my former life with King Henry. I did not bray of it. In any case, I was furious with Henry for marrying me to this idiot.

'I will gladly send your good wishes to the king, Lady Nest,' Lady Alice said uncertainly. Everyone knew I had been the king's mistress, that my eldest son Henry was the king's son, but even this girl knew it was in poor taste to refer to it openly.

I kept my face turned from both of them. Ida had been sitting silently reading, and intervened to mitigate the embarrassment that my husband's thoughtless words had created. 'We all send our kind regards to the king,' she declared, 'and thank you, Lady Alice, for bearing them.'

'Do you know the king, yourself then, Mistress Ida?' Alice asked rudely.

Ida coloured and put her head down. 'Oh no. Only by repute, of course.'

Ida did, indeed, know King Henry. Her brother was the king's best friend and Ida had nursed the king through a serious crisis of madness over the maiming of his granddaughters and she was there at his side when Henry learned of the drowning of his heir, but she could not admit to these facts. King Henry had known her as Sister Benedicta, a nun from Fontevraud Abbey in Anjou. She had run away from the religious life and it was impossible to reveal anything of her former life or she would be dragged back to the abbey and horribly punished.

Ida's well-intentioned remark had made matters worse. 'Is there... is there, in fact, a message, I should convey to the king, on your behalf, Lady Nest?' Alice asked. I relented at last, in the face of her discomfort. It could not be easy for her, a young girl far from her home in England, married to a man considerably older than herself, forced to give space in her household to a notorious woman like myself and all the baggage I came trailing from my affair with the king, my Welsh royalty, and the scandal of my abduction by a Welsh prince. The odour of good opinion did not waft in my wake.

'Thank you. You are kind,' I reassured her. 'But there is no special message from me. If I have a message for the king, I will write to him direct.' I stood. I was a full foot taller than Lady Alice and several inches taller, too, than my idiot husband. In my head, I composed all manner of messages for Henry: Damn you for putting me in this position! For not allowing me to marry Haith! Damn you, Henry, for being you! I stalked from the hall, before my 'messages' should be blazoned across my face or escape from my mouth. Behind me, I heard Ida gather her pile of books in haste and follow me up to my chamber, to the consolations of Amelina and Robert, and the view of the bleak, rushing river.

Richard de Clare and Lady Alice left this morning and de Marais assiduously set about his task of overseeing the garrison and the work of the steward. At mid-morning he sent a boy to ask that I attend him in the hall.

'Husband?' I asked, standing before him as he pored over the accounts ledger.

'You have ordered the feed for the horses from Merewald,' he stated without looking up at me.

'I have.' As the constable's wife, it was my duty to run the household in the absence of Lady Alice.

'I always order it from Borgred. It is cheaper by far for such quantity,' he asserted, his tone disapproving.

'Cheaper in price and quality,' I maintained. 'At Pembroke, I judged that Merewald's was the better value. It lasted longer and the horses were fitter for it.'

He regarded me. 'You are not at Pembroke now. You are no longer the chatelaine of Pembroke. You will not countermand me.'

'I had not thought to do so. Only to carry out my responsibilities to the best of my ability. And,' I added, 'knowledge.'

'You will keep things as I have arranged them. You will not introduce your own innovations. I do hope we will not argue on such matters,' he smiled unagreeably at me.

'As you wish,' I said angrily.

'Furthermore, you will put a bridle on your maid's tongue. I know it is in women's nature to banter aimlessly and you cannot help it, but your Breton woman steps too often over the boundaries of her place.'

I nodded brusquely, not trusting myself to open my mouth and allow the words to fall out that were brimming behind my lips. I feared that I would only endanger Amelina's tenure with me by arguing with him. I turned on my heel.

In my chamber, I told Ida that she should undertake all the household management on my behalf and not change any of de Marais's habits even if they were stupid.

She stared at me. 'My lady?'

'Can you do that?'

'Of course, I can, but …' She looked at Amelina who shrugged sympathetically at her.

'There is no point in me doing it,' I complained. 'He wants nothing of me except a royal-blooded heir and the start of his line. He scorns my abilities and experience. What if I should bear an idiot? Or bear no child.'

'I expect you will bear one soon enough and no idiot,' Amelina remarked. 'They've dropped from you easy enough with all the rest of your men.'

'Don't be impertinent,' I snapped, though that was like commanding the incoming tide to stay back.

Within a few hours we had forgotten our cross words with each other. Ida had been down to the hall and swiftly organised all the household orders to my husband's liking. Now, she was singing quietly as she stitched and Amelina was making out a puzzle picture with Robert. A long hank of Ida's pale blonde hair hung down across the front of her tunic. Like Haith's, her hair was thick and straight. When she had first come to me, a renegade nun, her head had been shaven and was a soft burr of blonde stubble.

I mused to myself that if I could conceive a child, I could find a way to then live apart from my husband, but if I proved to be past childbearing, I must find another pretence. At least with the de Clares gone, I did not have to be constantly reminded of my diminished status, and my husband's additional duties during their absence would keep him busy and out of my way.

Bored with the child's puzzle, Amelina stood and began pacing up and down, sighing to herself and casting her eyes at the ceiling each time she turned at the limit of her pacing. Evidently I was required to ask: 'What's wrong with you?'

'I can't bear it, is what,' she grumbled.

'You can't bear what?'

'I can't bear that you can sit here still calmly married to that de Marais, when Haith is just down the road, when he is alive after all, and you could be with him.' Ida looked at her in surprise. 'Don't look at me like that,' Amelina retorted. 'Look at what *you've* done! Running away from a nunnery.' Ida coloured.

I deflected Amelina from her assault on Ida. 'You know how hard won my calm is,' I told her, 'and you've changed your tune since I was first wed to de Marais.'

Amelina nodded, admitting that she had.

'I dream of riding to Haith,' I declared, 'but if I did that, he would lose everything. I'm not sure he would welcome such a rash action from me, anyway.'

Amelina came to a halt in front of me and put her hands on her hips. 'I think he would.'

'I would be shaming my sons and daughter, my brother. Haith and I would lose the king's love. I would be shunned and have no standing in Wales. I know I do little enough but I think my existence, my presence here is something for the people, something to give them hope that the old order is not gone entirely, that we, the Welsh inhabitants and the Deheubarth royal family, might come back from this Norman occupation and resume our place.'

'Do you think that is any more realistic than running away with Haith?'

'Perhaps not, but my brother Gruffudd and his wife Gwenllian have not given up. I cannot either, even if all I do is simply be. If we were gone, if their children were gone, there would be no trace of what went before, of my father's kingdom and all the family that I have lost. It would be as if the sea had closed over the heads of the whole Deheubarth royal family.' I turned to Ida. 'Do you find it detrimental to be of Flemish origin here?'

'Some Welsh and Normans that I encounter in the market have remarked on my accent, some in neutral fashion, and others with disapproval in their tone,' she responded. 'It does not concern me greatly. There are many Flemings hereabouts, but I do not speak with them much. I cannot invite curiosity about myself from anyone.'

That, I thought, amounted to a lonely existence. I must take more care of Ida's welfare.

'And you, Nest,' Ida asked, 'how do you reconcile your Welsh heritage with your Norman surroundings?'

'With great difficulty,' I replied. 'When my brother Gruffudd returned from Ireland to make a bid to win back his kingdom from the Normans, my loyalties were torn between my Norman husband, Gerald, and my brother.'

'I can't imagine how I could react if there were a conflict between my affections and loyalties towards my brother and towards a lover,' Ida said.

'Nuns, on the whole, do not have lovers,' remarked Amelina, and raised her eyebrows in curiosity to Ida, who turned her face back to me.

'My brother Gruffudd had some successes before being captured and humiliated by the Normans,' I told Ida. 'He was not always reduced to nothing as he is now. My brother is the rightful king of the whole of south west Wales, but he subsists these days in the barren commote of Caeo. I admire the uncompromising stance of my sister-in-law Gwenllian and wish that my own position could be as pure and simple. In her view, my brother is king of Deheubarth and the Normans are parasites to be purged. But I know enough to recognise that the Normans will not easily be dislodged from Wales. I have counselled integration to my brother and Gwenllian, but they ignore my advice.'

'What will your brother and his wife do? What *can* they do?'

I shook my head. 'Gruffudd has no resources to mount another campaign to win his kingdom back. And if he tries and fails again, King Henry will execute him.'

'You Welsh are an occupied people,' Ida said.

I sighed. 'Yes. But I cannot hate the Normans. Not all of them. My sons consider themselves to *be* Normans. I cannot take the stance of Agnes of Wales, the Welsh princess who was the wife of Bernard de Neufmarché, the murderer of my father. She hated her Norman husband so bitterly that she disinherited her own son to revenge herself.'

'That man deserved everything he got,' Amelina announced with relish, 'including the piles.' She followed up her pronouncement with a heavy sigh.

'Yes?' I asked her, responding to the cue she was surely giving to me.

'Couldn't you do more than just be a symbol?'

'Yes. I have been circumspect, playing safe, but my older children are grown now—they are taking their own ways. You are right, Amelina. I could do more to assist Gruffudd and Gwenllian.'

Amelina was alarmed. 'But, I did not mean … you must be careful! You would put yourself at great risk if you helped them commit treason against the king!'

'Of course. Yet Gruffudd *should* be acknowledged by Henry as king of Deheubarth, as the Welsh king is acknowledged in Gwynedd and Madog is acknowledged as king of Powys.'

'You mean to lobby King Henry?'

'No, that would be pointless. There is no reason for Henry to cede what he has. But his hold here is tenuous. There are a handful of Norman lords and a handful of Welsh. The balance is finely tuned. It could be tipped. I am of a mind to pay a visit to my kin, Amelina. You will organise the packing and I will go tomorrow.'

'I did not mean to prick you to grave danger, my lady,' said Amelina, alarmed.

'Visiting my brother and his family is hardly grave danger. In any case, I have braved much worse dangers in my life and I can skirt this one too.'

Amelina wrung her hands dramatically. 'Oh I hope so. I do hope so. Would be best to do nothing perhaps, after all.'

I smiled grimly at her. *Was* there anything, I wondered, that I could do to support the efforts of my brother to regain his kingdom.

Amelina frowned mightily at how her prompting about Haith had led me to this decision, but she moved to the chest at the foot of my bed to begin the packing. I started to rehearse in my head the words I would use at the meal to inform my husband of my decision to travel to Caeo.

4

Butchery

August 1122, Pont Audemer, Normandy

Haith did not have to wait long to attempt an exit from the castle. Most of the men lying on the floor of the hall were more unconscious with drink than sleep after the wedding feast, but there would be a few who were not unconscious, who were coming to despatch him. It was not easy to be surreptitious when you were over six feet tall, but Haith stood quietly, extricating himself and his cloak from his snoring neighbours. He pulled his black felt hat down over his blond hair to avoid catching the light of any torch stumps still flickering and gestured to his hound. Together they moved towards the buttery. His sword would have to lay abandoned in the pile on the threshold of the main hall door. Extracting it from the other weapons would create too much noise, and it was very likely that du Pin had stationed men at the door to intercept him. Haith did not know the layout of this stronghold but most castles had some kind of back route for the servants. He looked around the buttery. Casks were stacked on their sides from floor to ceiling along two walls, and haphazard piles of barrels were ranged against the other walls. Red wine that had leaked from the taps in some of the casks pooled in depressions in the uneven stone flags of the floor. There was no other door from here.

Haith and the mastiff moved on to the pantry where loaves of bread and breadknives were laid out on a wide table in the centre of the room. A threadbare tapestry covered the far wall, its bottom edge wavering in a draught. Haith lifted the edge of the tapestry and found an unlocked door. He slipped through, latched the door closed again behind him, and waited for a moment in the stagnant dark. He could sense nobody. His dog would alert him to any lurking presence. His eyes became accustomed to the blackness and he could dimly discern the shape of the passageway ahead. Haith and his dog moved on silent feet down the dim tunnel to another door that led out onto an exterior stone staircase. At the top of the stairs, Haith crouched behind his dog and rested his cheek against his warm flank, allowing his eyes to adjust again to the gloomy evening light so that he could observe the courtyard. As he suspected, du Pin had stationed four men at the hall door, but he could see no others between himself and the stables. He and the dog moved down the steps. He took care not to release any loose stones on the stairway that might alert the watchers to his presence. He sidled around the walls towards the stables. It was likely that more men would be posted there. Haith gave his mastiff the command to lie and wait in long grass close to the stables. The dog might spook the horses and give away Haith's presence.

He moved closer to the stables, hearing muffled voices coming from inside. Perhaps two or three men. Avoiding the main door, he found a gap in a side wall at ground level and rolled himself inside one of the horses' stalls. His nostrils encountered the familiar stench of horse urine, the familiar waft of horse heat. He pulled a handful of hay from a net hanging on the wall and held it out to the warm occupant, who nuzzled him in gratitude. In the darkness, Haith was disorientated and unsure where his own horse might be tethered. A spade had been thrust into a pile of muck just outside this stall. He slid the spade from its excrement sheath and moved towards the voices. If he stumbled around looking for his horse, they would hear him. Better to use the element of surprise against them.

Two men had their backs to him, watching the stable door. He slammed the spade against the head of the first one and, then, against the surprised and turning other. He took the swords from their inert bodies and did not have far to look for his horse and gear. He was swiftly reunited with his hound. He had to find a way out of the castle that was not through the guarded drawbridge, and quickly, before his absence from the hall was noticed or the men sprawled in the stables regained consciousness and raised the alarm.

Leading his horse, he moved towards where he would expect the postern gate to be. Surely this too would be guarded. The snoring was audible before the dark form slumped next to the gate could be discerned. Two emptied bladders of strong ale from the wedding feast pillowed the head of the sleeping man. Gingerly, Haith lifted the gate latch and let his horse and dog amble through before him while he kept an eye on the unconscious guard.

Haith took his horse at a slow pace down into the dark town, with the hound padding alongside and found his way to the deserted marketplace. He rode through and found a small copse of trees adjacent to the market square, where he rolled himself in his cloak for a few hours' sleep.

The cock crowing woke him and he mounted and rode back towards the marketplace where the traders were in the process of setting up stalls. Coloured awnings fluttered in a slight breeze and masters shouted at sleepy apprentices. Haith rode past the booths of leather and textile merchants, past bakers and cobblers, straight through the centre of the market, making his way towards the river, where four butchers' stalls stood in a row. The butchers and their boys were laying out slabs of meat and suspending skinned carcasses from hooks. The air was grimly stodgy with the stench of dead flesh.

A market was not the most private place to corner his quarry, but Haith did not know what the butcher Berold looked like and it was very likely that he would be at this market. Haith did not want to ask around for a man named Berold and give the butcher the opportunity to flee from him. He rode a little way along the river's edge and looked back over his shoulder to check that he was no longer visible from the market stalls. He veered from the path to a stand of trees and pushed into the greening gloom, urging his horse to step carefully over fallen logs. He swiped low-hanging vegetation from before his face or lent in the saddle to avoid it. Deep in the wood, he came to a clearing where he dismounted, tethered his horse and told his hound to stay. Haith took a thick sack with a heavy coil of rope inside it from his saddle. He slung the sack over his shoulder and moved back nonchalantly along the river path. One of the bakers' boys sold him a hunk of fresh bread and he sat on a log, just behind the butchers and within earshot of their banter, breaking fast, feigning an interest in the view of the fishermen on the Risle.

A butcher's boy fumbled a bucket at the edge of a table to catch the ooze of dark brown blood as his master swung a thudding chopper into a side of beef, dividing it into smaller joints.

'That's as fresh as my wife's mother,' laughed another of the butchers, gesturing at his neighbour's display of a spreadeagled sheep's carcass. He had a point, thought Haith. The mutton flesh was a darkening purple, shot with green. It looked stripped and exposed.

'And your pig's head appears to be one of *your* relations,' returned the competitor, pointing at a shrivelling snout.

'Have a care, Berold,' laughed the first butcher, good-humouredly. 'I have a knife in my hand!'

Haith scoped the area. The four butchers' stalls were next to the river, so that their slops could easily be disposed of in the water at the end of the day's trading. Behind the stalls, a stand of thorny bushes quickly developed into the small copse where his horse and hound were waiting. It would be best to take the man named Berold before more people arrived at the market. Haith moved round to the back of the stall, inching closer to the butcher, noting that the man was built like an ox and was wielding a vicious-looking butcher's hook. Haith assessed the positions of the other butchers and their apprentices.

Berold leant forward to set the hook down and carefully wiped his bloodied hands on his apron, swiping the cloth between his fingers where bits of flesh had snagged. He moved back into the recess of the stall to reach for a mug of ale. Swiftly, Haith stepped close behind the butcher, slipped the long sack over the man's head and torso, yanked the rope tight, pinioning Berold's arms, and dragged him backwards with his hand over the butcher's mouth. Berold was a massive weight to manoeuvre unwillingly and he grunted and floundered in the sack. Sweating heavily, Haith dragged his captive towards the bushes, with the man's feet scuffling vainly to gain some purchase and break their backwards progress. Haith's head was covered with a leather cap tied under his chin and he was protected by his jerkin and gambeson as he crashed through the thicket. The butcher's arms, however, were bare inside the sack and his clothes were thin for hot work. Berold was cruelly pierced and scraped by the thorns, which reduced his struggle temporarily. His cries of pain were adequately muffled by the sack.

Having dragged Berold far enough to be out of earshot, Haith dumped his burden and stood panting, the rope in his grip. 'Be silent!' Haith lent over the squirming sack and pricked his knife into what he thought must be the vicinity of Berold's throat. The thrashing, trussed man went still. 'No harm will come to you if you are silent and still. Good. Get to your feet. Try anything and I'll slit your belly and you'll see your own tripe.' No doubt, Berold could hear the Flemish twang of Haith's accent and would know the fearsome reputation of Flemish mercenaries. For once, Haith's provenance told in his favour. The man lumbered to his feet, breathing noisily, and Haith pulled him further into the undergrowth, until they reached the clearing. Haith's grazing horse looked up at their approach and skittered nervously at the sight of the sack with legs.

'Sit! And remember, silent!' Haith roped the seated man to a tree, knotting it brutally so that Berold grunted with the cut of the rope into his belly and forearms. Haith bent to slice a square opening in the sacking to reveal Berold's eyes, nose and mouth. The butcher glared fury but tempered his expression at sight of the knife so close to his face.

Haith let Berold look for a moment at him, at the mossed trees surrounding them and the dark pond in the centre of the clearing, at the massive hound that obligingly bared his teeth in a vicious growl. Taking his time, Haith sauntered to the horse, poured a cup of ale from a bladder suspended from the saddle and regarded the trussed butcher.

'Do you know who I am, Berold?'

The man shook his head. 'No, master, no. What have I done to offend you? Is it money you want?' He looked confused, as well he might. Haith did not have the look of a bandit of the woods.

'Not money, no Berold. Information. If you can give me satisfaction, I can let you go about your business and no harm done. I am a sheriff of Duke Henry, Berold.'

The man's red, sweating face paled. 'I mean no offence to you or the great duke, sir.' No matter if it was king or duke, England or Normandy, Henry's stern, unrelenting character towards wrongdoers was known everywhere.

'Of course not. Do you know why I am here, asking you questions in this unfortunately rude manner, Berold?'

Berold looked all around him again, as far as his constraints would allow. It was evident that escape was not an option and that some answer must be provided. 'Perhaps it's to do with that ship is it?'

'Ah, I see you are clever, Berold,' Haith said pleasantly. He took a sip of his ale. Then he moved back to Berold swiftly, crouched and gripped the butcher's chin through the sack, putting fear into his eyes. Haith tipped Berold's head back a little, brought the beaker to Berold's surprised mouth and allowed him a gulp of the ale. 'Yes,' Haith insisted quietly. 'I need to know what happened that night, the night of the wreck of *The White Ship* and the drowning of the duke's heir. It seems, by God's providence, you were the only survivor of the tragedy, lucky Berold.'

'Yes! I am a lucky man.'

'You are, indeed.' It went against Haith's innate kindness to put fear into a man, but he knew he would get nothing from him without terror. He had considered pushing Berold's head into the waters of the pond until he told the truth, but now that he had the man's measure, he dared not loosen the butcher's bonds. Haith was big, but Berold was bigger, and given a chance, might overpower him, although a lot of his size was lard, whereas Haith was lean, war-hardened muscle. 'You see, I was there myself, Berold, on the ship.'

Berold nodded his head up and down, trying to appease his captor.

'I saw two lords disembark,' Haith recalled, as if he were telling a tale. 'Count Stephen de Blois and Count William de Roumare and thought, given the rowdy passengers and crew, that they might have the right idea, so I followed them.'

Berold nodded enthusiastically again. 'You had a lucky escape, sir, indeed! All those poor souls drowned in that cruel, grey sea— three hundred in all, they say.'

'So they do.' Haith drew an enormous, serrated hunting knife from his hip and began to needlessly sharpen it on a whetstone. Berold watched him, his pallor growing and his eyes widening. A man of Berold's profession would know that this was a particularly good instrument for cutting flesh.

'Sir, do you mean to murder me after all that I survived the long night in the cold waters of the English sea, clinging for dear life to a splintered spar? Don't do it, sir! I did no harm. I'm just a poor butcher.'

'Yes, you are. So, why is it that you were aboard that ship? A ship full of nobles and the sons and daughters of the duke?'

'For provisioning,' mumbled Berold.

'Come, Berold. I don't have time for lies. Let's make a deal. For each lie you tell, I will cut off a sliver of your flesh. So, provisioning is it? That is one lie to begin with.' Haith moved the knife swiftly towards Berold's fat thigh.

'No!' the butcher screamed, his voice surprisingly high for such a large man. Haith arrested the movement of the knife, poising it dramatically with its tip touching Berold's brown hose. 'I'll tell no lies, sir. There was a man that sent me onboard.' Sweat was trickling unimpeded into Berold's eyes and from the furrow beneath his nose into his mouth.

'A man. That is not terribly informative, Berold.' Haith carefully slit a long gash in Berold's hose, close to his groin. He touched the tip of the knife against Berold's exposed white skin.

'No!' Berold's efforts to squirm away from the knife, only caused his tight bindings to carve into his tender flesh. 'I didn't know his name, but I saw him in the company of the lord called Ranulf de Gernon.'

Haith concealed his surprise. He had been expecting Stephen de Blois's name to be on Berold's lips, not Ranulf's. 'You are sure of that?'

'Yes, sure.'

'What did he look like? This man.'

'Very curly brown hair. Unusual scar cutting straight down through his left eyebrow, leaving it bald....'

'De Pirou? Was his name William de Pirou?' Haith asked. He recognised this description of the king's dapifer. De Pirou and Haith had served together in battle in Normandy on several occasions. He had, himself, recently seen de Pirou in the company of Ranulf de Gernon at Henry's court, and been suspicious since de Pirou was listed on the victim list of *The White Ship* and yet stood breathing and laughing at Westminster. Nobody else had noticed the discrepancy.

'I never knew his name,' Berold responded. 'I saw him treacherously abandon me to the sea's embrace when he took the raft, though.'

'The raft?'

'Yes, there were two small rafts onboard. We were supposed to scuttle one and escape in the other. The man—de Pirou you say—did scuttle one but then he left without me. Left me there to drown.' Berold was indignant and Haith tried to keep the contempt from his face. For whatever reason, in whatever way, these two men, perhaps acting on commands from Ranulf de Gernon then, had deliberately caused the drowning of so many young nobles of Henry's court. It was unthinkable and yet it had happened.

'And why did the man get you onboard, Berold?' Haith watched resistance crystallise on the butcher's face and knew he would only get at this truth by actually hurting him. Swiftly, consciously avoiding any blood-letting that might be life-threatening, he pushed the tip of the knife into Berold's soft groin and held it there for a few seconds, while Berold screamed. Haith withdrew the knife.

Berold panted and slumped against his ropes. 'Please, please ....'

'Why, Berold? Or the knife goes in again, and deeper. Will you have me joint you like your carcasses on the stall back there?' Haith held the bloodied knife in Berold's line of vision.

Berold's feet scrambled in the dirt, desperate to move away from the implement of his pain, but he was held fast and could go nowhere. 'I repent of it. It was a dreadful thing. I owed money.'

'I don't need to hear *your* reasons, Berold. Focus. I just need an answer, quickly.' Haith slowly wiped each side of the knife against Berold's hose, high on his other thigh.

'No! Please, master! Don't! I was paid to drown a man.'

'Drown a man!' Haith exclaimed incredulous. 'And you drowned three hundred in error instead?'

'No!' Berold wailed. 'That wasn't my fault. The crew were dead drunk. The captain was drunk. That was part of the plan. To cover up our actions. We put barrels with heavily fortified ale and wine aboard. But the crew, those sots, drove the ship onto the rock and it foundered. That *wasn't* the plan.'

'Go on....' Haith waved the knife before Berold's face, which was slick with the butcher's tears, snot and spittle.

'I was paid to drown a man in a barrel of water and throw him overboard, like it was an accident at sea.'

'What man?'

'I don't know who he was. That was de Pirou's job. To point him out to me and get me alone with him.'

'Well, and did you do it? How could you commit this murder on a ship with so many people on it?'

'We had the barrel ready below-decks, concealed from the oarsmen by the freight and the horses. All the nobles were above-decks, swilling wine. De Pirou got our mark down to us on a pretence. I had him head-first in the barrel sharpish, kicking and twisting, and then he stopped. So it was accomplished. De Pirou was supposed to help me get him out of the barrel and sling him overboard, but then the pilot interrupted us.' Berold's account ended on a whine, as if he had been terribly wronged in this sorry tale.

'And then what?'

'I don't know why the pilot was there. Came looking for wine, most likely. He took in the sight of the legs sticking out of the barrel, looked both of us full in the face, and then de Pirou stuck him.'

'Killed him? The pilot?'

'Yes.'

'These legs, this man you murdered, Berold, tell me more. It was a young man?' Haith asked, wondering if it had been Prince William, or Earl Richard of Chester, perhaps, who had met such a humiliating death. Could Earl Richard be the reason that Ranulf was implicated? Ranulf's father had inherited the earldom of Chester after Richard's death in the wreck.

'No, not a young man.'

'Most of those onboard were young, Berold. Was it the prince or an earl? Tell the truth!' Haith warned him.

'It *is* the truth!' Berold wailed. 'He was sixty or so, scrawny, a clerk I'd say. It was an easy job.'

'A clerk!' Haith frowned. 'The only clerk I know of onboard was Gisulf. Was that his name?'

Berold did his best, in his constrained position, to shake his head. 'I didn't know his name.'

'Well, what then?'

'The ship had no pilot,' Berold moaned sulkily. 'It struck the rock and the great ship was holed! Being so large and overloaded, it tipped so fast and horribly and we were all swimming or sinking. I thought rescue would come, for sure, from the shore or the king's boat. They must have heard us all screaming.'

Yes, thought Haith, bitterly, such a course of events would explain why the ship had veered so far off course as soon as it had left the harbour. Those on the king's ship and on shore, like himself, had, indeed, heard cries from the water, but assumed it to be a continuation of the celebrations of the prince's party. It was a dark night and it was only in the morning when shards of the shattered longboat, and then, eventually, bodies began to drift ashore that they understood what had happened in the dead of that moonless night.

'I saw the prince on a raft later when I was in the sea, holding onto that spar for dear life,' Berold volunteered. 'I knew de Pirou had cut the lashings of the raft and the prince would soon be done for, in any case. I saw the raft go under with him. He was calling out to a woman who was in the water: "Mathilde, Mathilde!" And she was screaming to him, "Will! don't leave me, Will!"'

Mathilde and Will. It had to be King Henry's illegitimate daughter, Mathilde, countess of Perche, and his legitimate heir, William *Adelin*—the throne-worthy. King Henry was struggling to recover from the grievous blow and Haith doubted that he would every truly succeed. So, Ranulf de Gernon, perhaps, had paid de Pirou to murder Gisulf, but the plan had gone hideously awry. Stephen de Blois had not been the culprit, then. Yet, it still made little sense.

'Is that it? That was the whole plan?'

'Yes,' Berold was sobbing. The pain of his wound was throbbing now past the first shock of its infliction, but Haith noted that it was not bleeding copiously. The butcher would survive it, unlike his drowned victims.

There was nothing more this butcher could tell. It was de Pirou that Haith needed to hunt down to discover Ranulf de Gernon's motivation for murdering the royal clerk, Gisulf. He wiped his knife on the grass and sheathed it. Berold's own conscience at being responsible for the deaths of three hundred people should mete out fair justice to him, and if it did not, then God would be his final judge. Haith stood and walked to his horse, checking the girth strap and stoppering his ale bladder, before mounting. The mastiff got reluctantly to his feet.

'Sir? Sir?'

Haith turned his horse in the direction of Tiron Abbey. He would send a fast messenger to the king with news of the Beaumont sisters' marriages when he reached Tiron. He planned to say nothing to Henry about his enquiries into *The White Ship* until he had the whole story.

Berold's cries grew fainter as Haith spurred his horse on, keen to escape from the gross corruption of what he had heard. That those two men, Berold and de Pirou, should be the only survivors of such a horrible tragedy was more wicked than he could bear to think on.

5

Kin

August 1122, Caeo, Wales

The ride to the village of Caeo took several hours. Gruffudd was restricted to Caeo and its environs by order of King Henry after my brother's rebellion seven years ago. I left Amelina and Ida at Cardigan with Robert and travelled east with four guards. The road inclined gently all the way, so that we were obliged to rest our horses on occasion, whenever we passed through a village. I noticed that the people all around were in great poverty and gazed with hatred at the Norman soldiers accompanying me, until I spoke to them in Welsh. Then they softened and told me something of their tribulations. 'You be the sister of the king,' one old man gasped when I gave him my name. He doffed his cap and his wife made a clumsy attempt at a curtesy.

'The king?' I answered, a little confused at what he meant. 'My father was King Rhys ap Tewdwr.'

'Aye, and you be the sister of King Gruffudd ap Rhys.'

I smiled my agreement and did not show my consternation. King Henry would not be pleased if it should come to his ears that my brother was named king, whether Gruffudd encouraged it or not.

'God bless him and his queen for their charities.'

I turned back to the elderly couple. It was the woman who had spoken. 'You speak of Gwenllian ferch Gruffudd ap Cynan, I think?' I named my sister-in-law.

'Aye, my lady. They saved our children from starvation and I thank them in my prayers each morning and night for it.'

I had brought gifts of silver and food with me from Cardigan, as much as I could stuff into my saddlebags away from the watchful eye of my husband, thinking that my brother and his family would be suffering privation. If they were distributing largesse, what was the source of their wealth? I did not wish to linger in the village causing too much wonder and gossip that might get about all over the place and would have to push on to find the answer to my question. Our horses were watered and rested and we mounted again for the last leg of our journey. The road continued to rise through thriving woodlands as we approached the mountains. Ravens called from trees and rocks. Buzzards circled high ahead. Nearing the village of Caeo, I gazed at a vast mountain region that extended for miles to the north, looking for all the world like a petrified, storm-tossed sea of rock. Specks in the far distance were sheep and sure-footed ponies grazing on the rugged terrain. The village of Caeo was located at the confluence of Afon Annell and Nant Frena and was traversed by an old Roman road, now used by drovers. We had arrived on market day but as we rode slowly past the stalls, waiting for people and carts to get out of our way, I could see that the wares on display here were sparse compared to the opulence that I was used to seeing in the markets of the Norman-held towns.

A baker pointed out a large residence to us as the household of my brother and we rode into its yard. A fair-haired boy ran out to gape, alerted by the sound of our horses' hooves on the cobbles. 'I am looking for Gruffudd ap Rhys,' I called out. The boy continued to stare open-mouthed at me. I repeated my request. 'Gruffudd ap Rhys. Do you know where I might find him?'

One of my soldiers leant down and gripped the boy by the ear,

'Answer the lady, boy!'

I heard the sound of a sword drawn from a scabbard by someone concealed from my view behind the horses' great flanks. The sword whipped around and lay in threat against my soldier's throat. 'You will take your hands from my son,' declared a quiet but commanding female voice and my man let go of the boy's ear, sharpish.

I craned around the horses for a view of the red-haired woman who stood there.

'Gwenllian?' I queried.

'Nest!' she cocked her head in equal astonishment.

'Lady,' muttered my soldier, still at threat from her blade. She withdrew it from his neck.

I jumped from my horse and ran to clasp her in my arms and she returned my embrace, laughing. I was delighted to see her. I held her face in my two hands, marvelling anew at the rich, dark red of her hair that swirled wild around her, uncovered by any headveil. 'Are you well? I see you are well? And this is your son?'

'This is Cadell. Don't you remember him?'

He grinned at me. 'Ah, yes,' I smoothed down his spiked, blond hair. 'I recall you, indeed. You visited me and my husband Gerald when you were very young. I am your aunt.' This Cadell was around eleven years of age and was one of my brother's sons from his first marriage to a Danish woman, when he lived in Dublin. He was Gwenllian's stepson.

'Nest!'

My brother stepped from the doorway of the large house and I rushed to embrace him. He, Gwenllian, and Cadell led me inside. It was a mean home for a 'king'. Two younger boys stood there waiting to be introduced to their aunt: Morgan who was six and Maelgwyn, a lively three-year-old. The oldest brother, Anarawd, they told me, was out gathering firewood. 'And where are your sisters?' I asked them. They glanced shyly to their mother.

'Gwladus and Nest are betrothed and gone to live in the

households of their prospective husbands,' Gwenllian said. Gwladus and Nest were also the children of my brother's first marriage and it made good sense, in the family's impoverished circumstances to send them from home as soon as possible.

'Who are they betrothed to?'

'Gwladus to Caradog ap Iestyn in Morgannwg and Nest, your namesake, to Ifor ap Meurug of Senghenydd.'

'They are good matches.'

'And why not?' Gwenllian demanded. 'They are daughters of the king of Deheubarth.'

'Indeed,' I placated, seeking to mollify her with the gestures of my hands and my expression. I bit back my question concerning the daughter that I had helped her to birth at Llansteffan when she and Gruffudd were on the run. I did not see that child about the place, but could ask the question later. Instead, I produced my gifts of silver, food and a fine quilt. They were received gracefully by Gwenllian. My brother's circumstances here were, indeed, straitened and I was puzzled. 'At a village on the way here, a man and his wife told me that you had saved them from starvation, but now you have fallen on hard times yourselves?'

Gwenllian and Gruffudd glanced at each other. 'We have always had hard times here,' Gruffudd said, 'but we find ways to help the local populace who are much oppressed by the Norman occupiers. All the good grazing land has been taken from the Welsh and they are taxed overhard besides.'

I waited to be enlightened further but Gruffudd said nothing more. He went out a little later with Cadell to check that my men were adequately billeted and I took the opportunity to press for more information. 'But, Gwenllian, how do you help the villagers when you have nothing yourselves?'

'We rob rich foreigners passing on the roads hereabouts and redistribute their greedy wealth.'

I gaped at her. 'You rob?'

'Yes. I am not ashamed of it. It is they who should be ashamed of their gluttony and cruelty.'

'But, you mean you rob them at swordpoint? By violence?'

'Yes.'

'You and Gruffudd and your followers.'

'Yes.'

'And by foreigners you mean?'

'Normans. Yes.'

'But, Gwenllian, if the king or his justiciars should hear of it they would hang you all!'

'Everything they have is stolen from us.' She stared at me hard to see if I would disagree, but I could not. 'We cover our faces. There is no evidence that it is us.'

'But you run the risk.'

'We have to. My own daughter died when we arrived here and I'll not watch other Welsh children die of privation and illness with no money to aid them.'

'Your daughter. I am so very sorry, Gwenllian.' She kept her face turned away from me, the set of her mouth hard and fragile. I recalled that child's birth, her first child. 'Do you keep some of the proceeds of these robberies yourselves?'

'Nothing,' she declared. 'Only what is needed to feed those here. The bare minimum.'

It was an astute action as well as a charitable one on the part of my brother and his wife. It garnered the inhabitants' love and gratitude to Gruffudd, allowed him to give alms and gifts as a king should, kept his fame alive, despite the constraints that had been foist upon him.

Cadell slipped through the hole in the compound fence and ran up to the den in the woods above the village to find his older brother, Anarawd. 'A black-haired princess is come to visit us,' he told him.

'What are you talking about?'

'Our aunt, it is. Our Aunt Nest.'

'The one that's fucked all the Normans?'

A guffaw burst from Cadell and he slapped his hand over Anarawd's mouth, withdrawing it quickly again when Anarawd licked his palm. 'Yuck!' they exclaimed together. Cadell wiped his palm against his jerkin. 'Don't speak ill of her. Father would whip you. Besides, she's nice.'

'I'm sure she's nice.'

'She's beautiful.'

'You think all females are beautiful, including the backward girl who shovels the horseshit.'

'Come and see for yourself then. She has long, thick, black hair.' He gestured at its length to his waist. 'Great blue eyes like the dark pools of a bottomless sea. Dimples.' Cadell poked two indentations into his own cheeks and opened his eyes as wide as they would go. 'Truly, she is the most beautiful woman you have ever seen.'

'More beautiful than Gwenllian?'

Cadell paused and considered. 'They are both beautiful, but one red and one black. Her skin....'

'Oh, stop, you bard! I don't want to hear any more of your ecstasies. I shall come and see the Normans' whore for myself.'

'Anarawd, please don't!' Cadell screwed his face up in distress at his brother's words. He scrubbed his sleeve across his nose. Hefting himself up, he ran in pursuit of his brother, hoping that Anarawd would not offend the beautiful princess.

At dinner, Cadell stared open-mouthed at me until Gwenllian frowned and he glanced away briefly, but then looked back again. 'We have gold here, Aunt Nest,' he blurted.

'Gold, Cadell?'

'He means the old Roman mines,' Gruffudd told me. 'They haven't been worked for many years.'

'Still gold there though,' Cadell asserted and winced. I guessed that Anarawd had kicked him under the table.

'Have you seen it, Cadell?' I asked.

He nodded enthusiastically. 'There's great white streaks on the surface of the rock and flowing down and down the tunnels all the way into the centre of the world.'

I smiled with delight at his description and Cadell squirmed in his seat and blushed.

'Well white isn't gold is it,' Anarawd scoffed. Anarawd was thirteen and looked very like my black-haired brother, whilst Cadell had the blond colouring of his Cambro-Danish mother.

'No, white isn't gold,' Cadell countered. 'It's quartz, but the gold glitters inside that vein. That's where it is.' He was clearly pleased to display his knowledge to me.

Gruffudd raised an eyebrow to me. 'It's true enough. I found a gold hoard, Nest,' he told me, 'from the Roman times. But no one has the art now to know how to release the gold from the rock's grasp.'

'No one?' I queried. 'I heard there are master miners in the north of England working the silver mines there and the Norman king, Henry, plans to visit them. I believe they are from Germany.'

Gruffudd shrugged.

'I have told you before, Cadell, you must not play near the mines,' Gwenllian complained. 'Do you want to be sucked in by Gwen and never return to the land of the living.'

Cadell hung his head.

'Gwen?' I asked.

'It's the legend of the mines,' Gwenllian responded. 'There is a standing stone there, Carreg Pumsaint, where five saints rested during a great storm. They lay down on the stone and left their magical imprints—five ovals where they slept. It is said that they sleep for ever in the mine. A woman named Gwen who was too curious for her own good,' Gwenllian elbowed Cadell, who looked chagrined, 'ventured in to take a peek at the sleeping saints. But she lost her way and she too sleeps there for ever, except on the nights of the full moon and a storm.'

'What happens then?' I asked, gripping Cadell's hand.

Gwenllian waved her arms ghost-like in the air. 'She emerges sobbing and yowling as a white vapour and may drag you down into the mine with her forever!'

We all laughed at the tale. 'You tell a good story, Gwenllian!' I declared.

'To bed, boys,' Gwenllian told Cadell and Anarawd. The younger children had retired before dinner with their nurse.

As Cadell passed me I reached out and took his hand again, which caused him to flush hot and red-faced. Anarawd was of an age to feel he was a man and he sniggered at his brother's embarrassment. 'I have a request,' I declared, looking at Gruffudd. 'Would you send Anarawd and Cadell to come and stay with me for a while at Llansteffan?' It had occurred to me that I could alleviate some of the financial strain on my brother's family by taking some of his children under my wing. I could also arrange schooling for them and teach them how to comport themselves as princes, which Gwenllian and Gruffudd were hard-pressed to achieve here in Caeo. I glanced at Cadell's face. A slow smile budded, and then became full-blown at his father's enthusiastic response.

6

Missing

August 1122, Normandy and Anjou

Haith made a brief stop at the bishop's palace in Lisieux to perform a search of the papers at the clerk Gisulf's former lodgings. Lisieux was the seat of the king's main administration in Normandy. Standing on the threshold of the palace, Haith watched a messenger gallop from the courtyard. The rider was bearing Haith's news to King Henry in England of Waleran's involvement in rebellion with Amaury de Montfort and William *Clito*. Haith's letter described the marriages of Waleran's sisters and the gathering of lords aligned with William *Clito*, which he had witnessed. There was nothing in Haith's letter concerning his investigation into the wreck of *The White Ship*. When the messenger was out of sight, Haith ducked his head to avoid the lintel and stepped back into the lobby, heading towards the stairway up to Gisulf's small room.

The clerk's office was stuffed with papers of all kinds from laundry lists to rough drafts of charters, but nothing that explained why Ranulf de Gernon might have ordered the murder of the king's clerk on *The White Ship* with all its terrible consequences. Haith sat back hard in the flimsy chair he was perched upon and it protested at his sudden movement. Why would Ranulf de Gernon murder Gisulf? Or had Ranulf, perhaps intended the *whole* thing—the sinking, the deaths? Surely no man could countenance that massacre, could have no reason for it? He had suspected Stephen de Blois because the heir's death brought him nearer to the throne. What did Ranulf gain? Richard, earl of Chester had also died on the ship and de Gernon's father had been made earl of Chester in his place, but that was hardly such a great gain. The earldom of Chester was not overly rich and was troublesome due to the forays of the Welsh across the border. De Gernon's father was better off before his elevation to the earldom, when he had commanded the rich lands of Carlisle and Cumberland instead. King Henry had obliged de Gernon's father to give up those lands in exchange for the earldom, lest he become too all-powerful in the north. Perhaps the earl had not expected that, had expected to become a veritable king of the north? Haith was wearying himself with the ceaseless speculations whirring in his head. He tidied the papers up into a neat stack.

Frustrated in his search, Haith refused the offer of a comfortable bed for the night and pushed on instead towards Tiron Abbey. His road wound through valleys where the trees were starting to turn towards autumn. A few yellowing leaves stood amongst the green, or fluttered softly to the ground. An incised stone marked the turnoff to the abbey, which took him on through dense woods. Many had beaten a broad track to the abbey gate and Haith had no difficulty in finding his way. Once inside the courtyard, he led his tired horse to the stables and sat for a while watching the boys from the abbey school chase each other around the green quad laughing and calling out taunts. He and the king had once been like these boys, during their own schooling together. How much heavier were their responsibilities and the weight of their years and experiences now. When they were children, Henry had three older brothers and no expectations of ever becoming king. He and Haith thought their course was to become priests and court chaplains, with Henry, no doubt, rising to bishop and perhaps archbishop. How different a life that would have been for them both. On balance, Haith considered that he preferred the active soldier's life that he had led and his current posting as sheriff. He felt an anxious twinge of guilt that he was not at his post right now, but he knew that the deputy he had left behind him in Pembroke was an able man.

The abbey porter who had admitted Haith ambled towards him. 'Are you looking for a bed for the night, sir?'

'Yes, many thanks,' Haith told him, 'and a word with your abbot.'

The porter's face expressed his query and also conveyed that he was far too lazy to be made to actually voice it.

'My name is Haith de Bruges, sheriff of Pembroke, in service to Duke Henry,' Haith announced. 'My business with your abbot is brief but necessary.'

The porter nodded and strolled off again. Haith considered that if the porter's speed was anything to go by, he might hear nothing back in response to his request until the morning. However, ten minutes later an altogether brisker-looking man approached Haith. 'Sheriff Haith is it?'

Haith rose to his considerable height and tried not to give the abbot the impression that he was looming over him. 'Yes, Lord Abbot. Thank you for speaking with me.'

The abbot indicated the stone bench that Haith had risen from and they both subsided onto it.

'I am here on a delicate matter,' Haith opened. 'It concerns the awful tragedy of *The White Ship*.'

'Ah, yes. Awful indeed.'

'I was on that ship myself,' Haith ventured, hastening to add in response to the abbot's raised eyebrows, 'but disembarked shortly before she sailed. I watched a number of others disembark before me. Stephen, count de Blois and two monks of your order.'

'Yes.' The abbot's voice and face were animated with the relief that the monks had disembarked.

That much was true then. Haith was relieved to have gotten this far. He had feared that the 'monks' might simply have been disguised in the voluminous grey habits of the Tironesian order, and in that case, he would have had very little hope of ever identifying them.

'You know who they were, Lord Abbot?'

'Certainly. There was talk of nothing else in the abbey for many weeks. The tragedy, and their lucky escape from the cruel sea. Brother Paul and Brother Bernard.'

'Might I speak with them?'

'To what purpose?'

'I am hoping to bring some peace to my lord, King Henry, with any further details I can glean for him.'

'Poor, poor man,' replied the abbot. 'To lose three children and so many members of his court in one cruel blow. His grief is beyond imagining. Very well. Of course, if there is any consolation we can offer … I will have you seated with these two brothers at the meal.'

Haith soon found that Brothers Paul and Bernard did not have much in the way of new information for him, except to confirm that they, like Count Stephen had disembarked because of the rowdy drunkenness of the crew and the passengers. 'Did Count Stephen appear ill to you?' Haith asked.

They exchanged glances and Paul spoke. 'In truth, no. He appeared hale and hearty. We were surprised later when we heard the rumours that he had disembarked due to illness since we saw the count head straight to *The Trader* with another lord, William de Roumare.' He named a tavern in Barfleur where Haith had heard more or less the same tale from a friendly barmaid.

'Sir Haith,' the abbot called his attention with a question. 'Has the duke indicated who he will name as heir?' It was the question everyone was asking, in Normandy and in England, after the drowning of Prince William.

'No,' Haith replied. 'King Henry has made no announcement on the succession yet. As you know, he is lately married to Adelisa de Louvain, and they hope that their marriage will soon be blessed with a child.'

The abbot nodded. 'Of course, of course.'

There was a moment's silence as the monks around him contemplated the question and kept their thoughts to themselves. An uncertain succession bred instability, created vulnerability, and presaged war. When the queen gave Henry a new heir, the insecurity of the succession would still remain. Though in good health and as robust as ever, King Henry was, undeniably, hurtling towards old age and it would be many years before any child born now could step into his shoes. There would need to be a regent appointed to keep control of the kingdom of England and Wales and the duchy of Normandy on behalf of a child heir. Henry's senior lords were already gearing up to contend with one another for that role, and Haith, along with everyone else sitting at the refectory table, knew those lords might be wondering why they should not simply take the crown or the duchy for themselves, rather than waiting out the time while a child grew to manhood. And then there was William *Clito*. Until Henry had a son, William *Clito* had the strongest claim to the duchy, but the king would never acknowledge that. Henry's oldest, illegitimate son, Earl Robert of Gloucester, was certainly a contender to be appointed regent of a new heir, as was Henry's nephew by his sister, Count Stephen de Blois. Robert was the more solid man, whilst Stephen was mercurial and ambitious. Haith knew these questions would be haunting the king's thoughts, just as they worried in the minds of his subjects.

After the meal, Haith made his way to the abbey's guest dormitory and stretched his long frame on one of their beds, which, inevitably, was a good foot too short for him. He stared at the ceiling, but there was no relief for his frustration up there in the dusty cobwebs hanging from the beams. His interrogation of Berold had garnered valuable information on what had happened on the ship and how the murder of Gisulf had been the instigating incident, but he was no nearer being sure who had commissioned that murder or why. Should he put Stephen de Blois back on his suspect list, along with Ranulf de Gernon? Stephen's tale of illness might have been a deception, yet there could have been many innocent reasons why he made the decision to leave the ship. Haith's diversion to Tiron had gained him little and now he was anxious to reach Fontevraud and Benedicta as soon as he could. The ride from Tiron would take him two days.

Haith broke his journey near Tours, staying in the guesthouse of Marmoutier Abbey. The ride to Fontevraud was uneventful aside from driving rain on the first day, followed by brilliant sunshine in the Loire Valley on the second day. The wet leaves sparkled in the sun like washed jewels. Haith's arrival at the abbey, on the other hand, was far from uneventful.

Haith sat in the office of the abbess and gaped at her. Growing aware that he was staring foolishly, rudely, he closed his mouth and shifted his gaze to the floor where his own hound lay next to the abbess's dog and tentatively licked the other's haunch in friendly fashion.

'I assure you that both things are true, Sir Haith,' Abbess Petronilla told him. 'Your sister is not here, and she is safe.'

Recovering from his initial surprise, Haith began to feel angry. His journey had been a wild goose chase. 'Well, where the … (he bit back the blasphemy) is she?'

'I cannot tell you that. I can only say that your sister was a small child given as a gift to God before she was old enough to make that choice herself and, nowadays, the Church begins to frown on such practices although they are not so nimble in making changes. Here at Fontevraud, we strive always to be at the forefront of Christian thinking.'

Haith stared at the serene, quietly-spoken woman. 'Are you telling me, Lady Abbess, that Benedicta has abandoned the cloister? For good?'

'I regard her as being on an extended pilgrimage,' the abbess suggested, smiling gently. 'I told her that I could collude in her decision and that, perhaps, so would you, but that there was still the matter of her soul and her word to God. The only remedy there was to make a confession to a priest and soon, but any priest would return her to the retribution of the Church and in that case, things would not go gently with her. I advised her of all that.' Defensiveness crept into the voice of the abbess and she averted her eyes.

'But she went, nonetheless?' Haith asked. 'When did this happen?'

'Perhaps two years ago,' Petronilla remembered, casting her eyes to the ceiling in an effort to calculate the time.

Haith's control over his surprise deserted him and he openly gawked at the abbess. Benedicta had written to him many times in the last two years. She had deceived him, or at least allowed him to think that she was here all that time. 'Well, where is she? Give me a clue, Lady Abbess. I need to be assured of her safety.'

'Will you return her to the Church?' the abbess asked, suddenly holding his gaze.

'No,' he asserted. 'What my sister wills, there my support will follow, whatever her reasoning. I am simply anxious for her.'

'Well, then, I think you could do worse than seek news of her in the household of a Welsh noblewoman named Nest ferch Rhys. I do not know a great deal about this lady but perhaps you …'

Haith ceased to hear the words that the abbess was speaking. His astonishment reached its apex. What, in God's name, could any connection be between Benedicta and Nest?

'I have been forwarding your letters to Benedicta in Wales,' the abbess continued, 'but I suppose there is a lapse of quite some time before she receives them. Your sister, as I am sure you are well aware, knows her own mind. She will make her own peace and find her own way to God, I have no doubt. Please give her my affectionate wishes when you find her.'

'Thank you for your candour, Lady Abbess. And for your great kindness to my sister. I must make haste to return to my post in Wales and find her there, it seems.'

The abbess smiled. 'Tell me, Sir Haith,' she said, 'has the duke made an announcement on the succession yet?'

Haith gave the abbess the same unsatisfactory answer he had made in Tiron. 'The king has recently taken Adelisa de Louvain as his new queen and they pray that their marriage might be blessed before long with a child and heir to England, Wales, and Normandy.'

The abbess nodded.

'Before I leave, I have another kindness to ask,' Haith said.

The abbess raised one eyebrow and inclined her head. 'How else may I help you, sir?'

'I would make confession,' Haith said. He had been feeling the burden of guilt at his torture of the butcher in Pont Audemer, but he had not made confession for a long time, and there was a great deal more besides that he needed to unburden.

The abbess directed Haith to the abbey priest who had just finished hearing the confessions of the nuns in the great abbey church. The nuns looked sidelong and curious at Haith as they filed out. When they were gone, Haith took his place beside the priest and, first, listed the men that he could remember or was aware of having killed in battle.

The priest shook his head dolefully and gave Haith a stern penance. 'The path of the warrior is your duty, my son, but it stains your soul and does not lead you to God's grace.'

Haith cleared his throat. 'Well, there's more, I'm afraid, Father. Recently I … well, tortured a man.' The priest blanched and looked askance at Haith. The small man fought to regain his composure. No doubt Haith's litany of violence was out of the ordinary from the confessions he heard from the nuns of Fontevraud. The priest increased the terms of Haith's penance and was about to conclude the confession. Haith took a breath. 'There is more that I must confess.'

The priest glanced up. 'More?' He looked away from Haith's face again quickly, studying the rosary sliding between his fingers. No doubt, he judged Haith to be the usual, brutal, Flemish mercenary. Haith itched to justify his actions, but that was hardly showing penitence or remorse, so he resolved to stick to the bald facts.

'Yes, my son?'

'I love another man's wife.'

'That is a grave sin ...' the priest began.

'I have always loved her,' Haith blurted. 'When she was the mistress of the ... (he could not name the king) my master, when she was married to her first husband, and now that she is wed to a second.'

'You must put all such longings aside,' the priest told him sternly. 'Else you will go to your maker steeped in mortal sin.'

Haith baulked at the idea that loving Nest was somehow more heinous a sin than torturing Berold or killing men in war. Could love, the kind of love he felt for her, be sin?

It was only as Haith heard the gates of Fontevraud Abbey clang shut behind him and his horse began her steady walk back along the long road they had travelled together that he realised he still had the gift from Count Amaury de Montfort in his saddlebag. The small wrapped book was addressed to 'Benedicta' in the count's elegant hand, and so that was where Haith would carry it, together with his questions. Was Amaury de Montfort the reason why Benedicta had left the convent?

As a long stretch of road opened up before him, suppressed emotion began to well up in Haith at the thought of Benedicta free of the cloister. It was the first time, since Nest's marriage to de Marais that he had felt anything resembling joy and he savoured it for several minutes and then startled his horse by slapping his thigh and laughing out loud at his delightful sister.

7

Desperate Measures

September 1122, Bristol Castle, England

I looked down onto another river—the river Avon lapping its serene curve around the foot of the curtain wall at Bristol Castle and caressed my rounding stomach. I could be sure now. I was with child and could leave my husband.

I had been visiting with my foster-sister, Mabel FitzRobert, countess of Gloucester, at Cardiff Castle, where we had grown up together. I planned to stay for a few weeks' respite from de Marais, but news that the king would be passing nearby at Bristol galvanised me to action. Desperate measures were necessary if I were to escape my marriage.

The journey from Cardiff to Bristol was harsh at this time of year with autumn seas, rains and mired roads to contend with. Mabel, Amelina and Ida accompanied me on the journey, together with an escort of Mabel's armed men. We rode first towards Striguil and crossed the Severn near there by ferry. I was drenched to the bone and nauseous with the child I carried. 'This reminds me of my first journey out of Wales,' I shouted at Mabel above the bluster of wind and waves. Her round face, framed by a dark wimple, glistened white and shiny with the drenchings from the salt water.

'Yes?' she yelled back.

'I travelled with your parents, crossing this channel on our way to Glastonbury where your mother asked the saint to intercede and give her a son.'

The boat rocked furiously and Amelina kept her eyes tight shut. The sudden swoops of the ship as it fell down tall waves were unkind to us all and we reached dry land in a state of disbelief that we were still alive.

To get down-country to Bristol from our place of landing we were obliged to traverse a landscape criss-crossed with rushing waters loaded with rain. The roads were founderous everywhere. Crossing several fords and quagmires, we teetered on improvised planks of wood. At one fast watercourse all the ford could offer us was a guide-rope slung across the river between trees that we must cling to, hand over hand, to reach the other side. 'We can't do that, Nest!' Amelina declared. 'We have to turn back.'

'It's not so deep,' Mabel said. 'I've crossed it before.'

'In spate? Like this?' exclaimed Amelina.

'We have no choice,' I declared. I pulled my horse's reins over his head and led him towards the edge of the river.

'Nest!' Amelina cried out behind me but I did not turn back. With my free hand I gripped tightly onto the guide-rope. At the river's edge, my horse and I sunk into soft mud knee-deep and the freezing water tugged hard and fast at us, longing to carry us downstream in its headlong tumble. I knew I must not pull in terror on the bridle and transmit my fear to my horse. I kept my grip on the bridle soft and my grasp on the guide-rope fierce and was glad that Amelina had laced my boots so tightly this morning. I felt with my foot for something other than mud, knowing that the riverbed itself would likely be more stony. I found something harder beneath my foot and advanced hoping to find more stones and rocks mid-stream. My sodden gown and cloak weighed heavy on me.

I heard splashes and screeches behind me and glanced back to see some men of the guard, then Ida, Amelina, Mabel and the rest of the men following me into the churning, brown waters. At mid-stream, we were wading up to our necks. We had to evade the panicked kicks and thrashing of the horses as the men struggled to lead them through the water and keep an eye out for broken trees and tangled mats of vegetation carried by the flood that might knock us from our hold on the rope. The river dragged at me. My teeth chattered. I struggled on and my horse pulled me in its keenness to emerge from the river. I felt the water swilling around my knees and saw that I had made it. There was more mud at this bank, making a last attempt to haul me under, but I tugged my leg from its grip and clambered up the bank where I watched the men assist Ida, Amelina, and Mabel to reach the land. We stood gasping and shivering, waiting for the whole party to assemble on the bank, astonished to be free of the river and to see each other grimed as golems.

On our arrival at Bristol Castle, Mabel had the servants show us to a fine room with a good fire blazing. Mabel's husband, Earl Robert of Gloucester, King Henry's oldest illegitimate son, held Bristol and Cardiff. The castle at Bristol stood on a narrow strip of land between the Avon and Frome rivers and had very stout defences.

'No more water, please! Ever!' declared Amelina as she stripped us of our sodden, muddied clothes. 'If thou wilt become unwell, wash thy head and go to sleep,' she muttered.

'We will soon be warm and dry,' I tried to reassure her. We squirmed into clean shifts, pulling them unevenly down over our resistant damp skin with chapped fingers. Ida held her chilled hands towards the fire to help the blood flow again to her fingertips.

When we were fed and warmed, Ida sat with stylus poised, ready to write my letter. I was capable of writing my own letters, but I did what I could to make her feel necessary in my household. And besides, not to write to my husband in my own hand put yet more welcome distance between us. I dictated the letter:

> *'To Stephen de Marais, Constable of Cardigan Castle. From Nest ferch Rhys.*
> *Greetings. I have happy news that I am carrying a child. I would not risk myself to a winter journey ... '*

Amelina snorted and she and Ida trained accusatory glances upon me.

'....journey,' I carried on firmly,

> *'and will remain in the care of my foster-sister, the countess of Gloucester, at Bristol Castle. I will send you word when the child is born. It will be sometime in the spring of next year. I have all the help and care that I need here. I know your duties are heavy in Cardigan and you must remain at your post.*
> *Stay in health, husband.'*

'No further embellishment?' asked Ida, looking up from the scroll and blotting her work.

'No. That's it.'

'Double delight!' declared Amelina. I shook my head at her, warning her to stop talking but she continued, nevertheless. 'A baby! *And* an unwanted husband held at bay!'

'Amelina!' exclaimed Ida. 'You may think such things, but you should not say them aloud.'

'That has never been Amelina's strong point,' I said.

Mabel entered in a hurry. 'I've found out that the king holds court *now*, Nest, and will only stay here this one night. You had best seek audience with him immediately.'

Ida and I considered each other with anxious expressions. Apart from her brother Haith, the king was the only person in England and Wales who would recognise her as a runaway nun.

'Stay here and do not show yourself,' I told her calmly. I looked down at myself. Amelina had just swapped my mud-smeared travelling clothes for an old, plain dress.

'That won't do,' Amelina exclaimed, finding a new burst of energy that enabled her to jump up from the pallet to tackle her area of expertise. 'But all your dresses have been drenched on the journey and need to be aired. They are damp at best and sodden on the whole. What to do?' She turned a stricken face to Mabel, who smiled her amusement at Amelina's dramatics. Amelina had been my maid since I'd grown up in Mabel's family and Mabel was as familiar with her manipulations as I was. 'Come and look through my wardrobe, Amelina, and see if you can find a gown that will not look too short on Nest.'

'And ribbons I'll be needing too,' Amelina emphasised, shooting a determined glance at me over her shoulder as they hurried out.

In a surprisingly short time, Amelina had me looking like a fine court lady who had taken all day preparing for her audience with the king. She tricked me out in one of Mabel's best floor-length, long-sleeved undertunics of pale green wool and covered part of that with a richly embroidered sleeveless tunic. My shoes were embroidered with gold thread and pearls, my borrowed mantle was light brown with a high ermine collar that caressed my neck and chin. As Amelina fussed around me, I wondered whether I would find Haith travelling with the king's court. I had heard nothing of him in Wales. Amelina stepped back from threading bright green ribbons through my dark plaits and pinning a short, delicate veil onto my head. She moved the beaded girdle so that it was slung more alluringly across my hips. My pregnancy was visible but not yet far advanced. Amelina's expression was smug.

'What I look like, is one thing,' I said, 'and I thank you, Amelina, for your trouble and, Mabel, for your loans, but it is what I can find to say that really matters.'

'Nonsense,' announced Amelina. 'You could talk gibberish

Welsh for half an hour straight and the king would not notice what it was that you said at all.'

I could not feel so confident. I was twenty years older than when Henry had first loved me and though he had aged himself, of course, his current mistresses and his wife were more than half his age.

I sidled in at the back of the hall where the king was holding court, intending to first assess the situation, see who was present, judge the mood of the king. However, I had only been standing looking about me for five minutes when the drone of the clerk's voice suddenly stopped. The king called out, 'Lady Nest? Is that you there?'

I looked up, embarrassed, as the crowd all turned to see where the king was enquiring. 'I … yes, sire.' Henry was on his feet and beaming at me.

'Well, let the lady forward, do!' exclaimed the king, waving his hands towards himself. The people jostled me forward, pushing me where I was not moving fast enough for their liking in their efforts to obey the king with alacrity and avoid his anger.

I found myself at the front of the hall, facing Henry far sooner than I had expected or wanted. A few hours ago, I was wading a river. I was not ready yet to venture all my future and happiness on this moment. The king smiled broadly at me. I was not inclined to return his smile. I was still angry with him. But I supposed that I must smile and smile, if I were to win my way here. I tried to inject some sincerity into the movements of my facial muscles.

'Lady Nest! This is a surprise. You are a delight for my sad eyes.'

I saw from his expression that his words were not mere formula. I reminded myself that he had recently lost three children in the wreck of *The White Ship* and softened a little. This must have been an unspeakably hard year for him.

'You wished to speak with me, Lady Nest? What brings you so far?'

'You were not so keen to speak with me last year,' I said frostily, referring to the occasion when he had decided, with no warning, to marry me to de Marais and would not hear, then, my desperate pleas to negotiate with him.

He leant forward and responded in a low voice. 'No quarter for me, then, Nest?'

I knew that if Amelina were beside me she would stand painfully on my foot to remind me that I must lie through my teeth to get my way and not speak plain truths. I took a shaky breath. 'I have come to present a petition, sire.'

He raised his eyebrows. 'On behalf of your husband?'

'No, sire. On my own behalf as Principissa Walliae, a princess of Wales.'

A slight smile curved his mouth for a fleeting moment. Henry was delighted by women in every way and he was delighted when a woman lay claim to her rights and status. His delight did not mean that he would agree but it meant that he would listen at least. 'Then you must present your petition, Principissa.' He nodded to a scribe sitting at the side of the raised dais where his throne was placed. The scribe dipped his nib in brown ink, smoothed his parchment and looked expectantly at me.

'I ask that the king confirm my rights to my dower lands at Carew and Llansteffan that were bequeathed to me by my mother Gwladys ferch Rhiwallon, queen of Deheubarth. I would gladly swear my oath on a holy relic that the lands were left to me as my dower.'

'There is no need to swear,' the king declared. 'I am well aware that these are your dower lands and do so confirm them in your hands as long as you use them for the benefit of my government of Wallia.'

I drew a deep breath. 'Thank you, sire. And I ask that you grant me right to reside on my lands at Llansteffan.'

He raised an eyebrow.

'My scribes,' I announced grandly (though I referred, in fact, to Ida) 'have drawn up this charter,' I drew a rolled parchment from my sleeve, 'and I ask that you consider it and, if it pleases you, that it be duly signed and witnessed.' I heard people muttering in low voices behind me but kept my eyes trained on the king's own.

'Do you, indeed?' He took the rolled parchment that I held out to him and bent over it, holding it flat across his knees. I realised that his eyesight was not what it once was since he had to peer so close over the charter. The document confirmed my right to Llansteffan—the castle and its demesne and the small town at its foot. It confirmed my right to reside there and take a proportion of profits from the town market, by order of the king. It was my escape bid from de Marais.

'There is no need for a written charter,' Henry declared. 'My confirmation of your dower lands is written down as the record of this court, as you see.' He gestured to his own scribe.

'Nevertheless, Deheubarth is far from your courts in England and a charter that I might carry would be of use to me.' I took a step closer towards his knees and lowered my voice in a vain attempt to gain some intimacy and privacy between us. 'I never asked you for anything before, sire.'

He pursed his mouth at me. He did not like the precedent it would set. 'I will review the document and think on it,' he stated loudly.

My heart sank. I knew him well enough to translate this statement to 'no'.

In my chamber, I told Ida what had happened and we discussed my disappointment.

'Well, all is not lost yet, is it?' Amelina insinuated, glancing at the great bed behind us. 'He's here for the night.'

'Amelina, your thoughts do not contribute anything helpful to this discussion,' I told her tersely. I turned to Ida. 'There is no need to be concerned for your safety. The king has no idea you are here. You simply need to keep to my chambers until he leaves tomorrow.'

'Unless, of course, the king finds his way to said chambers,' Amelina persisted. 'As he used to.'

'Please! Be silent,' I told her, exasperated. The notes of a lute being tuned rose up the stairwell to us and Amelina danced around the room, laying out my best red dress, which she had succeeded in drying, and my best jewels, and, of course, red hair ribbons.

Ida began to laugh at Amelina, but her laughter ceased abruptly. 'No!' She pushed herself up lopsided from her chair with one hand and clutched at her collar with her other hand. Amelina and I moved swiftly to support Ida, each taking one of her elbows. She had gone as white as fresh snow and I feared she would fall.

'What is it?' I asked, bewildered at what might have suddenly frightened her.

'It's him.' I realised that she was listening to the melody of the voice spiralling up from the hall. I could hear, now, the Welsh tones of the song.

'Sweet appletree of crimson colour, / Growing, concealed, in the wood of Celyddon / Though men seek your fruit, their search is vain.'

The voice stopped for a moment and I asked her, 'Him?'

'Breri.'

'The king's minstrel?'

'He is a bard. A travelling bard. I last knew of him in the service of the king's sister, Countess Adela de Blois. He knows me. Like the king, he knows who I am. He knew me as a nun at Fontevraud.'

8

Gisulf's Box

September 1122, London, England

Emerging from the shadow of the gatehouse, Haith rode into London hearing the curfew bell at Saint-Martin-Le-Grand. Saint-Martin-Le-Grand offered sanctuary from law to anyone who could lay hands on the altar and he wondered how many fugitives might be sheltering there right now. He had arrived with little time to spare before he must appear at Bishop Roger's Upper Exchequer Court at Westminster. The court was scheduled for the following day. He dismounted and pushed open the gate of his townhouse. Two armed men confronted him in the courtyard and, then, recognising him, bid him welcome. Haith was pleased to see that his deputy had thought to post guards. There would be a quantity of silver sitting in a chest inside the house to pay the taxes at the Exchequer that needed to be well looked after. Haith led his horse across the courtyard and his grinning stableboy came running to take the reins. 'Welcome home, Master!'

Haith ruffled his hair. 'Thank you, lad.' Haith glanced up with satisfaction at the black and white columbage of the house. It was good to be home.

Haith's deputy, Gwyn, had heard the horse and voices in the

courtyard and he emerged from the door, shouting a greeting. 'Sir Haith! Welcome back!'

'Thanks!' Haith gripped Gwyn's shoulder. 'All well here?'

'Yes, sir.' They moved inside and Haith subsided onto the comfortable chair close to the hearth to take off his damp boots. A good fire was burning and he stretched his stockinged toes out to its heat, looking expectantly at Gwyn. 'So, what's the news?'

Gwyn waited while Haith's housekeeper held out a bowl of water for Haith to wash his hands and face and provided them both with beakers of wine before responding. 'I travelled up from Pembroke with the taxes last week.'

'No trouble on the road?'

'No. All was well. I had a solid guard of five men with me. The weather kept dry for us.'

'Is the coin good?' Haith asked.

'I hope so, sheriff.'

'Your hopes are my neck, Gwyn, you'd best be right,' Haith rebuked.

Gwyn held up a reassuring hand and stated in a tone of greater certainty. 'You can depend on it. I had Gilpatric check the quality of the silver.'

Gilpatric was the minter at Pembroke and Haith knew that both he and Gwyn were dependable men. 'Good,' declared Haith. 'Thank you for your work and care. What other news?'

'The king's in Bristol and planning to go north to York and inspect the silver mines at Alston.'

Haith nodded and wondered if Henry had received his message yet concerning the rebellion that Waleran and Amaury were brewing in Normandy. 'And back in Pembroke?'

'Lady Isabel birthed a girl and they are both well.'

Haith nodded again. This girl was another of Henry's numerous illegitimate brood. He thought with a pang of his own son with Nest, Robert, who was unacknowledged by him and did not know his father. The boy must be three years old now. Perhaps

Nest would let Haith take the boy into his household when he was old enough to train and then they could grow to know one another.

Haith listened with only half an ear to Gwyn's litany of new shops and inns that had opened in Pembroke and Tenby, of husbands or wives caught out in adultery in the towns, of a fight on market day. Gwyn made no mention of Nest and Haith forced himself not to ask. He could not keep running away from the loss of Nest forever. Soon, when the king was finished with him, he would have to return to Wales, to his office in Pembroke, and he would have to face it, to face the sight of her with de Marais. He had sent a letter to Ida at Cardigan Castle but received no reply as yet.

Haith left the guards and his sword at the door and entered the hall at Westminster with two of his men carrying the heavy studded chest of silver. Bishop Roger of Salisbury was presiding over the exchequer court session. At the extreme far end of the great length of the hall, most of the other sheriffs and clerks were already gathered around the exchequer table set up before the bishop. All other people were excluded from this morning's closed session. The clerestory gallery that ran all around the upper level of the walls was usually crammed with onlookers, but stood empty today. The roof soared high above Haith's head and when the hall was packed with all the people of the court, it was still a vast space. Reaching the table, Haith inclined his head in greeting to Miles of Gloucester who was here to pay the dues for Carmarthen. The other sheriffs all answered for counties in England. The king's empty marble throne with its lion's feet was beyond the exchequer table, raised up on a dais. Haith found that he was looking forward to seeing Henry, but it would be a while yet before he caught up with him on his progress north.

It came to his turn and a clerk read out what was owed to the king by the sheriff of Pembroke for the annual farm of the counties, the proceeds of justice, and the national levies of Danegeld and feudal aids. Haith lifted the lid of the chest and the clerks set about weighing the purses and recording the payment on a wooden tally stick. The treasury clerk retained one half of the stick and Haith kept the other half as his receipt and then the transaction was recorded on a sheet of parchment. At the end of the long day of payments, all the sheets would be carefully rolled and sealed, ready to be placed in the royal archive. Haith breathed a sigh of relief when the announcement of the assay, the blanch payment, was made. His payment was not to be one of the random sampling of coins that would be melted and checked to ensure that the silver was not debased. Since he had not checked it himself this time, he was taking an enormous risk on Gwyn's assurance and even his friendship with the king might not save him, if he was accused of cheating the crown of its dues. Relieved to have successfully concluded his business at court, Haith found his horse and headed towards the eastern edge of the city.

He had made enquiries amongst the king's household and had been surprised to discover that the murdered clerk Gisulf had held a soke and burh in London. This was a private estate and residence of some importance and an indication of the wealth that the clerk had managed to accumulate. A summons had come from the king this morning to attend him in Carlisle. Henry had received Haith's message concerning the fermentation of rebellion in Normandy at Waleran's castle. The king's command meant that Haith had only one day to spare in London and would have to set out tomorrow morning to catch up with the king's entourage.

Haith found Gisulf's house on the edge of the city, close to a stinking and clogged ditch in the vicinity of Smithfield. Haith wondered at the choice of location. This place was as far away as it was possible to be from the royal palace and administrative offices at Westminster where Gisulf's duties as royal clerk had lain when the king was in residence. From the outside, the house had an air of neglect. Haith banged on the door, which quivered on loose hinges beneath his fist. The person on the other side of the portal took their time opening up. Haith regarded the door with scepticism. It was so badly maintained and flimsy that a quick kick would have easily collapsed it, despite the barrage of locks that he could hear being unlocked and the bolts being slid back.

The door opened a crack and the hostile gaze of a very fat and slovenly looking woman scoured Haith from head to foot. Finally, she asked him his business.

'I am on the king's business, madam,' Haith told her. She looked alarmed. 'I am required to collect all papers belonging to Gisulf the clerk, who formerly lived here.'

'We don't want no Flemings here,' she blurted, voicing the prejudice of many Londoners against the foreign traders and especially against the numerous Flemings. 'Get away.'

She began to close the door and Haith inserted a boot in the gap. 'I told you madam, I am on the king's business. I am one of his sheriffs.' Haith neglected to mention that his shrievalty was far away in south-west Wales.

'Master Gisulf told me that he held this soke from the archbishop of Canterbury himself and no writ, not even the king's, runs here. Get away or I'll be calling the reeve on you.' Her words were bold, but the fear in her face told a different story. She must have been holed up here for the last year, since report of Gisulf's drowning would have reached her, just waiting for the day when an official of some sort would knock on the door and turf her into the street.

Gisulf's burh was a defensible walled house, and during his

lifetime it would have been staffed with guards and well-nigh impossible to breach but Haith had the impression that following her master's death, this slatternly woman was the only person remaining. Gisulf's other household staff would have long since left when the payment of wages abruptly dried up.

'I know the law,' she went on. 'No one can be arrested in their house in a soke. It's protected, private property. Only place you can arrest me is standing in the middle of the road.'

'Well, perhaps you would care to step out and join me here, then,' countered Haith in exasperation. 'What are you defending woman?' He tried another tack. 'Your master is dead. I have been instructed to search his papers in case he has left bequests for his retainers that must be honoured before his affairs are wound up and this very soke is returned to the jurisdiction of the archbishop.'

She heard the twin hint of something in it for her and the threat of eviction and gaped at him for a long moment, perplexed. 'Master Gisulf didn't want *anyone* knowing he was secreted away here,' she complained, 'but, true enough, he's dead now.' She opened the door to allow Haith over the threshold.

'Indeed,' Haith said, impatient in his hope that this run-down residence might give him a crucial piece of the puzzle of *The White Ship*.

'He kept his paperwork all upstairs,' she said, 'but there's nothing there now.'

'Lead the way, please.'

The woman turned her broad back upon him and led him up several flights of narrow, precipitous stairs to the attic room. 'This was his writing room,' she said, throwing her arm wide as if she had led him to a palatial chamber rather than the sorry little room he was looking at. 'I haven't touched anything.' Haith raised an eyebrow at her. He strongly doubted that. 'I didn't take in any tenants in respect for poor Master Gisulf.' Haith ignored the hint that she might like some remuneration for her delicacy.

'Leave me, mistress. I will let you know when I am finished here.'

She humphed, turned on a heel, and eased herself back down the creaking stairs.

Haith looked around him. A narrow bed, a desk, and chair. A candlestick on the desk. If there had been a candle, the woman had taken that long ago. A sliver of light came in through a skylight. More low beams for Haith to avoid. And these beams were rough and splintered and of many differing widths and woods, as if they had been collected in the forest and leant against each other, temporarily, to hold up the roof, rather than being carefully dressed and knit in place by a master carpenter. That was probably exactly what had happened. It gave the room the appearance of a kind of treehouse. Haith wound his head carefully around the treacherous beams to look at the desk. There was nothing on or under it. He sat on the chair and regarded the empty room. The woman would have ransacked its contents long ago. He rose up again, gingerly, to avoid braining himself on the 'treehouse' structure. He moved slowly and quietly down the stairs in search of the woman's quarters.

He heard her chopping vegetables at the board in the kitchen. She had her back to the open door to the kitchen. Haith moved past the doorway to the next room, which appeared to be her bedchamber. There were clothes strewn around the room. He dropped to all fours to look under the bed and fished out a small chest. He sat back on his heels regarding it. It was a good quality waxed canvas coffer strapped with leather. It did not look like the possession of the woman next door, but rather more like something Gisulf himself would have used to store parchments and carry about with him. It had a stout hasp and was locked. Haith tested the weight of the coffer. Whatever was inside was not heavy. He could carry it. Better to take it back to his own quarters and break it open there, rather than sit here hammering at the lock, and dealing with the woman's resistance. He hefted the chest to his hip, draped his cloak about it and made for the door, calling out a cheery goodbye and thanks when he was clear of the threshold and closing the door behind him.

In his own townhouse, Haith rocked back in his chair, more shocked even than when Abbess Petronilla had told him that Benedicta had left Fontevraud. He had not thought it possible that he *could* be more shocked than *that*. Gisulf's box contained scrolls and letters. Haith thought he had found the reason here, amongst these papers, for Berold and de Pirou's commission to murder the clerk, but then he had found another, second letter from Robert de Bellême and it was that one, that letter that had given him the great shock.

The parchments in Gisulf's coffer were in many different hands and they were all originals. This was a crime in itself. The king's correspondence should be stored in his scriptorium at Westminster and not in a clerk's obscure attic room down a back alley. It was quickly apparent to Haith that Gisulf had been a blackmailer. Clerks and messengers were in highly trusted positions, carrying secrets as they often did. Clerks who could read, where many messengers might not, were an especial vulnerability. These letters that Gisulf had kept back or copied were all incriminating for some poor unfortunate. Most of the contents related to sexual misdemeanours by husbands, clerics, wives, but reading through the top layer, Haith had come across a letter from Waleran de Meulan addressed to William *Clito*, assuring him of his loyalty and his wish to see him in his proper place as duke of Normandy. This was a much more serious matter than all the rest and surely the reason for Gisulf's drowning in the barrel. The letter had been folded within a slip of paper addressed to Henry from his sister Adela, countess de Blois. 'Brother,' she wrote, 'see here what my trusty network of spies have discovered now of the plotters, and weep. This ingrate was your beloved protégé and he betrays you so easily.' Waleran's letter was indeed damning. It was a stupid letter. It was the letter of a young man eager to show that he would gladly bite the hand that had fed and nurtured him. The king did not deserve such treatment from Waleran.

It was likely that Haith was holding in his hands the seed of all those deaths on *The White Ship*. Instead of sending Countess Adela's note with the letter on to the king, Gisulf must have attempted to blackmail Waleran, who had ordered Gisulf's murder. Waleran had not sailed with the ship, or sailed at all at that time, pleading that he had business to attend to on his estates and Henry had graciously let the new, young lord, who had just come of age, go free to flex his muscles on his own lands. Yet de Pirou had an association with Ranulf de Gernon rather than Waleran and Haith could make no sense of that. Why had de Pirou been involved?

Haith puzzled over the mystery of *The White Ship* yet again. Stephen de Blois's own sister, Matilda, had died in the wreck. It was hard to believe that he would conspire to that. Stephen had been the third male in line for Henry's throne before the wreck, and he was second in line now, behind his older brother, Thibaut. Ranulf de Gernon's father had gained the earldom of Chester as a consequence of the death of his cousin Richard in the shipwreck. Perhaps there was motive there after all. Perhaps it had been a conspiracy of several lords acting together.

As Haith sat tapping Adela's letter against the edge of the table, his eye had fallen on the corner of another letter buried further down in Gisulf's chest. Only three words were visible on that corner, but Haith immediately recognised the distinctive hand of the traitor Robert de Bellême. Haith fished it out and unfolded the two pages of this letter. De Bellême addressed King Henry from prison where he had been confined after his last rebellion. He asked the king to allow him to return to his French estates, to at least allow his son to inherit his French estates, but supplication did not come easily to de Bellême, and Haith was soon reading recriminations against Henry's treatment, and then,

> *That I should come to this because that whore-nun took it upon herself to steal my correspondence with de Montfort is unconscionable. That letter was taken by the nun Benedicta at Fontevraud after she had lulled de Montfort with a disgusting excess of sexual favours, or so he says.*

Aghast, Haith dropped the letter as if it had burnt him. He sat staring at it on the floor, his heart beating as though he had run a great distance. He bent and retrieved the letter, reading the words again. He knew that Benedicta had indeed assisted Henry in the matter of convicting de Bellême with some correspondence. He had assumed that it was letters from Bertrade de Montfort that she had supplied, not something from Bertrade's brother, Amaury. He did his best to unread the words, 'disgusting excess of sexual favours' but it was impossible. He moved across the room to wrestle with the buckles on his saddlebag until it yielded to him the small wrapped book that de Montfort had given to him to convey to Benedicta. He tugged at the black fleece wrapping, shaking the tangling shreds from his hand to the floor. Ovid's *Amores*. A finely bound copy. Hardly an appropriate gift from a man to a nun. Against his own instincts, telling himself no, Haith opened the cover and read the inscription.

> *Benedicta, I will never forget you and will always think of you, wherever you are in the world. I read and reread Ovid's words: 'thigh to thigh'.*

The inscription was followed by the confident flourish of his signature: Amaury de Montfort, count of Evreux.

Haith resisted the urge to hurl the costly book at the wall. What had Benedicta done? What had she gotten herself into? He should have been able to protect her from it. And now, he could not follow her trail to Nest's household, but instead must dance attendance on Henry far to the north of the country. He dropped his forehead to the comfort of his large hand and closed his eyes, whispering, 'my dear sister?'

A new thought hit him like the near-miss of a thudding boulder from a trebuchet. Were his suspicions that Stephen de Blois or Ranulf de Gernon or Waleran de Meulan were responsible for the sinking of *The White Ship* all completely wrong? Was it possible that it was Amaury who had commissioned the murder of Gisulf, to protect Benedicta? That it was *this* letter that had led to the wreck of the ship and the loss of all those lives?

9

Reunion

September 1122, Bristol Castle, England

'The bard, Breri, is a spy,' Ida whispered, her eyes enormous with fear. 'He has great powers of discernment.'

'Well, he cannot see through walls or doors. Keep the door locked, Amelina, when I am out of the room. Trust no one to come in. If there is a knock, you must open the door and Ida must stay hidden from sight.'

Amelina nodded solemnly and I gripped Ida's shoulders reassuringly. 'They will not discover you. You are safe as long as we all hold our nerve. Nobody is dragging you back to the cloister. I must go down to the feast now.'

Regardless of Ida's account of his espionage for Countess Adela, it was an immense pleasure to listen to Breri's songs at the meal. 'My compliments on your new bard,' I told Henry. 'The Welsh singers are the best.' I was seated next to the king and my foster-sister, Mabel, his hostess, sat on his other side.

'Breri is not mine, alas. I cannot keep him, though I have tried,' Henry grumbled. 'He assures me that he must go on into his homeland.'

'To Wales?'

'Yes. He is destined for Gilbert de Clare's household at

Pembroke, he says, and scorns the service of the king of England!' Henry went on to speak obsessively of portents, forecasts, hermits and scryers throughout the rest of dinner. Mabel and I exchanged anxious glances. Such matters skirted close to magic and blasphemy.

'Did you experience this great battering of hail in Wales, Lady Nest, just after Christmas?'

'No, sire.'

'Hail balls the size of my fist,' he exclaimed, holding out a curled hand to me as demonstration. 'They were hurled down hard from the heavens and punched holes in roofs, killed cows and sheep in the field. I had some collected afterwards and those frozen shards shimmered of the Otherworld.'

'It sounds … dramatic, sire.'

'We have to ask what did it portend. I have been warned that there will be terrifying tribulation on the Earth, and very many illustrious people will succumb to destruction.'

The king's chaplain called up the table to us from the far end, where he was seated: 'We are occasionally afforded a glimpse of the Otherworld for our edification. At Ely, last month, for instance, there was a sign. A pregnant cow was order to be sliced open and three piglets were revealed. We must persevere in good and turn away from evil.'

Henry stared at his trencher for a while, seeming to ponder the chaplain's words. 'And Nest, I have had reports of stars streaming from the sky in brilliant rivers of light. Why would stars so fall from their orbits? I would know the secret causes of things.'

'We cannot know the future, sire,' Mabel stated.

'And if we could, we might wish we did not,' I added.

'There are those with great wisdom,' was all that Henry would concede on the point. 'I have summoned Abbot Walcher of Malvern to me. He is famed for his knowledge of the heavens.'

'I know of the abbot, sire,' Mabel said. 'His fame as a scholar and an astronomer is unparalleled.'

'Yes,' the king said. 'He writes to me that Muslim Spain has great aqueducts and fountains in the cities. And there are vast libraries of learning there that he has studied. He says it is not blasphemy to study the stars that have been ordained by God to influence the terrestrial world. He has predicted solar and lunar eclipses using a device called an astrolabe. He can calculate the time of the new moon, which can be of great value for medicinal purposes.'

'But we cannot reckon the grains of sand on the beach, the drops of water in the ocean, or the days of the world, sire,' I said, feeling argumentative.

'When he joins me,' Henry continued, ignoring my interruption, 'I will ask him to tell me what he sees in the heavens and their alignments with regards to deaths and births in my vicinity.'

'But the abbot is not a fortune teller, lord king,' I protested. 'He is a scholar. I can tell you that there will be more deaths—there are always more deaths. And births.' Alarmed by the direction of conversation, I did my best to divert Henry to a different subject.

After the meal, I returned to my chamber and told Ida about the peculiarities of Henry's dinner conversation.

'He was very sick when I last saw him in Normandy,' Ida said, 'after the maiming of his granddaughters. He lost his wits for a while, Nest. He became obsessed with the powers of relics and greatly fearful of his own death. The loss of his heir, his other children and his wards on *The White Ship* must have placed even more pressure upon his sanity.'

'He seems quite sane to me, but, just … overly reliant on these ideas of prophecy and dream, which I never knew in him before.'

Ida opened her mouth to respond, when there was an near inaudible scratch at the door. Ida's eyes widened in alarm. There was something decidedly odd about that scratch. It was not the sound that a servant would make seeking entry. It sounded deliberately surreptitious. I gestured to Ida to conceal herself behind the curtains of the bed. I watched her feet disappear from view and heard the bed creak as she climbed up onto it. Amelina positioned herself at the foot of the bed ready to ensure that no sudden draught might part the curtains and reveal our secret nun.

I rose and opened the door a crack. The tall, portly bard Breri stood there, a wide smile on his florid face. His lute was slung across his back and he held a very large glass of wine in one hand and his bow in the other. I guessed that he had scratched at the door with that bow. Had he been eavesdropping? Could he have heard Ida's voice through this thick wood? Or heard our conversation about the king's sanity?

'Sir bard?'

'You are the *gwawr*, Nest ferch Rhys, I believe,' he said in Welsh, meaning the noblewoman.

'Yes.'

'I am here with a message from the king and wonder if I might beg a moment's audience with you, *Principissa*?' He flattered, or mocked me perhaps, with the title of princess that I had used in court that afternoon to impress my rights, so ineffectually, upon the king.

'What is his message?' I asked, without opening the door any wider.

'He asks that he might bestow a visit upon you in your chamber for a taste of fine wine and conversation. For old time's sake, he declares.' Breri spoke in a melodious Welsh and overegged his words deliberately.

I could not allow the king to discover Ida here and sought quickly for a solution. 'My ladies are sleeping after an arduous journey through foul weather. It would be better if I went to the king.'

'I will convey your response to your king.' Lascivious amusement danced in Breri's eyes. He bowed to me, bending briskly, one foot forward, both arms quite straight and parallel with the floor, his bow held out to one side and his glass of wine to the other.

I wanted to slap the man for his impertinence, but I was caught in a quandary and could think of no other escape. Exposing myself to gossip and to Henry's advances by going to his chambers was the last thing I wished to do. But there: it was done.

Ida and Amelina remonstrated with me in hushed tones when we judged that Breri had moved away from the closed door.

'It can't be good for your reputation, my lady, to go to the king's chamber!' Amelina declared. 'Will you buy your freedom from one unwelcome man in your bed by climbing into the embrace of another?'

'In that moment, I could think of no other solution. I can't let Henry in here with Ida here. Anyway, I doubt that I have any reputation left to cherish. It is in shreds already after my abduction by Prince Owain. And no, you fool, I have no intention of resuming my relationship with Henry. That is far from my mind.'

'It can't be right, surely,' Ida said, more mild in her objections than Amelina, 'to go to the king's private chamber?'

I looked down at my dress. I was still wearing my splendid gown and jewels from the feast. 'Undress me quickly, Amelina, from this finery and pass me that everyday dress there. Is it dry?'

'This one?' Amelina was aghast as she held it up in enquiry. 'It's dry, but you can't wear this for an audience with the king,'

'It's perfect,' I declared. 'And get these ridiculous ribbons out of my hair.' I began to tug at them myself. 'I know what I am about. And that wimple.' I pointed at a particularly unbecoming, plain wimple made from heavy brown wool.

Reluctantly she did as I asked and I was soon clad in the drabbest clothes in my wardrobe. I took a breath, nodded to their anxious faces, closed the door quietly behind me, and heard them lock it as I had instructed. As I moved down the long, dim passage towards the king's chamber, my candle guttered in a draught. I glanced back over my shoulder, sensing someone behind me but could see nothing in the blackness beyond the circle of light circumscribed by my candle.

I found Henry relaxing in his shirt and britches before a fire with a glass of wine. With increasing age, he was losing the taut, hard muscles of his younger days and the increased bulge of his stomach was evident. His robes of state were slung across a chest. He saw me at the door and gestured that I be admitted swiftly. Loitering on the threshold of his private chamber would soon set rumours flying around the court. A woman known to have been the mistress of this king and the abductee of a Welsh prince could hardly hope that she had a great deal of reputation to protect. Henry stood and dismissed the two servants who had been packing up his possessions in preparation for his journey north tomorrow. He led me back to chairs set opposite each other and close to the crackling hearth, which was pungent with pinecones newly scattered on it. He poured wine for us and we sipped, looking at each other for a long time over the rims of our beakers.

'Are you unhappy, Nest?'

'I persist.'

'Me too.' He refilled our beakers. Our stance and the atmosphere between us was redolent with memories of the old days, long ago, when we had been lovers, when I had been the king's mistress and one of the most powerful women at court. I had been more powerful, at times, even than Henry's first wife, Queen Matilda, who was gone now and blessed, at least, not to have to live through the loss of Prince William, as Henry must.

'I am grieved beyond words for you Henry.'

'Thank you.' We sat in silence, nursing our wine and our pains for a few more moments.

'I intended to give you to Haith, you know, as you and he requested,' he ventured, and I instantly held up my palm to him begging him not to continue but he did. 'Like you, I thought he had perished on *The White Ship*. I am sorry for it, Nest.'

It was something, I supposed. I was glad that I concerned him enough to apologise to me for my unpalatable marriage to de Marais.

'Well, thank you for your sorry.' I raised my beaker and smiled. He smiled in return, his gaze directed at my dimple, which had always amused and fascinated him. 'Is Sheriff Haith travelling with your court?'

'No. I haven't seen him for a while and assume he is about his business in Pembroke.'

As far as I had heard, Haith was not at Pembroke, but I kept that to myself. 'I am with child, sire. So de Marais has his heir. I have done my duty to him and that marriage and would go my own road now.'

'Of course you are with child, Nest. You are always with child, my fertile Welsh princess!' He pulled his stool a little closer to mine, so that our knees were touching. 'How many sons do you have?'

'Five.'

'So far,' he stated, nodding in the direction of my stomach. 'If only I had married you. I would not be in this quandary, without an heir to the throne. I am truly glad to see you, Nest. You always gave me consolation and advice when others could not.'

Other women he meant. Well, I thought sharply, it was perhaps asking too much of the young mistress he had abandoned at Pembroke (as he had me, many years before) or a fourteen-year-old queen. 'I hope the queen is well.'

'Yes. Adelisa is a pleasant girl, but she arrived knowing nothing of the politics here or in Normandy and, I suspect, that none of it is of great interest to her.'

'She will be busy rearing your heir soon, no doubt.'

Henry said nothing for a while longer than I had expected. 'If it pleases God,' he said, at last. The poor girl. She had only been wed a year and already they were casting doubts on her fertility. No one could have the least concern about Henry's own virility, despite his fifty-four years in contrast to the queen's youth. Henry's trail of illegitimate children tracked all across Normandy, England, and Wales.

'Adelisa will give me a son but even if I live long, he is likely to still be a minor when he inherits the throne. I have to decide how best to safeguard him and the legacy of my reign. When that heir is born,' he said, 'I will need to think about the appointment of a regent for my son, after my own demise.'

'That time is far off yet, sire.'

'A king must think far ahead, Nest.'

'A regent for a minor on the throne? Has that happened before?'

'Yes, with my own father, when he stood to inherit the duchy of Normandy. There were attempts to kill my father, and successes at killing his regents.'

I was silent for a moment, thinking. 'In Wales, this does not happen. The most able, adult male relative inherits—he who is most aggressive in his claim and can muster the most support. Who would you appoint as regent? Your nephew, Stephen de Blois, is your closest kinsman in the court,' I said, careful to inject a note of hesitation into my tone. I disliked and distrusted Stephen.

'Yes, but that would be a great deal of power for an ambitious and not always circumspect young man. If Stephen were so close to the throne as regent, he would think to take that throne himself. I am thinking of my son, Robert, and my daughter, Maud.'

I frowned and considered what such a responsibility might mean for my foster-sister and Robert's wife, Mabel. Henry's daughter Maud, his only remaining legitimate child, was married to the Emperor of Germany. 'Maud is far from here and has a husband herself who is in need of an heir,' I said, my tone laden with my doubt.

'This is true. But I have asked Emperor Henry and Maud to stand ready to act quickly should Robert need their support in ensuring a regency. Depending on circumstances, depending on timing, I am hoping that I can obtain Maud's oath to come and give at least a year of her time to support Robert, in the event that he must become regent.'

'This seems very complex. Why not allow Robert to be regent alone, or appoint someone else who is already here, in your realm.'

'Such as?'

'Is there no-one else?'

'No one of the younger generation with the right qualities. No one I trust. Remember, Nest,' his voice sank to a whisper, 'how many of that generation died on *The White Ship*.'

I blinked slowly to express my sympathy and we both sat in silence for a while, thinking of the rollcall of the drowned, so very many of them. Henry reached for the jug of wine and refilled our beakers. 'Maud is my legitimate child and used to command,' he said, recovering the certainty of his voice. 'I have spoken with Robert and asked Maud to come to consult with me. She was due to meet me in Kent earlier this year and I waited there for her but she did not arrive. The Count of Flanders would not give her passage through his lands. If I were to have a child heir and they were to take sick and die, Maud would be the rightful heir. It would be best, then, if she were already on English soil.'

I blinked at his words. Did he imagine that the Norman lords would allow a woman to rule?

'Robert would make the best regent,' Henry carried on. 'His own interests would make no headway, more's the pity.'

I raised my eyebrows. This conversation felt as if we had stepped back twenty years and nothing had passed between us. No other mistresses and wives on his part, no husbands and lovers on mine. If was as it had been between us in the days of our great affection for each other, when he was newly king and mulled over all his affairs of state with me. I gazed into the dark red pool of my wine, suppressing my welling emotion. Now, we were both so old and had lived through so much. Now, we must sit and discuss how our children would replace us.

'Robert would make me an admirable *heir*,' Henry continued. 'I could ask for no better. I wish wholeheartedly that it could be so. That I could appoint him, my eldest and my most loyal son. But his maternal lineage does not make him throneworthy in the eyes of my unruly and ambitious barons, and his illegitimacy means that opposition from the church would be relentless. He would be untenably weakened as king by his birth. It seems ridiculous, when you consider that a few years back, my own father, who *was* a bastard, was crowned king of England. But there it is. I have to be realistic. You agree? Robert would be the best choice of regent?'

'Yes. I have no doubt of that.'

'Nor I. All I need is an heir now! Perhaps you could give me some practice for that, Nest?'

'Henry, you are incorrigible. I will do no such thing.'

He pulled a face. 'Let's see later,' he murmured, filling my beaker again. 'I'd rather take an experienced woman to bed than a young girl. A woman that I know I fit with very well.'

I laughed. It was impossible not to laugh with him. It was the first time I had laughed since I had heard the news that Haith had drowned, since I had learned that news was false and been forced to wed de Marais in the same moment. And Henry laughed, and I guessed that this might be the first time he had laughed too for a long time. 'I can sympathise with that,' I joked, 'since my own husband is fifteen years my junior, thanks to you!' I raised my goblet to him, and he looked with warm affection into my eyes, while I did my best to evade that liquid black gaze that I had known so well as a young woman, that had led me astray so often before. 'What about Adelisa herself as regent?' I asked, to remind him he had a wife and keep him distracted from his flirtation with me.

'She will have a role, of course, as the queen mother but she does not have the political acumen and experience of my daughter, Maud. Nothing like.'

I thought of our own son, Henry. I could have raised and supported a king. The king had so many sons, all frustratingly useless since they were illegitimate and their mothers were, for the most part, low-born. Alone among the king's mistresses who had given him sons, I had royal blood. Our son had royal blood on both sides but he was also the only one of Henry's illegitimate children who had not been raised at the king's court. The king had granted me that, in love for me, that I raise my child in Wales. So our son Henry had not been raised to rule or to aim high, and a part of me was glad of that.

'If Adelisa and I should not be blessed with a son, then I am determined that a son of my daughter Maud will inherit my kingdom. My grandson.'

'England and Normandy together with the empire of Germany and Italy!' I exclaimed. 'This is a vast kingdom. Too vast, surely?'

'Yes. It would have to be her second son, of course. Her first son will be heir to the empire.'

I opened my mouth and then closed it again. I had been on the verge of mentioning that Maud had not yet birthed any living child in eleven years of marriage, but, then, I saw a look of fevered hope in Henry's eyes and did not speak my scepticism. He leant forward and whispered. 'It has been prophesied.'

I said nothing in response to his prophecy. I had allowed this meeting to go on too long. The fire was beginning to burn low and the huge bed in the room, with its lavish green quilt and hangings, seemed to have grown more present. 'Will you excuse me, sire?' I said. 'I had a long, arduous journey to get here and was readying for bed when I received your message. You find me in my old, everyday frock, as you see.' Presenting myself as an aging, plainly dressed woman was not giving me the protection from his importuning that I had expected.

'Naked is good, as I recall,' he persisted. 'Readying for bed is good.' I cast my eyes to the ceiling and he shrugged. 'You would make a peasant's smock look like a ermine and pearl-encrusted robe, Nest.' He took my hand and touched three gossamer kisses to the first knuckles of my fingers. My body responded to the contact with his mouth. I slipped my hand quickly from his and made my way to the door.

'Nest.'

I had my hand on the latch of the door. I would do a great deal to elude my horrible husband, but I could not go so far as to sleep with Henry.

'I will begin my progress north at dawn tomorrow and would be glad if you would accompany me for the first few hours of my journey. Break fast with me at the hunting lodge that lies on the route.'

I said nothing, keeping my back to him and my expression to myself. I knew that hunting lodges were always places of sexual tryst for him.

'I would speak more with you of your charter,' he stated.

I turned back to face him. 'I will be ready to ride with you at dawn, sire.'

We were all up with the lark in the morning but so was the rest of the household and a great deal of clattering and neighing broke through the swirling morning mist that lifted and lowered around the castle courtyard in waves. The air was damp and Amelina forecast more rain. Readying to dress me, she laid out an oiled riding cloak and heavy boots. She would remain at the castle and wait for my return, but I asked Ida to accompany me and keep her face well concealed. 'It's too dangerous,' she gasped.

'I have a notion,' I told her as we stood at the window watching Breri leave to continue his journey into Wales. Through the swirling mist, we glimpsed his flamboyant hat and his back, as he swayed in the saddle, disappearing down the road.

'I have an idea about this threat.' In response to her inquisitive glance I continued. 'While Breri is in Pembroke, you are at great risk in Wales. I'm thinking you might be safer at Henry's court for a while.'

'What are you talking about, Nest!'

'Henry would not betray you to the Church. I assure you that he will find the notion of a renegade nun a great amusement, and he was very grateful to you for nursing him through his sickness before.'

Ida's expression showed her hesitation at my idea. 'But then, I would have to leave you.'

'Not for ever, just until we are sure that Breri is no threat.'

'I believe Breri would have no compunction in betraying me for a handful of coin.'

'Whereas the king would protect you.'

'I don't know, Nest.'

'I have two motives, I confess. I think the king needs you, Ida. I was a little concerned at his speech last night on prophecies of death and births. Perhaps you could help keep him stable, keep him well?'

She nodded, but her face showed her reluctance and anxiety at the risk we would run in exposing her situation to the king.

Amelina's prediction was true and we rode for half an hour through sheets of cold rain that blustered at our cloaks, penetrated beneath the brims of our hats and under our collars, slid wet fingers inside the tops of our boots. 'You'll be regretting this, Nest!' Henry laughed.

'I hope not, sire.' First, I saw the long, curving line of the grey wall of the deer park running far across the fields, as far as the eye could see. We trotted through the gateway into the park and the trees gave us some respite from the downpour. Then, the hunting lodge came into view through the trees. Halting before the lodge, two of the king's men came to help Ida and me dismount. We ran for the shelter of the door. 'Stay close to me,' I told Ida in a low voice.

'Come in, Nest, and ....' Henry turned, holding his hand out to me. Ida stood close behind me with her face swathed in a veil. He stopped mid-sentence at the sight of her, thinking that I had come alone, perplexed that my chaperone persisted in accompanying me even into private conversation with him. I pulled her fully into his chamber and closed the door behind us. The king had already discarded his sopping cloak and Ida and I followed suit. Then Ida slowly removed the veil that was moulded wet to the contours of her face.

'Sister Benedicta … Haith's sister,' Henry said slowly.

'Yes.' She cast her eyes to the ground and Henry looked at me bewildered.

'You are a long way from Fontevraud.' I saw his eyes roving over her clothing. 'And from your nun's habit.'

'Sister Benedicta is known as Ida de Bruges now,' I told Henry. He opened his eyes wide to me and then to her, but she only glanced briefly at him, her face flushed. 'She has temporarily left … she is on an extended pilgrimage.'

'I see.' Henry's voice was loaded with amusement. I was relieved to find that my prediction about his reaction was correct.

'Henry, I have two favours to ask of you.' I spoke quickly.

'Ask away.' He was chuckling openly now at Ida.

'Would you keep Ida with you, in your court for a while, and safeguard her. She is at risk of exposure as a runaway nun and I want to protect her from that.'

'I would, certainly,' he assented warmly. 'I owe her a great deal.' Ida thanked him quietly.

'And would you sign my charter and ask witnesses for it from your household members breaking fast in the next room.'

He narrowed his eyes, distracted for a moment from his amusement at Ida's renegade status. 'Hmm. You wish to be away from your husband, Nest?'

I did not respond. 'Very well. It is the least I can do for you, my beloved.' He took my hand and I let him.

'I would have it in writing,' I persisted.

He rummaged in the saddle bag that he had brought in with him and produced my rolled charter. He unrolled it on the table, weighting it at either end with two stones that were left on the table for just such a purpose. He read it through again, and looked up at us both, his eyes glinting with humour. He took a few steps to the door, opened it a crack and called out, 'Give me a stylus, quick.' He closed the door and returned, stylus in hand to stare again at my charter spread out on the table.

'Was it a man?' he asked Ida, without looking up from his perusal of my charter.

Ida kept her lips tightly pressed together and her gaze directed at her feet.

He signed the charter with a flourish. 'My scribe will see this witnessed for you, Nest, and sealed with the royal seal.' Now he looked up. 'I have no doubt it was a man,' he said to Ida, smiling delightedly at us both, and holding the charter out to me.

10

Gold

November 1122, Caeo, Wales

Cadell ran with his brother, Anarawd, up the last stretch of steep hill on the Caeo to Pumsaint road. At the brow of a hill, they caught their breath, gripping their thin, knobbled knees, then straightened up to survey the ruins of the Roman goldmine before them. Their stepmother, Gwenllian, had told them tales of how the mine had occupied this dip in the Cothi valley. The whole area was strewn with lumps of fist-size quartz. The bards sang of the Romans as a race of giants who had left behind them so many extraordinary feats of construction: roads, town walls, the long wall keeping out the Scots, forts, houses with mosaic floors, heated baths.

Anarawd was sceptical that these Romans could really have been giants, yet the mine was undeniable. If Cadell's father could mine gold, he could rebuild his army. Cadell's aunt had told him that she was serious about finding out about the mine. She had even written for advice to a German who was an expert working in the silver mines in the north of England. Cadell and Anarawd had recently returned home from a visit to their aunt in Cardigan and would very likely have a chance to return there again before too long. His aunt was intent on ensuring that they were well-versed in how to behave like the princes of Deheubarth, which, she told them emphatically, they were. It would be excellent, Cadell considered, if next time he visited his aunt he could go bearing a rich lode of information on the gold to further his father's fight to regain the kingdom of Deheubarth. That would impress her, for sure.

Cadell's heart beat fast with trepidation as well as exertion. He and Anarawd had agreed that they would venture into one of the dark, cavernous openings today, wade down the flooded, underground tunnels and find gold. Autumn had stripped away much of the vegetation from the site and heavy rains had filled the river and gullies, making it easier to see the layout of the mine and to distinguish between natural formations in the landscape and features that had been built by the Roman giants. 'Or their Welsh slaves!' Cadell exclaimed.

'See, the leat they built, marked by that reed-filled depression?' Anarawd asked. He gripped Cadell's shoulders and twisted him to look to the right at a straight gully carved in the hillside. 'That's the aqueduct. And those are washing tables.'

'Washing tables? What, like the Roman baths Gwenllian told us about in the city of Aquae Sulis?'

Anarawd laughed. 'No! For washing and crushing the ore—to separate out the gold.'

Before Cadell, and to his left, were three overgrown ponds, which Anarawd guessed could be a series of 'tanks' that the Romans had made. Down there, amongst the tanks, were the entrances to the shafts. Their stepmother, Gwenllian, often told them stories from the distant past when the Romans had marched and built here, in the Welsh hills. It was hard to believe now, looking around at this neglected terrain. Parts of the structures were broken and eroded, and others had fused back with the rock and vegetation and were in the process of being reclaimed by the land. Gwenllian had told Cadell not to go near the mine-workings, which might collapse and were filled with poisonous air and ghosts, she said, but he and Anarawd had decided to shrug off her warnings. Their father had found a buried hoard of Roman golden jewellery that had gone to fund more men and weapons. Who knows what they might find. They might be able to contribute something really valuable to their father's struggle.

The boys ambled down the hill towards a water-filled depression where Cadell picked up a long stick and poked it into the murky pool, stirring up pebbles and shimmers. 'Gold!' he shouted.

'Just gold dust, faery dust,' Anarawd laughed. 'Not much use. How can you render something from dust specks?'

'It's still gold though,' Cadell said stubbornly. 'And if there's still gold here, why isn't the lord of this land mining it? Or Father?'

'We've forgotten how to do it. Us and the Normans, both. We don't know the Romans' secrets of mining anymore.'

'Well, can't we read the ruins, the landscape we're looking at right now?' asked Cadell. 'Figure it out, somehow?'

Anarawd shrugged.

One day, Cadell's father would regain his kingdom, which meant that one day Anarawd would be king of Deheubarth. An operating goldmine would be a very useful thing for a king, and his brother ought to realise that, Cadell considered.

At the sound of a bird's screech, Cadell looked up to the distant ridge in time to see not only the circling bird of prey, but also a group of riders breaking from the dense tree cover on the slope. They were heading for the drovers' road, the road he and Anarawd had come along from Caeo.

'Quick,' Anarawd gripped Cadell's jerkin so that the stick in Cadell's hand dropped into the water. 'We have to warn Father. We'll take the shortcut through the woods.'

Cadell briefly mourned his goldstick swirling out of reach, and followed the line of Anarawd's pointing finger to the riders. Swiftly, they turned and, shoulder to shoulder, ran as fast as their coltish, teenage legs would carry them, crashing past trees and through undergrowth, sure of the path. Visitors were an unusual occurrence here. Cadell's thoughts buzzed chaotically between excitement and fear. They ran along the ridge above the village of Caeo where they could see below them their father and the red head of their stepmother, seated near a smoking fire. They traversed the steep hill at a run, on the diagonal, braking their gallop down the hill with their knees and hips, balancing with outstretched arms.

'Father! Father! Riders are approaching!' gasped Anarawd, his face hectic with the run and the unwarranted event.

Gruffudd and Gwenllian looked up at the sweating boys, as they gestured behind them. 'How many?' asked Gruffudd.

'Ten,' Anarawd replied with certainty.

'Norman or Welsh?'

'Welsh.'

Ten was a warband and they could do plenty of damage against an unprepared village if they were so inclined. Gruffudd began to issue orders to the men in his vicinity. Gwenllian swept up her small daughter and thrust her at the nurse who had been alerted by the shouts of the boys and had emerged to stand on the threshold of the house. 'Stay inside with her.' Cadell followed Gwenllian inside and watched her lift the lid of a chest. She strapped on her gambeson and then her sword.

'May I have a sword?' asked Anarawd, coming up behind Cadell.

Gwenllian nodded. Anarawd was big and strong enough to be of some use. 'You have done well in training.' She handed him one of her own swords. 'But only draw it if your father or I do so. A drawn sword is an invitation to attack you.'

'What about me?' Cadell asked.

Gwenllian handed him an ornate but wickedly sharp dagger. 'Put this in your belt and, similarly, keep it there unless I tell you otherwise.' Cadell pouted at his lesser armoury but his eleven years had not yet given him the muscle to wield a sword—even the lightweight ones that the smith had made for his stepmother, whereas Anarawd would be able to swing the weapon she had handed to him.

All three re-emerged to stand behind Gruffudd and his men who were armed and drawn up in ranks. They were not all here, but it was enough to face off ten men. Though their existence in Caeo was meagre, many of the men who had followed Gruffudd to such battle successes against the Normans a few years back had returned to him, finding their way through the dense forest and along mountain paths to this barren, upland commote where he was living out his banishment on orders of the Norman king. Where else would those men go? What other Welsh prince had offered any real resistance to the invaders? It was a constant strain for Gruffudd and Gwenllian to ensure there were provisions for the men, but, at this moment, Cadell was glad that his father had persisted with it and not forced the warriors to disband and seek a wealthier lord elsewhere.

The riders approached. There were three horsemen leading the group: two men, and a youth around Anarawd's age, judging by the size of him. They halted and surveyed Gruffudd's party. The helmeted head of one of the leaders swung in Gwenllian's direction. A smile curved the mouth that was all that was visible of his face beneath the helmet. The two leaders and the youth dismounted and removed their helmets. Cadell fingered his dagger hilt nervously and inched a little closer to his stepmother. He wondered if he would be able to protect her if the intentions of the visitors were evil. Cadell looked swiftly to his stepmother at her screech but saw that it had been a yelp of surprised recognition. She was smiling, but he noted that she still had her hand on the hilt of her sword, so he followed suit and did not remove his own hand from his dagger.

'Good day to you, Gruffudd ap Rhys. Sister.' The tallest man turned his face briefly to Gwenllian, and then back to Gruffudd.

'Greetings Cadwallon,' Gruffudd said. Cadell relaxed his shoulders a little and let his hand drop from his dagger hilt to his side. These were Gwenllian's brothers, and, yet, Gwenllian herself had warned Cadell that kinsmen were sometimes the worst enemy. Their father, King Gruffudd ap Cynan of the northern kingdom of Gwynedd was old and said to be blind. In his declining years, his two eldest sons were ruling Gwynedd in all but name.

'Perhaps you remember my brothers?' Cadwallon said to Gruffudd, gesturing to the other two princes of Gwynedd, 'Owain and Cadwaladr.'

'You are welcome,' Gruffudd told them all graciously.

There was a slight shift in the tense air between the two groups. Gwenllian's second brother, Owain, called commands over his shoulder to their men to dismount and disarm. The clattering pile of swords lowered the tension again several notches, although Cadell did not doubt that all these men retained at least one dagger as wicked as the one that Gwenllian had handed to him.

'Is it Cadwaladr?' Gwenllian asked the youth. 'You were just a small child when I last saw you.'

'You look the same, Gwenllian,' he grinned. His own dark red hair echoed hers.

'Here are my sons, Anarawd and Cadell,' Gruffudd introduced the two boys. Cadell acknowledged the greetings of the princes of Gwynedd awkwardly. It was rare these days for his family to mix with other royals, and he felt uncertain of the protocols despite his Aunt Nest's tuition.

Cadell's father led his guests into the small hall of their house where Gwenllian set about giving orders for a meal. Gruffudd's men were well-trained and would keep a careful eye on Cadwallon and Owain's troop billeted in the village. Cadell watched Gwenllian moving about the hall. She kept her head high and the stance of her body was regal and disdainful despite her chagrin that her brothers should see her and her husband living like this. The fine clothes of her brothers only served to emphasise the threadbare apparel that she, Gruffudd, and his sons wore. Cadell watched the youngest brother Cadwaladr cast a scathing eye around the space and across the few servants. He brushed at the bench with the gauntlets he had just taken off before sitting down on it.

Cadell noticed how his father's careworn features contrasted with the arrogant confidence of Gwenllian's brothers. Grey patches peppered Gruffudd ap Rhys's black hair and dark smudges beneath his blue eyes marred his handsome face. His father was growing old before his time. At least, Cadell remembered, they had the visiting bard, Breri, to bring a touch of nobility to the meal. It was a stroke of luck that he had chosen this moment to pass through Caeo on his way back to Pembroke.

The cause for the visit of the princes of Gwynedd did not emerge until late into the evening, when Anarawd and Cadell were yawning after their long walk to the goldmine and their sprint back to Caeo. Cadell noticed that the youngest brother, Prince Cadwaladr, showed no signs of fatigue, even though he drank strong wine along with the men.

'We came to discuss strategy with you, Gruffudd. You have the advantage of years and experience on us,' Cadwallon declared.

Gruffudd gave no immediate reply. The princes of Gwynedd were the sons of a strong king. Their family ruled a vast area of the north whilst Cadell's father was king only in name. Cadell guessed that his father was probably thinking that all his years and experience had done for him was lose him everything.

'You came the closest that anyone ever has to throwing off the yoke of the invaders,' Owain flattered.

'I came close,' Gruffudd agreed, referring to his attacks on Norman strongholds. He had almost succeeded but it had all ended in this ignominy. The Norman king allowed him only a commote—a handful of villages in the middle of nowhere. 'But the Normans have strengthened their hand here again with new men, refortified castles.'

'Have you given up, then?' asked Cadwaladr rudely and Owain

frowned him to silence.

Gruffudd laughed with good humour. 'Never that, boy.'

'The Norman king is weakened. He has no heir,' asserted Owain.

'There is always an heir,' Gruffudd retorted. 'It is just not always obvious who he is.'

It did not escape Cadell's notice that Cadwaladr smiled wryly at that remark. Prince Cadwaladr, with his bushy red hair and long, thin nose looked something like a fox, thought Cadell. His pale face was splattered with large, orange freckles and his blue eyes drilled intelligently into everything around him. Cadell assessed that he was treacherously ambitious for himself, despite his youth.

'King Henry is distracted with new instabilities in the north and in Normandy,' Cadwallon claimed.

'The biggest thorn in the Norman king's side,' declared Gwenllian, 'is his nephew William *Clito*, who claims Normandy and could claim England too.'

'Normandy and England are not of interest to us,' said Owain.

'No, but distractions and weakenings of the king are,' she insisted. 'We hear there is rebellion brewing against the king in Normandy on behalf of William *Clito*. We could join forces with these rebels.'

'With Normans!' Owain recoiled. 'You think they would not stab us in the back given the opportunity? You speak of matters you do not understand, sister.'

Gruffudd blinked his eyes slowly at her and she fell silent. Cadell thought angrily that if her brothers did not have the sense to know that his stepmother had the head and stomach for politics, that was their problem. His father would discuss everything with his stepmother in any case and she had warned him to trust nothing they said. Why would her brothers need to come to them, when she and Gruffudd had no power? Surely, they were looking for a cover or scapegoat for their own actions, and their own aggrandisement could be their only true motive.

'So what are you suggesting?' Gruffudd asked Owain. Cadwallon and Owain had the resources to raise a vast army. Gruffudd was lucky these days if he could raise a chicken that would lay eggs. 'Maredudd of Powys tested the waters when *The White Ship* went down and the king lost his heir and other nobles.' Cadell's father was referring to an attack that Maredudd of Powys had made on the lands of the earl of Chester. 'He got a hard slap-down from the Norman king for his troubles.'

Cadwallon and Owain nodded, and they all smiled for a moment remembering the many hundreds of cattle that Maredudd had been forced to deliver to the Norman king by way of fine for that incident, and how Maredudd had delivered the cows in a vast stampede on Cardigan Castle.

'Still, I did get to stick the king at least,' Gwenllian boasted, tossing her thick red plait back over her shoulder.

Owain gave a shout of laughter. 'We knew the rumours were true! It *was* you who winged the king! You always were the best archer in Gwynedd.'

King Henry had only suffered a flesh wound from her arrow, but it had felt like some recompense for all they had lost, all the Normans had taken from them.

'Does our father condone your thinking?' Gwenllian asked. Their aging father still had a firm grip on his northern kingdom and had retained it all these years through his careful dealings with the Normans. He would not put his accord with King Henry at risk.

Cadwaladr spoke out of turn again. 'Father is old and blind. *We* have ideas.'

Owain frowned him to silence one more time. 'Father is aware of our thinking. If we proceed with caution, he is behind us.'

'So what are your ideas?' Gwenllian challenged.

'We attack Ceredigion Castle between us,' Owain invited and sat back waiting for Gruffudd's response. The Normans had rechristened Ceredigion as Cardigan since they could not get their ungainly tongues around the proper names for anything. Cadell's thoughts immediately went to his aunt Nest. She was in Cardigan Castle. What might happen to her if there was an attack?

'The Normans are dug in there as elsewhere,' Gruffudd said. 'No Norman castle has been taken by attacking Welsh forces for the last two decades.'

'Then we should be the first to do so, no?' asked Cadwallon. 'It can be done. The Norman warriors Robert of Rhuddlan and Hugh of Montgommery were killed. Owain of Powys breached Cilgerran. The invaders are not invincible.'

'Montgommery was killed by a Norseman,' Gruffudd reminded him.

Owain swept the objection away with a careless wave of his hand. 'De Clare is frequently absent from Ceredigion and leaves the castle's security in the hands of his constable, de Marais.'

'I know it,' Gruffudd frowned. 'You think I don't scope information on the state of my own lands?' he said pointedly. Ceredigion was disputed territory and had swapped hands back and forth between the Welsh kings of Gwynedd, Powys, and Deheubarth for several generations, but it had been in the territory of Gruffudd's father and he intended to hold to that. Cadwaladr shifted in his seat at Gruffudd's assertion but said nothing. So he has eyes on Ceredigion himself, thought Cadell. 'De Marais is capable,' Gruffudd went on, 'and the garrison there is large and well organised.' Nobody referred to the fact that Gruffudd's sister, Cadell's aunt Nest, was married to de Marais.

'You consider the idea hopeless then?' asked Cadwallon.

Gruffudd shook his head. 'It could work. If I could gather more men about me here and march west, you would march south, and I could ask my Norse foster-brother, Raegnald, to support us with a sea attack from Dublin. If we have the element of surprise on our side, it could work.'

Owain leant forward, his eyes alight. 'This is what we hoped for.'

'But what is in it for you, brothers,' Gwenllian asked, 'when my husband takes Ceredigion, which is rightfully his?'

'We acknowledge that,' Owain soothed. 'We would ask only the secession of a sliver of the northern territory of Ceredigion to us as recompense. The Norman king seeks to manipulate and control us with his divide and rule policy. Let us disallow that.' He reached a hand across the table to Gruffudd.

Gruffudd sucked in a deep breath. Cadell watched his father resist the urge to look to his wife for her guidance. He could sense her distrust of her brothers in any case. Gruffudd had much more to lose than the princes of Gwynedd did. If this plan failed, King Henry would likely execute his father. He had only escaped summary judgement before because of the intervention of Cadell's aunt who was loved by the Norman king. And yet, what should his father do? Moulder away here for more years like a farmer, scraping a living from this barren soil, leave no legacy for his sons, allow the royal house of Deheubarth to dwindle to nothing at all? Cadell watched anxiously as his father leant forward and gave his hand first to Owain and then to Cadwallon. 'If Raegnald will agree to it, we will go forward.' Cadell realised that the condition allowed his father a way out if that should prove necessary.

With the deal struck between the two royal houses and beakers raised, Gruffudd nodded to Breri. The bard inclined his head in return, plucked a resonant chord on his lute, and began a stirring tale of the deeds of Gruffudd's father, King Rhys ap Tewdwr. At the close of this narration, Gruffudd's house minstrel took up the entertainment. Cadell saw Breri cross the hall and request permission to take a seat next to the young prince, Cadwaladr. Cadell narrowed his eyes and watched the exchange between the bard and the prince take place like a pantomime. The prince inclined his head graciously and waved Breri to the bench. Breri moved his head close to Cadwaladr's and cupped a hand to the prince's ear.

Shivering with cold and anxiety, Cadell stood concealed at the edge of the door to his parents' bedchamber, some hours later. He watched his stepmother comb out her extraordinary, dark red hair. The feast was over and Gwenllian was sitting in the bed in a white shift, and Gruffudd sat on the bed beside her, still clothed, with one stockinged foot on the floor. 'I don't trust them,' Gwenllian said.

'They are your brothers.'

'That's why I don't trust them. I know them. They want Ceredigion for themselves.'

'And we are aware of that. They think to use us, and we will use them. Raegnald will assist me in attacking the castle. If we can oust the Normans from there, I would have a base to work and expand from. It's what we need.'

'The Norman king would not accept it. He would take extreme punitive measures.'

'We will wait for the right moment when he is much occupied with affairs elsewhere, when he is in Normandy. Once I take Ceredigion, he would have to treat with me, as he does with the other Welsh kings. I would demand recognition as king of Deheubarth—as client king—a similar arrangement to those that he has with your father in Gwynedd and Maredudd in Powys.'

'It would be a regressive step for him. From his perspective, he has Deheubarth and no reason to give it back to you.'

'Then we must create a reason. We cannot sit here eeking out an existence like peasants.'

Gwenllian combed her fingers through the mane of her loosened hair. 'No, we cannot.'

Gruffudd heard Cadell at the door. 'What is it?' he asked,

beckoning him to come in.

'I had another nightmare.'

'Come here to me,' Gwenllian murmured, and Gruffudd shifted to allow Cadell to creep under the cover of the thick furs and settle beside his stepmother.

'Close your eyes and I will tell you a magical story.' Obediently Cadell closed his eyes.

'There once was a prince named Pwyll who ruled the land of Deheubarth. The prince was out hunting and saw a stag brought down by a pack of hounds but no sign of their master. He shooed the first pack away and allowed his own hounds to feast on the carcass of the fallen stag. But then, a rider approached, berating him, saying that he had stolen his quarry and was ill-mannered and would pay for it. Forgive me, stranger, said the Prince. I thought the hounds had no master. I am their master, declared the man, and I am King Arawn. How can I make amends? asked Pwyll. You will take my face and my life for one year, replied Arawn. Very well, but what of my own lands? asked Pwyll. I will take your face and your life for one year and rule your lands, said Arawn. And so it happened. Pwyll stepped into Arawn's shoes and ruled his lands and slept in a bed with Arawn's wife.'

'Is it … my aunt Nest and the Norman king, then?' Cadell asked, opening one quizzical eye.

Gwenllian put a finger softly to his mouth and went on with her story. Cadell closed his eye again. 'But in that whole year Pwyll did *not* make love to Arawn's wife, despite her *enormous* beauty.'

Gruffudd swung off the bed with a sudden humph! 'There's not much peace around here.' He strode out to the hall in search of a beaker of wine. When he was gone, Gwenllian and Cadell settled back cosily. 'One day, Pwyll sat on a mound and an extraordinarily beautiful woman rode past on a fast horse.'

'You?' asked Cadell.

Gwenllian smiled and continued. 'Pwyll sent several of his best men on the fastest horses to catch her but she was too swift for them. And so he set off to chase her himself but he, also, could not catch her, so he cried out, Won't you wait for me, lady, and tell me who you are? Gladly, she said. I am Rhiannon and promised to a man I do not wish to marry. I would rather, Prince, marry you. Then we will compel it so, declared Pwyll. One year later, Rhiannon invited Pwyll to feast at the house of her father and while they were feasting a rather ugly young man came in and asked Pwyll to grant him a favour. With pleasure, cried the ebullient Pwyll, whatever you ask. Oh why did you say that! wailed Rhiannon, for the man was Gwawl, her former suitor, and, of course, he asked for her.'

'Oh no,' murmured Cadell, drowsily.

'What can we do now? cried Pwyll. Rhiannon gave him a magic bag and instructions on how to use it. One year later, Pwyll visited the hall again where Rhiannon was seated next to Gwawl whom she loathed. Pwyll was in disguise. Grant me a boon, he asked Gwawl. Fill my bag with food. The servants began to put food and then more and more food into the bag, but it did not fill up. Will your bag ever be full? asked Gwawl in dismay. If a nobleman stamps it down, it will, answered Pwyll. So Gwawl came and put his feet in the bag and stamped and he disappeared down, down into the bottomless, magical bag and Pwyll closed it tight shut over his head and now Pwyll could marry Rhiannon.' The melodious flow of Gwenllian's voice halted.

'What about the rest?' asked Cadell in an aggrieved tone.

'Ssh.' She smoothed his fair head down onto her shoulder where his blond locks mixed with the dark red swathe of her hair. 'I can tell you the rest another night. It has been a tiring day.'

'Bravo, my lady! What a story!'

Gwenllian looked up, shocked at the stranger's voice on the threshold of her private chamber. The travelling bard, Breri, stood there, leaning against the door jamb.

'This is insolence!' Cadell exclaimed. He flipped back the quilt, intending to swing his legs from the bed, but Gwenllian stayed him.

'Forgive me. I can never resist a well-told tale.' Breri bowed, turned and disappeared, returning to the hall.

'This Breri is silent on his feet, despite his bulk,' Gwenllian said, looking at the absent space where the bard had stood on the threshold of her bedchamber.

Cadell had not heard him approach her door and did not know how long he had been standing there, listening to them.

11

Evasion

December 1122, Dunstable, England

'Are you writing to your sister, Haith?'

Haith looked up at Henry's young queen, Adelisa. She was counting out a pile of fine blue wool cloaks that she intended to give out to the knights of the household as Christmas gifts. 'I am,' he told her. 'Ida is comfortable and safe in your household at Winchester and I thank you for that. I am looking forward to being reunited with her at Easter.' Ida had written to Haith, at last, to tell him that she had resided in Nest's household for two years, but was now under the protection of the king and queen.

Adelisa smiled mischievously. She knew that his sister had absconded from a nunnery, was enjoying the subterfuge of concealing Ida, and was delighted to be able to converse on the secret in her own language with Haith. He had to frequently remind himself that this blonde fourteen-year-old, who he was inclined to interact with as little more than a child, was, in fact, a queen and must be met with sober respect. Her personality did not make that easy since she was inclined to jokes and games and was insatiably curious about her new context in England. Haith had been travelling for the last few months with the king and queen. Adelisa accompanied Henry everywhere in their ardent wish that she would soon bear an heir to the throne. The king was constantly kind and caring with his youthful queen but he was, nevertheless, old enough to be her father and had little time for frivolity or leisure. The king tasked Haith with keeping company with the queen.

Henry's entourage had spent a full year on the road with only brief stops everywhere. After reasserting his grip in Wales, Henry toured England, checking on his administrators and their exercise of his delegated authority. In the far north, the king had kept a weather eye on the aggressive tension building between the king and prince of Scotland, on the one hand, and the earl of Chester and his sons, Ranulf de Gernon and William de Roumare, on the other.

Adelisa unpinned the exquisite silver brooch from the neck of her dress and held it up to the pale sunlight coming through the window to study the fine craftsmanship. The king had given it to her during their visit to the Alston silvermines. The court had spent time in York, Durham, Carlisle, and then visited the silver mines at Alston, where Haith had joined them. King Henry was intrigued by the miners' methods of extracting the ore, and, of course, mightily pleased with the great piles of it they had shown him. The queen's brooch was shaped by two birds bending in a convolution toward one another, their beaks meeting in a kiss at the top of the circular brooch, and the plumage of their tails crossing at the bottom.

'What were the silvermines like?' Adelisa asked. 'Were there piles of such glorious silver, like a dragon's hoard?' Her eyes glinted with curiosity, gleaming like the fine brooch twisting between her thumb and finger. She had not been allowed near the mines themselves where there were many dangerous engines in operation and where the miners were stripped to their breeches to cope with their sweaty labour.

'No, my queen,' Haith laughed. 'I'm afraid it was no heap of glittering silver, more like a scene from the bowels of hell. It was hot, noisy, smoky, sweaty. It is not easy to extract such beauty from the rock,' he gestured at her brooch.

'Would you?' she asked, holding the brooch out to him. He rose from the writing desk, pinched the brooch carefully between his thumb and finger and stooped to pin it back in place, near the neck of her gown, his large fingers fumbling at its delicate fastening mechanism.

'How do they do it? Get the silver from the rock?'

Haith stepped back and assessed that he had got the brooch more or less straight. 'There are shafts sunk into the ground and miners are lowered down on ropes to hack at the rock face that glitters with veins of ore. They name it galena.'

'Galena,' she tried it on her tongue. 'It could be a beautiful name for a baby girl!'

Haith made no comment, knowing that any girl child that Adelisa birthed was likely to be named Matilda, after the king's mother, and perhaps in memory, too, of the daughter he had lost to the sea in the wreck of *The White Ship*. 'They bring up the glittering hunks of rock and must place it in a bloomery to separate the silver from the other parts of the ore.'

'What is that?'

'A bloomery? It's a little like a bread oven or a kind of chimney. A fire is lit below, very, very hot. The ore goes in the top and when it is hot enough, buttons of silver will separate out and emerge below.'

'I don't see why I couldn't witness it myself,' she said, pouting a little.

'It was intriguing, but it was not a pleasant place to be, lady. The miners laboured in extreme heat and wore little clothing. They were grimed all about their visage and hands and had the look of semi-naked demons!'

Adelisa clapped her hands in delight at his description. 'Truly, Haith?'

'It was terribly noisy, what with the constant hammering and crash of rocks, the gush and treadle of the waterwheels powering pleated bellows. There was such a racket it hurt the ears. The smell was very bad too.'

'What did it smell like?'

'I can't describe it. Like no smells that we are used to on the surface of the earth. Some other smell from the depths of the earth that grated on the senses. There were the smells of the charcoal burning. The cupellation vessels they used for refining the silver are made from burned antlers or fish spines, the miners told me.'

Adelisa shook her head slowly in astonishment, her eyes wide.

'They set fires against the rock face to heat the stone, then douse the fires with liquid, so that the stone fractures and the water hisses and steams. There were foetid vapours all around us, lady, and we had to retreat to a safe distance, holding our noses! Many of the senior miners were German and shouted in their language.'

'You could understand them?' Adelisa asked.

'Some, yes. They called the bloomery the wolf-furnace, but I don't know why.'

Adelisa's face beamed her fascination.

After Alston, the court had been in York for Saint Nicholas's Day and then moved south again for Christmas. The royal household had at last come to rest at Kingsbury Palace in Dunstable after the dizzying peregrinations of the last year, and Adelisa was immersing herself in organising a lavish Christmas celebration. King Henry was making plans for a new priory in Dunstable and the creation of a market for the town. With its position at the junction of two old Roman roads—Watling Street and the Icknield Way—the town was well suited for such developments. The king had been displeased to hear of robbers in the forests nearby and set about having the forest cleared and improving the poor state of the roads. Henry was ensconced now with a messenger from the Count of Anjou and Haith reflected that such a visitor was unlikely to leave Henry in a good mood. The count was undoubtedly insisting on the return of the dowry of his daughter Mahaut, who was the widow of Henry's drowned son, Prince William. The king never enjoyed the act of giving up money or lands. Furthermore, the Count d'Anjou had betrothed his other daughter, Sybil, to Henry's rival in Normandy, William *Clito*, which was a slap in the face to Henry. The king was secretly treating with the Vatican through the papal envoys to get that marriage annulled and would likely prevail, but it was more cash flowing in the wrong direction from the king's coffers.

Christmas at Kingsbury was the lull before the storm, thought Haith. In the coming year, Henry would have to tackle the rebellion in Normandy and that would mean a lot of time away from England, for the king, and away from Wales and Nest, for Haith. The packing had already started up again around them. Haith explained to Adelisa that they would be moving first to Berkhamsted, then to Woodstock where she would be able to see Henry's menagerie of exotic animals (and, which he did not mention, where Haith had first met Nest). Then they would go on to Winchester. Haith lifted his hand from an inkwell that a servant wanted to wrap. Adelisa laughed at Haith's observation that the servants had only just unpacked the last goblet and their fingers were still entwined in the packing straw when Henry gave the command to start packing for the next leg of their journey. The servant's face, on the other hand, was tight. He was less amused by the continual packing and unpacking. The queen, at least, had been able to gain a good sense of the English and Welsh parts of her husband's kingdom from this peripatetic year.

Haith shivered and turned back to the fire. 'Send the maid to build up the fire,' he told the packers and one left the room to find the girl. Haith returned to his letter to Ida. He wrote nothing in it about his discoveries concerning Amaury. He only told her of his trip to Fontevraud and asked Ida to reassure him of her welfare. It was strange after all these years to be addressing her by her birth name. He tried to produce a neutral letter and not to convey any of his extreme concerns about her, but a neutral letter between them was a cold letter and Ida would feel it so. He tried to convey a reassurance that he did not disapprove of her course of action in leaving the convent. He scored through a few words and changed them for others. The letter was looking messy now and Ida would read into that too. He advised her, in the letter, that he would meet her in Winchester when the court arrived for Easter. Now that this meeting was imminent, Haith felt anxious about the conversation he must have with Ida concerning Amaury and Gisulf. He blotted the letter, folded it and handed it to a servant, and then moved to stand beside the queen, where she was looking out of the window. Kingsbury Palace stood on a steep chalk escarpment overlooking the river with a fine view of the surrounding snow-covered countryside and the swift flowing river. 'A perfect Christmas snow scene,' the queen said, pressing her pink fingertips together beneath her chin and turning a glowing, smiling face to Haith.

The king's entourage rode up the steep incline towards the royal residence at Winchester with guards lining the route with their long, pointed shields facing the royal party as they rode past. Once inside the courtyard, King Henry wasted no time on niceties, such as allowing his retinue of barons to find their rooms and unpack. They were all summoned to immediate council in the hall to discuss how to deal with the rebellion in Normandy. Haith's warning after his visit to Pont Audemer had been the first signs and now there was no doubt that a rebellion was being led by Waleran de Meulan and Amaury de Montfort in favour of William *Clito*. Haith let himself down from the saddle, feeling the creak and stiffness of his aging joints. He wanted a hot bath and beaker of ale, but the king's patience did not allow for that.

'The king!' the usher shouted as the great doors parted before the royal party, and the people standing in the hall turned to face their lord. To Haith's eye, the lords and ladies massed in the hall presented a tense welcome. Waleran's twin, Robert de Beaumont, earl of Leicester, was one of the first to confront the approaching king and drop respectfully to his knee, proffering his loyalty. Such loyalty would have been hardwon since he must know that his twin would be declared a traitor in this assembly. The twins were close and usually acted in concert, but the majority of Waleran's lands were in Normandy, while most of de Beaumont's holdings were in England. The earl, therefore, had little choice but to act against his brother in defence of his own interests.

Since the death of the king's son, the younger members of the court had divided into factions focused around two rivals: Robert, earl of Gloucester, the king's illegitimate son, and Stephen, count of Mortain, the king's nephew. The enmity between the two men was no secret. The king had been married to Queen Adelisa for nearing two years and there was no sign of a child. The question of the succession was beginning to weigh upon them all, and not least upon the king himself. Haith clenched the muscles of his face to suppress any expression showing there, as he watched Stephen and Robert near race one another to get to the king first. Their trajectories brought them to Henry's path at the same time, and Robert stepped back respectfully to allow Stephen to kiss the king's hand. Robert might be the king's son and Stephen simply his nephew, but Robert was illegitimate and had to cede way to Stephen's more noble bloodline.

Henry waved the niceties away brusquely. He was never interested in the flattery of courtiers, but his grip on Robert's arm as he raised him was one of real affection and respect. Henry briefly rested his forehead against Robert's. 'I am glad to see you, my son.'

Haith followed Henry as he cut a rapid swathe through the waiting members of court, registering amongst the crowd that the de Clares had come from Wales: Gilbert de Clare from Pembroke and Richard de Clare from Cardigan. Richard was accompanied by his young wife Alice. Haith noted that Alice's father, Ranulf Le Meschin, earl of Chester and his son Ranulf de Gernon and stepson William de Roumare were present. Neither of the Ranulfs nor de Roumare were happy with King Henry at present and their expressions were guarded. Ranulf was angry at the king's arrangements for the northern territories since he had conceded a great number of holdings to the Scots, lands that the earl regarded as his. William de Roumare was also disappointed that the king had denied his petition for his mother's Bolingbroke lands.

'Any who have report of matters in Normandy, speak up!' Henry called out, his voice ringing against the cold stone of the hall, and a series of lords gave reports on what could be gleaned on the present activities of the rebels. These reports were always a mixture of genuine information and information displayed to gain the king's favour. When Henry wearied of the procession of courtiers jostling for attention, he held up a hand, brusquely interrupting the florid preface of one young lord. 'That's enough! The state of things is clear enough and will not be tolerated. I thank you all,' he said, briefly glancing at the interrupted and crestfallen last speaker.

'My lords Ranulf, earl of Chester, and Robert, earl of Gloucester, I call on you to go in haste to Normandy and make preparations for a campaign against these rebels. I will soon follow on your heels.'

That meant, Haith realised, that he too would be going to Normandy very soon. The closed session of the barons was concluded and the hall doors were opened to admit the other members of the court. Evening was falling and servants began to light the myriad lamps. Haith looked for Ida but did not see her and guessed that she would be keeping from sight in the queen's chambers. Across the crowded hall, he spotted de Pirou joining the retinue of Ranulf de Gernon. At last, Haith would have an opportunity to interrogate de Pirou. He was desperate to find proof positive that it was not Ida's lover, Amaury de Montfort, who had caused the sinking of *The White Ship*. Haith moved towards de Gernon's group but the king beckoned him over. Haith kept an impatient eye on de Pirou as he listened to the king.

'All these deaths, Haith!' Henry said. 'One after the other. First my daughter, Queen Sybil; then the archbishop; then Ranulf, my chancellor; Bishop Richard de Belmeis has been paralysed from a seizure and is like to die; and Robert Bloet died in my arms. Too many deaths of old friends, Haith. And children should not die before their fathers.'

'It is hard, sire.' Haith knit his brow. It was unlike Henry to be expressing such feelings, although Haith had no doubt that he felt these harsh losses. Haith had so far kept his counsel on his discoveries concerning *The White Ship*. All he knew for sure was that the spectacular tragedy was a consequence of the sordid murder of the clerk Gisulf by de Pirou and Berold. Perhaps Stephen de Blois, Ranulf de Gernon or Waleran de Meulan were involved and perhaps not. Such a tale would not bring Henry consolation or conviction and Haith needed to know more.

Haith saw de Pirou move towards the door and excused himself to the king, stepping fast to keep up with his quarry. At the far end of the corridor, he caught sight of the man disappearing around a corner. Haith knew that this corridor led towards the postern gate of the castle and he could not allow de Pirou to evade questioning. He ran at full tilt. De Pirou heard him coming, looked over his shoulder and sped up. Haith's legs were the longer and he caught his quarry by the collar of his cloak and held him fast against the wall. 'De Pirou! I would have speech with you.'

'Sir, what do you mean by chasing and pinioning me? Let go of me!'

Haith came straight to the point. 'I know that you and Berold murdered the royal clerk Gisulf and the pilot on *The White Ship* and that this led to the sinking of the ship and all those deaths. Do you deny it?'

The late afternoon light was failing but Haith still saw de Pirou's face pale in the gloom. 'That bastard butcher! I thought that tub of lard would sink straight to the sea's floor, but I suppose instead he floated to the shore like some bladder-borne Odysseus.' Suddenly, de Pirou kicked at the wall behind him and Haith found himself holding an empty cloak. There was a door concealed flat against the wood panelling and de Pirou must have known it. There was no time to gape. Haith flung the cloak from him and followed de Pirou through the door that let into a long, dark tunnel. It must go out under the moat. De Pirou was running fast and Haith set off in pursuit again. The other man had the start on him, but Haith still had the longer legs. He reached for and managed to grip de Pirou first just with his fingertips and then tugged the fabric of his shirt to gain a fistful. Haith spun de Pirou hard against the wall, knocking the wind from him, gripping his shirt hard and awry. Both men panted for a moment, regaining their breath.

Deep into the tunnel, it was damp and dark. Haith could only just discern the shadowy outline of his captive and hear his panting breaths. 'I know that Gisulf was a blackmailer,' Haith gasped. 'Was he blackmailing Ranulf de Gernon? Were you acting on behalf of Ranulf?'

'No, do not accuse him.' De Pirou's voice was close and leaching anxiety.

'Who, then, ordered the murder of Gisulf and why? I will have it from you, de Pirou,' Haith slammed the man's shoulder against the wall for emphasis, 'or I will haul you in front of King Henry. How do you think he might take the news that you had a hand in the death of his son? I know that Gisulf was blackmailing Waleran de Meulan.'

Haith could not see the calculations pursuing each other across de Pirou's face, but he could almost hear the whirring of de Pirou's brain as he strained for lies.

'What Lord Ranulf *does* do is pay me to listen and find out information for him. I'll tell you about a conversation I overheard in Chartres when the earl and I were visiting there, some months before *The White Ship* went down,' de Pirou whispered. 'The Countess Adela had a speculative discussion about the succession with her sons Thibaut and Stephen.'

Haith frowned. 'Go on.'

'She argued that if Henry were to lose his son, it should be Stephen and not Thibaut who ought to take the English throne.'

Haith said nothing, dissatisfied with this tale. The man was a murderer, an accomplished liar.

'Well, don't you think that set Stephen de Blois off thinking? And didn't he disembark from the ship?' de Pirou asked plaintively.

'What are you saying? That Stephen ordered you to murder Gisulf? You are just giving me misdirection here, de Pirou. I need to know who gave you the commission. You admit that you are in the pay of de Gernon.'

'The earl is expecting me. I should go to him, but I can meet you later today, and give you the information you seek, and proof of it too.'

De Pirou was playing for time. He would go asking advice from whoever it was that had commissioned him: Waleran, Ranulf, Stephen? They were all young hotheads who could have unwittingly committed the crime, but it was true that Stephen had the most to gain from the sinking. Yet Haith knew a crafted lie when he heard one. De Pirou twisted suddenly from Haith's grasp and set off back up the tunnel towards the palace with Haith in fast pursuit once more. De Pirou burst through the door just ahead of Haith.

Back in the palace corridor, de Pirou ran to the left and Haith skidded around a corner after him. De Pirou ducked through another door with Haith close on his heels. They were in the busy, steamy kitchen and de Pirou was knocking pans and platters from tables into Haith's path as he bent around astonished cooks and cooks' boys, brandishing ladles and skinned rabbits. 'De Pirou, hold!' Haith shouted but de Pirou sped past the kitchen hearth and its enormous cauldron. He drew his sword and lent to rock the cauldron with it as he passed, sending a cascade of boiling broth to the floor that Haith slipped around, barely managing to keep upright. Haith followed de Pirou out through the far door leaving the shouts and cries of the kitchen staff behind them. They were in another of the palace's main corridors and at last Haith got a grip on de Pirou's short tunic and pinned him to the wall once again, one arm tight across his throat. 'I want an answer now!' The two men stared at one another, breathing hard. Sweat ran down the crevices of de Pirou's face.

Voices approached and the king and Ranulf de Gernon rounded the bend and looked in astonishment at Haith and his captive. Haith let go of de Pirou's throat and stepped away from him. 'What is the meaning of this?' demanded de Gernon. 'Your man assaults your dapifer, sire. I insist that he is severely punished! He cannot be allowed to get away with this.' Haith read anxiety on de Gernon's face, despite his bluster.

'It's nothing, my lord, sire!' de Pirou called out rapidly. 'A friendly dispute over a card debt is all.' De Gernon studied de Pirou and Haith saw a look of complicit knowledge pass between them. De Gernon knew very well why Haith had cornered de Pirou. De Gernon gripped de Pirou's arm, glared at Haith, and they moved away. Haith could do nothing but look on helplessly as his quarry disappeared from sight.

'Gambling, Haith?' the king chortled. 'Not setting a very good example are you?'

Haith bowed to the king as he moved past him. He lent back against the wall, dispirited not to have gained the answers he sought. Recovering his calm, he wiped at his sweating face with a sleeve before making his way to his quarters. Opening the door, he was confronted by the back of a tall woman standing at the window. Perhaps he was in the wrong room. She turned and Haith stared, astonished, at Ida. It was extraordinary to see her out of a nun's wimple, with her pale blonde hair visible beneath the veil of a secular woman, to see her in a court gown rather than a nun's habit.

She smiled broadly and he took her hands in his, exclaiming at the ink that splattered the fingers of her right hand.

'I'm making a book for the queen,' she laughed. 'Sorry that I'm a mess, but I heard you had arrived and was impatient to see you, ink or no.'

'What's the book?'

'It will be a gift from Queen Adelisa to the king, so don't tell him about it and ruin the surprise. I am writing an account of the king's deeds indeed!' she declared with a mock-pompous expression.

'I look forward to seeing and reading this masterpiece.'

'So you should. It is costing the queen a pretty penny with the animal skins I have had prepared, and the inks. I just received the first pages today and have been making tests for the illuminations.' She held her inky hand out again. 'I haven't even started thinking about the vast outlay I will recommend for the covers yet!'

They had much catching up to do. Ida gave him news of Nest and his little son, Robert. 'It was wonderful for me to spend time with them, Haith. I hope soon that I will return to Nest. I am anxious for her. She will birth her child soon and I wanted to be there for her.'

Haith frowned his own anxiety at the news. 'She has Amelina. Do you have cause for concern? Has she been ill?'

'No, no. Nothing of that sort. We grew close and she is like a sister to me. But yes, be reassured, she does have Amelina as you say, and there is no reason to fear for Nest.'

'But you fear *you* are at serious risk of exposure from this bard?' Haith asked.

'Yes. He knew me at Fontevraud.'

'You were both working for Countess Adela de Blois there?'

'Yes.'

'Well, who do you think he is working for now? It's not the king, or I would know of it.'

'I don't know. Perhaps he is simply pursuing his poetic art.'

Haith shook his head. 'Once a spy, always a spy. Well, except in your case of course,' he apologised, holding out a conciliatory hand to her. It seemed like as good a moment as any to raise the question of Amaury de Montfort. 'I have a gift for you that I carry from a friend of yours.' He produced the book which he had wrapped up again.

Ida looked with innocent curiosity. 'From the abbess?' she asked. He handed it to her and waited as she unwrapped it, turned it over in her hands, opened it to the dedication. A deep blush crept over her face and neck, leaving them blotched as though wine had been spilt over her skin and then scrubbed to a pale taint. 'Thank you for carrying this to me, brother.' Her voice was low and cautious.

'What is he to you, Ida? Amaury de Montfort?'

'He was a friend to me.'

'Is he the reason that you left the cloister?'

She did not reply.

'He is a traitor to the king, and is in rebellion against him now.'

Still she said nothing and would not meet his gaze.

'Did he speak to you of *The White Ship*? Of Gisulf?'

Now Ida was bewildered and she looked at him, frowning. 'The ship? The drowned clerk? Why should he?'

But as the words left her mouth, Haith saw the doubt spread

across Ida's face. He was relieved to discern that she had known nothing of Amaury's possible involvement in Gisulf's murder beforehand, but he could see by the rapid expressions crossing her white face that she knew more.

Haith hesitated, searching for the words to question her further to see if she could tell him anything that might either exonerate or implicate de Montfort. He was both frustrated and relieved to have their conversation interrupted with a summons to wait upon the king. The king's business kept Haith occupied day and night over the coming weeks so that there were no further opportunities to speak with Ida in confidence before they left Winchester.

In June, Haith and the king were waiting in Portsmouth for a fair wind to Normandy. Henry was busy with a mountain of matters in preparation for leaving England in the charge of his viceregent, Bishop Roger of Salisbury, before they sailed to deal with the rebellion. Haith sat in *The Topsail* inn in Portsmouth waiting for de Pirou who had sent Haith a short note assuring him that he would meet and talk with him before they sailed. Haith had been intrigued to read de Pirou's words that heavy matters weighed on him and he would be relieved to speak of them. Would this be yet another attempt at decoy, at distracting Haith from the truth? Yet they were all due to board the same ship to Normandy: King Henry, Haith, Ranulf de Gernon and de Pirou. Ida would travel with Queen Adelisa in a week's time and would be quartered in Rouen. De Pirou knew he could not evade Haith's determined hunt for the truth forever. After Haith had downed a third beaker of wine, it was evident that de Pirou was not going to show. Haith knit his brow. Damn the man. De Pirou had been giving him the run around both literally and metaphorically for months. He rode directly to Ranulf's house and asked to speak with de Pirou, guessing that would be his billet here in Portsmouth.

'He hasn't arrived yet, sir,' a worried-looking servant told him.

'Shouldn't he have been here days ago? We may sail at any time today or tomorrow.'

'Yes, sir. He should have been here, and Lord Ranulf is concerned on the matter.'

'Let me have speech with Ranulf's steward.'

The steward soon appeared in the hallway. 'What can I do for you, Sheriff Haith?'

'I had an appointment this morning to meet with de Pirou but I gather that he has not arrived yet?'

'That's correct. We sent a man out to search for news of him. De Pirou should have been here days ago.'

'And do you *have* any news of him?'

'He left London to make his way here. We have ascertained that much from his servants and we found that he stopped in an inn in Farnham. But after that, there is no sign of him. We fear he may have been set upon by robbers. My lord has sent two more men to enquire and enlist the assistance of the sheriff of Hampshire in finding out what has happened. Can you enlighten us further?'

'I'm afraid not. I hope he is found safe and well.'

Haith turned away, thwarted yet again.

The royal galley was scheduled to sail for Ouistreham the following morning. Haith and the king arrived at the harbour with the king's escort and had to fight their way through a noisy crowd gathered on the pier. 'What is it?' Haith asked one of the sailors crowding there. 'What's going on?' The sailor grimaced and pointed down at the water. The king and Haith stared down onto the back and billowing white shirt of a dead man in the water.

'What the devil?' Ranulf de Gernon pushed his way through to join them.

'Well, get him out of the water,' the king commanded.

Two fisherman hooked the body, pulling it towards the pilings where a number of others were able to manhandle it out of the swell and up onto the planking. The body flopped onto it back. It was bloated and had been feasted on by sea creatures, but Haith knew who it was. 'De Pirou,' he said quietly.

The king turned to him. 'Are you sure? It's hard to see who it is.'

Haith nodded. Ranulf bent and inspected a ring on the hand of the dead man. 'He's right, sire. It is de Pirou. Poor soul. I gave him this ring. He must have slipped on the planking in the dark, drunk perhaps, and lost his footing.'

Haith guessed that de Pirou had gone to the commissioner of his crime with news of Haith's discoveries. Was de Gernon that commissioner? Had he drowned the man who had caused so many other deaths by drowning? Was he ultimately responsible for the sinking of *The White Ship* and had he murdered de Pirou to ensure that no one could testify to that fact?

During the hours on the boat, crossing the English Channel, Haith studied Ranulf, but no amount of looking at the surface of the man was going to give him evidence one way or another. The insouciant young lord conversing so easily with the king did not give the appearance of having murdered three hundred people, including the heir to the throne and two of Henry's other children besides. There was no doubt that de Pirou and Ranulf had been thick as thieves, but had Ranulf commissioned the murder of Gisulf, or was there someone else behind that commission? Haith sighed, thinking that all his investigation had achieved so far was to complicate matters. He had more suspects now than he began with. Stephen de Blois had seemed the obvious, first suspect, but now he had added Waleran, Ranulf, and Amaury to the list. Haith's questioning of de Pirou must have led to his death, suggesting that Haith was himself at risk now from whoever the guilty party was. And war was an excellent cover for murder.

12

The Charter

June 1123, Llansteffan Castle, Wales

I stood at the tower window looking south over the spectacular view of the estuaries of the three rivers and the widening bay beyond. Llansteffan stood high on the headland above the confluence of the rivers. I heard a shout from the fields behind me and moved to see the view from the other window that faced out eastward towards the village. It was the time for haymaking and the fields were busy with workers armed with scythes. Soon they would be celebrating *Gŵyl Ifan Ganol Haf*, Saint John's of Midsummer Eve, with dancing and a bonfire at the foot of the hill beneath the castle.

'He who sees fennel and gathers it not is not a man but a devil,' Amelina declared behind me.

I turned to her. 'Do we have devils in the house, Amelina?'

She smiled and shook her head. 'No! But those lazy gardeners are letting the fennel bolt,' she grumbled. 'Your sons have arrived below, Lady Nest. And the sheriff.'

I raised my eyebrows in query. I had written to the steward at Carmarthen Castle asking that they send a royal official to me to witness a charter. Miles of Gloucester, the king's official in Carmarthen, was with the king's court and I had thought that it might be Haith who would come.

'It's not Haith that's come,' Amelina immediately disappointed my thought. 'It's Maurice de Londres.'

I knew that de Londres was castellan at Ogmore, but we had never met and I could not guess at what his stance might be in the coming scene. 'Is my husband here?'

'Not yet.'

In the hall, I greeted my sons, Henry, William, and Maurice, and I welcomed de Londres. William looked askance at me when I spoke Welsh to one of the servants and I suppressed my irritation with him.

'I am happy to be of service, lady,' de Londres began, but had no opportunity to complete his greeting as de Marais entered at that moment. I had not seen my husband for several months. Surrounded by my sons who were all tall, de Marais's shortness was emphasised. He was momentarily taken aback at the unexpected sight of the other men in the hall. I saw that he would have liked to burst out with an enquiry as to their purpose here, but politeness held him back. It was best that I get matters started swiftly.

'I have asked you all to attend me,' I declared, 'because I am in dispute with my husband concerning the management of my estate.'

De Marais's expression darkened but he began by trying for a conciliatory tone. 'My dear wife,' he cajoled, 'as I have requested in my letters, I need you to return to your duties at Cardigan Castle now that you have birthed our first child. And I need you to sign the charters I have drawn up regarding your estates at Llansteffan and Carew.'

'I intend to stay here in Llansteffan. The king has given me leave to do so,' I said bluntly.

De Marais could not keep the fury from his face and de Londres turned back to me with surprised consternation showing on his.

'And,' I continued, emphatically, 'I will dispose of my own

lands as I see fit.'

'Mother,' my son, Henry, leapt in before de Marais could respond, 'no one wishes to take what is yours, but it is our duty to be strategic in its use to support the king's interests here in Wales.' He winked at me out of de Marais's line of vision to indicate that he intended to support me and to mollify and manipulate de Marias to suit us.

'These are wise words,' de Londres ventured.

'I know that you are right, Henry,' I said. 'I have decided to gift Carew to you, William,' I announced to my second son. Carew was too redolent of my former life with my first husband, Gerald, for me to bear to ever live there again. It was the place I associated most with my marriage to him. 'You are of age to make your own household as Henry already does at Arberth, which was gifted to him by the king.' It did not hurt to name our connection to King Henry as often as possible.

William smiled his delight at the prospect of his independence. Added to his stewardship of Pembroke Castle on behalf of Gilbert de Clare, my gift of Carew created him a considerable power in the region. I saw de Londres nod his recognition that I was within my rights to grant that demesne to my son and that he approved of the appointment.

De Marais, on the other hand, was furious. My gift significantly diminished the income from the estates that I brought to our marriage, to him. 'And Llansteffan?' he demanded.

'Llansteffan, I will keep in my own hands. The king has given me a charter confirming my ownership and permitting me to reside here.' I flourished the charter, and passed it to de Londres to examine. I listened to my husband breathing heavily through his nose as de Londres read. De Londres looked up from perusing the parchment, smiling lopsidedly at me, in recognition of my stratagem. Then de Marais and my sons, one by one, read it through. 'My son, Maurice, will be my castellan here.' Now Maurice was as pleased as his brother William. I knew that my attachment to Llansteffan was irrational. It was where my brother, Goronwy, had been killed by the first Norman invaders. It was where I had loved Haith. I knew that my husband, and even my sons, saw my ownership of it as nominal. Strategically, they viewed it as theirs, Norman territory, but I did not see it that way and in law it was mine. Maurice would be the custodian of Llansteffan, but it belonged to me and I would enforce that at law if I had to.

'These decisions seem lawful to me, and in the king's interest,' Henry declared swiftly, 'and I am happy to support them. What do you say, de Londres?'

'Yes, I am also happy to support Lady Nest's decisions regarding the disposal of her estate and confirm that this is the king's seal and signature commanding it so,' de Londres stated firmly.

It was done. De Marais could not argue with this ratification of the document that I brandished when it came from both my son Henry and from the royal official. There was nothing he could do to gainsay me or argue with me. He was caught in a bind, not wishing to lose any further face in front of these men, anxious not to affront my sons who were of importance in the region. My clerk had already drawn up the charter confirming my disposal of Carew to William and we duly witnessed it. Maurice told me he would collect his gear from Carew and return to me and his new duties with haste. De Marais was poleaxed by the swift sequence of events and looked more shocked and floundering than angry, although that would undoubtedly come later.

'Might I have a word with you, Lady Nest?' de Londres asked.

'Of course.' I led him to a seat at the hearth. From the corner of my eye, I watched de Marais ready to depart with great fuss and irritation. My sons kept him corralled and headed with him towards the door and the stables, while de Londres consulted with me on the coming harvest and the next tax collection. I waved to my boys as they turned smiling to me at the threshold and regretted their departure, wanting to celebrate our ridding of de Marais with them, but at least I could also watch my husband leave and hope to never see him again. De Londres refused my offer of a bed at Llansteffan for the night. He was a long way from his own base at Ogmore, but he told me he had business at Kidwelly and must go on there before nightfall.

'Rebellion against the king is brewing in Normandy,' de Londres told me, 'led by Waleran de Meulan and Amaury de Montfort. And there is news that the rebels' hero, William *Clito*, has married Sybil, the daughter of the count of Anjou.'

I frowned. 'Such a marriage furthers *Clito*'s claim to the duchy of Normandy significantly.'

'Yes,' agreed de Londres. 'Many of the lords from the south and west of Wales have been called to arms to the king and we will be rather thinly spread in the meantime. I thought, as a significant landowner here, Lady Nest, I should inform you about this. Your sons are already aware of it.'

We, I thought. He imagined that because my sons comported themselves as Normans that he could presume to also include me in this Norman 'we' who were holding the land against the rebellious Welsh. I longed to ask de Londres if he had any news of Haith. No doubt, he would know where the sheriff was and what he was about, but I knew that such a question would break the bounds of decorum and I could not speak Haith's name, much as I wanted to.

After de Londres had taken his leave, Amelina came into the hall with my new son in her arms and handed him to me. I looked down into his sweet face. 'And here is another Norman,' I said in a gentle tone, touching my fingertip to his soft cheek. He pursed his tiny mouth at me in response and I smiled into his eyes. 'Another sweet, sweet Norman.'

Part Two

1123–1135

'One generation is going away, another is coming. There are
men like the leaves of a tree, the leaves of the olive tree, the
laurel tree, or any tree that still retains its mantle of greenery.
Thus the earth bears men, as one of these trees bears leaves; it
is covered with men, some of whom die, whose others are born
to succeed them. The tree always has its bright dress; but see
below how many dry leaves
crowd you.'

13

The Crow

December 1123, Pont Audemer Castle, Normandy

Haith squinted through the sheeting rain, looking up at the rebel commander standing on the parapet of Pont Audemer Castle. The man had his back to the besiegers and was gesticulating at his troops, confident that the trebuchets and arrows of the king's forces were not yet in range. Concentrating, Haith blocked out the noise of the wind, the soldiers' shouts and the tramping and snorting of horses all around him. He struggled at the control rope of the crow with his companion, straining to keep both balance and direction in the swing of the enormous weight of the grappling iron. Haith focused on the position of the hook and their target standing unawares on the castle wall. The crow was incredibly difficult to control. The thing was like fishing, but with the weight of a bell rather than a feathered bait. Each tiny move on their part resulted in a major jerk from the grapple so that it swung wildly, too far one way and then the other, yet gradually they manoeuvred it nearer to the castle commander. Amid the smoke and noise of war engines being trundled into place, the commander had not noticed the huge iron claws veering towards him as if they had Saint Vitus's Dance. 'Yes!' Haith shouted as they found their target. Haith could see the soldiers close to the commander waving their arms in panicked signals. The commander turned too late to find himself hooked by the barbed iron talons of the crow. 'Swing it!' Haith yelled. Together, he and his companion slewed the commander from the castle wall. After a brief and desperate struggle to keep a hold on the crow's embrace, the commander plummeted the long drop to the stony ground. He did not rise.

'Let go!' Haith shouted. He and his companion released their grip on the crow's ropes and the blunt end of the pole swung up wildly into the air, recoiling against its wooden brace as the heavy, iron claws slammed down into the ground. Haith swallowed, keeping his eye on the still body of the commander at the foot of the castle wall. He staggered, unprepared, when his companion slapped him hard on the shoulder in congratulations. The king was fond of his constantly developing engines of war. Haith had to concede that, on this occasion, the ingenuity of the engineers had proven its worth. Leaderless, the garrison would soon surrender, yet it seemed a cowardly way to engage in combat, at long arm's length and no risk to one's self. This seemed an unseemly way for a brave soldier to die.

The siege had gone on and on, well past the usual battle season, and into this wet and frigid winter that both sides were forced to contend with. Haith hugged his gloved hands beneath his armpits, but they were excruciatingly cold. On his side of the wall, the troops and horses stumbled in semi-frozen mud. On the other side of the wall, inside the castle, he guessed that the well and pond were frozen solid and the food supplies were exhausted.

He had been inside the castle wall he was staring at, that they were working so hard to breach, two years ago. He remembered the great hall where he had sat watching the cheerful preparations for the weddings of Waleran de Meulan's three sisters, where he witnessed the arrival of the rebel leader, William *Clito*. He imagined the great hall would be a much sorrier sight now. He remembered the line of maids strewing sweet herbs before the marriage feast. Fleetingly, he wondered if the forward maid with the dimples was still in there, and how she might have fared amid the boulders that had crashed relentlessly into the courtyard for the last few months, or the arrows that had rained unkindly on the castle defenders.

When they first arrived in Normandy in the summer, the king refortified his strongholds all across the duchy: at Rouen, Caen, Falaise, Argentan, Arques, Gisors, Vernon, Exmes, Vire, Gavray, Domfront, and Ambieres. Henry spent most of his time in Rouen with Queen Adelisa and left the front-line duties to the earls of Chester and Gloucester and to his *familia regis*, which included Haith. The king's extraordinary arsenal of siege engines to be deployed against the rebels was under Haith's management: ballistas, mangonels, wooden towers on wheels, engines that hurled stones and javelins, and now the iron hand of the crow. William *Clito* had been attacking in the south and there was news in September of Waleran, Amaury, and the other rebels at La Croix-Saint-Leufroy. From then on, the autumn was stormy in Normandy with thunder, rain, and war.

In October, Henry grew impatient and set out with a vast army, summoning one of the rebels, Hugh de Montfort to him, demanding that he hand over the castle of Montfort-sur-Risle. Hugh, however, evaded the king, escaping from the castle before the arrival of the royal army. He had left Montfort-sur-Risle in the command of his heavily pregnant wife, Adelina, one of Waleran's sisters. Amaury de Montfort and William Crispin failed in an attempt to capture Gisors from the king. Earl Robert and Earl Ranulf had been, in turn, attacking Amaury's lands around Evreux. King Henry, usually so considerate towards women, had relentlessly besieged Adelina in Montfort-sur-Risle, burnt the town, fired Brionne, and then marched to lay siege to Pont Audemer, which had held out until now, until the middle of December.

The king called his council to attend him in his tent to announce the capitulation of the Pont Audemer garrison. Haith strode up the hill towards the royal pavilion, which was pitched on a rise to preserve it from the worst of the icy puddles and muck. The king's flag flew from the pinnacle of the brilliant blue and red striped tent. Two servants stood at the entrance securing the tent flaps back to allow the members of Henry's war council to crowd inside. The king was sitting on a portable throne and nodded to Haith. 'Good fishing with the crow, my friend!' he called out. When his commanders were assembled, the king addressed them: 'You all know that the garrison has surrendered and you will have heard the gentle terms I have given them for their valiant, if misguided, efforts.'

Not so gentle terms, thought Haith, for those many who had already died. He had overseen the bodies inside the castle being loaded onto carts that morning and then seen them off to be ferried out to the limepits for burial. The dimpled maid had been amongst the dead. He had recognised her in the pile of corpses despite the ghastly greenish pallor of her face. Her delicate neck had been pierced with the uncaring gash of an arrow.

'We have reports from Gisors,' the king continued, 'that Amaury de Montfort and William Crispin attempted to take the fortress by subterfuge but they have been repelled.' A cry of victory went up from the assembled men. 'I have decided to call a truce for Christmas,' Henry declared.

'But should we let up now, sire,' asked Stephen de Blois, 'when we are so close to hammering the rebels into the ground?' Stephen was an enthusiastic soldier. Haith could not recall ever feeling enthusiastic about war. Bowel-droppingly terrified, anguished, exhausted, nauseatingly disgusted. Those were his feelings about war, but it was not ever anything that could be dodged or ran away from. It had to go on until the king called a halt, as he was doing now, and Haith sent up a grateful prayer for that. There was no need for anyone to offer an argument against Stephen. Every man there, including Stephen, knew that the king did not change his mind. Stephen's bluster was just part of his constant efforts to prove his worth to the heirless king.

'Our troops are exhausted and sick,' King Henry declared. 'Fighting this late into the year is doing neither side any good. The people of Normandy, my people, are suffering from the ravages of war on the land all around us. They need a chance to recover themselves, so that there is no starvation next year. There will be respite for the Christmas period. We will return to Rouen, and then return to the battlefield to obliterate the rebels in the spring.'

All nodded and murmured their needless assent. Henry's councils were never occasions for debate. They were simply vehicles to convey information on decisions he had already made. In truth, all the king's soldiers, apart from Stephen de Blois, had little stomach to continue the fighting in this unseasonable season. Apart from the question of the succession, de Blois had other reasons for excessive battle zeal. His father had been accused of cowardice during the first crusade and Stephen went to great lengths to ensure that the same accusation could never be laid at *his* door.

Haith accompanied King Henry and Queen Adelisa inside Saint Romanus chapel in Rouen, but halted just inside the door to allow them to proceed towards the altar in privacy. They removed their heavy winter cloaks and loaded them over Haith's proffered arm, and heeled off the boots they had worn to cross the muddy courtyard outside. The king and queen stood in their plain linen shifts and, in the cold silence of the chapel, their breath showed white around their faces. It made Haith shiver just to look at them. The differences in their ages and physiques were emphasised by their state of undress. Henry's undertunic was taut across the girth of his belly, whilst Adelisa's slender, girlish body was swamped in the voluminous folds of her shift. As the king and queen processed solemnly towards the altar, wearing chaplets of white flowers on their heads, their bare feet slapped against the stone slabs of the nave. The tiny chapel was lit with a thousand candles for the royal visit and a small choir of novices sang softly under the discreet direction of a monk. To Haith's right, candlelight glinted on the gold leaf of a book of hours, open on a stand. From the walls, large colourful paintings of saints and the holy family looked down on Haith with doleful eyes. A solitary priest stood at the altar ready to raise the lid of the reliquary and allow the royal couple to touch the preserved remains of Saint Romanus. The king and queen prayed to the saint to intercede for them and grant them a son. The saint's mother, Felicite, had lamented her barrenness until she was visited by an angel and Henry was sure that the saint's bones could help them.

Saint Romanus was known for many miracles: levitation, quelling a flooding river, resisting the temptations of a demon cavorting as a naked woman, and vanquishing a dragon. To Haith's left, a wallpainting depicted the saint confronting the dragon with a crucifix. The dragon had batlike wings, a long neck, and breathed fire from its curiously human-looking face.

The cathedral at Rouen had been struck by lightning some years before and there was plenty of work for stonemasons, carpenters, and fresco artists there now. It would be a long time before it was rebuilt and could be used again. In the meantime, many of its treasures, including the relics of Saint Romanus and the tombs of the early dukes of Normandy—Rollo and William I—were temporarily housed here. It was strange to see the ducal coffins placed on the floor like mere packing crates.

Haith tried but failed to suppress his curiosity about the relics that Henry and Adelisa were so reverently huddled around up there. A mummified penis perhaps? More likely a finger bone, or dried out tongue, or a vial of blood. It was rumoured that there were numerous churches claiming to house Christ's holy prepuce, but it was forbidden to speak about that. Haith had to part company with Henry on the topic of the efficacy of relics. He could not give credence to this worship of bits of old bones and leatherised flesh, but he kept his opinions to himself.

The king and queen completed their entreaties and were coming back down the aisle towards him. Henry was intent on his hands joined in supplication before him, but Adelisa lifted a white face to Haith and sent an agonised glance in his direction. He did his best to send her a reassuring smile in return. This relentless and seemingly hopeless pressure to be fertile with an aging man could not have been what she had imagined as a young girl, dreaming of her future husband.

14

Miners

April, 1124, Manorbier Castle, Wales

My brother Gruffudd sat back, patting his stomach. 'I'm not used to such quantities of food!' he laughed. Almost all my family were reunited today for my daughter Angharad's wedding at Manorbier. The marriage was a small affair with just the remaining members of my kin and the family of the groom, William FitzOdo de Barry, in attendance. Given the Norman and Welsh complexity of my family and my separation from de Marais, I was relieved that none of the Normans had been invited from the castles of Cardigan or Pembroke.

The bard sang to us,

'Month of April—wanton is the lascivious;
Sheltering the ditch to everyone who loves it;
Joyous the aged in his robes;
Loquacious the cuckoo in the rural vales;
Easy is society where there is affection;
Covered with foliage are the woods, sportive the amorous.'

The song was reminiscent of Breri's poetry and the Manorbier bard had probably learned it from him. Was there no escape from the ubiquitous Breri? He seemed to pop up everywhere.

Maurice was seated beside me and smiled tightly at his uncle. Of all my sons, Maurice looked the most like my first husband, Gerald. At seventeen, he was much the same age as Gerald had been when I first met him. Maurice was a young man of few words but I was conscious of him listening carefully to the nuances in my conversation with Gruffudd.

Angharad was happy with her husband and his family. I had commissioned an illuminated manuscript as a gift for her and she and her husband were smiling over it, pointing out the details to each other. It showed Angharad and William standing either side of a tree covered in curling leaves and branches. The branches of the tree sprouted down below to the lines of their parents and kin. The top left corner of the manuscript showed a shepherd playing on his pipe and in the opposite top right corner was a hart leaping through trees. In the bottom corners were a huntsman with a spear and a mastiff on the scent. 'It's lovely, Mother!' Angharad declared.

Her oldest brother Henry presented her with a finely crafted silver casket and she opened it, exclaiming at the rings and brooches in the compartments inside. 'One from each of your brothers,' William told her.

FitzOdo was rebuilding Manorbier Castle in stone and it would be a fine place for Angharad to exercise her wifely skills. I swept my gaze over my family. My eldest son, Henry, the king's son, was a man and had married last year. William, my eldest son with Gerald FitzWalter, had also taken the opportunity of my gift of Carew Castle to take himself a wife. They had both chosen to marry Welsh girls of good stock and I approved of their matches and smiled at my daughters-in-law.

Only my son David who was a novice at Saint Davids was not here. I had left my two youngest sons at home with Amelina. It was a cause of some consternation to me that they were both named Robert, but since everyone thought the older Robert,

Haith's five-year-old son, was Amelina's child, I could not argue when de Marais insisted that his son should be named Robert. I resolved it by privately referring to de Marais's hale and hearty baby as FitzStephen.

Gwenllian had accompanied Gruffudd to the wedding and was in animated conversation with Angharad and her mother-in-law. Gwenllian's stepsons, Anarawd and Cadell, were a little younger than my grown sons and the conversation between the cousins was rather constrained. Sadly, they were not sure whether to consider one another as enemies. Gwenllian's own young sons, eight-year-old Morgan and five-year-old Maelgwyn, were wrestling and laughing with the hounds near the hearth.

'Come and see the fine view from the ramparts.' I reached a hand to my brother to haul him to his feet. 'Walk off your overeating.'

On the threshold, I glanced back over my shoulder to Maurice at the high table. He was eyeing us with a serious expression. He would be worrying that I was embroiling myself in Gruffudd's dealings. I worried, too, where such dealings might lead for Maurice and his brothers who had aligned themselves so entirely with the Normans. 'He does not trust me,' Gruffudd murmured, close to my ear.

'I know.' We rounded the corner and were out of Maurice's view and I felt the relief of it and the guilt at it, that I could not be honest with my own sons.

I led Gruffudd past the well in the upper ward and up the steps leading to the ramparts. 'Look at this masonry.' Gruffudd pointed at the herringbone style of placing stones to produce a distinctive pattern. 'My sons, too, will build castles here in Deheubarth in stone.'

I nodded and let his words ring in silence for a while to show my confidence in their truth. We stayed standing on the top step, holding the wall. The weather was too wild to risk standing on the wall itself. As we gazed out at the spectacular view, we were buffeted by the wind, our hair blowing awry.

'The Deheubarth royal family survey their domain,' Gruffudd said. His tone was light but both our hearts were heavy at his words. Here, where he should be king and his sons princes, they had a status barely better than outlaws. Gruffudd pulled me down to sit next to him on the step where we had some shelter from the wind and did not have to shout at one another. 'What of the German?' he asked, meaning the mining expert that I had sent to survey Dolaucothi. 'I sense you have good news from him.'

After Cadell had told me about the goldmine, I contacted one of the miners at Alston, named Werner, and asked him to assess the potential of my brother's mine for me. 'Yes!' I could not contain my excitement, despite my misgivings. 'He says there is certainly gold to be mined, both in the open surface veins and in the tunnels and he has the knowhow and means to do it. He is keen to make a start.'

'We must consider this carefully, Nest.'

'I know.'

'If the Normans get wind that I am mining gold two things will happen. They will deduce that I am using it to arm myself for rebellion and they will want a big cut of the proceeds.'

'The mine is on your land and you are entitled to work it and to pay tithes on the proceeds to the sheriff of Carmarthen for the king's coffers.'

'That much is true.'

'I have thought this through, Gruffudd, and my advice is that you instruct the miner to only work in the tunnels to attract less attention, not on the open rock faces and that you keep it all close.'

He nodded.

'That you do not declare the full extent of your profits to the sheriff, but you do declare some.' I stopped and took a deep breath. Now, here we were, both on the brink of flouting the king's law.

For Gruffudd, that had little impact. He flouted Norman rule each day, with his every action and his very existence. He had no choice in that. But I had never had an occasion to pit myself against Norman rule before. It was a big step and I saw these thoughts crossing Gruffudd's earnest face.

'I would not endanger you, Nest.' He paused. 'I could do as you suggest and the additional amount that I do not declare to the sheriff could go to arm my men in preparation for our next best opportunity. It is of some assistance that the sheriff of Carmarthen, Walter of Gloucester, is an old man and not as assiduous in his work as your friend, Haith, at Pembroke.'

I breathed a sigh of relief that my brother's lands did not fall within Haith's purview for I would not embroil him in any of this risk or deception. 'But Walter's son, Miles of Gloucester, *is* assiduous,' I declared.

'But often away at the king's court.'

'You should not underestimate Maurice de Londres, who acts on behalf of the Gloucester family. I have met him and sense he is a staunch character.'

Gruffudd nodded. 'The mining will cost money to establish. Did the miner give you an estimate of the initial outlay needed?'

'Yes and I will pay it. Meister Werner writes to me that the finding of the veins and seams progresses well. He says the sun draws the metal in the veins towards the surface and gold might be persuaded to part with other material through the application of acid, salt, or mercury. It is a fascinating topic, Gruffudd. He says he has to solve the flooding in the mine tunnels and find the means to win the gold from the other material it is fixed within. He writes that he can turn the water on itself, using waterwheels to power the drainage of the tunnels and he has a new design for a furious furnace that he used at Alston.'

'I see that you are an excited miner, Sister.' The expression in his blue eyes sobered. 'It will be costly. How am I to raise the funds?'

'*I* will pay for it, Gruffudd,' I repeated.

He was silent for a long moment. 'If the Normans discover it, Nest, you would be implicated in treason, along with me.'

'I am aware of that. Miners are used to keeping their art secret from prying eyes. Meister Werner will not blurt on us.'

'It is your decision?'

'It is. I would see you king of Deheubarth, but if all we achieve is to force the Norman lords here to curtail their oppression of the Welsh, this would be some progress.'

'They have not tended to compromise.'

I swallowed and knew that he was right. Most likely, if Henry and his delegates suspected anything of the skimming of proceeds from the mining operation that we were proposing they would hang everyone involved. I would, at the very least, be imprisoned and stripped of my lands.

'Your sons, Nest?'

'They must know nothing of it. This is the hardest part for me, Gruffudd. To support you and support our people, I must oppose my own sons.'

He looked at me with concern and waited.

'But I am resolved. Gruffudd, I think of our brother Goronwy every day and the rest of our slaughtered family and I think of our people harried up into the barren lands of the mountains and taxed as their children starve. The poets say that the grave is better than a life of want. I cannot sit and do nothing. I have written to the king to tell him that there is need to lessen the grip of tax in these lands, when we have faced consecutive years of famine. He squeezes us too hard.'

'How did he respond?'

'He has not replied.'

'He is busy with his wars in Normandy and our taxes pay for it. We have no choice but to give him wars here to look to.'

I nodded reluctantly.

'We cannot sit by mildly, Nest.'

'No,' I agreed, 'we cannot.'

'I will instruct the miner as you suggest. You must ensure that when you send the money to pay for the mining operation there is no way to trace it back to you.'

'Have you encountered a bard named Breri sniffing about, Gruffudd?'

He was surprised. 'Yes, he was at Caeo a few months ago. He sang for us on the occasion of a visit from Gwenllian's brothers. He is pretty good.'

'He is a pretty good spy too. News of your visit from the princes of Gwynedd will have reached the ears of the de Clares. This Breri roams between the castles of Pembroke and Cardigan and must be in the pay of Gilbert or Richard de Clare, or both.'

Gruffudd frowned. 'That is not good, but thank you for the warning. Cadell thought the poet might be in league with Prince Cadwaladr. They had a lot to say to one another at Caeo.'

I considered this information. 'From what I hear from Ida, I wouldn't put it past Breri to be working as a double agent—selling information to both sides, to the de Clares and to Cadwaladr. Take great care that, if he returns to Caeo, he gets no wind of the mining. We wouldn't want either the Normans or the princes of Gwynedd to find out about that.'

15

The Devil's Eloquence

April 1124, Caen, Normandy

Haith groaned at the cry of a cockerel and opened his eyes to stare at the pale light filtering in through the fabric of his tent. The city of Caen, where the king was in residence, was brimming with soldiers, mercenaries, and the usual rash of traders following the armies. Haith had no option but to accept billeting in the vast field of war tents outside the city walls. He should, he thought reluctantly, get up. His bones ached. He was too old for sleeping on hard ground. The war against the rebels churned on and there seemed no end to it. There was famine and heavy taxes all across Normandy and the king was forced to draw heavily on his English coffers. He had discovered bad coin in the pay of his mercenaries in Normandy and taken extreme measures against the coiners in England. Half of the moneyers had been maimed and dismissed. The minds of the English and the Normans alike stung with the ferocity of Henry's retribution. Haith closed his eyes again. A few more minutes.

'Get up, Haith!' He sat bolt upright as the king burst in, ducking his helmeted head under the low entry flap. 'Extraordinary news!' Henry exclaimed. Haith rolled himself swiftly out of his blanket and clutched it to his privates as he stood, his head pressing gently at the dome of the tent membrane. He knotted his blanket skirt-like around himself.

'What's happened?'

'Waleran has been captured and all the rebels with him. The rebellion is over! We're returning to Rouen.'

'Thank God!' Haith gripped Henry's upper arms to share his relief and joy. Beneath Haith's palms, he felt the slip of Henry's wrinkled skin and the slack of the once hard muscle of his biceps.

Dismounting, Haith looked around at the courtyard of the king's new palace at Quevilly, adjacent to the Priory of Notre-Dame de Pré in Rouen. The king's servants immediately began the task of unpacking the carts of his entourage in preparation for the Easter court. Behind Haith, Waleran de Meulan, Hugh de Montfort, Hugh de Chateauneuf, and twenty-five other rebel knights swayed wearily in their saddles, loaded with chains. One side of Waleran's young face was green and yellow with bruising where he had fallen hard in the brief battle at Rougemontiers. Waleran's horse had been shot from beneath him in a hail of arrows when he was captured. His dark hair, usually so perfectly groomed, stood from his head in unwashed, uncombed clumps. Haith looked up at the palace facade and thought he saw Ida's face at a window.

When the prisoners were secured, Haith made for his chamber and was not surprised to find Ida waiting there for him. 'Tell me what happened quickly, Haith? Amaury de Montfort? I did not see him amongst the prisoners.'

'He lives,' Haith reassured her. 'Waleran and Amaury had a small win, relieving the fortress at Vatteville when it was under royal siege. But Waleran won himself no love in the countryside thereabouts. We found a family on our patrol who told us Waleran had severed the feet of their father and his two grown sons for cutting wood in his forest.'

Ida grimaced and her eyes were liquid with empathy for the peasant family. 'There has been so much cruelty on both sides ….'

'Earl Ranulf had wind of the route that Waleran would be taking after Vatteville and ambushed them near Rougemontier. Waleran had a greater force but Ranulf had the experience. The horses of the rebels were shot down by the king's archers on their flank and Waleran, Hugh de Montfort, and Hugh de Chateauneuf were surrounded and captured. That foolish young man is in chains in the dungeons below and will soon be sent across the Channel to imprisonment in England. If he looks to the examples of the king's earlier opponents, Duke Robert de Normandy and Count Robert de Bellême, he will know that he has reason to fear a very long imprisonment.'

Haith saw the urgent question on Ida's face. 'Amaury was also captured by William de Harcourt.'

'But he was not with you when you arrived.'

'No, your friend has the Devil's own gift of eloquence. He charmed his captor into allowing him to escape and de Harcourt fled with him.'

'Amaury would never see the outside of a cell again,' Ida said, 'if he fell into the king's hands.'

'True enough. William Lovel also escaped from the field.'

'Ranulf Le Meschin has played an important role in vanquishing the rebels for the king.'

Haith nodded. 'That he did. He is the hero of the fight against the rebellion. The king is not inclined to clemency against his enemies and has ordered that the captured followers of these rebel lords have their eyes broiled from their heads.'

Ida gasped. 'Oh Haith! Can he not be prevailed upon to give mercy?'

Haith shook his head. 'They gave no mercy themselves, Ida, and many good men have died fighting them.'

Ida sighed heavily.

'But the rebellious hopes of the king's nephew, William *Clito*, are thwarted, for good, I hope. There can be an end to it now,' Haith said. 'The villages of the wretched country people have been pillaged to the very straw. Soldiers hunted for the poor people's meagre treasure concealed in wells and cellars. We are all weary of the strife. The king is past the age when the rigours of war can be easily endured or when war might be experienced as excitement. Me too! I grow too old for the campaigning. But on this occasion, the old men have defeated the younger and prevail.'

'Well, I am glad of that, at least, for this old man.' Ida hugged her lanky brother to her hip.

Haith picked up a candle. There was not much of it left. It had been a long night of celebration for King Henry's forces, but this candle stub would be enough to get him up the stairs and along the passages of the palace to his room. Haith dipped his head at each archway and bent his long frame around the tight bends in the stairwell, shielding the candle flame from the draught at each sliver of window slit. After the raucous hall, the silence and stillness of the passageway were emphatic. The door latch screeched metal and needed oiling. Haith entered the small private room that had been allocated to him and put the candle down on a table. He turned back to close the door as quietly as he could with both hands, in case others were sleeping around him in the hushed stone chambers. He hunted around the room and found a near-new candle to take up the baton from the sputtering one he had carried upstairs.

He sat bone tired on a stool for a moment, thinking of the grimness that had happened this evening along with the victory celebration. The king had ordered Geoffrey de Tourville, Odard du Pin, and Luc de La Barre to be blinded. Waleran was forced to stand in chains and listen to the sentence passed against his lieutenants and Haith saw the young man blanch as the punishment was pronounced. The count of Flanders remonstrated with the king, arguing that it was not customary to mutilate knights captured in war but Henry was adamant. They were his liegemen and had broken their allegiance and committed treason. Waleran and the two Hughs then stood quaking before Henry to hear their own fates. 'You will order Morin du Pin at Vatteville to surrender,' the king commanded Waleran, 'or you will also suffer consequences to your person'.

Waleran was still young, barely twenty, and had never encountered such danger. Even in battle he was surrounded by men who gave their lives to keep sharp blades far from him. 'Yes, sire.'

The king told the three young men that they would be sent to England in chains and would never see the outside of a prison again. The hairs on the back of Haith's neck stood in empathy at the thought of such a young man, a boy really, hearing that was to be his future, the rest of his life.

There was a knock on the door. 'Come!' Haith called.

A small, scrawny priest stood on the threshold, his pale feet in muddy sandals splayed at the hem of his habit in a wide V-shape. 'The prisoner, Luc de La Barre, has asked that you have speech with him, Sir Haith.'

'With me? I cannot intercede for him to the king. Once the king makes up his mind, it is not changeable.' Haith glanced at his bed. He was weary and wanted to wipe the scenes of war, and the sense of his own bloodguilt from his mind in sleep.

The priest shrugged his shoulders. 'I don't know why he wishes to speak with you, sir, only that he does and is most insistent that it occurs before his sentence is carried out tomorrow.'

Haith grimaced. Visiting a man about to have his eyes put out was not an appealing prospect for his evening. 'Very well.'

The bruleurs would be at de La Barre's cell at first light tomorrow with their hot irons. They had already carried out sentence on Odard du Pin and Geoffrey de Tourville and the whole court, Waleran, and de La Barre himself, had no choice but to listen to their screams.

Haith took a torch and made his way down to the castle dungeons. At the guard's station he divested himself of his dagger in case it was turned against him. He followed a guard down narrow, low passageways. More places not constructed to accommodate his height. More places where he must walk hunched and contorted. Haith began to think that he should buy a windmill to live in and take out some of the floors. He did his best to distract himself from the stench and misery all around him as the guard led him deep down to the worst cells. 'There's them that was blinded this morning,' said the guard, but Haith averted his eyes, conscious that he had some, and did not look in the direction the guard was indicating. 'And here he is. Next up.' The grimy face of Luc de La Barre gazed through the bars of the cell. Haith had known Luc at court before the days of rebellion. He was a gifted poet and had been an accomplished, flamboyant courtier. It was grievous to see him brought to this, but rebellion had its price and all knew that Henry was not a forgiving man when it came to disloyalty.

'The priest told me you wished to speak with me, de La Barre.'

'Thank you for coming, Haith,' said the prisoner, his courteous voice and manner belied by his surroundings. 'Won't you enter my palace, here? I am no danger to you.'

Haith gestured impatiently to the guard to unlock the door. 'I will call you when I'm done.'

There was nowhere in the grimy, stinking cell to sit apart from the floor and that squirmed with insects and the occasional glimpse of a bright-eyed rat, so they stood.

'There is nothing I can do for you, de La Barre. The king has made up his mind. I'm sorry for it.' It was hard to look into the man's eyes, knowing that they would be gone tomorrow. De La Barre's scurrilous songs on the king's failure of virility had not helped his case, but Henry had ruled harshly against him because he had already forgiven him for rebellion and let him free on two other occasions. De La Barre had exhausted the king's patience.

'I know that, Haith. I wished to speak to you on the matter of *The White Ship*. It weighs on my conscience and I would relieve myself of it. The information I can give you will not help me with the king but it will help me with my maker who I will see before long, though I see nothing else.'

Haith wanted to tell the man that he would likely survive the blinding. Most did. Homer had been a blind poet, but Haith could not bring words to his mouth that did not sound trite. In any case, it was not his job to bring comfort here.

'What do you know of the ship?'

'I heard from Morin du Pin that you had unravelled a lot of the tale but not all of it.'

Haith said nothing. Morin du Pin had been Waleran de Meulan's steward since the young count had been orphaned and the two were tight as father and son.

'I heard that you wanted to know who commissioned Berold and de Pirou to murder Gisulf on *The White Ship*, the act that led to the sinking and all those deaths.'

Again, Haith said nothing. His instinct was to let de La Barre do the talking.

'It was Morin,' Luc declared.

'Morin, on behalf of Waleran?'

'The count knew nothing of it beforehand. He did not know that Gisulf had intercepted a letter from him to William *Clito* and had him over a barrel as it were. It amused Morin to commission de Pirou to 'put Gisulf in a barrel' instead.'

'Why de Pirou? I thought he was working for Ranulf de Gernon?'

De La Barre looked perplexed at Haith's mention of de Gernon. 'De Pirou and du Pin are old fighting buddies. They do each other favours. I heard nothing in it of de Gernon.'

'I see. So that's the whole story.'

De La Barre nodded.

'And how do you know it?'

'I was there, when du Pin commissioned de Pirou. The butcher was de Pirou's own addition.'

'You are certain that Waleran de Meulan knew nothing of it?'

'I am certain that they did not know of it in advance, but when you came probing de Pirou, I know that Count Waleran panicked. They talked with du Pin and found out then about the order he had given concerning Gisulf's murder on the ship. It must weigh heavy with the count too. Three hundred deaths and the king's son. But I swear that Count Waleran did not know of the murder plot beforehand. I was there when it was discussed,' de La Barre said, 'but I had no part in it. And yet the information has weighed heavy on me.'

'Well, now you are relieved of it.' Haith considered that it was likely Morin du Pin who had done away with de Pirou to prevent Haith's enquiries coming any closer.

'Thank you. Will you tell the king? I know it won't help my case.'

'I need to know more before I speak to the king. I need to speak to du Pin.'

'Have a care, my friend. Du Pin is dangerous. Very dangerous.' Haith nodded. 'I know it.'

'I thank you that I am unburdened,' de La Barre said. 'This is more than a priest could do for me.'

'Go with God,' Haith said and gave his farewells briskly to the condemned man, shouted for the guard and collected his dagger on his swift way out. He was relieved to emerge into the fresh night air of the courtyard. He made his way to the well, took a beaker of cold water from the suspended bucket and poured it over the top of his head and the back of his neck. He filled another beaker and drank it down. He sat on the well edge, thinking. So Stephen de Blois and Ranulf de Gernon appeared to be exonerated of any hand in *The White Ship* crime, if Luc's testimony was to be trusted.

In the gloom, Haith was surrounded by mounds of building materials for the as yet unfinished wing of the palace. The sinking of the ship must have just been a chain of accidents, following on from the murder of Gisulf that was intended to protect Waleran. Du Pin was holed up, under siege in Vatteville, and Haith would have to wait for his surrender before he could question him. Du Pin would not be in a happy mood, with his liege lord, Waleran, in chains and his brother, Odard, blinded. Haith could not see how the story Luc de La Barre had told to him could give King Henry any comfort, just as it gave little to him, now that he had finally uncovered it. Something that de La Barre had said niggled at the edge of his mind. They. He had said '*they* did not know if… *they* talked with du Pin' when Haith had asked about Count Waleran. Who else did Luc mean? Who else had known about the commissioned murder of Gisulf? Waleran's twin, Robert, earl of Leicester, perhaps, but he seemed loyal to the king and was likely in England and not present. Amaury? Amaury de Montfort? He and Waleran were also close. Amaury was like a favoured uncle to Waleran and Amaury was the driver behind this rebellion and the ones before. Was it Ida's lover, Amaury, who de La Barre referred to? And, if so, did Amaury have more of a hand in the sinking than appeared after all? Amaury had his own reason—Ida—for complicity in Gisulf's murder.

Haith stared at the door down to the dungeons. He should return to the grim cell and question de La Barre further but the thought of returning to that stagnant air so full of fear and misery was too much in one night. He would speak with de La Barre again tomorrow, after the blinding, when he was recovered enough.

Haith woke late to the sounds of turmoil in the rooms beneath him. 'What is it?' he asked the servant who brought him bread and ale.

'That poet prisoner. He's brained himself in his cell rather than have the blinding carried out.'

Haith stared. 'He's dead?' The man nodded and moved on to his next chore.

Haith pulled on his clothes and hurried down to the cell. 'Where is he?' he demanded of a guard who was standing in the empty space with a mop and a bucket.

'Dead one? Already taken out. Killed himself rather than lose his eyes.'

Haith looked at the man, but he had nothing more to tell him. He looked around the cell. It was hard to see anything in the gloom. There was a splash of drying blood against the wall where de La Barre's head had hit. But did he do it himself or did somebody do it for him? And was Haith in jeopardy from whoever had murdered de Pirou and now de La Barre? Knowing that de La Barre had talked with Haith, would whoever it was be coming for him next?

16

Sanctuary and Pardon

July 1124, Rouen

Haith waited for the right time to talk with Ida about *The White Ship* and Amaury de Montfort, but no time ever seemed like a good time for such a conversation. His investigation stuttered on. It appeared that the culprit he sought was Waleran's steward Morin du Pin, but Haith was frustrated again there. After a long siege at Brionne, du Pin surrendered, on orders from his imprisoned lord, and the king commanded that du Pin be sent into exile. Haith raced to Brionne when he heard the news, hoping to force a full confession from the man, but arrived only in time to see du Pin ride out of the castle, heading for the harbour. Haith kicked his horse into pursuit. Du Pin looked over his shoulder, recognised Haith, and knew the cause for the chase. Du Pin spurred his horse on to a church, jumped down and ran for the door.

Cursing, Haith saw but was too late to prevent the other man from lifting the sanctuary knocker. Du Pin grinned smugly at Haith as he was admitted by a priest. The big studded door closed resolutely behind him. Haith dismounted and stood before the door. There was a dip in the marble floor where he stood, worn away by the faithful filing into church each week. Haith slid his fingers and palm around the lion-head knocker on the closed door. Du Pin was beyond his reach for at least forty days. The lion's mane on the doorknocker was arranged in two rows of coiled locks. It had prominent eyes, heavy brows, flaring nostrils, and gripped the ring of the knocker in its mouth. Haith curled his hand into the ring and rested his forehead on the closed church door. If only he had so tight a grip on du Pin.

Haith sat out the forty days, staying in a tavern, but inevitably du Pin chose to be escorted into exile rather than face Henry's retribution for the rebellion or Haith's questioning and had eluded an encounter.

In September, the king returned to Rouen and granted audience to the vanquished rebel lords Amaury de Montfort and William Lovel. It was a brave move by de Montfort to come here, Haith had to give him that. He could have continued to skulk in hiding, but he was risking the brutality of the king's ire in hopes of receiving pardon and the return of his lands and title.

Haith accompanied Ida into the crowded hall and jostled his way through the packed gathering to a place at the front where he might look both at Amaury and at Ida. He saw how anxiously she stared at Amaury's bowed, blond head as he knelt in supplication to the king, how she studied the king's face in an effort to discern what doom he might pronounce.

'Forgive me, my duke. I have been a fool,' Amaury said. It was a short speech indeed, but Haith saw that the dialogue taking place between the king and the count was a silent one, expressed in their faces and their contemplation of one another. Amaury was related to Henry. They were cousins a few times removed. They both carried the ducal blood of Rollo, the first duke of Normandy, in their veins.

'You reached outside your orbit, count,' Henry said, choosing to be equally crisp and concise in his response.

'I acknowledge my error and beg your pardon.'

Henry narrowed his eyes and turned his gaze to the second man, William Lovel, who proffered a rather more lengthy and shaky speech of contrition than Amaury's.

When Lovel had finished speaking, Henry let them sweat a while as he considered them, and then looked out over their heads to his assembled court. Lovel, certainly, was perspiring, Haith noticed, looking at the back of the man's neck, but de Montfort showed no sign of anxiety whatsoever. Either he was a consummate actor or a man of enormous bravery. Perhaps both. It was not difficult to see why Waleran had followed him into contention against the king. Nor was it difficult to imagine what Ida saw in this bold man.

'I give you my pardon, de Montfort, Lovel,' Henry declared loudly, and Haith heard Ida draw in a breath beside him. 'One time. And never again. You will suffer death not imprisonment if you ever betray your fealty to me again.'

Haith had hoped that he might get the opportunity to question Amaury concerning Gisulf or du Pin but, again, he was thwarted. Pardon granted, the two men wisely did not remain at court where they were surrounded by lords whose brothers, sons, and fathers they had seen to their deaths. They left immediately. As Amaury passed from the hall, Haith saw the warmth of the smile exchanged between the rebel lord and his sister. The heat and brilliance of such a smile might have cajoled a new moon out from its black hiding place.

17

Crossing

September 1124, The English Channel

Bracing for the next wave kept them all in a state of stress. Haith clung with one hand to the rim of the ship's bulwark and kept his other arm wrapped tightly around Ida's shoulders as the vessel was pummelled by the high seas and freezing water dashed intermittently over them. He fought to anchor them as far as he could in place on the bench but the force of each wave knocked them sideways, slid them apart, momentarily loosed Haith's hold on his sister and she cried out. Ida's skin was translucent white with her fear and her teeth chattered. The bilge water swilled calf-high around their legs.

Haith had lost count of the number of times he had made this Channel crossing, perhaps it was once every year of his life since he had been ten years old. First, he and Henry crossed back and forth with King William, Henry's father or with his mother, Queen Matilda, rarely staying put for long in either England or Normandy. Then he had followed Henry to and fro across the Channel in the difficult years after his father's death, when his brothers held ascendancy, Robert as duke of Normandy and William Rufus as king of England. Since Henry had taken the thrones of both realms, Haith's Channel crossings had become even more frequent. This time, he needed to return to his duties in Wales and was crossing alongside the prisoners: Waleran, Hugh de Chateauneuf, and Hugh de Montfort who were being conveyed to prison in Bridgnorth. Ida had decided that time had passed, and with the protection of both Haith and Nest available to her, she could risk a return to Nest's household.

There was no privacy on the ship for Haith to speak with Ida on the topic of the sinking and, besides, it seemed bad luck to speak of a shipwreck whilst they were making the same rough crossing themselves. Count Waleran was shackled and made a discomforting shipmate. He glared with bitter hostility at Haith, perhaps blaming his uninvited arrival at the three weddings of his sisters, which had heralded the rebellion and Waleran's subsequent downfall.

At Southampton port, Haith watched the heavily armed escort take the road towards Gloucester and then Bridgnorth with the prisoners. It was a grievous thing for three men, all in their early twenties, to be committed to close confinement probably for the rest of their lives, but Haith could summon no pity for them. They had arrogantly threatened King Henry.

He found a genteel inn where Ida could rest for a few hours while he went in search of horses for their onward journey. First, he needed a beaker of ale to recover himself after the choppy Channel crossing before a long ride and a second water crossing to Wales, and he needed to collect Gisulf's box, which was stashed with an innkeeper at another portside tavern. His steward had sent it on for him from London. He made his way back to that tavern, wanting to mull on things and think how he would broach conversation with Ida about Amaury. The alewife placed a brimming beaker carefully in front of him, and her husband placed Gisulf's chest on the bench, tipping his hat in acknowledgement of the coin Haith handed to him. The inn was quiet with just a few old regulars in one corner who were speaking together in hushed tones. A fire burned welcome in the hearth and Haith stretched his damp boots towards it.

Haith and Ida crossed the Bristol Channel on a small trading ship heading for Tenby and planned to ride on from there to Cardigan. It was good to hear the lilt of Welsh voices all around him again. In the pungent gloom of the stables, Haith counted three coins into the cupped hand of the ostler who was loaning him two horses. 'Do you hear news of the lady wed to de Marais at Cardigan?' Haith asked in as nonchalant a tone as he could muster.

'Princess Nest, eh?'

'Yes.' He could not say her name.

'Not at Cardigan.'

The ostler was not given to extended speech, it seemed.

'Do you know where she is?' Haith prodded.

'Might be Llansteffan.' The ostler, his mouth hanging slightly ajar, scanned Haith, starting at his boots (damp again) and slowly reaching up to his face. It took a while and Haith was reminded that he was taller than most men here, unless they were of Viking heritage.

'Flemish, are ye?'

'Flemish by birth, yes. I am the sheriff of Pembroke,' Haith replied, his tongue stumbling at owning his title and status.

The ostler raised one unimpressed eyebrow. 'What be wanting with Princess?'

'I am an old friend of the lady.' He bit his tongue on his intended addition: and my sister resides in her household. The less said in public of Ida the better for her sake. Haith and Ida had winced at the story of a renegade nun told to them by one of the sailors during their Channel crossing. She was captured in a village outside Caen. The villagers had stripped her naked and whipped her in the marketplace, before the nuns had bundled her bleeding into a habit and into a solitary cell in the convent. The story had sent a chill through Haith.

The ostler appeared to have no intention of volunteering any information on Nest and must be pressed. 'Lady Nest is not, then, at Cardigan with her husband, you believe,' Haith stated. 'Are you certain of it? I don't want to be riding your nag in the wrong direction do I?'

The ostler shrugged and Haith craned towards the road to see who else was about and might be more forthcoming on the subject. His attention was startled back to the ostler.

'Left her husband. The Norman.'

It appeared to be common knowledge that Nest was living apart from de Marais. Haith frowned, irritated by the unadorned gobbets of information delivered by the ostler. He mounted the horse and led the second to collect his sister. When she was safely mounted they turned their horses' heads towards the coast road, towards Llansteffan.

A more loquacious pie-seller at the edge of town confirmed the ostler's information that Nest was at Llansteffan. 'Aye, master. You'd think the lady would have been happy enough with another Norman between her legs eh, after all the others she's had!' The pie-seller's enormous grin was switched off abruptly at sight of Haith's furious expression and how he reached toward his sword hilt.

The pie-seller bundled up his display and set off at a trot, throwing back over his shoulder, 'No offence now, master!'

Haith kicked his horse too hard and the stallion sprang forward.

'Haith! Slow down!' Ida cried behind him.

But Haith gave his horse its head and sped along the clifftop, pebbles flying into the blue air on his right from the hooves of his mount. He did not rein his horse or recover from his anger until they reached the ferry at Laugharne that would take them across the Taf to Llansteffan. As Haith waited for Ida to catch up with him, he cursed himself for the gallop. The horse was surefooted but he needed more thinking time. He should have taken the journey from Tenby to Llansteffan at a slow pace. He had two reasons to be anxious about this visit—he had not seen Nest for three years, and, furthermore, there was the awkward conversation he must have with Ida concerning de Montfort. Could Nest truly have completely left de Marais? He had heard no rumour of it during his time in Normandy. How would she receive him and how might he respond? There was no use in speculating and he tried to turn off the buzz of questions in his head and focus instead on the road and his surroundings. Sunshine lit roses and blackberries in the hedgerow but a black cloud lowered on the hill above. They were in for another dowsing.

18

Interrogation

September 1124, Llansteffan Castle

I dipped my stylus in the ink pot another time to complete the letter to the German miner Meister Werner who I had brought down from the silvermines in Alston to assist Gruffudd at Dolaucothi. I did not sign the letter and had disguised my handwriting, but Werner would know who it was from. I took care that there was nothing in it that could incriminate me if it fell into the wrong hands. Perhaps nothing would come of this mining and then I could relax and return to sitting on the fence, kicking my heels, as Amelina put it. Amelina was standing at the window watching visitors arriving in the courtyard. Two riders, I guessed, from the sounds of their horses' feet striking the cobbles. We heard voices raised in greetings between the new arrivals and my servants in the hall below and Amelina turned to me, a look of delight on her face that I had not seen for a long time. I recognised what it meant immediately. I stood up too quickly and knocked the remaining ink over. It dripped brown as old blood onto the floorboards. 'Tch!' Amelina rushed to right the pot and take a cloth to the spilt ink. She straightened up and looked me up and down. 'You look well,' she told me. 'He will be dazzled.'

'Who will be dazzled?'

'Haith,' she said confirming my guess. 'It's Sheriff Haith and Ida who've arrived!'

'Bring Robert,' I told her. 'He will want to see his son. I will be down shortly.'

I blotted my letter, folded it carefully, and pulled my casket towards me. The small ivory casket had been a gift that I had received long ago from the king. Its cream surfaces were decorated with painted roundels depicting exotic birds. I unhooked the bunch of keys from my girdle and unlocked the casket. My best jewels were inside and a few treasured parchments: a love letter from the king, the ring that Gerald had given me on our wedding day, a lock of Haith's hair tied with a black ribbon that I had shorn gleefully one morning as we lay in bed. The layers of my life. I set my treasonous letter to the miner atop my treasures and locked the casket.

My pulse was beating hard. I had not seen him for more than three years, since he returned from the dead during my wedding to de Marais at Cardigan. Would he still care for me? Would he notice how I had aged, how grey streaked my black hair? I resisted the urge to linger in front of my mirror. There was nothing I could do about the fact that I was forty-three. As I moved down the steps, forcing myself not to hurry, the thought struck me that he might have married.

I paused at the bottom of the steps before entering the hall. Haith was standing with his back to me at the hearth, warming his hands after his ride. I took a moment to drink in his presence and brace myself, and then walked to Ida and hugged her. 'I'm so glad to have you back.' Haith turned and looked keenly at me and then at our son Robert who ran gleefully into Ida's wide-opened arms. 'I thank you for attending me,' I said softly to Haith.

Haith smiled warmly to me and turned his attention to Robert, who peeked at him shyly over Ida's shoulder. His delighted expression at the first sight of Robert shifted abruptly to sadness and I knew it was because he could not share in Robert's childhood with me. I noted the chime of Haith and Robert's pale blue eyes, when he turned back to me. 'He is a fine lad.'

I nodded. 'I am so pleased to have your sister returned to me,' I said cheerfully. 'Ida was a great comfort immediately after my marriage,' I glanced away from his gaze, 'and your return.' I gestured for him to sit and took my own seat opposite, focusing on my hands in my lap. 'Ida's safety from exposure is of great concern to me.'

'And to me,' he responded.

My servants were setting the board for a meal and I asked Haith if he would join us. Ida went upstairs to unpack her travelling chest and change her clothes. There was an awkward silence between Haith and I as we waited for Ida to return. He talked with Robert about dogs and Haith's mastiff was well-spoilt with admiration between them. When Ida returned, we shifted to the table. As we ate, Ida carried most of the conversation, which became stilted whenever Haith and I were required to speak directly to one another. The servants cleared away the trenchers and dishes and I invited him to sit in front of the fire again with a beaker of wine. Perhaps the wine would loosen the tension between us. Amelina scooped up Robert and took him to help her feed the chickens.

'The rebellion is over then?' I asked Haith, reaching for a topic that might keep the conversation flowing and not take us into any embarrassing or painful corners. 'The king has prevailed at last in Normandy?'

Haith answered Nest's questions politely, struggling all the while to look her in the face. Her gaze was like 'the deer's glance' as he had once heard a poet sing. It was impossible that he could have forgotten how extraordinarily beautiful she was, yet the sight of her seemed like the first time. He must have grown accustomed to it, before, when they had been lovers. He thought of another poet's words: a jewel grows pale on you and a crown does not shine. He wished he could tell these words to her. She was wearing a silver-grey robe. Her elegant long hands were caressed by the frilled cuffs of a wide-sleeved over-mantle. The scalloped edges of her veil framed her face that once had lain on a pillow next to his own.

The sight of her was like a continent lost under the sea for years that had suddenly risen to the surface again. If he looked too much at her his eyes took on a life of their own and required to roam over every detail of her face and body. He had not realised how hardfast he had held her absence from his life until now. He smiled awkwardly at Ida instead. 'The slow outcome of the king's negotiations with his son-in-law, Emperor Henry,' Haith found himself reporting rather formally to Nest, 'was that the emperor began an invasion of France, marching towards Reims in a show of force. The emperor's vast army turned back before engaging the French king's forces but it was enough to put fear into them. King Henry and Count Thibaut de Blois attacked the Vexin but they were repelled by Amaury de Montfort.' Haith noticed how Ida became alert at the mention of de Montfort's name. He lost track of the story he was trying to tell Nest in response to her questions on the progress of the campaign.

'I noticed that the king has developed a new obsession,' Nest said, 'an unhealthy concern almost, with auguries.'

Haith nodded. 'Yes, since he lost his son.' There was another awkward silence that stretched on while he reached in vain for something more to say to her.

She rescued them from the silence. 'Ida wrote to me that you have been investigating the sinking of *The White Ship*?'

He cleared his throat. 'Yes, that's right. I have.'

'Is the mystery clarified, now? Was it an accident as we all believe, as the king believes, or do you know a culprit? Is it possible anyone could have deliberately caused such a thing?'

'Well,' Haith felt ridiculously tongue-tied, like a teenage boy. Confronted with Nest in the flesh, rather than in his memory, his brain was refusing to work properly. 'Ida,' he blurted, 'I found a letter from Robert de Bellême among Gisulf's possessions. The clerk was blackmailing many people,' he tried to explain to Nest. He instantly regretted his words to Ida, but they were out there now and Nest was contemplating him with an expression full of curiosity.

'Robert de Bellême,' Ida said in a startled voice.

'He accused you ....' Haith swallowed. 'Well, he implied that you had extracted information from Amaury de Montfort.'

'Well, I did, Haith. You know that. I stole some of the correspondence between them. I did it for the king and it was important. It convicted de Bellême and removed that threat to the king.'

Haith glanced at Nest and saw that Ida's statement had not surprised her. She was in Ida's confidence on the matter of Amaury, then.

'What is your relationship to de Montfort, Ida? Won't you tell me that?'

'It is nothing to concern you. It was some time ago and of no significance—to him at any rate, I am sure.'

'Yet, I must press you and would know for reasons of my own. Perhaps you would prefer to speak in private?' Haith glanced at Nest again and was sorry to see that she was frowning at him now.

'No. I have no secrets from Nest. She knows everything about me. I owe her that since she shields me in her household.'

'You owe me nothing, Ida. I owe you love and give you anything willingly,' Nest said. She frowned pointedly at Haith. He must be appearing a bully to her and should desist with his questions.

Ida interrupted his thoughts with a bald declaration. 'Amaury was the reason I left Fontevraud.' She looked down.

Haith cast a guilty glance in Nest's direction. 'Sheriff, you should persist with your questioning of your sister,' she told him frostily. 'Since it seems that you are intent upon it.'

'The questions can wait for another time,' he tried to excuse himself. 'I discovered that Gisulf was murdered on the ship, you see, and that led to the sinking. The murder was commissioned by Morin du Pin, the steward of Waleran de Meulan.'

'Waleran!' Nest exclaimed, and Haith recalled that she had been very close with Waleran's mother, Elizabeth de Vermandois, long ago at court when they—Nest, Henry, Elizabeth and he— when they were all so young.

'The young count, it seems,' Haith hastened to add, 'did not know of the planned murder in advance. Du Pin acted to protect Waleran from Gisulf's blackmail—over the rebellion, you see.'

'How is Ida's friend, Count Amaury involved?' Nest asked.

He had hoped she would not ask that. 'I'm not sure... I don't know ...' Haith stuttered.

'You know I befriended Amaury, briefly,' Ida said. She was red in the face, but rushed on. 'He and I ... well you can know, Haith. You are my brother. We were lovers. Just one time. It was inadvertent on both our parts. An accident of happenstance. He took a fall from his horse. I was set by the abbess to watch over him. I ... it was the occasion when I took the letter that convicted de Bellême. Do not hate me Haith!'

'I don't hate you, Ida,' he protested. 'I can only hate myself for pressing you, for distressing you. You acted for the sake of the king. You acted against rebellion.'

'Yes, but no. The letter was that, yes. But the ... I took Amaury as a lover because I liked him. I liked him very well. Because I was not made to be a nun. I did not choose to be a nun.'

There was a long moment of silence between them all and Nest reached a hand to Ida's cheek briefly and stared back coldly at Haith.

'I understand, Ida. I do,' he stated, avoiding the angry pools of Nest's blue eyes. How could he be so stupid as to choose this moment, his first meeting with her after so long, to interrogate Ida. She was clearly unimpressed by his behaviour.

'He was kind to me. Interested in me,' Ida said, pulling his attention back to her.

'Of course he was interested in you. Any intelligent man would be,' Haith stated. 'He gave you the book of Ovid's poems.'

'Yes, we spoke of the poems together.'

'But only once? You were only together once.' It was Haith's turn to colour now.

'Yes. Just that one time, but I saw him again in Reims, during the papal council, at the bishop's residency.'

'Ah. Not long before the fateful sailing of *The White Ship*.'

Ida was bewildered. 'Yes, I suppose that is so.'

'Ida, can you tell me what you and Count Amaury spoke of on that occasion?' Haith had momentarily forgotten about Nest's disapproval in his keenness to at last gain answers to his burning questions.

Ida frowned at him. 'Why on earth do you want to know that, Haith?'

'I have a concern, a suspicion that I am trying to clear up, to eradicate let's say.'

'A suspicion against Amaury?'

'Yes.'

'He is a man of honour.'

'So I have observed myself. But still, I must ask you this, Ida. Was the clerk Gisulf a matter of discussion between you?'

Ida coloured again, the flush staining her face and neck. She pulled her wimple away from her skin to flap some air at it.

'You persist too much, Haith, I believe, beyond the bounds of care for your sister.' Nest's voice was distinctly wintry.

'It's alright, Nest. I will answer. I want to answer. Yes,' Ida said slowly. 'Amaury and I did speak of Gisulf when we met in Reims.'

'I'm sorry to press you, Ida.'

'You are truly sorry, Haith?' Nest asked in a tone of challenge.

She was staring at him as if he had been revealed to be another man. 'More wine, here!' she called out, looking around the hall to a young maid who was sweeping near the hearth. The maid dropped her broom with a clatter and ran towards the pantry.

A few moments later, a manservant came with a recharged jug and filled their beakers. 'Is there aught amiss, my lady?' he asked Nest, looking at Ida's flushed features.

'No, no. Just leave it there,' Nest told him.

The man bowed himself away. Haith lifted the beaker towards Ida and she took it from him. 'Don't fuss,' she said. 'I'm fine.'

'I'm sorry I have shocked you, Ida. I don't mean …'

'Whatever you mean, Haith, you have pressed me and you know what you are about.' Ida stared at him.

He swallowed and avoided the angry expressions of both women. 'Did you and Amaury discuss Gisulf? Will you give me an answer?'

'I will because I can only guess that it matters immensely to you that you should interrogate me in this fashion.' Her voice was laden with resentment.

'Ida, I'm sorry.'

She held up a hand, heaved a deep sigh, and took a long draught of the wine. Haith also drank and placed his beaker back on the table with deliberation, looking his question again earnestly with his expression.

'I don't understand why you must know these things, Haith, but I trust you and, so, I will answer you. Gisulf had scribed the letter from de Bellême in prison telling Count Amaury that he had been betrayed by his correspondence that I had stolen, whilst Amaury and I were … together.' Ida shifted with embarrassment on the bench and poured more wine into her beaker. She drank it off before continuing. Nest briefly gripped her hand and released it to reach for her own beaker. 'I was tasked to spy on Amaury and his sister Bertrade by Countess Adela, King Henry's sister. I did not want to stoop to dishonesty but these are powerful pressures, Haith.'

'I do understand that, Ida. Truly I do. I am moving among these pressures and dilemmas myself all the time. As is Lady Nest.' Nest nodded her agreement. Had he lost her good regard entirely with this assault on Ida's modesty? He looked at Nest earnestly but she would not look at him, although he knew she must be feeling his eyes on her face.

'Do not think that I lay with Amaury for that reason!' Ida cried, pulling his gaze back to her. 'That is *not* so! I liked him, Haith. And I believe he liked me, though doubtless I was merely one of very many—not nuns, I mean, but women at any rate!' They laughed together at her amendment and, since it was a relief, their laughter went on a little longer than the remark itself had merited. The sound of Nest's laughter conjured more memories that Haith worked to suppress. Nest's dimples disappeared and her mouth calmed back to a smile.

'Gisulf tried to blackmail me with his knowledge of my liaison with Amaury,' Ida said.

Haith took a deep breath. 'I had wondered if something of that sort had occurred.'

'I'm sorry you know any of it. But since you do, you should know the rest. When I encountered Amaury at Reims, I told him of Gisulf's importuning.'

'Did you seek Count Amaury out?'

'No! He found me and so I blurted out the information because it was concerning me greatly at the time. It was simply on the top of my mind when I spoke with Amaury. In the event, Gisulf drowned on *The White Ship* and so...' Ida stopped and gaped at Haith, appalled. 'No. You are wrong. Amaury did not commission violence against Gisulf on my account. Do not think it.'

'I think you are right, Ida, but I had a suspicion and I needed to shake it until I found the truth.'

'Why?' Nest challenged him abruptly. 'Why are you shaking this particular tree so hard? Finding out will not bring any of those drowned unfortunates back.'

'No, but whoever is guilty deserves to be exposed.'

'The sea is guilty,' Nest said.

'Not only the sea,' Haith countered but wished he could leave it, could escape the disapproval he was earning from Nest and the distress he was causing his sister.

Ida poured more wine for them. 'Haith?'

'I know that there was foul play on that ship, Ida. I do not know that the sinking was intentional but there was certainly foul play, and I am seeking to get to the bottom of it. You say that Amaury did not commission violence against Gisulf. Why do you say that?'

'He,' she began but then stopped, thinking, remembering. She resumed, her voice sunk low to a whisper, 'He did tell me I need not worry further about Gisulf. He would see to it. I don't believe it of him. I can't.'

Haith held up a hand. 'Don't speculate further, Ida. I know myself that only sleepless nights and no answers lie in that direction. Only Amaury can tell us the truth of it. Or some other first-hand witness.'

Ida's hand had been clasped in horror to her mouth and she removed it to speak again. 'It is easy for you to say don't speculate. Now, I must, Haith, along with you. Now, I must seek to know if Amaury was involved, is implicated in this awful thing. If I am.'

'*You* are not,' Haith asserted. 'If Amaury did take action against Gisulf, you did not know of it or condone it.' He looked at the floor. He had relieved himself of his own anxiety about Ida's guilt, only at the cost of causing *her* great anxiety.

'We have another concern, Sheriff, beyond your talk of *The White Ship*,' Nest continued, and it did not escape his attention that she had ceased to call him by his name. 'We will need your assistance in relation to a bard named Breri.'

Haith swallowed on the bitterness of having offended her. 'How may I help, my lady?'

'Ida is known to him. Known to him as a nun and a spy from Fontevraud. He is here, in Wales, in Pembroke.'

'In Pembroke!'

'He is well travelled as many bards are, and has taken residence with the de Clares at the castle. It is too close for comfort. He could reveal Ida's former identity.'

'I must go to my duties in Pembroke, so I will keep an eye on him and keep a watch on his intentions and movements.'

Nest smiled briefly. It was not her full smile. 'That would be a relief to us.' She rose at the entrance of her steward and, giving her apologies, left the room. Haith watched her go with a cold sense of loss. He had alienated her.

He turned back to Ida. 'I am sorry to have pressed you so hard, Ida. There are several mysteries around *The White Ship*, and threads I have been following.'

'Including Amaury.'

'Yes, de Montfort is one thread but there are others, perhaps more credible. Stephen de Blois disembarked from the ship before she sailed and stands to gain from the death of the king's heir, but I have found no evidence against him. The king's dapifer, William de Pirou, was certainly aboard the ship and survived the wreck in mysterious circumstances. He was the prime mover in Gisulf's murder. At one time, I thought Ranulf de Gernon might have commissioned the murder, since he is close with de Pirou, but then I received testimony from a prisoner in Rouen that implicated Waleran's steward. It is still a maze of possibilities.'

'But why must you know, Haith? As Nest says, a discovery will not return Prince William to life, to the king's side.'

'No, but if there was a deliberate conspiracy it threatens the king still and is a very great crime that should be exposed.'

'Yes.' Ida's tone was doubtful. 'Perhaps you feel guilt that you survived the wreck, Haith, that you disembarked.'

'No. That would be ridiculous,' he denied.

Ida sank her voice to a whisper and placed her hand on his arm.

'Perhaps you need this diversion from other grief?' She looked meaningfully in the direction of the doorway where Nest had disappeared. 'Perhaps this is *your* unhealthy obsession, Haith.'

Haith did not reply but studied the patterns of shadows on the floor.

'There is no benefit in your pursuit of this mystery,' Ida asserted. 'You need to get on with your life, with your duties as sheriff at Pembroke, and perhaps, in time, the situation here at Llansteffan might change too.'

Haith nodded without looking at her. He knew it was good advice, but he knew he would not take it.

19

Threshold

May 1125, Pembroke Castle, Wales

Haith stepped to greet Lady Nest as she rode into the courtyard at Pembroke accompanied by two men at arms and another lady. He hoped that he might gain a second chance to recoup the damage he had done to Nest's opinion of him during his questioning of Ida at Llansteffan. He lifted Nest from her horse and she stepped away from his touch briskly. 'Sheriff.' She acknowledged his greeting, but moved past him towards the hall. She was still angry with him then. The second lady dismounting was swathed in veils and a heavy, hooded cloak but Haith knew that it was his sister. He gave her his hand to steady her as her foot touched the cobbles. Why was she here with the bard Breri, who could identify her, in residence?

'Can you take me somewhere out of sight quickly, Haith, while Nest greets the de Clares?'

He nodded and took Ida's elbow, steering her towards his own quarters. 'Why are you running such risk of being here?' Haith asked as soon as the door was closed behind them.

'I have been pondering our last conversation concerning Gisulf and had an idea. I troubled Lady Nest with it so much and so often that she resolved we must come and speak with you. Do you have these letters of Gisulf's, where you found the evidence?'

'Yes.' Haith gestured at the small chest in the corner of the room.

'Are there other letters or just the ones from Bellême and from Waleran?'

'There are many. This is the whole collection from his house in London. They all look to be letters for blackmail of some sort.'

'May I look through them?'

'Why?'

'I was the librarian at Fontevraud Abbey, if you recall. Sifting through scrolls is my specialism.' She rolled up her sleeves and pushed the dangling ends of her headscarf behind her shoulders. 'Perhaps I will find something else to illuminate this mystery that is now vexing us both.'

Haith nodded slowly. 'I'm sorry for the vexing, Ida. You will find de Bellême's letter distressing,' he warned as she lifted the lid of the chest and reached inside to the scrolls and parchments.

'Will you bring me a jug of wine for my labour, Haith?'

'Yes, but please stay inside. Breri is about the place somewhere. I am always coming upon him in unexpected places.'

'He is a skilled spy.' He had to decipher her words as she mumbled with her head down, already engrossed in her task.

Haith returned with a jug of wine and watched Ida work. In this light, she reminded him of his mother. He smiled at the memory.

'I'm going to be a while yet, Haith. You're putting me off, staring at me. Go and find Nest. You know you want to.'

'Don't jest with me on that topic, please, Ida.'

She glanced up for the first time from her perusals. 'No. I'm sorry. No jest. I know how it is for you. And for her,' she said meaningfully.

He was torn between wanting to know more of what she could tell him of Nest's feelings and a sense that this would be unfair to both Nest and Ida. He rose abruptly. 'Well, I'll leave you to it for a while.'

In the hall, Nest was in conversation with Lady Isabel and her daughter. They were speaking of the shocking news that Prince Cadwallon of Gwynedd had murdered three of his uncles, his mother's brothers, as he worked to remove all opposition to his rule. 'These Welsh barbarians are ruthless!' exclaimed Lady Isabel. Haith saw Nest flinch at her words, but Isabel was oblivious to the fact that she was conversing with a 'Welsh barbarian'. The three ladies were intent on their conversation and Haith was loathe to interrupt them. Nest glanced up in his direction just as he made the decision to back out again. He bumped into a man standing close behind him, stumbling heavily onto his foot. 'Oh, so sorry.' He turned. It was Breri who had been pressing close behind him and who now was wincing in pain. 'I changed my mind,' Haith apologised for his sudden movement. 'I did not want to interrupt the ladies.'

'Who *ever* wishes to interrupt ladies.' Breri accepted Haith's apology gracefully and leant back against the doorjamb to observe the ladies' conversation as Haith turned back towards his quarters.

He secured the doorlatch of the chamber behind him. 'Breri is on the prowl,' he told Ida urgently. 'We have to find a way to get you out of here without him seeing you. We will have to wait for nightfall.'

'Darkness will have little effect for him. He is used to poking around in the dark.'

'Doubtless. Did you find anything?' He gestured at the great pile of papers she had been working her way through.

'Yes, look at this.' She cleared one pile of papers from the bench beside her so that he could sit close. On the table in front of her, she had singled out three letters. He recognised the two that he had found himself: Waleran's letter concerning William *Clito*, with Countess Adela de Blois's covering note, and de Bellême's letter concerning Amaury and Ida. He reached for the third, which had been torn. 'What is this one?'

Ida did not reply but let him read it.

To William de Roumare, my dear brother, Ranulf de Gernon, heir to Chester, Carlisle and Cumberland sends greetings and love. I urge you to have urgent speech with SB at the first opportunity on our dissatisfaction at the king's disposition of our mother's lands. SB is most likely to succeed this aging and tyrannical king and we might make better headway on the matter with him. If he might promise us reparation of our lands, and to you gift Lincoln and its earldom, then we might offer him good service in return. You may give reply with the Welsh bard I send with this. He is discreet and can be trusted. I have instructed William de Pirou to carry the sum of

The letter was torn there. 'He names himself heir to lands that do not belong to his father,' Haith said, puzzling at the meaning of the letter. 'SB must be Stephen de Blois. He and Roumare disembarked from *The White Ship* in company together. Good service—it could mean anything!' Haith blew out his lips exasperated. 'More obfuscation!'

'Whoever it refers to or what the service was,' Ida said, 'the king would have been most displeased to have read those words from de Gernon's hand.'

'Yes. And the Welsh bard mentioned here? It must be Breri, working for de Gernon, as well as the de Clares. He seems to be everywhere.'

Ida nodded. 'That seems more than possible. Breri was in the pay of Countess Adela de Blois. The countess's network of spies was extensive and more than effective. That network fed information on events in Normandy to Countess Adela and she conveyed it to King Henry. Now, Breri appears to be replicating his work, spying in Wales and feeding information to whoever will pay him well. I've been trying to think through the provenance of these three letters. Waleran's with Adela's note,' she put her palm flat against that parchment, 'was doubtless carried to Gisulf by Breri. Gisulf should have given it to the king but kept it back.' She moved her hand to de Bellême's letter. 'Gisulf will have received this letter from de Bellême on behalf of the king and may have kept this back too. And this one,' her hand moved to de Gernon's letter, 'was clearly carried by Breri and implicates him in whatever was afoot.'

Haith nodded at her analysis. 'Where does that leave us?'

'I am wondering if Gisulf and Breri were in this blackmailing business together, or alternatively if Gisulf was in turn blackmailing Breri.'

'No more potential murderers, please!' Haith pleaded. 'I already have too many suspects.'

'Can't we figure this out, Haith? Morin du Pin's involvement in Gisulf's murder was asserted to you by Luc de La Barre and that implicated Waleran, or was to protect him at any rate.'

'Yes.'

'William de Pirou's involvement was told to you by Berold, which implicated Ranulf de Gernon, because you know they are compatriots. It seems they tried to involve Stephen de Blois in their conspiracy against the king, but we have no way of knowing whether or not he accepted their bribes. Perhaps Waleran and Ranulf were in it together, a conspiracy to rid themselves of their blackmailer?'

'They are an unlikely collaboration,' Haith said. 'I know of no connection between them. By the same token, Amaury could have been involved in such a conspiracy on your behalf. He is close to Waleran. Very close.'

'I don't believe that. He is not a man to murder another in the dark. He would have cut Gisulf down face to face, by his own hand, if he decided to. There is no evidence of Amaury's involvement but you have heard evidence against these other two.'

Haith hesitated. This was simply what she wanted to believe.

'In any case, Haith, whatever the truth of the matter, there is no further threat to Henry. Waleran is incarcerated. Amaury is distant and reconciled with Henry. But if Ranulf is guilty he is surely a threat to you if you continue to pursue this? He must already know that you are on his trail from your questioning of de Pirou.'

Haith bit back the urge to tell her of the murder of de Pirou. It would only worry her. 'Well, you have uncovered another piece of the puzzle, Ida. Come, we must find a way to smuggle you out without encountering Breri.'

'Will you let this matter go now, Haith? I tell you, it has become a fruitless and a risky obsession for you.'

He swallowed. 'I fear I cannot, just yet.'

She sighed and began to wind the swathes of veil around her head and face again. There was a knock on the door and Haith opened it a crack to a boy with mussed hair. 'Princess says see you in the stables,' he announced in Welsh, clearly relieved to be free of the memory of so many words. Behind Haith, Ida laughed softly as he closed the door on the young messenger. 'Stop that!' Haith told her, smiling. 'She is waiting for you, not for me, as you well know. I will escort you to your horse and take my farewells of you both.'

In the stables, Nest allowed him to assist her into the saddle, but her demeanour did not encourage anything further than that. 'Was your visit satisfactory?' she asked Ida.

'In some ways, yes, and in other ways, no,' Ida said, looking ruefully in Haith's direction.

20

The Heir

December 1126, Westminster Palace, London, England

'The young men are gathering around me like vultures readying for a feast,' Henry complained, 'each wondering who will step into my shoes'.

Haith sat with the king in his private chamber in Westminster Palace sharing a companionable last beakerful of wine as was their frequent habit before Haith retired and Henry made his way to Queen Adelisa's still barren bed. Haith grimaced, knowing that Henry's words were true. 'The Queen will bear a son,' he asserted in as confident a tone as he could muster.

'Will you stay for the Christmas festivities at Windsor?' Henry asked. 'It would be a kindness to me.'

'Of course, Henry.' Haith had submitted his accounts at the Michaelmas exchequer court some weeks ago and was impatient to return to Wales, but the king's request would only delay him a little longer. Henry's business had kept Haith away from Llansteffan for the best part of a year, and he had had no opportunity to try to repair the damage to Nest's opinion of him. The court would move soon from Westminster to Windsor for the Christmas feast, and Windsor was partway to Wales at least.

The celebratory procession, in their finery, moved down the narrow corridor from the chapel to Westminster great hall with Stephen de Blois and his new bride, Matilda de Boulogne, at its head, followed by the king; his widowed daughter, Maud, who had lately returned from Germany; and all the members of the king's court. Haith followed in the wake of the nobles, towards the back of the gleeful crowd. Matilda de Boulogne was a great heiress and Stephen de Blois strutted smugly as the group broke into the vast space of the hall. Like everyone else, Haith had heard the court gossip that Stephen aimed to curry favour with the king and be made heir to the throne with a marriage to a descendent of the Saxon English royal family. Haith, however, knew that the king had betrothed Matilda to Stephen years before, soon after the death of the bride's mother. It had not been in the king's mind then that he would find himself without a legitimate son. This marriage, now, was likely intended by Henry as a sop for the blow to Stephen's aspirations that he was about to announce. Such timings and stratagems were Henry's way.

In the great hall, Haith watched the king mingle with the members of his court. Henry de Blois, another of the king's nephews, and the younger brother of Stephen de Blois, cupped a hand loaded with jewelled rings to his own mouth and Henry's ear, to whisper something to the king. This Henry de Blois was an intriguing character. His interest in relics bordered on an obsession mirroring the king's own. It had become a topic of frequent conversation between them. 'A penny mitigates heavenly indignation no less than a pound of silver,' was one of this nephew's unctuous and frequent sayings, although Haith doubted that Henry de Blois would ever be satisfied with a penny rather than a pound himself. King Henry had recently made him abbot of Glastonbury. To Haith, the new abbot reeked of untrustworthy ambition, but the king was evidently enjoying his flattery. 'I am an athlete of God,' Henry de Blois had told the king on the previous evening. Haith might have found him entertaining were it not for the fact that there was threat in such vaulting arrogance.

When the king had returned from Normandy in the autumn, his widowed daughter, the Empress Maud came with him to England after an absence of many years. King Henry had recalled her to his side after the death of her husband, and rumours were rife concerning who the king intended to give her to in a second marriage. If Henry did not get himself an heir very soon, then a son of Maud's might become the heir instead. Haith had known Maud as a child but she left England at the age of eight to go to her splendid marriage in Germany and this grown woman was an exotic stranger to Haith and the rest of the court. She was imperiously handsome with the solid, stern features of her father and luxuriant brown hair that hung in two plaits down to her knees.

Haith made a mental note of the empress's appearance to write on it to his sister, who was curious to know what everyone looked like, what they wore and said at court. The empress was ostentatiously dressed in what Haith assumed must be German fashion. Her gown was a rich orange-gold. She wore a deeper orange-coloured bustier over it that was studded with rubies, stiffened with metal strips and laced at the front. Her gold belt cinched her waist, crossed at the back and was tied at the front low on her hips. The sleeves of her gown were full and hung well below her knees. When she raised her arms in the imperial gestures that she was fond of making, the blue silk lining of the sleeves and the yellow embroidery around the cuffs were fully visible. As empress, she wore a crown holding her pale yellow headveil in place. Her red mantle was embroidered all over with the image of Christ and trailed around her on the floor. She wore no rings or other jewels, apart from her crown but her mantle was held in place at each shoulder with an enormous ruby-studded golden disc. Even at Henry's rich court, she seemed a figure too opulent, too glinting, for her surroundings. She far outshone Queen Adelisa and Stephen's bride although they were finely dressed. Maud's vivid splendour entirely surpassed any other woman or man at court, including the king himself.

The king summoned a select group of men to private conversation in his chamber in the evening, and asked Haith to wait upon them. Haith moved along the clerestory gallery, arriving before the king's guests so that he could set out beakers and jugs of wine. The king's son, Earl Robert of Gloucester arrived first, in company with the king's brother-in-law, King David of Scotland. Next the viceregent, Bishop Roger of Salisbury, arrived with Geoffrey, archbishop of Rouen, and John, bishop of Liseaux, who was Henry's main administrator in Normandy. Finally the counts, Conan of Brittany and Rotrou of Perche, both sons-in-law to the king, entered the chamber. With this set of guests, it was evident that there was a serious matter of state to be discussed, and the only likely topic was the succession.

'My wife and I are not yet blessed with a son,' Henry opened, making straight for the point. 'I must form alternatives while we wait for that outcome.'

'Sire,' interrupted Bishop Roger. 'Forgive me, but this should be a most private conversation, I believe.' He glanced at Haith.

'It is a most private conversation,' Henry said, testily. 'I trust Sheriff Haith with my life.' Haith did his best to fold his long legs and his brilliant blond head into the shadowed recess at the side of the room. They settled again to hear what the king had to say. 'For now, I plan to create my daughter, Empress Maud, my successor.'

The men exchanged glances, wondering which of them would speak first.

'The empress is of course an excellent woman,' began Roger,

'but, sire, your lords would never countenance a woman as your heir. That way dissension and anarchy lies.'

'My lords will do as I tell them. She is my blood and she has the mettle for it. If it came to it, she could carry forward the kingdom I have built. Further, she is of the stock of a long line of English rulers that stretches back to King Alfred. She stood regent in Italy for her husband and has years of experience of rule.' When the king's words were met with an uncertain silence from the other men in the room, Henry carried on: 'There are instances of female rulers. Urraca inherited Castile-Leon, on behalf of her two-year-old son. It was a similar situation. Women need not only transmit the right to rule. Some have shown themselves capable of exercising that right, at least until a male heir is of age. I will expect all my barons to support my daughter. David?'

'If this is your wish, sire, it is also mine,' David replied. 'And I will give my niece my wholehearted support, should the occasion arise.'

'Robert?'

'Of course, sire. As you command, I will give my sister my full support in that eventuality.'

'Yet, sire,' risked Bishop Roger, 'you have nephews. Thibaut and Stephen de Blois—also experienced at rule.'

'Thibaut has his hands full in Blois and has no knowledge of my kingdom here across the Channel. Stephen, well Stephen is as enriched as he should be. I have, on occasion, had reason to doubt the wisdom of his rule of his own lands. I would not entrust the entire kingdom into his hands. And I *will* have *my* direct bloodline on *my* throne.' Henry's voice rose to its full thunderous timbre punching out his emphatic final sentence.

The men fell silent. Haith reflected that William *Clito*, as the eldest son of Robert de Normandy, Henry's older brother, was the rightful heir to Normandy and England should the king fail to get himself an heir and yet none of them would dare to voice that thought to the king. Henry had spent years and many pounds of silver suppressing William *Clito*'s claims.

'Sire, may I mention one more matter. You ask for our thoughts and advice, no?' Bishop Roger ventured.

Henry gestured impatiently. 'Tell me. I'll listen.' And not take any notice, thought Haith.

'Your daughter is young. She will remarry and she will have heirs herself.'

'Exactly so. My line.'

'But, sire, whoever she marries would be king of England.'

'No, they would be her consort and the father of the king of England.'

The men exchanged glances. 'Do you have someone in mind, sire?' asked Bishop John.

'Not as yet.'

Henry's answer was hardly credible and every man in the room knew it.

'Immediately after Christmas, you will organise an oath-swearing ceremony to my daughter, Bishop Roger,' the king instructed. It was a typical move by Henry to select the most vocal opponent against his will to enact it. Haith refilled the goblets of each of the men, that they might drink again and give their assent to the king's command.

Haith watched the court with interest over the next few days. The empress was clearly aware of her father's plans and perhaps had also been apprised by the king of Bishop Roger's opposition, even though it had been reasonably voiced. Stephen de Blois and Henry de Blois appeared decidedly subdued and they had, no doubt, be made aware of the king's intention to name his daughter as his heir. Haith was standing in conversation with Countess Mabel of Gloucester, Richard de Clare, Gilbert de Clare, and Pain FitzJohn, the sheriff of Shropshire and Herefordshire. The empress approached them and asked Countess Mabel how she was proceeding with the training of her new falcon. To Mabel's gentle account, the empress responded briskly: 'With an unruly hawk, if meat is offered to it and then snatched away or hid, he becomes keener and more inclined to obedience and attentiveness. Try it.' Mabel inclined her head in thanks.

The king rose to make an announcement and held out his hand to his daughter to come and stand beside him. The empress progressed in her stiff skirts towards her father, and Mabel leant to speak close to Haith's ear. 'I am learning her character, you know, as well as how to train my hawk. Do not imagine for a moment that the empress will ever vacillate in any way. She is like her father in that.'

The king announced to the assembly that he had decided to move some of his prisoners. His brother, Robert de Normandy, would be moved from Bishop Roger's custody at Devizes Castle to Robert of Gloucester's custody at Bristol Castle. Haith glanced at Mabel who appeared to be surprised at the news. Waleran de Meulan and Hugh de Chateauneuf, King Henry declared, were to be moved from Bridgnorth Castle, which was held by Pain FitzJohn, to the custody of Brian FitzCount at Wallingford. Now Haith looked at Empress Maud. A self-satisfied smile hovered on her lips. Standing close to her, Bishop Roger wore an expression of chagrin. The empress and Brian FitzCount were close friends and Mabel's husband, Robert, was the empress's half-brother. This was likely her doing, and intended as a deliberate affront to the bishop, and perhaps to FitzJohn too, if he had demurred at the idea of Maud as heir to the throne. These prisoners were the symbols of harshly suppressed rebellion, and this moving of them was a signal to any who might oppose the king's will with regard to his daughter's appointment as heir.

The assembly was over and Haith negotiated the narrow staircase and passageway of the castle and let himself into his small chamber. A breeze moved the embroidered wall hanging next to the window. Haith frowned at the open casement, realising at the moment that he stepped to close it that he had not left it that way.

He sensed rather than saw movement to his left. Light glinted off a dagger and the assailant was upon him. Haith caught the man's wrist and struggled to fend the blade away from his body. The attacker was as big as Haith. Their laboured breathing and grunts, the birds tweeting from beyond the open window, sounded unnaturally loud in Haith's ears. He was acutely aware of the vulnerability of his lungs gasping for air as he wrestled with the man, his blood pumping through veins so close to the surface of his skin, his jangling nerves and clenching muscles, his heart thumping its alarm in his chest. The assailant's lower face was covered with a cloth and he wore a tight-fitting cap low on his forehead. All Haith could see was his furious, dark eyes. How easily that slender filleting blade pressing closer might slide into Haith's delicate organs, lacerate and shred the fine structures of his body. One of them would die in this savage confrontation. The man jerked his arm up, making it harder for Haith to keep purchase on the assailant's wrist. The cold knife tip touched Haith's neck, penetrating his skin. One more small push and the knife would sever his artery, spill his lifeblood to pump in a spreading ruby pool around him. Haith tightened his hold in desperation, crushing the attacker's wrist. The man cried out and dropped the blade. Haith took a breath, readying to go on the attack, but the assailant stamped on Haith's foot, making him release his grip on the intruder. The man ran, threw himself over the window-ledge, and disappeared from view. Haith took a moment, bent over hands on his knees, breathing hard. He touched his fingertips to the beads of blood at his neck as he limped across to look from the window and caught sight of the man running through the gateway. He considered shouting out but the assassin was already past the guards.

Haith collapsed down onto the window seat and rested his head back against the wooden panelling behind him, his mouth open, his breathing slowing, his body taking its time to step down from full alert. Who would want him dead? It could only be to do with his enquiries into *The White Ship*. Waleran de Meulan was incarcerated and Morin du Pin was exiled overseas. Surely they could not be implicated in this murderous commission. Ranulf de Gernon and Stephen de Blois were both at court. This attempt on his life strengthened the possible case against them and weakened the case against Amaury. Yet, Haith reflected, money could have a long arm.

21

The Beard

March 1127, Caeo, Wales

'Hold still, man!' Gwenllian cried. Einon, one of the men serving Cadell's father, sat before her as she struggled to weave the tiny, folded message into the strands of his bushy, red beard. Cadell pinched a hand over his nose and mouth to stop his snort of laughter, but it was near impossible to hold it all in, and his stepmother Gwenllian glanced sidelong at him. 'You're not helping, Cadell!' she exclaimed.

Einon was also doing his best not to laugh. 'It's a mite ticklish, my queen.'

Gwenllian sat back to take a frustrated break from her third attempt to entwine the parchment in the beard. Twice before she had almost got it suspended in the wiry red hairs so that it was invisible and carefully couched. But as soon as Einon stood and drew himself up to his considerable height, the tiny letter dropped to the floor. 'This is no good! It won't work!' Gwenllian groaned, her face pink with frustrated effort.

'You've so nearly done it, mother.' Cadell's stepmother was not renowned for her patience. 'Here, let me try.' Cadell held his hand out for the small folded square. He had penned the letter. His parents did not write, but he had learnt to do so during visits to his Aunt Nest's household and he had written the message to the Norse lord Raegnald in a minuscule script. It read,

Gruffudd, King of Deheubarth, sends love to his foster-brother Raegnald. I mean to attack the Normans at Cardigan, aided by the sons of Gwynedd. Will you send boats and men to assist me in this endeavour and help me to regain the kingdom that is rightfully mine?

Cadell's slender fingers nested the message deep into the beard. He plaited strands around it so that it could not fall—not when Einon rode, or rolled over in his sleep, or stood in a gale-force wind on the ship taking him to Dublin and Raegnald's hall. 'There!'

The man looked down. 'Can't see it at all.'

'It will hold?' Gwenllian asked.

'It will hold,' Cadell said with certainty, looking at Einon. Then he turned to Gwenllian. 'But is this wise, mother?'

'Wise?'

'To trust our lives and throne to your brothers?'

'Go, with my thanks and hopes,' Gwenllian told Einon, her brusque manner belying her words.

'My brother and I will be ready at the gate shortly,' Cadell told him courteously in an effort to mitigate Gwenllian's tone.

Einon tucked the forked ends of his loaded beard into his belt, bowed low to them and strode from the room.

'I don't want to speak in front of him. That is why you wrote the letter rather than sending a message by mouth,' Gwenllian told Cadell.

'Yes, I know.' This way Einon could not have the message tortured from him if he were captured by the Normans at the port. He would be travelling from Llansteffan. That had been Cadell's idea too. Nest had invited her nephews to visit her again and Einon would travel as part of the boys' escort, and then slip away to Ireland by boat at night.

'No, it's not wise,' Gwenllian stated. 'I don't trust my brothers at all, but is it wise for us, the royal family of Deheubarth, to sit here in this backwater stirring potage all day long?'

Cadell shook his head. 'No, for sure. That is not wise.'

22

Flotsam and Jetsam

April 1127, Llansteffan Castle, Wales

The arrival of my teenage nephews Anarawd and Cadell at Llansteffan this morning stirred memories of my brother Goronwy. He had died here at Llansteffan, at around their age, with all that promised life lost, leaked into the sand on the beach below with the cruel blow of a Norman sword. But I suppressed those memories and beamed a smiling welcome to them. It had been a while since I had had the pleasure of conversing in Welsh and I knew that they valued the time they spent in my household, which offered them considerably more comfort than my brother's straitened circumstances.

They were accompanied by a massive hulk of a man with a long, orange beard that he had tucked into his belt in a style that would definitely not be regarded as the height of fashion in Norman circles. My son Maurice cast a scathing glance at his cousins in their Welsh attire and was undoubtedly horrified that I did not keep my Welsh connections hidden away. When the greetings and arrival was over, the dogs had ceased to bark, and the babies had ceased to cry, Amelina ushered the boys upstairs to unpack their sparse belongings and settle into the comfortable chamber we had prepared for them.

The timing of their visit was fortuitous since I had recently had to part with Ida again. King Henry and his queen had a deal of business with the courts of Flanders and Louvain and had need of a clerk skilled in those languages. The king had asked that Ida return to court to serve the queen for some months. I judged, too, that Ida would be safest out of Breri's way again.

Anarawd and Cadell came bounding down the stairs noisily. 'Where is your huge companion?' I smiled at the boys.

'Oh,' said Cadell breezily, 'he just accompanied us here to make sure we were safe on the road and now he is returned to Caeo. Is it near dinner time, Aunt Nest? I am famished!'

'You are always famished,' I laughed.

We took our seats at the table to eat and the servants brought in the dishes to a stirring commentary from Cadell. 'Poached eggs in a ginger and saffron sauce; pike in ale sauce; pork meatballs with almond milk and thyme!' he announced, as he reached for each dish.

'Enough!' I said, tapping his arm and laughing. 'Use your mouth to eat with instead!'

He grinned and obeyed me.

After dinner I sat with Anarawd and Cadell, playing tables. 'The goldmine is going well, Aunt,' Cadell said in a low voice, his head close to mine. 'Meister Werner has sunk an immensely deep shaft with a wooden shed above it. Many ladders are lashed together and the miners descend down on these rickety contraptions into the very centre of the earth. They work with picks and wedges and hammers. The ore is lifted in buckets all chained together.' Rapidly he sketched some of the things he described for me with a piece of charcoal on wood. 'What they bring out is washed on the old Roman washing tables and fired in crucibles.' Cadell's eyes shone at me and my own face mirrored his excitement. 'The gold,' he whispered, 'is moved in packs slung onto ponies or in little minecarts that run ingeniously on wooden plankways.' When I had looked at his sketches long enough, he spilt water on the drawings and scrubbed them away with a cloth.

'You should not speak of this to your cousins,' I told them in a low voice, adding bitterly, 'my sons'.

The following morning passed cheerfully in the bailey, as I stood observing my nephews playing with my sons, Robert and Fitz-Stephen. The boys stood about the fishpond watching the big fish floundering among the stalks and crying out 'There's one!' or 'That red one's so fat!' There was a sudden rumpus at the gateway and one of my servants came over to us at a run, his face an unnatural puce colour.

'What is it?' I asked, alarmed.

'A man has been found on the beach, washed in by the tide. He is drowned.'

'How terrible! We will go to see who it is.' I owed that to the poor soul if he were one of my peasants. And I knew the boys would be ghoulishly pleased to look at a corpse. It was the way of boys to revel in gore and others' misfortunes. Robert and FitzStephen clamoured to come with us but I insisted that they stay behind with Amelina.

I led the group across the castle bailey, out beneath the gateway tower and down the steep hill to the sandflats. The tide was out and snakes of water left behind meandered in incised channels here and there. Clumps of greenery decorated the sand and waited for their next immersion. The sun glinted on small white shells and crab pools. Lines of wading birds looked up briefly at our interruption of their study for insects marooned by the absent sea. Growing closer, we could see the black silhouette of a man laid on his back, bloated, discoloured and washed up by the tide like an eroded tree branch. As we grew closer it became apparent that we were looking at the drowned bulk of the man named Einon who had accompanied Cadell and Anarawd from Caeo.

Cadell was white in the face and let out a series of gasping sobs. I looked at him in alarm. I should not have allowed them to accompany me and witness this. 'Take Prince Cadell back to the hall,' I said to a servant.

'No, please, Aunt, no. I want to honour Einon. He was a good friend to me and did us bold service.' He scrubbed the tears from his face and sniffed hard. 'I don't need to be sent back to the hall with the children.'

I hugged him to my hip.

My steward had gone closer to inspect the poor corpse and called out to me: 'Seems like his body has been deliberately thrown from a boat to marry with a tide that would bring him in here on the beach. I'd say the man's been tortured, lady.'

Before I could reach out a hand to stop him, Anarawd ran to crouch down beside the man's ruined face. He knelt over him weeping. I let go of Cadell and moved nearer to Einon's body. I stooped to lift Anarawd up and away from the poor carcass. 'We cannot help him now, Anarawd. He is gone.' I frowned as I caught sight of a meaningful glance exchanged between the two boys.

I waited until we were back at the castle and they were sipping hot drinks laced with strong wine to warm them after the chill shock of the beach, then I sat down and looked at them earnestly. 'What is it, Anarawd, Cadell? What is it about this man's death that you are not telling me? I can see in your faces that there is something.'

They looked at each other and reached a decision. 'The man carried a message from my father to Raegnald in Dublin,' Anarawd told me.

'A written message?'

They nodded.

'In Welsh.'

They nodded again.

'It was missing,' Anarawd stated.

'Missing?'

'It was woven into Einon's beard. It was gone. I checked on the beach.'

I admired his bravery to have searched the corpse under the concealment of grief. 'Well you had best tell me what the message said.'

They were silent.

'So, I am to guess that it was a dangerous message for your father. Did he sign it?'

'I'm not sure of that, Aunt,' Anarawd answered.

Cadell, however, nodded. 'I penned it. It gave father's name. That was stupid of me.'

'It's not your fault.' Cadell swallowed and I paused to think. 'It is doubtful that Einon's capture and the taking of this message could have been happenstance.'

They continued silent, studying the table.

'If we are to protect your father, you had best trust me.'

'Are you not on the side of the Normans, Aunt?' asked Cadell.

'No,' I found myself saying, vehemently. 'I am Welsh. My sons have chosen to live as Normans, but I cannot be anything other than Welsh, and since that is so, I must support your father in his quest to regain our kingdom.'

They stared at me, their eyes gleaming with proud affection. I looked around hastily to ensure no one else was in earshot. I dropped my voice again. 'Who could have known that he carried such a message and known of his whereabouts?'

Anarawd shrugged. 'We travelled only with Einon. Only father, Gwenllian and we knew of it. No one else could know. I don't understand it.'

'Very well, then, who else knew about whatever was contained in the message?'

'The princes of Gwynedd,' Cadell declared.

I shifted in my seat to face him more fully. 'There is a tale here that you need to tell me if we are to safeguard your father from whatever treachery is afoot.' They told me of the visit of the princes of Gwynedd to their home in Caeo, of the plans to attack Cardigan together with the aid of Raegnald.

'Why would they betray us?' Anarawd asked. 'We were working together.'

'Gwenllian said she did not trust her brothers,' Cadell volunteered. 'I did not trust that youngest one most of all.'

'What is his name?' I asked.

'Cadwaladr ap Gruffudd ap Cynan.'

'I will send word to your father and Gwenllian to warn them that the message has likely fallen into the wrong hands and has not reached Dublin.'

'In another message that might be found and used against us?' asked Anarawd, aghast.

'No. I will send a trusted messenger.' I would not tell them who, but I already knew that I would send Dyfnwal, Amelina's husband. I was in the simmering conflict between Welsh and Normans now, up to my neck, I reflected.

The following morning I came down the steps to the hall and could hear Anarawd laughing with one of the Welsh men of the garrison. I stopped in the doorway and they had not heard my approach. Anarawd was reading from a paper he held out in his hands. 'She who for a long time, filled with a sevenfold demon, had raced about in pestilential madness, through the seductive chambers of men at Babylon, whose god Baal rejoices in damnable naked sports, and in the sanctuaries of voluptuousness sirens chant echoing antiphons, where satyrs leap, the lamia suckles her brood.'

'What's it about, the Norman king?' the soldier asked.

'No,' laughed Anarawd, 'what makes you think that, you ignoramus. It's about Mary Magdalen, of course.'

'Don't know about that,' responded the soldier stubbornly, 'that King Henry is accustomed enough to concubinage and his court is a Babylonish furnace they say. You can be asking your aunt about that.'

I saw Anarawd frown, then he caught sight of me standing in the doorway. 'Get out!' he told the man, 'Get about your business.'

The soldier swallowed at the realisation that I had heard him, pulled down his cap and hurried to the great doors leading out to the courtyard.

'What is that, Anarawd?' I held out a hand for the paper and he passed it to me. It was scribed in a fair hand in Welsh.

'It's a poem about Mary Magdalen,' Anarawd said, his tone guilty. 'But after this rather lurid bit about Babylon, it's about the remission of her sins by Christ.'

I glanced over the paper and recognised it as a poem by Hermann de Reichenau. 'Yes, it is a fine poem. Where did you come by this?'

'From the bard.'

I looked at him in alarm. 'What bard?'

'I … I supposed he must be your bard. He was here yesterday in the hall or perhaps it was the stable, I can't remember, talking with me and Cadell and some of the men. He gave the paper to me.'

'Was his name Breri?'

'I don't know his name. What's the matter, Aunt?'

I asked Anarawd to describe the man to me and it answered to Breri's description. There was no doubt. He had been here at Llansteffan, poking around, asking questions of my nephews and my son's men, making implications about me with this Magdalen poem I supposed, and he had been here when Einon was murdered and the message in his beard had gone missing.

23

Snake in the Grass

April 1127, Llansteffan Castle, Wales

'The king has made his barons swear an oath to his daughter as his heir?' Gruffudd asked Maurice. In response to the message I had sent with Dyfnwal, my brother had ridden in to collect his sons an hour ago and we sat in the hall waiting for the boys to pack up their belongings. I had not expected him to come himself. He was surely in grave danger.

Maurice nodded. 'That is the news. Excuse me please, Mother. Uncle.' He went out to see to the practice of the squires in the courtyard.

Gruffudd waited until Maurice was out of earshot. 'I received another interesting message, Nest, besides yours. From your kinswoman.'

'My kinswoman?'

'Cristin, who is married to Gwenllian's brother, Prince Owain of Gwynedd. She has had a hard lot. Forced to marry into closeness with those who murdered her father and uncles.' Gwenllian's oldest brother, Cadwallon, had murdered Cristin's kin and she had been married to Owain as a peacemaker between the feuding families. 'She has written to me to give me news of treachery. I wanted to make sure you had the full picture.'

I raised my eyebrows.

'She wants vengeance against her husband's family. She told me that she has no proof, but it is likely, from words she has overheard whispered about that it was the youngest prince Cadwaladr who had Einon murdered as he carried the message to the Danes for me.'

'What might Cadwaladr do with this evidence against you? Why would he oppose you? I thought they were your allies against the Normans?'

'Cadwaladr wants to be king of Ceredigion. His older brothers take Gwynedd and he would have the lands that belong to me. He is likely to treacherously give the evidence to the Normans, I imagine. And then, I suppose the king will hang me anyway,' he concluded gloomily.

'Gruffudd! What are you doing about it?'

'What can I do?'

'You could treat with Cadwaladr before he takes this step. Regain this message that you so rashly entrusted to paper.'

Gruffudd grimaced. 'It was Gwenllian's doing. She is ruing it.'

'You should not be sitting here. You should be riding to Cadwaladr.'

'It's likely too late for that, and, anyway, I could not trust that Cadwaladr would not hand me over to the king's agents. I will return to Caeo now. I do not want to be taken here, with you.'

'Gruffudd, for God's sake! Why did you come? You should be far away.'

'I wanted to speak with you before I have to leave, Nest. I may not see you again.' He took my hand. 'I had to wait until Maurice was out of earshot, but I wanted to tell you that I will have to cross to Ireland if there are charges of treason laid against me. Ensure that you stay clear of it, Nest.'

'But I can go to Pembroke. See what is to be done. We could speak with Cadwaladr. You could offer him land. That's what he wants isn't it? Part of Ceredigion for his own kingdom?'

Gruffudd shook his head and said vehemently, 'I'll give him none of the land that is mine. Do not endanger yourself, Nest. I had best go now.'

I held onto his hand for a moment longer. 'I'm sorry Gruffudd! I know I will see you again.' My mouth quivered, undermining my intention to sound firm on his behalf. My poor brother who should be king here had spent most of his life in exile, in hiding, in poverty. He was the only brother I had left, when I had started out with five, and the only person who had any conception of what I had lost when the Normans massacred our family.

He smiled sadly at me, stood and took his leave. I stood in the shadow of the gatehouse and watched him ride from the castle with Anarawd and Cadell. Cadell turned in the saddle and waved to me and I returned his gesture, holding back tears. If my brother must flee and seek shelter with his friend Raegnald in Ireland all our efforts to regain the kingdom of Deheubarth were set again to nought.

I could not stand the thought of another brother killed and if treason were proved against him for a second time he would hang for it. I did not stand staring after their absence from the horizon for long. 'I'm going to Pembroke,' I informed Amelina.

'Alright,' she said bewildered.

I strode to the stables, ordered my horse saddled, and hurried back inside to change into my riding clothes.

'Lady Nest! This is a pleasant surprise.' Gilbert de Clare and Isabel rose to greet me as I walked into the hall that once had been my domain. Haith was there and had a worried expression on his face. The bard, Breri, also stood and flourished a bowing greeting to me, with a hypocritical, unctuous expression on his face. I was already too late perhaps. I had hoped that I might come and assess the lay of the land for Gruffudd. Perhaps there was a way for me to alibi him, to refute charges against him.

'We have received grievous news concerning your brother,' de Clare declared, confirming my fears.

I halted a few feet from the dais. 'My brother?' Now I must flounder and find some cover for my visit. I could not appear to be complicit in the evidence they had against Gruffudd.

'Breri here,' de Clare indicated the bard, 'has given me a missive from your brother that has fallen into his hands.' Breri's expression was smug. 'It speaks treason against the king,' de Clare announced sternly. 'A plot to attack Cardigan with the aid of the Irish Danes.'

'There must be error,' I retorted. 'My brother lives quietly in Caeo with his family. This is forgery. I don't doubt it comes from someone evil-minded.' I glared hard at Breri.

'The provenance of the message is convincing,' said de Clare. 'What is the purpose of your visit, my lady?'

I opened my mouth but could not find my excuse. How could I have been so stupid? Why had I not found a story on the ride here? Breri raised an eyebrow at my hesitation.

'I invited Lady Nest,' I heard Haith say. 'Sorry that I neglected in all this business of the treasonous message to mention it before now. I needed to go over the accounts of Llansteffan with the lady for my renderings to the court of the exchequer.'

De Clare observed Haith steadily before returning his gaze to me. 'We are remiss. You need refreshment after your ride, Lady Nest.' He gestured to the seat next to him and Breri shifted to make space for me there. I could not be trapped here.

'Thank you but before I sit, I must see to my horse, which has taken lame on the way here. I will return shortly.' I turned and moved swiftly from the hall before there could be any argument.

In the stables I spoke softly in Welsh to the groom who knew me well from my previous time as Lady of Pembroke. 'I need to send a message to my brother in all haste and privacy.'

'I will take it for you, my lady.'

I knew that I could trust him and had done so before. 'It is dangerous for you.'

'I will have care, my lady, and I will deliver your message.'

'Take these words, then, to my brother: You are exposed. Find refuge in Ireland.' The man repeated the message to me and swung up into the saddle. I watched him ride out through the gatehouse.

'Sending a messenger?' I turned to face Breri who was standing too close for comfort.

'I had hoped to stay some days visiting Lady Isabel but I will return to Llansteffan early since my favourite horse is lame and I wish to walk her back slowly to my groom who will care for her. I have sent a messenger ahead to Llansteffan to let them know of my change in plans.'

'He appears to be taking the wrong road,' Breri remarked, peering at the direction of dust left by my messenger on the road beyond the gatehouse. Suddenly he stepped close to my horse and ran a hand down her legs. 'Ah! And your horse's legs have cooled now despite her lameness.'

I made no response. He offered me his arm and I had no choice but to place my hand there and be escorted by him back into the hall. Haith rose and came down to speak quietly to me. He waited for Breri to move off, which reluctantly he did after a moment's hesitation. 'Thank you,' I told Haith, referring to the excuse he had made for me. Breri was whispering into de Clare's ear and the two of them looked up to stare hard at me. A chill shivered through me. No doubt Breri was reporting his suspicion that I had just sent a rider to my brother.

'Lady Nest.' Haith's whisper was urgent. He took a firm grip of my elbow and steered me from the hall. When we were out of sight of those sitting at the high table, he swung me round so that my back pressed hard against the exterior stone wall. 'What the hell are you doing?'

I glared at him, saying nothing.

'De Clare has evidence of treason against your brother. A note inciting the Irish Danes to attack Cardigan. Now, that snake in the grass, Breri, is whispering to de Clare that you are somehow involved. Are you?'

I held my tongue.

Haith looked up at the sky, despair and distress written large in his expression. 'Let's get you out of here. I will ensure that the story is discredited with de Clare.' He pulled me roughly by the arm towards the stable.

'You're hurting me.'

'Sorry.' He loosened his grip. 'But we need to be quick. I need to get you away. I'm not sure Llansteffan is far enough. Can you go somewhere else?'

'I can go to Mabel in Cardiff, I suppose,' I panted, as he bustled me along, almost lifting me in his haste.

'Do that and do not delay.'

'What about Ida?' I asked him. 'Since Breri was able to infiltrate at Llansteffan and get his hands on this message from Gruffudd, then he may know that Ida has been there.'

Haith nodded. 'I will look to it.'

We reached the stable, and he hoist me into the saddle of my not lame horse. I felt a wash of desire at his hands on me, at his desperation for my safety. He lent his hand briefly against my thigh and then looked up at me with an expression of intense concern. 'Please, Nest, please, take care. The king would never harm you but there are many others, in Wales, who would see you humiliated after your treatment of de Marais. The king is far away. They are not.'

I bent down, reaching a hand to his cheek. 'Thank you, Haith.' Impulsively, I bent further, my feet pressing in the stirrups, and kissed him. He opened his mouth in surprised response and the kiss became long and hard until my horse shifted with the awkward lean of my posture pressing against her.

'Go,' Haith whispered and let my fingers slide reluctantly from his.

24

Death of a Hound

August 1128, Llansteffan Castle, Wales

Haith's horse wound its way up the steep path to the hilltop fortress at Llansteffan. Nest had stayed for the best part of a year with her foster-sister, Mabel, in Cardiff, and Ida had written to tell him that she had joined her there. Last month, Mabel had travelled to be reunited with her husband in Rouen, and Nest and Ida had decided that the threat of repercussions in the wake of Gruffudd's treason had subsided and they could return to Llansteffan.

The guards gave him access and he rode into the courtyard where two small boys, one with brilliant red-hair, came running from the stables to see who had arrived. 'My nephews, Morgan and Maelgwyn.' Nest's voice was close behind him. He turned to greet her. 'With Gruffudd fled to Ireland, I invited Gwenllian and her sons to live under my protection.' They watched as the boys shifted from their curiosity at Haith and began to chase a squealing piglet that had wriggled out under the willow hoarding of the pen. 'Don't hurt that pig!' Nest shouted after them. 'She's Amelina's favourite and she'll have your hides!' Nest turned back laughing to Haith. 'My older nephews, Anarawd and Cadell, have gone with their father to Ireland. It's a pleasure to have

Gwenllian's young boys here.'

Haith nodded. 'And you have someone to converse with in Welsh.'

'Yes. I do take pleasure in that. I am blessed to have three great friends staying here now: my sister-in-law, your sister, and, of course, Amelina. And a fourth?' She looked her question shyly to him.

'Of course,' he paused and they exchanged a warm look. 'I get the odd opportunity to be speaking Flemish,' he said, 'with Ida, with the queen, and with some of the settlers here. It's relaxing to speak in your own tongue now and then.'

She smiled her agreement. 'Come in, Haith. You are very welcome.'

Nest's sister-in-law, Gwenllian ferch Gruffudd ap Cynan, was seated in the hall, her flame-red hair splayed uncovered on her shoulders. Looking at Nest and Gwenllian together in this fortress, Haith did not find it hard to remember that not long ago they would both have been queens here, rather than subservient to Norman overlords. Haith greeted Nest's sons Maurice and William who were also present. 'William has just arrived too,' Nest told him.

William acknowledged Haith's greeting, but Haith could see that he had something on his mind that he wanted to broach with his mother. Greetings and news were exchanged between them all, and William's impatience grew palpable, and he directed irritated glances in Gwenllian's direction.

Gwenllian rose and gathered her skirts about her. 'I will see to my boys,' she told Nest and sauntered from the hall.

As soon as she was out of earshot, William glanced at his brother and launched into the topic that had obviously been burning to leave his tongue. 'Mother, it's bad enough to take the risk yourself of returning, given the suspicions that you were involved with your brother's treason. Can't you see that having Gwenllian and her boys here is not helping your case? Excuse me, Haith,' he turned briefly to Haith, 'for speaking out on this family business, but I must have it said and I know you will agree with me on this, that mother should not consort with the family of a traitor.'

Haith opened his mouth to respond, but was pre-empted by Nest's angry retort to her son. 'What would you have me do? Throw your cousins and my sister-in-law out to roam the countryside like beggars?'

'She could go to her own brothers in Gwynedd, Mother.'

'Yes, that would be better, for sure,' Nest said sarcastically. 'They will stay here with me. You and your brother,' she glared at Maurice too, 'would do well to remember that Welsh blood flows through your veins. You are not all Norman! And I thank you to stay out of it, Haith!'

'I intended to, my lady,' Haith stuttered.

'By God's bones, Mother! It'll end on the gallows, with our family stripped of everything.'

'The king would never allow that,' Nest asserted, drawing herself up.

'I've said my piece,' William declared, exasperated. 'I leave you two to try to talk some sense into her,' he told Haith and Maurice. He turned on his heel to leave the hall and head back to Carew. Maurice sustained his usual taciturn stance, merely raising his eyebrows to Haith before following his irate brother out to the courtyard.

'Despite William's assertion, Nest,' Haith hurried to say, 'I don't concur with his position. It is a kindness that you have taken in Gwenllian and her boys and what else should you do for your kin?'

'Thank you, Haith.' Nest struggled to regain her composure. 'Won't you sit?' She gestured to the chairs near the hearth that were loaded with furs. Haith's massive hound followed them towards the fire and licked at Haith's gloved hands before settling at his feet. Haith used his teeth to remove one of his riding gloves and pulled off its fellow, laying them on the side table next to him.

'We live as if we are two separate households within the castle, Haith, with Maurice and his cohort of Norman soldiers and hangers-on behaving in an increasingly aloof fashion from the Welsh contingent. I know that it is not only their half-Welsh blood that my sons have to live down with their Norman peers, but also my soiled reputation,' she said, blushing. 'With the king, Prince Owain, and leaving my husband,' she elaborated. Haith leant towards her. The heat of the fire was making him sweat and he loosened the thong fastening at his neck. 'Soiled reputation be damned, Nest,' he told her. 'You are the most honourable woman I have ever known.' She smiled. 'I am sad to see this division between you and your boys,' Haith said.

She nodded. 'I can find no resolution for it.'

Maurice returned and they had to cease discussion on the topic. Ida came down the stairs to greet Haith, with Robert in hand. 'Are you well, Haith?' she asked him, 'You look a little strange.'

'I'm hot, that's all,' he said, loosening the neck of his tunic a little further. 'It was a hot ride and I'll move away from the fire.' He made to push himself up from the chair but fell back feebly against it.

'What is it, Haith?' Nest asked alarmed.

His throat was constricted and a foul taste thickened his tongue. He made another determined effort and succeeded in getting himself upright. At his feet, his dog began to keen. Haith saw Nest blur and the hall around him swung, his hold on verticality failed as the floor sprung to meet him, and darkness swallowed him.

Maurice and his men hastily carried Haith upstairs to the guest chamber where Amelina ran to administer to him. 'He is seriously ill,' Maurice told me, looking askance at Haith's dog, which had shifted from a loud high-pitched whining to pitiful whimpers as it lay on the floor, twitching. 'I will go to Haith,' I told Maurice in panic.

'No, Mother.' He pulled me back down to my seat beside him. 'That would not be fitting.' He knew of my past relationship with Haith, and was anxious that I should not embarrass him. 'You know Amelina can help him with her medicining. You know she will do everything that can be done for him, and his sister is with him too.'

He was right that Amelina was skilled with herbs and would be more useful, but I found it hard to sit and wait while Haith suffered or was in danger. I looked at the dog. 'Something ails Haith's dog too.'

'Yes,' Maurice said, frowning. 'I'll look for the fewterer and see if he can bring remedy to the dog.'

As soon as he was out of sight, I rushed to the stairs and ran along the stone corridor to Haith's sickbed. Amelina was grinding charcoal in a pestle with water and trying to force the black liquid between Haith's pale lips, while Ida mopped at his face and neck that were beaded with sweat. He lay in the white bed deadly pale, looking all the world like a corpse. 'Amelina, tell me he will recover!'

'It's too early to say.'

'There's something wrong with the dog too.'

She looked up at me. 'Really? Will you sit with him while I take a look at the dog?'

'But surely you must nurse my brother, before you see to his dog!' Ida wailed.

'The dog may give me a clue as to how to help Haith.' Amelina moved purposefully away. Haith began to toss in the bed and his colour flipped from an unnatural pink to white and red. I dipped a cloth into the bowl that Ida held on her knee, wrung it, and applied it to his fevered forehead.

Amelina, Ida, and I sat with Haith through the night and there were a number of occasions when I thought we were about to lose him, but in the morning, Amelina assured us that his fever had broken. 'Go and eat something, Nest,' Amelina told me. 'He will not die now and you must be strong to help him when he recovers.'

I went down to the hall and told Maurice and Gwenllian how Haith was. 'You had best leave his medicining to Amelina and Ida now, Mother,' Maurice insisted again. I suppressed my urge to tell him to mind his own business and my own to rush back up the stairs to Haith.

Maurice decided to take the news of Haith's sickness to Pembroke. His absence from the castle provided an opportunity for a messenger to come from Caeo for Gwenllian. My sister-in-law and I received the man together in an outhouse where he gave us a whispered account of the profits of the mine. The miners had found a major lode and the proceeds were accumulating fast. 'I will send to Ireland to let Gruffudd know this good news,' Gwenllian said. 'When he returns he will be able to arm a great cohort of soldiers with it.'

'No more messages, I beg you, sister. We have already been betrayed once.'

'Then I will go myself.'

'No! Let me think on it. I will find a way that is safer.'

I looked down on the winding path from the castle and watched another messenger making slow progress past the donkeys and sheep on the path. I went out to meet him at the gate and took the letter that he carried, which came from my foster-sister, Mabel. It was a long letter with momentous news from Henry's court. I glanced over it and then called Ida to me to hear the news:

1128, The Royal Residence, Rouen

Mabel, countess of Gloucester, by the grace of God to my dear Nest, Lady of Llansteffan, perpetual health. Events here in the court are like the tide to and froing. I miss you greatly. We received news that William Clito *had married the sister-in-law of the French king and on the strength of that made a formal claim in arms to the Duchy of Normandy. Then Count Charles of Flanders as you will no doubt have heard, even distant as you are, was cruelly murdered while he was taking mass. King Henry supported the claims of Thierry of Alsace to replace the murdered count, but the French king installed William* Clito *as Count of Flanders. This was all, as you will imagine, quite counter to King Henry's interests. Henry sent Stephen de Blois to do battle with William* Clito. *Amaury de Montfort has also been supporting Henry's campaign. De Montfort turns coat to support Henry against* Clito *now, but the king is not adverse to that when the turning is sincere.*

To counter the growing power base of his rival, William Clito, *the king has married his daughter Maud to Geoffrey d'Anjou who is a mere boy of fifteen to her twenty-six years. The empress is severely displeased with the match. You will feel for her yourself in this matter. You can imagine how she has railed at her father and you can imagine, too, how her remonstrations have made no dent in his resolve. Henry's barons are angry since they fear, in times to come, they will have to take Geoffrey not only as duke of Normandy but also as king of England. So, my husband feared that William* Clito *might gain the high ground and be in a position to at last carry the Norman barons with him against the king. But the tide has turned again and the* Clito *is dead! He took a small injury to his hand in battle but the injury festered and that sad young man died on 28 July in this year.*

Amaury de Montfort arrived at Rouen with the news for the king who sincerely mourned his nephew and the loss of such a genteel knight. Amaury carried, too, a letter for the king written by William Clito *on his deathbed, which begged Henry for clemency for all his followers who have contested against the king, including Waleran de Meulan. The king is resolved to free Waleran as testament to his regard and grief for his extinguished nephew William* Clito.

I go now with the king's court to Westminster and must wait for a time when I am in your presence and can hold your hands and look in your face. In hopes this time will be very soon, with the great affection of your sister.

Ida and I exclaimed at all the twists and turns of fate and she, of course, wanted to discuss the part that Amaury de Montfort had played in these events. I mused to myself on Mabel's letter, tracing the inked words across the bumps of the parchment with my finger. If William *Clito* could successfully sue for clemency to the king, then I wondered if I might do so on my brother's behalf in time. Gruffudd had been in exile in Ireland for over a year.

After a few days, Amelina at last joined us at the meal in the hall, deciding that Haith was sufficiently recovered to be left alone for a short time. 'He is recovering well, apart from his eyesight,' she told us, 'but less so his dog.'

'What do you mean, Amelina?'

'The dog is dead. I think a would-be assassin saturated Haith's gloves with poison. The dog licked at the gloves,' she mimed the licking herself, 'took in a great deal of the toxin and died. There were signs of poison about the dog and in the symptoms of Haith's illness. Luckily Haith probably merely brought the gloves to his mouth, wiped his mouth perhaps, and so took in very little.'

I glanced over to the hearth where I remembered Haith removing his gloves when he arrived. Seeing the direction of my gaze, Amelina said, 'I threw the gloves on the fire, to be safe. I'm fairly sure I'm right in my surmise.'

'You mentioned his eyesight?' I asked, anxiously.

'Yes, he's seeing in green and yellow at the moment, but that will pass.'

Ida and I exclaimed together: 'Green and yellow!'

'Yes, it's a symptom of foxglove poisoning,' Amelina said, smug at the extent of her knowledge.

'Could it have been an accident?' asked Ida. 'Haith picked a plant on this ride here without realising its danger, perhaps?'

'Oh no,' Amelina asserted. 'A quantity sufficient to kill a mastiff and bring a large man like Haith to death's door must have been a deliberate lacing of the textile.'

'But who at Pembroke would poison him and why?' I asked. I turned to Ida. 'Do you think Breri could be a murderer as well as a spy?'

'I think he could do whatever was necessary.'

'But then who is Breri working for? I had assumed it was the de Clares but I cannot find any reason why they would want Haith dead.'

Ida shook her head. 'It has to be about *The White Ship*, but none of those possible culprits are at Pembroke. Perhaps Breri is in the pay of more than one master. He would be capable of that.'

'I thought he might be a double agent for the de Clares and for Prince Cadwaladr who covets my brother's lands in Ceredigion. But that could not explain this threat to Haith's life.'

'There is a third person Breri could be working for,' Ida said. I raised my eyebrows in query. 'When I searched Gisulf's chest, I found an incriminating letter from Ranulf de Gernon, that mentioned Breri's name. If he is working for a third master, for de Gernon, that might give reason for Haith's poisoning since he has been so intent on finding evidence of who might have caused the sinking of *The White Ship*.'

'Spying for three different masters!'

Ida nodded confidently. 'It's not impossible for that man, Breri,

I assure you.' She was silent, thinking, for a moment. 'For such an act, to go to the lengths of poisoning Haith in Pembroke, there must be some great secret belonging to someone powerful who fears that Haith will uncover it and tell it to the king. Haith is right in his quest to discover the truth about the ship and the drowned court after all.'

25

Runaway Bride

September 1129, Llansteffan Castle

'I want you to start packing for a journey to England,' I told Amelina.

Amelina opened and closed her mouth like a floundering fish. She frowned angrily at me, turned on her heel and stomped to my clothes chest, muttering loudly, '*Up* and *down* the country, over and over!' Nevertheless, she was soon enjoying herself, holding up tunics and mantles as we sorted those that were fine enough for court and others that could be worn on the journey itself. She sorted them into two piles on my bed. 'What are we going for this time?'

'I mean to ask the king for clemency for Gruffudd. He has been exiled in Ireland for more than two years.'

Amelina was about to give me her response to my intention, when we heard the sound of horses, a lot of horses, in the courtyard below. Amelina stood on tiptoe to look from the window: 'It's Gilbert de Clare, with that bard, and a lot of soldiers! That's not good is it?'

'No, it's not. Quickly, warn Ida to get out of sight.'

Amelina ran down the stairs to the hall where we had left Ida stitching and keeping an eye on the children. I fixed my veil onto my head and followed her down and was appalled to see that we were too late. Ida was standing between two soldiers, her face white, her arms held tightly in their grip. Maurice had followed the visitors in from the courtyard and stood observing the scene with a frown on his face. Gwenllian and her children were also staring at the Normans and Ida.

'What is the meaning of this?' I demanded of de Clare. 'That you bring armed men into my hall?'

'This woman is a renegade nun that you have sheltered in your household,' he stated coldly.

'This is nonsense.' I looked amongst the group of strangers, hoping that Haith might be here, but he was not one of their number. I swallowed when I recognised another prisoner as the Welshman who regularly brought news of the goldmine to Gwenllian and myself. His face was bruised and bloodied and he looked very afraid.

Breri pointed a finger at Ida. 'She was a nun at Fontevraud. She was named Sister Benedicta there. She consorted lewdly with Amaury de Montfort.'

'My name is Ida de Bruges,' Ida said shakily.

A scrawny priest stepped from the group of soldiers and began to harangue Ida. 'You take from God his bride. You will be damned if you do not return to the convent. In hellfire, you will kiss the bare teeth from which the flesh of your paramour has fallen.' He turned to the others. 'The Devil made her consort in lewdness with a man. The Devil cajoled her to cast off the veil of religion and causes her to persist shamelessly in wearing secular clothing. We must compel her to return to the Order that she has arrogantly despised.'

'You are mistaken,' I continued to address de Clare. 'This is no Sister Benedicta. She is my companion Ida de Bruges and I do not take kindly to this abuse of her by your wandering jongleur.'

Breri drew himself up. 'I am no jongleur, but a bard.'

'This accusation is nonsense and holds no water,' I declared. 'I demand that Breri is imprisoned for bearing false witness.'

'Have a care, Lady Nest,' de Clare told me, 'that you are not convicted of bearing false witness yourself. I see that you shelter here the family of your brother who has been convicted of treason against the king. Falseness swirls about you.' His eyes swept across Gwenllian and her family. Morgan was twelve and looked defiance at de Clare, although he must have been afraid. Maelgwyn was nine and Gwenllian hugged him to her side. Maurice was red in the face, staring at his boots and biting his lip. 'The evidence against this renegade nun is certain,' de Clare asserted. 'She will be incarcerated in a religious house and made to recant her gross sins. Take her!' he commanded and the men dragged Ida away, her eyes beseeching upon me.

De Clare took one more look at the occupants of my hall, stared stonily at me and then followed his men to the horses. They took the battered Welshman with them. I exchanged a frightened glance with Gwenllian. They had not managed to extract anything damning enough from him yet or they would have clapped she and me both into irons. I refused Maurice's attempts to speak with me. 'I will deal directly and only with the king on this matter,' I told him and he left the hall, exasperated with me. 'Gwenllian, you are not safe here. I am going to the king and you should seek refuge. Is there somewhere you can go?' I glanced miserably at my nephews.

'Yes,' she said firmly. 'Don't worry about us, Nest. I know where we can go. I thank you for your kindnesses to us and hope that you are able to gain Ida's freedom.'

When de Clare's men had cleared the gateway, I ordered two messengers to ready their horses. I penned one note to Haith informing him what had happened to Ida and another for the king, telling him also of the calamity. 'Come, Amelina,' I ordered, when the messengers had galloped out on their missions, 'we must swiftly follow my letter to the king.'

26

Clemency

September 1129, Westminster Palace, London, England

Approaching the palace of Westminster by boat, memories crowded me: memories of Sybil de Montgommery, my Norman foster-mother, after my family were slain; of my first meeting with Haith; and with King Henry too. The Thames was even busier than my memories. Numerous boats of all sizes moved around me. Small jetties and myriad stalls with bright awnings lined the banks. The whole merchandise of the world was set out and enticing us to open our purses. The shouts of traders and boatmen mingled with the high cries of gulls that pursued the boats and rode the currents of the air as we rode the waters. I had travelled from Wales to London with the entourage of Mabel's husband, Robert of Gloucester.

My boat bumped against the buffers at the palace pier on Thorney Island. The pilot handed me up the steps and I looked around me. Behind me, I heard Amelina stridently berating the porters as they manhandled my travelling chest from the boat. The palace and abbey, set amidst the island's marshy ground and surrounded by green fields, was a splendid sight. The distance to the palace was too short to require horses, so I lent on Earl Robert's arm and we walked on planks covering the mud beneath to the moat bridge and palace gateway. There were many more guards than usual crowding the gates and the doorway to the great hall.

Inside, I craned my neck looking for Mabel. Earl Robert assisted in parting the crowds for me and looking for my sister and his wife. I was, at last, relieved to see her. Stephen de Blois recognised me and gave a nod of greeting across the crowded hall. Next to him, I recognised Ranulf de Gernon, the new earl of Chester, from Haith's descriptions of him. He wore his moustaches very long and turned up at the ends, stiffened with wax, which had been a Saxon fashion that was now adopted by some Norman lords.

King Henry and Queen Adelisa sat on the raised dais. The young queen looked out, bright-eyed and intent on the throng of people, but I was shocked at Henry's appearance. There were dark patches beneath his eyes and he was, very unusually for him, a little dishevelled. 'Does something ail Henry?' I asked Mabel.

'There has been terrible news from Normandy,' Mabel told me. 'Geoffrey d'Anjou has repudiated Empress Maud as his wife.'

'They can be reconciled, surely,' I glanced back at Henry. 'Henry will work on it.'

'Yes he is already doing so and please God that such a reconciliation is possible. I believe the king has slept badly for several nights. He has been subject to terrible nightmares, where he says apparitions of his subjects accuse him.'

I raised a querying eyebrow. 'Accuse him of what?'

'He does not say, only that shades of vengeful lords, clergy and peasants crowd his bed and he cannot sleep. He has weapons and relics filling every inch of space around his bed and changes where he sleeps each night in fear of murder. His physician and astrologer, Grimbald, sleeps in his chamber and interprets his dreams on the instant of his waking when he does manage to sleep at all.'

'He is unwell? In his mind?'

'Perhaps.'

I had intended to make my plea for a pardon for Gruffudd in public at this assembly, but hearing Mabel's words and looking at Henry's condition I resolved that it might be best to approach him privately on the matter and to see if I could bring some comfort to him for the anxiety that he suffered.

Mabel pointed out Peter the Venerable, Abbot of Cluny, who was visiting England and other members and visitors to the court that I did not know. Once upon a time, I had been acquainted with everyone at court and they had known me, but it was decades since I had held the position of king's mistress and I was out of touch with the whirling currents of power here now. The place buzzed with discussion of the separation of Henry's daughter Maud from her husband. It had not been a popular choice of bridegroom, but the lack of an heir was an even greater concern. The first business of the court concerned Waleran de Meulan and Hugh de Chateauneuf.

The names of the two former rebels were called and they stood before the king. They had been freed by Henry from five years of imprisonment when the court was in Normandy and, now, he was reinstating them to their lands and honours. Waleran was the son of my great friend, Elizabeth de Vermandois. I had been with Elizabeth when she had birthed Waleran and his twin brother. No doubt, the two men had been kept imprisoned in some comfort, yet it was harsh punishment to idle away the vividness of one's short life in captivity and constraint. The king told them that due to the dying request of his nephew William *Clito*, he had granted them their freedom. They swore again their sincere allegiance and their oath not to conspire in rebellion against him.

Mabel pointed out the king's other nephews who I did not know: Thibaut, count of Blois, who was visiting and Henry de Blois, abbot of Glastonbury. The abbot was called to stand before the king and was well pleased to be created bishop of Winchester.

'This makes him the second richest man in England, after the king,' Mabel whispered in my ear.

The king's dulled eyes found me out at that moment and he nodded slightly to register my presence, but his attention was soon distracted elsewhere. 'Will you plead for your brother today?' Mabel asked.

'No, I've decided my plea will be best heard in private. Let's go to my chamber.'

We moved off to my room where my chest had already been delivered and Amelina was busy unpacking. Mabel and I sat down comfortably together to catch up. First, I wrote a note to the king asking for a private audience with him when he was able, and sent that to him with a servant. Mabel caught me up with the news of the court and we listened to Amelina complain about the smallness of the room and its draughts.

'And … Mabel, how do you feel to be reunited with your husband?'

'Good.' She laughed lightly and looked down at her hands in her lap.

I wiggled my eyebrows when she glanced up again. 'Not adequate!' I declared.

'Very good?' she tried. We laughed and I opened my mouth for further interrogation, but there was a knock on the door and one of Henry's servants entered to request my presence with the king. 'That was quick!' Mabel remarked, arching an eyebrow. I rose and Mabel squeezed my hand to wish me luck.

Henry was in his chamber, sitting with his broad shoulders rounded before a great fire. There was a large jug of wine on the table at his knee. He had, as was his habit, stripped off his robes of state and sat in his white shirt and a pair of grey breeches. When I entered, his back was to me. The king was 61 and his hair had receded significantly from his temples and forehead. His remaining hair was cut short to his head in a dark burr. He turned at the sound of my entry and I was grieved to see the battle between stress and a false cheer in the expression he gave me. The hair that curled thickly at the neck of his shirt that I had once delighted in combing at with my fingers was iron grey. In the privacy of his own chambers, he looked even worse than he had in the hall. 'Leave us,' he told the page standing in a corner and the boy slipped quietly out.

'Nest. Your name is like oil soothing me. Your face is the sweetest flower. You envelope me in the fragrance of delight, my dear.'

'Stop, Henry!' I laughed.

'No, truly. It's no exaggeration. You find me in a most lugubrious mood, dear Nest. Still no heir. You should have given me that bed practice I asked you for in Bristol.' His attempt at joking convinced neither of us.

'Henry!' I could not help myself. I went to him and took his head in my arms, cradling it against my stomach. He turned his face further into my body and wept almost without sound for long, long minutes. I held him hard, trying to absorb his grief, as I might hold and rock a swaddled and sobbing infant. I had never seen him so unmanned before. He had shown me many sides to his personality in our time together, but never this.

'Forgive me.' He extracted himself and dried his face on the voluminous linen of his sleeve. He took my hand. 'Sit and talk with me, Nest?'

I took the chair he indicated across from him in front of the hearth. Our customary composition. I poured wine for us.

'But you are here, Nest, of course, because you want something of me. I have already dealt with your nun. She is released and I have ordered that no harm may come to her. An escort is bringing her here to me. She should arrive in a few days. I owe her much and her brother too, and you of course.' He gazed at me warmly.

'Truly, Henry? Ida is safe?'

'She is. You didn't need to travel all this way to sue for her, but I'm glad that you did.'

'There is something else,' I admitted.

'Ah!'

'But that can wait a moment. I am sorely grieved to see you so troubled, sire, and would speak with you of your own cares first.'

'I have not slept for many nights, Nest, and am not myself. You find me in a sorry state.'

'What is the cause of your sleeplessness, Henry?' I caressed his hand on his knee, thinking how his knuckles had thickened and his hands had the splotched appearance of those of an old man. 'You can speak with me.'

'My sleeplessness is no doubt caused by my guilt, Nest.'

'Guilt? At what?'

'Everything,' he moaned glumly and stared into the fire.

'Everything! Sire, how can you say so. You have shouldered the burden of ruling England,' (I did not say Wales) 'for so many years and you have done well. More than well.' I considered, fleetingly, that there was hypocrisy in my speaking kindly to King Henry on the one hand, and conspiring in treason against him on behalf of my brother on the other, yet my kindness was for the man that I had loved long ago, and politics could not overwhelm that.

He gave me a quick, small smile, more grimace than grin. 'You think so.'

'Everyone thinks so. Why do you torture yourself with guilt? You have done your best. And it has surpassed that of any other king in living memory.'

'I have tried.'

'You have kept peace and prosperity in England for thirty years, sire! This is a great achievement. No one could have done better.'

'Perhaps. Yet, there is constant warfare in Normandy, conflict in Wales,' he glanced meaningfully at me, 'and I have no heir so when I die everything I have done will dissolve to ruination.'

'No, no, Henry. You will have an heir soon enough and there will be no ruination.'

'The queen and I have been wed for seven years. She does not quicken.'

'She has had no pregnancies at all?'

He shook his head. 'God punishes me for my delinquencies.'

I compressed my lips on the thought that God might see countless mistresses and hordes of illegitimate children as more than delinquency.

'Nest, I need comfort,' he said, standing suddenly and lifting me to my feet. He took me in his arms and I did not have the heart or the will, in truth, to push him away. His tongue thrust into my mouth and he pulled my wimple from my head, dragged down the shoulder of my tunic, and pulled my chemise from my breast. His mouth encompassed one nipple and then the other as he pushed down my clothes, and the old desire for him coursed through me. He looked briefly in my face and saw no resistance there, so lifted me to the bed. We were both stripped before I could take many more breaths and he was moving inside me and fast crying out in climax. Afterwards, he slept for many hours close against me, our sweat pooling and cooling together and his penis and then his semen slipping from between my legs. After a while, a servant knocked quietly and put his head around the door, quickly averting his eyes at sight of us on the bed. I waved him away wordlessly and Henry slept on. I was past childbearing, but I considered that if I had not been so and if I had quickened with Henry's child again now, I might have found myself queen regent in due course. I watched Henry's sleeping face and pushed down a fleeting, guilty thought of Haith. Life was complicated. I loved Haith but I also loved Henry in a nostalgic way and I was married to de Marais. My eyelids dropped down over my eyes in fatigue at it all.

I woke to see Henry dressed and washing his face. As I stirred and stretched in the pungent sheets, he turned to me, an expression of affection in his eyes and on his mouth. His eyelashes were clotted with the water he had splashed on his face. 'You save me again, Nest! I feel much better. As if I have slept for a thousand years. You have lifted the clouds of sadness in which I was wrapped. You brighten the nebulous gloom of my soul. I wish I could put aside my royal dignity, spurn my crown, trample my purple and run away with you.' I laughed at him as he towelled his nose and chin and then sat on the edge of the bed offering me a beaker of water. 'So, my most beautiful princess, my longest treasure (notice I do not say old), what do you want?'

I smiled with my eyes at him over the rim of the beaker as I sipped and handed the emptied beaker back to him. 'I would rather be dressed for that conversation,' I declared and slid from the bed in hunt of my clothes, my hands cupped modestly to one breast and another to my private parts, bending away from his embraces as I dressed. I pushed him gently from me and sat in the chair before the hearth. 'May I have audience with the king?' I asked.

'As many times as you like,' he joked.

I bowed my head for a moment. 'I would not have you think that I lay with you for the sake of the plea I wish to make to you. That is not the truth of the matter.'

'Don't worry about that. I have a clear sense of why you lay with me and am most grateful for it,' he responded, his eyes alight with amusement. I was relieved to see him return to his former confidence.

'I am glad of that.'

'Have you forgiven me yet for roping you to de Marais?'

I frowned, but quickly relented. 'I forgave you that when you signed the charter that released me from him. And,' I said, quietly, 'I understood why you felt you had to do it.' Henry had feared that if I remained a widow and unwed, I would become a liability again for his rule in Wales. I had already made that rule vulnerable when the Welsh prince, Owain, kidnapped me from my first Norman husband, Gerald, aiming to make fools of the Normans with his theft of me. Henry could not allow that to happen again and so he had callously done me the disservice of marrying me to de Marais.

'What is it then, Nest? Need to reject another husband? Have another abductor hanged from the walls of Pembroke?'

I laughed and then sobered my expression. 'Sire, it is my brother.' His expression sobered in return. 'I would ask you for clemency for Gruffudd, sire.'

He pursed his mouth sourly. How many times had I seen that look, known what it presaged. 'Don't say no,' I cried out quickly. 'He was at grave fault, it's true. But as the one who would have ruled in Deheubarth in former circumstances, his pride is injured with his disinheritance and the reduced situation in which he must live. You gave clemency to William *Clito*'s followers. Will you not give clemency to Gruffudd and let him return to his family, and to me?'

Henry swilled wine around his mouth. 'If I do grant clemency, will you stand surety, Nest, that Gruffudd ap Rhys will not act against my interests?'

I swallowed my own mouthful of wine. I had known that he would ask me this and that I could not be certain of Gruffudd's actions if he returned. In fact, I felt quite certain that he *would* act against the king's interests, that he *must* do so, and that, perhaps, I would too. 'I will so stand surety,' I stated with conviction and prayed I would not rue it.

Henry's mouth continued pursed for some time. 'You *will* rue it, Nest,' he retorted, echoing my thoughts.

'I hope not, sire,' I whispered, looking away from him.

'Very well. I will issue the pardon in tomorrow's court. I can gainsay you nothing. But if your brother causes me any more trouble in Wales I will not hesitate to hang him on the next occasion and no dillydallying on our parts will save him. Are we clear on this?'

'It is clear. Thank you, Henry,' I said, regarding him gravely. 'And,' I added in a more pert tone, 'you can be certain there will be no more dillydallying.'

'That's what you said a few years back,' Henry laughed, 'and a few more times before that.'

I rose to take my leave of him, shaking my head and smoothing down my gown. Mabel would be worrying about what had happened to me in all this time, or would have guessed at it.

I lent a hand on his shoulder. 'Go safely, dear Henry,' I whispered in his ear and brushed his lined cheek with my mouth.

'And you, my Nest.'

I backed into the corridor and dropped the latch on Henry's door. Turning to the corridor, I was appalled to find myself confronted with Haith. It was clear from his expression that he knew that I had been with the king. The dishevelled state of my clothes and hair were evidence against me. 'Haith!'

'I have come to treat with the king for Ida. Perhaps you are about the same mission,' he said slowly.

'Yes. I … Henry … the king assures me that she is already freed and on her way here.'

Haith's face briefly showed relief at this news, but then returned to his stare of consternation at finding me emerging from the king's chamber.

'I … Mabel is waiting for me.' He stepped aside so that I could move past him. When I reached my room, I was relieved to find it empty. I flung myself on the bed and hugged my knees, rocking and weeping. Oh what had I done! I had only meant to give Henry comfort for old times' sake, but I had affronted the man I loved and there was no cure for it. Amelina came in and was appalled to see me grieving. 'What is it? You are breaking your heart! Has someone hurt you?'

'Me. I have hurt me.' I wept hard and could not, would not speak of it.

'Nest, Nest.' She embraced me, trying to comfort me.

'What's happened. Has Ida been harmed?'

I shook my head. 'Ida is safe. The king has freed her and sent for her. She will be here in a few days. The king will give pardon to Gruffudd.'

'What is it then, Nest?' she asked bewildered.

'I need a bath, Amelina. Order a bath for me.'

27

Suspicions

September 1129, Westminster Palace, London, England

Haith stood dumbfounded at the door to the king's chamber, taking deep breaths. Nest had bedded the king. He was sure of it. He took his hand from the latch. He could not speak with the king now. Ida was safe in any case. He turned on his heel and moved back down the corridor. He avoided the hall and feast later that evening since he could not bear to have to watch Nest in company with the king. Should he simply turn tail and return to Pembroke? No, he wanted to wait and see Ida, see that she was safe. Nest owed him nothing. He did not own her. She had once loved the king, long ago. He tried to drive the speculations from his mind.

Haith went to the stables in the morning to see that his horse was provisioned and noticed that Nest's palfrey was not there. 'Is the lady out riding so early?' he asked the groom.

'I think she left, sir.'

'Left?'

'She and her maid.'

Haith avoided the king, spending as much time as he could at his townhouse rather than at the palace. He had intended to take this opportunity to share his findings concerning *The White Ship*, but he could not bring himself to a long conversation with Henry after discovering Nest in the act of leaving the king's chamber, the king's bed. He forced the words to take solid shape in his mind.

He decided to write out a summary of his findings on the ship in a letter addressed to the king instead, to be given to him along with Gisulf's chest in the event that Haith should die. After all, there had been two serious attempts on his life already. Haith wrote of his search for the truth about the sinking of the ship and that he had found no evidence to support his initial suspicions against Stephen de Blois. The accounts of Berold and Luc de La Barre and the letters in Gisulf's chest evidenced the fact that the royal clerk had been blackmailing Waleran de Meulan and Ranulf de Gernon.

He lifted his stylus from the parchment and paused in his account. The chest also contained a letter concerning Ida that might have given Amaury de Montfort motive for murder. Haith did not write that down.

He continued writing that Berold and de La Barre had attested that Berold and the royal dapifer de Pirou were commissioned by Waleran's steward, Morin du Pin, to murder Gisulf onboard *The White Ship*. They had carried out that murder and also killed the ship's pilot who had caught them in the act, and they had, thereby, caused the sinking of the ship and the deaths of 300 people including the king's heir. The witnesses swore that Waleran de Meulan had not known about the murder plan beforehand. De Pirou had since also been murdered. Morin du Pin had disappeared beyond reach into exile.

Waleran was incarcerated when the two attempts were made on Haith's life: one at Westminster during the Christmas court in

1126, and the second at Pembroke in the summer of 1128. There were reasons, therefore, to suspect the involvement of de Gernon in these murderous attempts against Haith, derived largely from the fact that he had opportunity to commission them, from his association with de Pirou, and his treasonous correspondence stored by Gisulf. There was, however, no concrete evidence against de Gernon. The bard Breri had also been implicated in the treasonous letter from de Gernon that Gisulf kept in his blackmail chest, and it seemed likely that he had some hand in the attack on Haith in Wales.

That was all Haith could write. It was a dissatisfying haul after all this time casting a net for truth. The perpetrators had died or disappeared and de Gernon, if arraigned, would simply deny any knowledge of Gisulf's murder and the sinking. Haith would be speaking against a powerful lord who could crush him if he accused him without proof.

Haith blotted the parchment, folded it and addressed it to *Henricus Rex*. He sealed the letter and allowed a long red ribbon to adhere in the solidifying wax. He lifted the lid of Gisulf's chest. So much misery and greed rustled in these papers. He reached for Robert de Bellême's letter concerning Ida and transferred it to the small casket of his own important mementos. He closed and locked Gisulf's chest and tied his letter to the king to the hasp. Perhaps with this summary, he could let the matter go as Ida had told him he should. He summoned two servants to carry the chest into the small, secure room where quantities of silver, his seal, and papers relating to his work as sheriff were kept.

Hooves sounded in the courtyard outside and Haith went to the door to see Ida arriving with an escort of the king's men. Haith sped down the stone steps to the hall two at a time and hurried to the door. Outside, he quickly crossed the small cobbled courtyard to help his sister from her horse. 'Ida, thank the Lord!'

When his sister was divested of her travel cloak and settled comfortably before the fire, he looked her over. He was relieved to see that she was unharmed and had recovered swiftly from her ordeal at the hands of de Clare. She told him cheerfully that she had been locked up at Pembroke for a week and harangued daily by de Clare's chaplain, but the king's summons had arrived before she was forced to endure any further punishment. 'I believe they intended to immure me in an anchorhold,' Ida said, her face sobering, her shoulders shivering at that imagined fate.

'Nest was here at court, I believe?' Ida asked him. 'Suing with the king on my behalf.'

'Yes,' he replied and moved away to leaf through a pile of papers on the table, making it clear that he did not wish to speak further on that topic.

28

The Librarian

July 1131, Fontevraud Abbey, Anjou

'Are you looking forward to your return to Fontevraud?' Haith shouted to Ida over the noise of the rough sea. Conversation offered them some distraction from the fear of the turbulent waters and the whipping winds buffeting their small ship.

'Yes,' Ida shouted back, 'as long as I leave again on this occasion!'

Haith grinned back to her. 'Have no fear, we'll not leave you behind.'

The king had decided to visit the abbey of Fontevraud and to take Maud with him, hoping that the abbess and nuns might make an impression on the devout empress and persuade her back to her marriage. The king's daughter Juliana (one of his many children born out of wedlock) had decided to take the veil at Fontevraud and join her daughters who had entered the convent as children. The king wished to made a substantial gift to Fontevraud for the sake of his daughter and granddaughters, and had asked Haith and Ida to accompany him. This gift to Fontevraud from Henry was one of many large donations he had made in the last few months. He had also richly endowed Cluny and La Trinité in Caen. His gifts and ongoing negotiations with Pope Innocent all had one end as far as Haith could see. To win favour with God, bring about a repair to Maud's marriage and, therefore, a resuscitation of Henry's hopes of a grandson. Haith was concerned about Ida's safety at Fontevraud but she reassured him that she would keep her face concealed and the king would allow no harm to come to her.

Haith had kept his distance from both Nest and the king for a while, but Henry was his oldest friend and his king. Eventually, it had been necessary to obey his summons, and try to erase any thoughts concerning Nest and Henry.

The abbess welcomed Ida as a laywoman and feigned no recognition of her. She took care that Ida was quartered where no one who had known her before would remember her and, true to her word, Ida went about heavily veiled. After their first night at the abbey, Ida met Haith in the refectory to break fast. When they had finished eating, she took her brother's hand and led him to her former kingdom: the library. He watched her make herself comfortable in a particularly secluded corner where she told him she had often sat before in her former life here. With the exception of themselves, the library was empty and Ida removed her veil to sit with her eyes closed, enjoying the warmth of the sunshine on her face.

'Do you think of de Montfort here?' Haith asked her.

'Yes,' she admitted startled, opening her eyes and blushing. 'Part of me thinks it is not fitting to think of him here, in God's house. But you know, Haith, it was an act of affection, of hope somehow, between us. I am not ashamed of it. I hope that God will see it in the same light.' She sat up straight and bent to the desk in front of her where she had laid out parchment, ink, and stylus. 'Do you think of Nest in this place?' she countered.

'I think of Nest everywhere. Who are you writing to?'

'To her, to Nest.' She looked up at him. He realised that she had grown aware of his reticence on the subject of Nest. 'I have hopes that you two will find happiness in time,' she said, but he did not meet her gaze or respond.

'How lucky we are, Haith, that our bodies, our hearts, and our children (in your case) are not indentured to the state as are those of kings and queens.' Haith's thoughts went to Nest. There was some application of that idea to her lot in life.

'Yes,' he said, 'you are thinking of the empress?' The king's business had lately been dominated by his efforts to repair the breach between Empress Maud and her husband.

'Yes, but the king too, how all his efforts now are to secure this succession and the future of his kingdom.'

'I wouldn't feel too sorry for Henry, Ida, from a personal angle, on account of his love life, I mean. I assure you that he sowed plenty of his wild oats in his youth, before he ever became king, and after too.' He was silent for a moment. 'He has followed his own heart for most of his life.'

'And you are thinking of how my idea applies to Nest,' she stated.

He did not reply.

'May I read my letter out to you?' She did not wait for his answer. He looked up at her desk, as she prepared to read and noticed that she had two sheets of parchment she had been writing on. She moved the second sheet to the top and read out:

Felicitations to you on the return of your brother Gruffudd and the safe delivery of Gwenllian's new son, Maredudd. I am grieved to hear of the death of Elizabeth de Vermandois. I know that you and she were close friends as girls.

'Did you know her, Haith? Elizabeth?'

He nodded and thought of Nest and Elizabeth as laughing and lovely young girls at court, of how he had first met Nest, escorting her on the king's orders on several journeys. It was hard to believe that Elizabeth was dead. He and Nest, Henry, and Ida, they were all in the twilight of their lives now, with not much time left to them. Could he find a way past the most recent causes for distance between himself and Nest, or had she made her decision that it was Henry who was the love of her life, after all?

'What is it, Haith? Something about Nest.' Ida had read some unguarded expression on his face.

'It's nothing. What else do you write?'

'I told her not to fret that Robert has gone to de Marais in Cardigan.'

She meant de Marais's eight-year-old son, Robert FitzStephen, not Haith's son Robert who was twelve. Nest's youngest son had gone to Cardigan Castle where his father had placed him in training with Robert FitzMartin. Ida continued to read out her letter:

FitzStephen will thrive at Cardigan. He will be in his element. You will see.

I return to England with King Henry and Empress Maud next month.

'Tell her that I know FitzMartin well and he will take good care of her son,' Haith said.

Ida was pleased at the additional comfort she could offer to Nest and dipped the stylus in the pot of ink one more time.

'Who is your second letter to?' asked Haith.

'No second letter,' Ida remarked, not looking up from her task. 'I just blotched my first copy.'

Haith frowned. His sister was an accomplished scribe. The last time he had known her to blotch her writing, she had been six years old. He studied her bowed, blonde head but found no explanation there.

The cry of a small animal in the night woke Haith, a mouse in the cruel claws of an owl perhaps, and he struggled to get back to sleep. The bells of the church rang out, adding to his inability to slip into drowsy unconsciousness. He grew tired of tossing and turning and sat up abruptly, swinging his legs to the edge of the bed. He slipped his cloak and boots on, determined to make a circuit of the abbey. He hoped a stroll would clear his head and allow him to find sleep on his return to his truckle bed in the abbey guesthouse. He felt carefully with his boot at the threshold. It was a pitch-black night and he could not remember if there were steps here or not that he might tumble down and break his neck. He fumbled his way carefully along the dark path, stopping abruptly at the sound of a man's voice, close by. 'My love.'

Haith kept stock still. He could hear rustling as if the man and his love stood against a hedge to Haith's right.

'You should not have come here, Amaury.' Haith recognised Ida's voice.

Haith could not retreat. They would hear him. He would have to wait it out and hope he remained undetected.

'How could I not, when I heard you were here, received your note? I was so close. There was no choice in the matter.'

There was an interruption in their speech and Haith imagined that the silence might be bracketing a kiss. He could not lurk here in the dark while his sister engaged in a sexual tryst with this man.

'It's been a long time,' Ida breathed. 'I did not expect you to come to me.'

'As I said, my love, no choice. I never forgot you, Benedicta.' Amaury called Ida by her nun's name, the name he had known her by when they were lovers. There was another silence. Haith took one silent step, backing away.

'I have to ask you something, Amaury.' Haith stopped moving.

'We have no time for words, sweet Benedicta, only for this.'

After another long pause, Ida's voice whispered through the darkness again. 'Amaury,' she was admonishing him. 'No, listen. Stop. I mean to ask you it.'

Haith's curiosity burned but he started to move silently away again. It was not decent to eavesdrop on his sister. He would have to hope, instead, that she would tell him whatever she found out from Amaury de Montfort.

29

Circling

'Take this, boy!' Haith slapped the slopping bowl of water with its bloodied towels into the boy's palms.

The young page was pale and alarmed. 'Yes, sheriff.'

'Keep your eyes on the king and run for help if there is any change in his condition. Do you understand?' Haith shook the shoulder of the shocked page. 'I'm going for the doctor but I will be back as fast as I can.'

The boy raised frightened, saucer eyes to Haith's face, but then nodded. Haith hesitated on the threshold of the king's chamber. Where was he most likely to find the doctor? He took a chance that at this time of the evening, the man would have already retired from the hall and taken to his own quarters. He pulled Henry's door closed behind him and heard the latch click back into place. The doctor's lodging was on the other side of the castle since Henry rarely had cause to keep a doctor near but he had cause now.

Haith jogged along the covered stone passageway. His own days of sprinting were at an end. He knew he would feel even this light run tomorrow in his overworn muscles. He hammered with his closed fist on the doctor's door. A female shriek and a blurred cry emitted from the room, 'One moment!' The king had no time for modesties. Haith tried the latch but found the door locked. He hammered again. 'Open up, *now*! The *king* has need of you!' He regretted the words as soon as they were out of his mouth. A number of servants passing in the corridor behind him stopped to gape. The news would soon be all over the palace that the king was taken ill.

The doctor opened up and Haith glimpsed the bedcurtains trembling behind the man, but who he was in bed with was of no consequence. 'The king is ill,' Haith said in a low voice. 'Get your medicines and instruments and follow me immediately.' The doctor nodded and they were soon back at the king's bedside.

'Wait outside,' the doctor told him imperiously, having recovered his dignity on their rapid walk back to the king's solar.

Reluctantly, Haith moved to sit on the bench opposite the king's door. He put his head in his hands. This illness had come on swiftly, with no forewarning. Henry had been pushing himself even more than usual for the last two years, hellbent on ensuring the repair of the empress's marriage. She had, finally, returned to Count Geoffrey last autumn, but there was still no news of an heir. The king worked tirelessly to lay the ground to ensure that Maud would inherit his throne. He had forced the barons to swear an oath to her again, before she returned to her husband in Anjou, but this time, there had been no ambiguity about it. They had sworn to recognize the Empress Maud as the king's heir in her own right. Over the last few months, Henry had been greasing the palms and pouring argumentation into the ears of the Archbishop of Canterbury and Bishop Roger of Salisbury. Both men would be instrumental in confirming Maud on the throne in the event of the king's death.

Haith lifted his head and stared anxiously at the closed door of the king's chamber. The king had lost consciousness and fallen, hitting his arm and face hard against the carved wooden chest at the end of the bed. Haith had picked him up, carried him to the bed, and staunched the flow of blood from the wound on his cheek and mouth. Henry had regained consciousness quickly, but lay moaning feebly at the pain in his broken face. The doctor was taking his sweet time in there.

'Sheriff Haith!'

Haith looked down the passageway and saw Stephen de Blois approaching fast, followed by a retinue of men. The faces of Ranulf de Gernon and Waleran de Meulan were at Stephen's shoulders, as they jostled to keep their places in the melee of men striding towards Haith. Stephen halted and Haith rose to his feet.

'What's happened?' Stephen demanded.

'The king fell in his solar and has injured his face and arm. The doctor is with him, my lord.'

Stephen looked at the closed door and hesitated.

Waleran butted shoulders with Stephen to step forward and glare aggressively at Haith. Since Waleran's return to court, he had been unremittingly hostile towards Haith, except in the king's presence. Haith could only assume the hostility derived from a combination of his unwelcome presence at Pont Audemer before the rebellion and the threat to Waleran if Haith informed the king of du Pin's role in the wrecking of *The White Ship*. 'We should go into the solar at once,' Waleran declared. 'The king may have need of speech with his lords.'

'It might be best to allow the doctor to make the king comfortable,' Haith ventured. 'I'm sure the doctor will come soon to tell us how the king fares.'

Ranulf stepped forward to join Waleran in an aggressive posture aimed at Haith. 'It is hardly your place to tell us what to do,' Ranulf snarled.

Haith ignored Ranulf and looked back to Stephen's face. He had the authority here, as the king's nephew. Stephen frowned, contemplating Haith. 'We will wait. Give me room here,' he pushed at Waleran and then Ranulf who were crowding him. 'And,' he said, lowering his own voice, 'we will have no raised voices in the vicinity of my uncle if he is sickening.'

Waleran's face showed his displeasure at being told what to do, but he drew back from the confrontational stance he had taken towards Haith. He lent, instead, on the panelled wall beside Haith and faced the bedchamber door.

Ranulf was not so easily silenced. 'You should be in the chamber, Stephen,' he hissed.

'Shut up,' Stephen said with uncharacteristic rudeness. 'Shut up, Ranulf. Let me think, here.'

Bishop Henry de Blois belatedly joined the throng outside the king's door, rustling in his silken bishop's robes. 'What's going on?' he demanded of Haith.

Haith repeated the story of the king's fall and the doctor's examination. He watched Bishop Henry exchange a glance with his brother, Stephen. Haith saw the glee cross the bishop's face fleetingly and be concealed as quickly. The bishop turned a look of concern upon the gathered men. 'We should pray for our lord king's deliverance.'

'Not here,' Stephen said irritated at the press of men in the hallway. 'The chapel, perhaps, brother,' he said. 'You might lead the court in prayers for the king's good health in the chapel, and I will wait and hear what Doctor Grimbald has to say.'

Bishop Henry flashed a look of annoyance at his brother and Haith saw the alarm on Ranulf's face at the suggestion. None of them wanted to miss any event that might occur in the king's solar. Stephen turned to the crowding courtiers. 'You will go to the chapel or the hall and await further news. You do no good creating a disturbance here at my uncle's door, at his sickbed.' Reluctantly the majority of the men dispersed, however, Bishop Henry, Waleran, and Ranulf remained waiting alongside Haith and Stephen. There was an awkward silence. They were, no doubt, Haith mused, all brimming to speak of the possibility of the king's death and what happened next, but could not. Booted footsteps resounded loudly and they looked up at the approach of Robert of Gloucester. Seeing their faces, Robert broke into a run. 'Haith! What's happened?'

'Your father took a fall,' Haith began, but Robert had burst through the doors of the king's chamber before Haith could complete his account. Stephen, Bishop Henry, Waleran, and Ranulf seized their opportunity and entered the solar behind the Earl of Gloucester. Haith judged that he would do best to follow suit. The doctor looked up at the disturbance and they were confronted by the king's glare from the canopied bed, his hands pale against the dark fur coverlet. In the shafts of light cast from the two tall windows at the side of the room, Haith could see that the king's cheek and one eye had already coloured black with streaks of red. His lip was sorely split. 'Father?' Robert asked.

'It looks worse than it is,' Henry declared, around his swollen mouth. 'I tripped.' He looked at Haith, daring him to gainsay the lie and Haith merely raised an eyebrow out of sight of the lords. Unobtrusively, he bent to collect the cushions that had been swept from the chest in the king's fall. He placed them on a bench set against the wall.

'Doctor?' Robert demanded.

'The king was in some pain but I have made him comfortable and there is no life-threatening injury here.'

There was a brief silence. 'Thank God!' Stephen declared.

Bishop Henry sank to his knees at the king's bedside and clasped his hands in silent prayer.

'There's no need for fuss,' the king said, 'but, Robert, I will keep to my bed for a few days while the bruising heals.'

'Of course, sire. Stephen and I can deal with the business of the court during your absence. There is no cause to worry over it.' He looked to Stephen who nodded his assent and the king likewise nodded.

'Good.' The king waved a weary hand. 'I'm tired. Withdraw!' he said. Bishop Henry rose from his knees and the lords moved towards the door. 'Not you, Haith,' Henry commanded and Haith turned and moved back to the king's bed, encountering the glares of Waleran and Ranulf as he crossed their paths.

When the doctor and everyone else were out of earshot, Henry contemplated Haith. 'Vultures,' he said.

'They are concerned for your welfare, sire.' Haith moved to the hearth and loaded more logs onto the fire. The afternoon light was beginning to dim and he used the flint hanging at his belt to light the lamp dangling from a chain slung over a beam.

Behind him, he heard Henry snort. 'Only concerned in so far as it impacts on their own welfare, with the exception of Robert, that is. I know that he truly cares for me.'

Haith turned back to the king. 'He does, sire. You look like one of your exotic beasts, Henry, with your face piebald.'

Henry tried to laugh but winced at the movement of his facial muscles.

'Did you tell the doctor that you lost consciousness?'

'I fell and hit my head,' Henry said with determination, and Haith compressed his lips. There was a knock at the door.

Haith opened the door to a messenger. 'An urgent missive from the empress,' the young man told him. Haith took the letter with its red seal from the man's hands, closed the door and took the letter to the king. 'Open it for me, Haith.' The king's hands were shaking still with the trauma of his fall. Haith took the king's letter opener from a side table and slid it under the seal. He handed the opened letter back to the king and watched his face light up. Even beneath the purple and black bruising, Haith could read what Henry's face meant. The king looked up, his eyes dancing, holding the letter as if it were the precious host from an altar. 'She is with child, Haith. At last. She is carrying my heir.'

30

Disturbance

March 1133, Beaumont Palace, Oxford

The king held court at his new palace in Oxford, which he named Beaumont Palace. Haith, with some concern for his own safety, noted the sour presence of Earl Ranulf, who only rarely came to the king's assemblies. The king had recently been building up the power of Alexander, Bishop of Lincoln, with the barely concealed intent of balancing out the grip that Ranulf and his half-brother, William de Roumare, exercised in the north of England. No doubt Ranulf was here to attempt to persuade the king to counteract these policies. The king, though, was, as always, eminently unpersuadable.

'Here is a messenger from Le Mans, sire,' the king's herald announced, fighting to keep excitement from his voice. The buzz in the hall dropped to a sudden, still silence. A message from Le Mans must concern the empress who was due to birth her child. Queen Adelisa slipped a hand over her husband's fingers reassuringly. King Henry reached out and took the ribboned scroll that the messenger proffered. He broke the seal, began to unroll the parchment and read it through at what seemed like an interminably slow rate to everyone watching. Could the letter really be that long? The king rose slowly to his feet, his face giving nothing away.

'My daughter, Empress Maud, sends word that she is safely delivered of a boy child.'

The court erupted in jubilant cries and whoops and Haith joined them. The king and queen's faces were wreathed with irrepressible smiles. Henry and Haith exchanged a delighted nod of acknowledgement. 'Oh, at last,' Mabel breathed softly next to Haith. 'Oh this is good news.' Haith glanced in the direction of Stephen de Blois and Bishop Henry. They wore the same smiles as everyone else but were they sincere? A child of Henry's bloodline, if he lived, knocked away their hopes that the Blois family might step into the breach at the king's death.

There were tears in the king's eyes as he shouted over the cacophony. 'We will celebrate…' With difficulty, the noise and jubilations were hushed and the king announced that there would be a week of celebrations to herald the birth of the new prince. 'He is to be named Henry,' he said, and fell back happily onto his throne shaking Adelisa's hand up and down in his own.

As the king was quitting the hall a little later, he beckoned to Haith. 'Attend me.'

Haith followed Henry to his chamber. They gripped joyful hands together. 'I will cross to Normandy as soon as the weather permits and meet my new grandson,' Henry declared. 'And, Haith, you will go to Wulfric of Haselbury and ask for his prediction for my crossing. I would like to go myself but I am piled to my eyebrows with work I must get done here before I sail. You can go, take him my gifts, and bring back his answer.'

'I will go at once, sire.' These days it was the king's habit to consult with one of his favourite sages before making the Channel crossing. Two years back, the king had nearly been shipwrecked making the crossing. Ever since the sinking of *The White Ship*, each journey between his kingdoms held a little more terror for the king. Reassurance from predictions, relics, and prophecies were all that could calm him adequately to place one foot before another to board a boat.

Before setting off to Somerset, Haith went briefly to his townhouse, intending to pack his saddlebags, since he would likely travel straight from Somerset where he would find the anchorite to meet Henry at the port for the crossing. His steward greeted him at the door with an unaccustomed frown.

'What is it?'

'Sir, we are fairly certain that we had thieves in the house last night.'

'Fairly certain?' Haith raised an eyebrow.

'There was a rumpus that woke a number of us in the middle of the night,' his steward explained. 'We fetched torches and heard someone escaping through the back gate and running away down the lane, but we were too late to catch whoever it was. We've searched, though, sir, and found nothing amiss, so perhaps they were scared off before anything could be taken.'

Haith frowned in his own turn. He gave orders for his packing and the readying of two horses for the journey, and then went to his strongroom. Gisulf's chest was there and at first glance his letter to the king attached to the hasp appeared to have been untouched. However, when Haith handled the letter and hasp more carefully, he could discern signs that the letter's seal had been broken and skilfully replaced with new wax and there were scratches on the lock of the chest suggesting that it too had been interfered with. He lifted the lid of the chest. Nothing had been removed but he was certain that someone had read his letter and very likely had found the three most pertinent letters in Gisulf's chest, which had sat on the top. They were still there, but some unlicensed fingers had sifted here. He turned then to his own casket, sitting on this desk, where he had secreted the letter concerning Amaury and Ida. He could not be certain but he thought that the ordering of things in this casket had also been disturbed although nothing was missing.

It was a two-day journey to Somerset and Haith stopped overnight to rest his horses and his own buttocks at Romsey Abbey. Abbess Wulfyn greeted him warmly, invited him to sit with her at her private dinner in her residence and complained bitterly of all the stone dust being generated by the building work that Bishop Henry had commissioned at the abbey. Haith listened politely and made his excuses as soon as he could, to get some sleep.

Haith had heard the king speak of Wulfric of Haselbury before, but had never met the man in person and was curious to see what he would encounter. A boy fishing in the river pointed towards the church in answer to his enquiry. 'You'll find the hermit on the north side of the church,' he told Haith, in answer to his enquiry, 'like as not sitting in a cold bath wearing chain mail,' the boy smirked, and Haith smiled back. 'Don't offend him, though,' admonished the boy. 'He can give you the paralysis, you know, if you deserve it.'

'I've no intention of offending him,' Haith responded.

Wulfric was not sitting in cold water in chain mail. Instead, he was working on binding a book. The man was gaunt from years of fasting and had alarming, black bags under his eyes from nights without sleep. He was in his early fifties and spoke in a heavy Bristol accent.

Haith greeted Wulfric politely and offered the gift of a splendid prayer book that the king had sent.

'The king needs to know something?' Wulfric asked, desirous of returning to his bookbinding.

'Yes. His daughter has birthed a son, an heir, in Anjou, and the king intends to cross the Channel to greet his new grandson. He asks for your prophecy for his journey.'

Wulfric touched his fingertips together and closed his eyes. Haith contemplated his tonsured head for five minutes or more as the hermit communed with himself, or his God, however it was that he arrived at his prognoses.

'He will go, but he will not come back; or if he does, it will not be safe and sound,' Wulfric pronounced.

Haith stared at him and then repeated the words, aghast. 'He will go, but he will not come back; or if he does, it will not be safe and sound?'

Wulfric nodded calmly. 'You have it.'

'I can't tell him that.'

'Those are my words. That is what he asked for.'

Haith left the cell and put his foot into his stirrup, his heart sinking. What could he tell Henry?

Haith rode into Fareham at dusk. He had left very early in the morning to make the journey in one day, but he wished that he had broken his journey and prolonged it, to give himself more thinking time about how to convey Wulfric's prophecy to the king. He found the king in the hall with Bishop Alexander of Lincoln and Bishop Nigel of Ely, both nephews to Bishop Roger of Salisbury. The court had been at Fareham since May and Haith had already heard from the gossip of his serving man that Henry had been giving numerous benefits to the bishops, including a new bridge at Newark for Alexander. All this munificence, Haith was sure, was intended as a means of controlling and diminishing Earl Ranulf.

'Ah, welcome back, Haith. What does Wulfric say?' Henry asked.

'He says, 'you will go and you will come back, safe and sound.''

Henry smiled. 'All is well, then.'

When he could have private speech with the king, Haith asked, 'I wondered, sire, did you have any interesting bards at court before you left Westminster?'

The king cast his eyes to the decorated ceiling trying to remember. 'Ah, yes!' It came to him suddenly. 'That Welshman was there, who used to be bard to my sister Adela. He is really very good.'

'Breri?' Haith asked.

'I think that's his name, yes. Very talented.' Haith compressed his lips. It was no doubt Breri then who had rifled through his belongings at his townhouse and by now Ranulf, Waleran or whoever he was in pay to would know everything that Haith knew.

At the beginning of August, the king and Haith boarded the ship at Portsmouth, readying to sail. Haith spent a great deal of time wondering at his own lies concerning Wulfric's prophecy and if he would do better to tell the king word for word what the hermit had divined.

'Come look at the sky, my king,' the ship's captain called down the wooden steps to the king's chamber. 'It is extraordinarily strange.'

Haith and Henry made their way rapidly up on deck. A sudden, huge cloud had appeared, turning daylight prematurely to dusk, so that the sailors had to light candles to go about their tasks of preparing the ship for departure. The wind died down entirely. 'The doldrums,' Haith breathed.

'The day darkens over all the land,' the king pointed, his voice trembling.

'Don't look at the sun directly,' Haith told the king. 'The light is too fierce and will burn your eyes.' They stood on the deck with many other members of the court, watching the darkening sky. It was midday and the sun slowly disappeared behind a black disk leaving them plunged into darkness. A priest beside the king voiced a prayer in a low, monotonous tone.

'What does it mean, Haith?' the king asked.

'The evils of men and women are visited upon us,' the priest declared.

'The End of Days?' Henry said, shivering at the sudden loss of the sun's heat as well as its light.

'The sun will return, surely,' Haith murmured.

'I'm glad I'm with you.' The king gripped his arm.

'It will come back,' Haith said firmly. They were all plunged into complete darkness and it was as if the world had stopped completely. There was no birdsong or other sound. It was like the blackness behind closed eyes at night. Haith was aware of Henry standing beside him. He was aware of all the others lining the deck, standing in fearful silence, but he could see nothing. A faint breeze lifted the hair around his ears. 'Yes! See!' the king cried. A sliver of light began to appear at the back edge of the black disc. The disc slowly moved across the face of the sun. There were shouts now all along the ship's side, welcoming the return of the dazzle of light. The return of clarity felt like being reborn, like having one's eyes pinned open to look on the world at the first dawn. Haith turned to smile at the king. There were tears of joy and relief streaming down his face. 'This loss and return of the sun shows how your reign is reborn with the new prince,' Haith said.

Henry clapped him on the shoulder. 'Are you become a prophesying anchorite yourself now, Haith?'

31

Henry FitzEmpress

April 1134, Argentan, Normandy

Haith threw the ball to the red-haired child. 'He is very early to be walking and catching balls,' Ida remarked behind him.

Here, in this small child, was the consequence of the empress's reconciliation with her husband and King Henry's fragile hope for an heir.

'The king says that his grandson is a prodigy and he certainly lives up to that.' Haith had to bend quickly to the left to catch the ball that the boy had returned with a hard but wild throw.

The boy could barely get his chubby arms around the bran-stuffed leather ball, with its colourful woollen pompons, and grew frustrated at his failed attempts. He kicked the ball in anger and the expression on his face swiftly changed to pleased surprise as the ball trickled towards Haith, and his kick was rewarded with a laugh from Haith and Ida.

'Shrovetide football is it?' exclaimed Haith.

'He's going pink in the sun,' Ida said. 'We should take him in.'

Haith nodded, looking at the boy's round, freckled face. 'I have a feeling he won't respond well to that. Give him a few more minutes.'

Haith and Ida had accompanied the king to Argentan to meet

with Empress Maud on her journey to Rouen. But the empress was carrying another child and was unwell. They had remained in Argentan longer than expected to give Maud a chance to recover her strength and the delay had given them all ample opportunity to get to know the prodigy, Henry FitzEmpress. At last, King Henry had his wish: a grandson and an heir of his own direct bloodline.

Haith turned to see the king emerging from the palace, clapping his hands to the child. 'Throw it to me!' he called out, but little Henry showed off his newfound kicking skill instead, losing his balance and falling over backwards. Ida rushed to right him and comfort him but there were no tears and he needed no comforting. Instead he looked furiously at the ground that had unfairly moved beneath his feet and come up to meet him. He screwed up his face and looked down in surprise at the blood starting to ooze from a graze on his knee.

The king laughed. 'Well kicked, darling!'

'I *not* darling! I Henry!' declared the podgy toddler, stamping a foot.

'Indeed, indeed you are,' laughed the king. 'You are Henry.'

A maidservant came out and whispered into Ida's ear and Haith noticed that his sister's expression sobered. 'What is it?' he asked.

'The empress is not well. I will go and see if I can be of assistance.'

Haith frowned as his sister disappeared inside. Empress Maud had been sickening throughout this pregnancy. 'Ida thought the boy was getting a little sunburnt,' he told the king. 'Should we play inside, sire?'

'Oh, yes. No sunburn for my boy. That hurts doesn't it, Henry, and you've already got a poor knee.' The king beckoned the child to him. 'No hurt shall come near you, my darling boy, my darling Henry!' the king amended hastily as the child opened his mouth to express his dissent again at being called anything other than

Henry. He was hale, hearty and strong-willed and they were all in his thrall.

The empress had recovered for long enough to make the ride from Argentan to Rouen but had then taken to her bedchamber again for the last few months of her pregnancy. The midwives plied her with their remedies, trying all and sundry in their efforts to help her regain her strength for the birth. Outside in the courtyard, the women of the household sat under a canopy in the shade of a tree weaving long hours into the evening, taking full advantage of the light. Ida was washing Henry FitzEmpress in a half-tub. A thankless task, reflected Haith, since the boy would be smutted and grubby again minutes after he left the tub. In the meantime, he swirled and splashed and got everything and everyone around him saturated. Laughing and struggling with her slippery, wriggling captive, Ida lifted little Henry from the water and wrapped him in towels on her lap. 'You are a special parcel, a special gift,' she told him.

'I a parcel,' his eyes gleamed mischievously from a gap in the towels.

'You are sweetness in my lap.' He pouted at that. It was too saccharin for his liking. He threw off the towels and ran naked and giggling from Ida. He began to score a picture on the wall with a piece of chalk left by one of the masons. 'Stop that, Henry! You know it is naughty!'

'But I drew a picture of you, Idooo,' he inveigled her and Haith could not help but laugh.

The empress was in long and arduous labour for three days and Haith and the king sat anxiously waiting for news. Ida was amongst the women assisting at the birth. At last, they heard the sound of a baby's cry and the king was able to sigh his relief. 'You have a brother or sister, Henry,' the king told the little princeling, who stood at his knee, playing with a wooden toy horse.

Ida emerged from the bedchamber carrying a swaddled baby and showed him to the king. 'It is a boy, sire.'

'He will be named Geoffrey, after his father,' the king said and angled the swaddled bundle downwards so that his clamouring brother could also see the baby. Both Henrys studied baby Geoffrey. The king smiled but little Henry frowned.

'Where's my mama? I want my mama. She is *my* mama.'

'You will see her soon, Henry,' Ida told him. 'But she is tired and sleeping now.'

Little Henry flung his arms around himself in a sulking gesture and protruded his bottom lip. 'Soon, boy!' The king ruffled his wild, red hair.

Little Henry ran to the far end of the hall galloping his horse in the air. Ida glanced anxiously at Haith and addressed the king again. 'The midwife is concerned for the empress, sire. The birth has gone hard with her and she is sick with fever.'

The king's smiles turned to an expression of concern. 'I will come and sit with her.' He glanced back over his shoulder. 'Keep an eye on little Henry, Haith.'

'Yes, sire.'

Ida and Henry retreated with the new baby and Haith looked back towards Prince Henry. If Maud should die, the king had already laid plans that he would take the boy back to England with him and raise him at his court as his heir, regardless of what the wishes of the boy's father, the Count of Anjou, might be.

32

Portents

November 1135, St-Denis-Le-Ferment, Normandy

While the king remained at Rouen, Haith was happy. Surely the danger in Wulfric's words was related to Henry's return to England? As long as the king stayed in Normandy, Haith persuaded himself that his inaccurate report of the hermit's words was warranted. If the king decided to set sail for England then he would have to wrestle with his own conscience again as to whether or not to give Wulfric's precise sentence to Henry.

Haith entered the hall and was horrified to see Breri sitting at the hearth, tuning his lute. He sat down, at some distance to the bard, next to King Henry who was occupied with a pile of correspondence before him on the trestle. Haith kept an eye on the bard for a while, vaguely aware of Henry shuffling papers. 'Nest!' the king said suddenly, in a tone of disapproval.

Haith looked at Henry in alarm. 'What is it?'

'Bad news from Wales, borne by this bard,' Henry gestured in Breri's direction.

'Bad news?' Haith felt his world begin to tip and placed both his palms flat on the trestle, his arms spread, to steady himself. 'Nest is not ill or …'

'No, no, would that it were as simple as that,' Henry said testily.

Haith took a deep breath. 'What is it, sire?'

Henry said nothing, gathering up the papers into a neat pile and stood with them, slotted firmly under his armpit. 'Nest is in health. We'll talk about it later.' Haith watched Henry's back, as he disappeared up to his solar. He looked back to the bard and encountered Breri's smug gaze.

Henry had had no cause to 'kidnap' his grandson after all. The empress had recovered from her sickbed after the birth of her second son but she had been sorely ill for quite some time. Now that she was recovered, both small princes were back with her and her husband in Anjou, but relations between the king and his daughter and son-in-law grew colder every day. Geoffrey and Maud demanded the castles that the king had offered as dowry but Henry showed no sign of handing them over. 'They all wish me dead before I am so,' the king grumbled. And now what mischief had Breri brought with him over the sea?

In November, the court moved to St-Denis-Le-Ferment, where the hunting was good at this time of year. Haith had left the lodge with the rest of the hunting party early that morning and Ida was alone with the king. She was surprised when King Henry asked her to pass his apologies to the others because he was feeling too unwell to hunt today. The king was usually the most avid of all in the chase, but perhaps the frigid November air was getting to his aging joints and chest. Ida sifted through the correspondence just delivered by the fast courier and passed most of the papers to the king's clerk. One of the letters, however, was addressed to her, and she sat frowning in distress at it.

To my most dear friend, Ida de Bruges, Nest ferch Rhys, Lady of Llansteffan. Ida, I quake to tell you that I have been summoned to attend Lord Richard de Clare at Cardigan Castle and fear that he may have obtained evidence concerning the shining element. He invites me to the betrothal of his daughter, Alice de Clare to Prince Cadwaladr. This is a surprising match but Gwenllian tells me that Cadwaladr is in close allegiance with Ranulf de Gernon, the earl of Chester, who is uncle to Alice de Clare. It seems that Prince Cadwaladr is furthering his own interests in Wales in league with de Gernon. It makes some sense. Sadly, Welshmen have conspired with Normans before now to gain ascendancy over other Welshmen. I am so afraid, Ida, that I might be constrained by de Clare and my sons to live again with my husband, Stephen de Marais, or worse.

By 'the shining element' Nest meant the goldmine and her letter expressed in a roundabout way that she was afraid that she might be accused of helping her brother's cause. Ida looked up with concern in the direction of the king, wondering if and how she could broach Nest's peril to him, but it was not certain that Nest had been exposed and the king would hardly take kindly to the fact that Nest had been supporting her brother treasonously against him in the mining enterprise. Ida would have to wait for more definite news from Nest before attempting to intervene with the king. In any case, the king was not in fine enough fettle himself to be offering help. He had been concerned by a series of what he saw as alarming portents in the sky and had been confined every day for several hours consulting with his astrologer.

The king waved a hand at the clerk who had asked him a question concerning the new batch of correspondence from England. He coughed uncontrollably for many minutes and was unable to speak. Ida tried to suppress her memory of one of Amelina's 'quotes': A dry cough is the trumpet of death. When the coughing finally subsided, the king was alarmingly grey in the face, with lurid red streaks traversing his cheeks. Everything about his appearance, Ida thought, indicated a coming fever. 'Sire,' Ida asked, 'would you be more comfortable abed? Should I send for your physician?'

He nodded and that alone was cause for great concern. The king was usually so robust and not at all given to wallowing in physical aches and ailments as some people did. Ida helped him to stand but he cried out in pain. 'Sire?' Ida asked him in alarm.

'My stomach,' he gasped. 'It's an agony to move, but let's get to it.' He gritted his teeth on the pain as Ida helped him to the bedchamber. 'Send for Archbishop Hugh of Rouen and my son, too, Ida.'

Ida looked at him alarmed. If he wanted the archbishop, he feared for his life. 'Your son, Robert?' she asked and he nodded. 'Tell Haith to take care of Nest, to see that no harm comes to her.' Ida nodded, too alarmed to ask him to expand on what he meant. 'I'm thirsty, very thirsty.'

Ida poured one, then another beaker of water for him and he gulped them down, nodding to her, gasping for breath, and leaning back against the pillows. His colour was still high and his breathing was stressed and rapid. Grimbald, the surgeon, arrived before the return of the hunting party and went into the bedchamber to examine the king.

Ida sat outside waiting impatiently for the surgeon's prognosis. Amelina had said 'An ague or fever at the fall of the leaf is always of long continuance or else is fatal'. Ida was terribly afraid that Amelina's words might come true today. She latched on to another of Amelina's sayings and tumbled it over and over in her head, hoping to ensure its truth through repetition: 'whilst the urine is clear, let the physician beg'.

By the time the doctor emerged from the king's chamber, the huntsmen had returned and Ida had informed her brother of the doctor's visit, along with the other lords of the king's entourage: William de Warenne, Rotrou de Mortagne, Robert of Leicester, and his twin Waleran de Meulan. Grimbald's expression was serious. 'I am sorry to say that the king's situation is grave. Despite a great thirst, he is passing very little urine and his whole body is inflamed. I have seen such symptoms before and they do not auger well.'

The men looked around at each other. 'Should we send word to Thibaut and Stephen de Blois?' Waleran asked. Waleran's estates were principally in Normandy and he belonged to Stephen's faction at court rather than to Maud's.

'The king has sent for his son, Robert of Gloucester,' Ida ventured to tell them. Waleran frowned at her as if she herself had thwarted his intentions.

The earl of Gloucester and the archbishop arrived the following day, together with Bishop Audoin of Evreux, who had always been a good friend of the king's. The king's condition had worsened overnight and he grew less and less responsive. They waited for five more days in a state of decreasing hope of the king's recovery. Robert told the assembled lords that he had written to his sister Empress Maud in Angers to inform her that her father was gravely ill. As the days passed and the king's condition worsened, no reply came from the empress. She was with child again and it was possible that she was unable to travel, or perhaps it was the recent disagreements and petulance between herself and her father that kept her away.

On the sixth day of his illness, Ida sat wringing wet cloths in a bowl and applied them to the king's forehead. She tipped small quantities of water at his mouth as she had been instructed by the doctors. The king's breathing was laboured and he was often confused and wandering in his speech with occasional bursts of his old lucidity that made Ida's heart ache. Ida had told Haith about the king's words concerning Nest, but there had been no good opportunity to discuss them with him. The king beckoned to Robert who knelt at the bedside, his face close to his father's. 'Take 60,000 pounds of silver from the treasury at Falaise to pay the wages of my household and soldiers.'

'Father!' Robert remonstrated, tears on his cheeks.

'I'm going, no use denying it,' the king mumbled. There were long pauses between each phrase as he struggled to find the breath and energy for words. 'Call them all, the barons here. I want to talk to them.' Robert rose and soon the barons shuffled in behind him and circled the bed. Henry waited for them all to be still, to train their eyes on his face and to prick their ears to reach for his strained, hoarse whisper. Even near death, he could command the room. 'When my father died,' Henry said, 'that great king, his body was abandoned and maltreated. I will have you swear that you will not abandon me at my death, but will carry me to Reading Abbey in England for burial, which is my wish.'

'Sire, you will recover,' pleaded Rotrou.

'Swear it,' Henry insisted. And each one of them did so swear. The king closed his eyes, exhausted.

Ida watched Robert look around at the ring of faces. 'You have to ask him, Robert,' Waleran whispered.

Robert took his father's hand, so suddenly white and frail. 'Father,' he asked gently, 'won't you name your successor to us?'

Henry opened angry black eyes upon them all again. 'You have made your oaths to her.' He subsided back into the pillows.

'Which oath does he mean?' hissed Waleran to his twin. 'The oath concerning staying with his body?'

Robert frowned. Waleran and everyone there had heard Henry's words as he had. He meant the oath to his daughter, to the Empress Maud. But Robert's father was dying and Ida saw that he could not, at this moment, in his great grief, argue over the king's still breathing body.

Part Three

1135–1139

'The whole aspect of England presented a scene of calamity and sorrow, misery and oppression… These unhappy spectacles, these lamentable tragedies, were common throughout England… The kingdom, which was once the abode of joy, tranquillity and peace, was everywhere changed into a seat of war and slaughter, devastation and woe.'

33

High Tide

December 1135, Le Bec Hellouin Abbey, Normandy

Ida and Haith travelled through stormy weather with King Henry's funeral entourage to Rouen and then on to the abbey at Le Bec Hellouin. The king had wanted to be buried at Reading Abbey but December was the worst time of year to attempt a crossing of the English channel. They could not pause in Rouen since the repairs to the cathedral after the lightning strike were still going on, and the place was full of masons and stonedust. Henry's body was laid out in Le Bec Hellouin Abbey instead where hundreds of candles lit the dead king's temporary resting place.

Haith had been down at the harbour to assess the weather and water and found no change. He entered the abbey library where he knew he would find Ida, stamped his frozen feet and shook the rain from his cloak and hat.

'How do things look?' asked Ida.

Haith gestured at the window where his sister could see the boughs of the nearby trees being battered by the storm. 'Not sailing weather for some time yet. The ships' captains all say we could be waiting for weeks. A council has been called in Neubourg to discuss the succession so I will travel there tomorrow with

Robert. Will you stay here?'

'Yes. I will stay with Henry.'

While Haith was at the barons' council in Neubourg, Ida and the funeral entourage moved on to Caen and were still waiting there for sailing weather. Haith rode into Caen feeling as glum as the wet, grey weather. He went first to Saint Etienne Abbey where Henry was laid out in an open coffin beneath huge candelabra suspended from chains, and surrounded by monks chanting sonorously. Haith still could not believe that Henry was actually dead. He looked at the altar, desperate to find another lighting place for his eyes than the grim view of Henry, his skin pale greenish, his forcefulness emptied out from the corpse. The sleek, silver curves of two small cruets on the altar held the wine and water. 'A' was incised in the lid of one for aqua and 'V' on the other, for vinum. A nauseated-looking monk flapped a fine flabellum to keep the flies away from the body. The flabellum had a carved ivory handle and a decorated parchment fan. All around them, colourful saints painted on the walls looked down in pity. Haith could no longer resist the urge and raised a hand to pinch his nose and cover his mouth. He was forced to step back from the palpable stench of the coffin. Haith took one last glance at Henry and had to leave, his eyes watering with grief and dismay.

In the cloister, on his way to find Ida, Haith encountered another of the monks. 'With our loss of the good duke, Normandy is become a forest of wild beasts, a brood of vipers, of ravening wolves!' the monk declared, distress writ across his pale, round face.

Haith bleakly nodded his assent to the assessment, feeling aggrieved on Henry's behalf at the chaos. King Henry, his friend Henry, had deserved so much better from his nobles than the treachery he had found at every turn. The barons' council had achieved little to calm the situation in Normandy, and now there was the news from England.

Ida was sitting waiting for him in his chamber and rose swiftly at his entry. 'What's happened, Haith? There are crazed rumours flying that Stephen de Blois has taken the English throne.'

'It's true,' he said bluntly.

'How could this have happened?'

'The assembly at Neubourg offered the duchy and the English crown to Stephen's older brother, Count Thibaut, but the following day news arrived from England of Stephen's imminent coronation and Thibaut acquiesced and withdrew from both.'

'He did not wish to retain Normandy at least? He acquiesced easily?'

'The barons did not want their lands torn between two masters and Stephen sent a substantial financial compensation for Thibaut who has no stomach for war with his brother.'

'But what of the Norman barons' oath to Empress Maud? How could this move to crown Stephen be accomplished so swiftly?'

'Stephen had news of Henry's death and was in Boulogne.'

Haith and Ida exchanged a meaningful look and Ida could not resist voicing their mutual thought. 'He had the news from Waleran?'

Haith nodded. 'Stephen was able to sail immediately for England despite the storms. He was refused entry at Dover by Robert of Gloucester's men, but managed a landing further down coast.'

'What then?'

'Stephen reached his own estates in London and gained the support of the Londoners as the new king.'

'I suppose he is well known in London and England.'

'Yes and Thibaut is not, has rarely set foot there. And many men made their oaths to Henry for Maud but never truly wanted a woman on the throne.'

'Even Bishop Roger, who was regent and held the keys to the royal treasury?'

'Especially him. He and the empress were never allies. Quite the opposite. I suppose that Roger hopes that Stephen will give him preferment, where it is likely that Maud would not have done so. Stephen went from London to Winchester and his brother, Bishop Henry, of course, supported him. Hugh Bigod swore that Henry had changed his mind about Maud on his deathbed and Bishop Roger handed over the treasury keys to Stephen.'

'But Henry did not change his mind on his deathbed!' gasped Ida.

'No,' Haith said. 'Yet Stephen was consecrated and crowned at Westminster the day after Christmas. He is king now.' He smiled wryly. 'At least Henry would have been impressed by such swift, decisive manoeuvring.' Henry would have done this, thought this, was a constant refrain between Haith and his sister. It was so hard to go forward in consciousness of the hole in the entire fabric of the life around them that was left by Henry's absence, by his absolute goneness. Everything felt unmoored.

'I spent some time in Stephen's company when he was a young man,' Ida said. 'I do not see him as good king material.'

Haith shook his head, agreeing.

'But what of the empress and the Count d'Anjou? What of Henry's grandson? Will the Count mount an assault on England to take his wife's crown back from her cousin?'

Haith shook his head again. 'The empress is ill and with child, and Geoffrey will not commit Angevin forces and resources to the attempt. Earl Robert is assessing if he can assemble the money and men another way, but I am not too hopeful of his success. I suspect that his concerns will soon turn to his estates in England and Wales and he may have to make his peace with King Stephen.'

'King Stephen,' echoed Ida in disbelief.

A few days later, the storms abated and the monks sewed Henry's body into an ox-hide in preparation for his last journey across the channel.

34

Food for Wolves

January 1136, Cardigan Castle, Wales

I sat in the cold hall at Cardigan Castle, my breath clouding white around my face, listening to Breri practising his songs for the evening.

'Month of January—smoky is the vale;
Weary the wine-bearer; strolling the minstrel;
Lean the cow; seldom the hum of the bee;
Empty the milk fold; void of meat the kiln;
Slender the horse; very silent the bird;
Long to the early dawn; short the afternoon.'

The new year dawned grim for me at Cardigan where Richard de Clare compelled me to live again with my husband, Stephen de Marais, because he suspected that I was aiding the Welsh rebels. And the cold new tide of 1136 brought with it news of the death of the king in Normandy. Despite everything, I had loved Henry. In a different way to Haith and to Gerald. Henry was not a good man as they were, but he was a great one. Brief and, afterwards, bitter as our affair had been, it had resonated through my whole life.

Breri looked up at me and took a sip of wine. He set his wine down again and returned to retuning his instrument. His well-fleshed fingers looked too big to pick out such delicate notes from the lute.

'I heard a crane that cried out on a pond
far from dwelling places.
That which may not be listened to fell silent.'

'Your song is exquisite,' I told Breri, wondering how beauty and brutality could be so combined in one man. I wanted to tell him that he would do better to stick to song and stay out of the vicious politics around us, but perhaps murder and treachery were at least as, or more, part of who he was as the beautiful melody of his poetry.

My son Maurice visited at Cardigan each week and brought news of the goings on at Llansteffan. Through Maurice, I heard of Henry's body waiting for a month in Caen to cross the channel and then progressing to Reading Abbey, and we heard that Stephen de Blois had taken the throne. 'Better that than the empress,' Maurice said.

'Why do you say so?'

'A king must needs be a warrior.'

'And you do not think a woman can be a warrior?' I thought of everything I had fought through since my father had been slain.

Maurice smiled and shook his head.

I sat over my needlework, sighing. My husband had instructed that I must keep to my chambers and the hall and with the exception of Maurice's occasional visits and news, I was bored with inaction and confinement.

'Any news from Westminster?' Amelina asked anxiously for the umpteenth time.

I shook my head. 'Nothing yet.' Amelina picked up a pile of linens to take downstairs. Richard de Clare had gone to

Westminster to speak with King Stephen. He had a signed confession from one of the men belonging to my brother who had been captured and tortured. The confession asserted that I was involved in the goldmining operation at Dolaucothi on behalf of my brother and had committed treason against the crown. I told de Clare that the confession was false witness, but he did not believe me. He would be in Westminster now, showing the confession to the new king, discussing what to do with me and my brother. With Henry gone, I had no protection. Before de Clare went to court, his men had taken me under armed escort from Llansteffan to Cardigan, where de Clare handed me over to the custody of my husband. When we arrived in the hall at Cardigan, I was miserable to see my youngest son, FitzStephen, sitting amongst his friends, staring at me. I regretted that he, that any of my sons, must witness my disgrace. But, I reminded myself, lifting my chin, I was a princess of royal blood fighting for the rights of my disinherited brother, King Gruffudd. With Henry gone, any ambiguity I had felt on naming Gruffudd king in my own mind was evaporated.

As we entered, de Marais stood and looked me up and down. My hands had been tied by the soldiers with a leather strap and I had no choice but to hold them before me. 'Lady Nest is accused of acts of treason,' de Clare stated in a loud voice and the hubbub of chatter and clattering around the hall stilled and silenced. I tried to look reassurance in the direction of my son's white face. 'De Marais, you will take charge of her while I travel to court and speak on the matter with the king.'

De Marais looked appalled. 'But I have no wish to take her up again as wife,' he exclaimed.

'I'm not asking you to bed the woman,' de Clare retorted, 'just to keep her in custody until I return with the king's decision on her punishment.'

'Ah, that I can do,' de Marais declared. Despite being kept in close confinement at Cardigan, I knew that my older sons, Henry and William, were working on my behalf with their lawyers and that was my only hope. I was glad, at least, to have the company of FitzStephen.

I looked up from the needlework in my lap and smiled at Maurice's arrival on the threshold. He stepped aside to allow Amelina to pass on her way out, her arms full of linens. 'Mother! Are you well today?' He came forward into the room.

I smiled and lied and he took a seat beside me. We had not been talking long, when we heard Amelina's steps as she ran back up the stairs. It was rare these days for her to engage in such a burst of action and I swallowed at the thought of what might have occasioned it. Was it the news come at last from Westminster? Might I suffer now a much worse incarceration as a consequence of my treason, or might this usurper king have ordered my execution? Amelina burst into the chamber. 'There's been a big battle fought and the Welsh have won it!'

'What are you talking about?' demanded Maurice.

'It's all over the castle. You should come down, my lady, to hear it. Can she?' she asked Maurice.

He nodded, shamefaced to be my gaoler. 'It seems an extraordinary occasion,' he said.

In the hall, I curled my lip at the sight of Breri but listened intently, nevertheless, with everyone else to the news he carried and was reporting to de Marais. 'The Battle of Llychwr was fought between Loughor and Swansea on the Common of Carn Coch. Hywel ap Maredudd led a Welsh army against five hundred Normans.' This Hywel was a prince of Powys and a cousin of Owain who had abducted me years before. 'All five hundred of those Normans are food for wolves now. Left on the field to rot and be torn at. And the Welsh are victorious.' The Normans in the room exchanged looks and words of disbelief. Maurice suggested that they send out a scout to verify the facts of this report and de Marais saw to it that a man was dispatched.

Breri sat down to compose while we waited for more news.

'Listen, O little pig! don't sleep yet!' he sang, making the children laugh, but the rest of his song was more bleak,

'Rumours reach me of perjured chieftains.
And tightfisted farmers.
Soon, over the sea, shall come men in armour
On armoured horses, with destroying spears
When that happens, war will come,
Fields will be ploughed but never reaped.
Women will be cuckolds to the corpses of their men.'

'Can't you find something more pleasant to sing to us, bard!' de Marais snapped at him, which only made Breri, perversely, dig deeper into his repertoire of gruesome narratives of war. The scout returned later in the day with confirmation that the initial report was true. The Welsh had, at last, achieved a victory against the Normans, and, perhaps, I thought to myself, my goldmine had helped them to do it.

De Marais was too distracted to notice that I had broken the bounds of my confinement and said nothing about my presence in the hall. However, just before the evening meal was due to start, Amelina bent close to my ear. 'My lady, there is one who needs urgent speech with you in your chamber.' I rose and moved as inconspicuously as possible to the stairwell, with Amelina on my heels.

In my chamber I was greeted by the extraordinary sight of a giant of a Welsh man armed to the teeth with a small child in each arm. 'I let him in the postern gate and nobody's seen him,' Amelina told me.

The man set the two small boys who were around five and three years old on their feet in front of me. 'Princess Nest?'

'Yes.'

'I am the guardian of these princes,' he told me, 'and am bid by

Queen Gwenllian to bring them to you. The queen asks that you give her small boys shelter, my lady.'

'Of course. I will.' If Gwenllian was calling herself queen then she and my brother were in hopes of regaining the kingdom. These were her two youngest sons. I gestured to the boys to approach me. Slowly, looking over their shoulder at the warrior who was familiar to them despite his formidable appearance, they came nearer. I knelt beside them. 'Maredudd and Rhys?' They nodded and Rhys smiled. I saw that he had my dimples. 'I am your Aunt Nest and you will be safe here with me. We shall play some good games together?' They gazed at me with uncertainty. The warrior took a deep breath of relief.

'What news of my brother?' I asked the warrior, quietly.

'King Gruffudd has hastened with his army to meet with the Gwynedd princes, Owain and Cadwaladr, with the news of the Welsh victory. His sons Anarawd and Cadell have gone with him.' Owain was King of Gwynedd now in all but name since his father was decrepit and the oldest brother, Cadwallon, had been killed by his uncle and cousins in vengeance for his killing of their kin.

'His army,' I echoed softly. The gold had done its job then and prepared him for this moment. The Welsh were rising up to throw off the yoke of Norman rule. I quaked at the thought. On both sides I had dear ones at risk—my sons, my brother, my nephews. 'Where are the rest of the family? Their mother?' I asked quietly. He stayed tight-lipped. 'You think I would betray her?' I asked astonished.

'We will hear news soon enough,' he said.

'You may go,' I told the warrior, 'Gwenllian's children are safe with me. I will guard them with my life.'

I instructed Amelina to keep Maredudd and Rhys out of sight in my chamber. I did not want the Normans in the castle, especially my husband, to know of their presence and to think of using them as hostages. I decided I had had enough of keeping to my chamber and returned to the hall. Maurice had been speaking with de Marais and turned to me with a pleased look on his face. 'Maurice de Londres is leading warriors now to put down this rebellion. It will soon be quelled.'

I made no response and saw his pleased look falter. For a moment he had forgotten that I was the enemy. We turned as the door to the great hall opened, blowing in a gust of leaf-loaded wind. I was astonished to see Haith and Ida entering. This was a day for astonishment it seemed, after so many long days of nothing and waiting. Ida rushed to embrace me and Haith gave me a civil greeting. 'We looked for you first at Llansteffan,' she said.

'Come to my chamber and we can catch up with our news. Both?' I asked Haith tentatively, thinking he might spurn the invitation, but he nodded and followed us up the stairs. Amelina made us all comfortable with beakers of wine and had a servant stoke up the fire. Maredudd and Rhys sat on the hearth rug playing with a few wooden toys that Amelina had found for them. The boys stared openly at the newcomers.

'Nest! What's happened?' Ida asked. 'Why are you here?'

'I am under house arrest,' I replied, trying to make light of it. 'Richard de Clare has accused me of supporting the rebels and has ridden to the king to make judgement against me. In the meantime, my husband is my jailer.'

Haith took a deep breath. 'De Clare has evidence against you that he is taking to the king?'

'One of Gruffudd's men was tortured and signed a statement that I was involved in backing the goldmining operation at Dolaucothi on behalf of my brother, to arm my brother.'

'And were you?'

I did not reply. Ida wrung her hands. 'What can be done, Haith?'

'I don't know. All is changed now, with Henry gone. The king asked me to take care of you, Lady Nest, when he was on his death bed, to ensure that no harm came to you.'

'He spoke the words to me, Nest. He wanted you to be safe.' Ida said.

'My sons are talking with lawyers. They hope to make the argument with the king that a man may say anything under torture,' I told Haith.

He nodded but his worried expression showed that he had little hope of the success of this argument.

Ida told me about Henry's death, their journey through Normandy and across the channel with Henry's body and his burial at Reading. 'Robert of Gloucester has given his fealty to Stephen de Blois after all. We thought he would support his sister, the empress, but his estates here in England and Wales would have been forfeit if he had done so, once Stephen took the crown, so …' Ida shrugged.

'It's possible we could sue to King Stephen for your pardon via Mabel and Robert, if it comes to that,' Haith said.

I nodded. The thought had crossed my mind.

'Henry de Blois, the new king's brother is a rum one,' Ida remarked.

'How do you mean?'

'He took the relic of Saint James's hand that the empress gave to Reading Abbey back to Winchester with him, for safekeeping, he said. Henry would have been distressed if he knew that.'

We were silent for a moment at the recognition that Henry would never know anything again. 'It's impossible to imagine him gone,' I said. He had been so loud, stubborn, certain, reassuring, carrying us all relentlessly forward. Now, there was a void where he should be. It felt as if the tide had washed out and, then, forgotten to make its crashing return to the shore, leaving it forever silent, empty, and still. Ida put an arm around my shoulder. 'We will miss the king and I fear that his kingdoms will feel his loss in these coming times.'

'Stephen's wife Matilda de Boulogne has been crowned

queen,' Haith said. 'King David of Scotland and Earl Robert of Gloucester, who were likely to be the empress's most staunch supporters have signed Stephen's coronation charter at Oxford. And the Pope has confirmed Stephen as king.'

'It's fixed then, final.'

Maurice entered and exchanged greetings with Haith and Ida. 'I have some good news for you, Mother. De Marais has given me leave to take you back to Llansteffan. There is a Welsh army reported gathering on the Gwynedd border, likely to march on the Ceredigion castles and he thinks you would be safer away from Cardigan.'

Did de Marais really think I would be safer away from here, or less of an evident symbol to fight for in an attack on Cardigan. 'Good,' I said, but grimaced at the thought of the coming conflict. 'Let's get ready to leave quickly, Amelina.'

'Do you think Llansteffan is any safer than Cardigan?' Haith asked Maurice. 'There are armed Welsh bands everywhere and they may try an attack at Llansteffan too.'

'I think if I am there they will not attack,' I said.

Haith shook his head. 'I'm not sure.'

'Whatever the case of it, Haith. I would rather be away from here.' They all knew that I meant away from de Marais.

'Who's this?' Maurice asked, pointing at his little cousins.

'A friend's children I am taking care of,' Amelina responded quickly. 'We will take them with us.'

I nodded complicitly to Amelina. We needed to get Gruffudd's sons away from Cardigan before my husband or any of the other Normans realised who they were and thought to use them as hostages.

35

Queen Gwenllian

May 1136, Llansteffan Castle, Wales

I was relieved to be home again at Llansteffan, to have the added reassurance of Ida's return to my household and knowing that Haith was nearby at Pembroke. Looking after Maredudd and Rhys was a pleasant distraction from the worry about what the new king would decide on my case and what was happening in the countryside with the Welsh uprisings. Once we were all safely at Llansteffan, I took the risk of explaining to Maurice who Maredudd and Rhys were. He looked at me askance for my deception, but I did not think he would betray his cousins, such little boys, to mistreatment.

'Nest!' Amelina's cry interrupted a complex Welsh melody that I was in the middle of singing with Maurice, Maredudd, and Rhys. My nephews were amusing themselves with making their older cousin dust off his rusty Welsh, and their charm had won over his reluctance. 'You must come quickly!' Amelina declared, her face anxious as she gripped the edge of the door to the great hall.

'What is it?' I moved to stand beside her and look out onto the courtyard. A man was riding in, half-hanging from his horse. 'It's William,' we chimed together, recognising him at the same moment. I sprinted out to catch him as he slid from the saddle.

'Maurice! We need your help with your brother!' Maurice and his cousins had followed us to the door of the hall, and he ran to assist us. Between Maurice, Amelina, and I we aided William from his frothing horse. William's clothes were smeared with blood and the muck of a hard ride. His legs buckled when his feet reached the cobbles. Maurice called one of the soldiers over who was standing staring at the commotion in the courtyard. Together, they carried William into the hall and set him on a fur, close to the hearth. Amelina bustled up the stone staircase to fetch her medicines from my chamber.

'Are you injured?' Memories of Gerald injured and dying flashed through my mind. William looked like his father.

'Just exhausted,' he groaned.

'Help me strip off his armour,' I told Maurice but Ida moved Maurice aside and aided me instead. Amelina bathed William's face and torso and we found no serious injury beyond scrapes and bruises.

'What's happened, William?'

'I have much news, Mother. When I can catch my breath.'

'You should sleep, rest,' Amelina told him.

'There is time for that later,' he replied, 'now I must be unburdened.' He looked to where Maredudd and Rhys were playing at the other end of the hall. 'They are Gwenllian's children?' he asked me. I nodded. 'Of course they are,' he smiled. 'The little one has the look of her. Good. They are out of earshot.'

I began to panic. 'Has something happened to my brother? Tell me quickly, William.'

'No, it's not Gruffudd. It's Gwenllian.'

'What of her?' asked Maurice.

William took my hand and his own were shaking. 'Mother, I am sorry to have to tell you that Gwenllian is dead.'

'Dead?'

'She led an army against Kidwelly Castle, against Maurice de

Londres.'

'An army?' I was bewildered.

'It's true.' William nodded his head. 'I fear that my cousins Morgan and Maelgwyn died with her.'

'No.' Amelina and I looked wildly at each other. 'You are sure of it?'

'Yes.'

'Have you come from Kidwelly?' I asked. 'Did you fight against them?'

'No, not from there. I have come from another fight. But Gwenllian has become the battle cry for the Welsh rebels. I heard of it from them.'

'My brother will be devastated.' I looked across at Maredudd and Rhys again. I would have to stand as their foster-mother now.

'What fight have you come from, William?' asked Maurice.

'I went with Richard de Clare to Westminster, Mother.'

I raised my eyebrows.

'I thought there was a chance that if there was serious risk to you, I might be able to treat directly with King Stephen on your behalf.'

I squeezed his hand.

'Did de Clare present his accusation against mother?' Maurice asked.

'Yes, but the king is much distracted with the business of the realm. He agreed with de Clare that you should be stripped of your lands, of Llansteffan, and that they should come into de Clare's possession. De Clare asked for much more besides but the king did not grant it and he was not pleased at de Clare's overreaching in his requests.'

'What does the king order regarding Lady Nest herself?' Ida asked.

'He ordered that you should be returned to the custody of de Marais to do as he saw fit and de Clare was of a mind that you should be imprisoned. Fully imprisoned,' he grimaced. 'In a dungeon, Mother.'

Amelina gasped. 'We have to make a run for it then! To the mountains, Nest.'

William held up a hand. 'Wait, Amelina, before you go rushing into any mountains. Wait for the end of my story.'

'Well get on with it then,' she told him.

I exchanged fond smiles with my sons at Amelina's impatience. 'There is no need to run,' William said, 'De Clare is dead.'

'What! How?' exclaimed Maurice.

'We were riding back near Abergavenny. I was thinking to send word to you to do exactly what Amelina has suggested. '

Amelina made a smug noise and crossed her arms.

William continued. 'De Clare was worried about me and kept a close eye on me but I thought there would be an opportunity, sooner or later, to send a surreptitious messenger. We were ambushed as we rode through a woody tract rightly called the Ill-way of Coed Grano. A Welsh war band came at us yelling "For Queen Gwenllian".'

I saw Rhys look over in our direction. He had heard his mother's name. How would I tell them the terrible news that their mother was gone?

'There was a rain of arrows,' William continued. 'Many of the men went down with that first piercing blizzard and did not even have time to draw swords. De Clare and I got to the trees, and then had to fight hand to hand. They overwhelmed us. There were too many of them. They asked us who we were and we gave our names. They killed de Clare on the spot. The king's writ against you died with him, Mother.'

I stared at him. 'They spared you?'

'They spared me because I was your son.'

'Who were they?'

'The men leading the war band told me they were Iorwerth and Morgan ap Owain, the grandsons of Caradog ap Gruffudd of Gwent.'

'Gwent,' I echoed. 'The Welsh are rising everywhere, all around us.'

William nodded. 'They are.'

'What do you mean the king's writ died?' Ida asked.

'It was in de Clare's scrip. I took it from his body and I burnt it as soon as I was away from the Welsh warriors. They rode with me through the mountains and cut me loose near Carmarthen.'

I looked into his eyes and squeezed his hand again. My sons were not fully Norman then, after all. William glanced at Maurice who told his brother, 'This was well done, William.'

'Will you join the Welsh?' I asked them both earnestly. 'Join the rebellion.'

They looked at each other. 'I won't do that, Mother,' William asserted. 'I can't, but by the same token, I won't see you suffer if I can help it.'

'My position is the same as my brother's,' Maurice concurred.

'Your troubles are not over with, though, Mother. The king will have written about the accusation against you to the royal justice, Pain FitzJohn, who is due to visit Pembroke later this year. I expect it will come up again when he arrives.'

'Well, then,' I declared, 'we will tackle it if it does. And, in the meantime,' I said heavy-hearted and glancing again in the direction of Rhys and his brother, 'I must find words to tell them that their mother will not return for them.'

36

Crug Mawr

October 1136, Llansteffan Castle, Wales

I slid my finger over the intricate carving of the tableman, waiting for Maredudd to make his next move on the board. For a six-year-old he had a good grasp of the game and was giving me a fair fight. His brother, four-year-old Rhys, was sitting next to me. I showed him the carving in the disk of walrus ivory, which depicted a cat looming over and about to attack a rat, its fierce claws extended. I would do all in my power to protect these two boys—as long as I had any power myself.

My own situation was parlous. I had been worried towards the beginning of July when we heard that the royal justiciar, Pain FitzJohn, was heading towards Carmarthen to relieve the Norman garrison who were being besieged by Welsh forces. We expected FitzJohn to go from Carmarthen to Pembroke and then it was likely that I would be called to answer to the charge of treason that Richard de Clare had laid against me, which would now be taken up by his successors. I was like the cowering rat in the sights of the stalking cat on my tableman. My sons counselled that I should flee to Ireland and I made preparations for it, but then news came that FitzJohn had been ambushed by Welsh warriors and died from a javelin blow to the head.

Another fortuitous death had saved me. These ambushes were the favoured method deployed by our Welsh warriors who knew the mountainous, forest terrain much better than the Norman occupiers.

When the early summer flowers were in bloom, I took Maredudd and Rhys to visit the field below Kidwelly Castle where Gwenllian, Morgan, and Maelgwyn had died. We stood on the steep scarp overlooking the Gwendraeth Fach and looked up at the formidable earth and timber ringwork fortification that Gwenllian had attacked. Its landward side, which we had ridden past on our way here, was protected by a crescent-shaped earthwork with a wooden palisade. Inside the wall, the great hall was built in stone. I led Maredudd and Rhys to a spring on the hillside and we laid three bunches of flowers in memory of their mother and brothers, my sister and nephews. 'We cannot linger here,' I told them and we walked with grieving hearts back to our horses for the short ride to Llansteffen.

Unrest and skirmishes were everywhere. Rumours flew that my brother was returning towards Cardigan at the head of a great Welsh army, together with Owain and Cadwaladr, the princes of Gwynedd, and they were intent on avenging the deaths of Gruffudd's wife and sons. A messenger had just come from Pembroke to warn us that the Welsh and Norman armies were likely to join battle today, somewhere near Cardigan.

The weather had turned chill and Amelina ordered the servants to stoke up the fire in the hall. I sat near the hearth, hoping that this game of tables could distract me from my anxiety. I moved my skirts aside for the servants to carry the logs in and place them close to the fire. Amelina sighed, sat down beside me and took my hand. She knew what I suffered with this waiting. She had been there at the births of all my sons who were now, almost all, in mortal danger. Henry, William, and Maurice had all gone to join the Norman forces preparing to defend Cardigan, and FitzStephen was in the castle too, though I hoped too young for fighting. Ranged against my sons, were my brother and their older cousins, Anarawd and Cadell. I would surely lose someone this day and perhaps all.

'Stop thinking about it,' Amelina said.

'How can I stop?'

She bent to the small table beside her and poured one of her medicines into a beaker of wine. 'Drink this.'

'No!' I pushed the beaker away. 'I want none of your tinctures. If I am to lose a son, a brother, a nephew this day, I want to feel it.' It was my lot to wait at home in anguish whilst my kin fought each other in bitter and bloody battles. I had already lost Gwenllian, Morgan and Maelgwyn. 'Must I look on the young faces of my sons and nephews, pushing a shroud from their foreheads to give them my last kiss?' I sobbed.

'Stop it, Nest. You're frightening Maredudd and Rhys,' Amelina hissed in my ear.

She was right and I tried to get a grip on myself. 'I cannot bear the waiting,' I said in a low voice, fighting for calm after my outburst.

My steward pushed the doors open a sliver, ducked his head in briefly to call to me: 'Norman warriors in the bailey, my lady.' My heart plummeted. 'Keep Maredudd and Rhys out of sight in my chamber. Quickly!' I hissed to Amelina, bundling Rhys into her arms. She moved swiftly towards the stairs, with Maredudd trotting at her heels. I wiped my cheeks with the sleeve of my gown. My thoughts flashed to another troop of Norman warriors here. A troop who had burned Llansteffan to the ground and beheaded my teenage brother Goronwy on the beach, maimed my brother Hywel soon after he was born. I rose and walked to the door where I recognised Alice of Chester, the widow of Richard de Clare, dismounting. She was surrounded by the big destriers of her escort. They must have come from Cardigan Castle.

'Oh Nest!' She flew to embrace me. 'Will you give us shelter to rest our horses for a short while?' Her distressed face was streaked with soot. Her usually immaculate dress was hastily thrown on and wrongly laced. She had no maid or female companion with her.

'Of course. What has happened, sir?' I asked a tall, broad man who shouldered his way through the others to head the group.

'This is Miles of Gloucester. Nest ferch Rhys, wife of *de Marais*,' Alice said with an emphatically meaningful tone aimed at him.

'Ah, yes, I recall you, sir,' I said. 'We were married alongside each other in Cardigan many years ago, were we not?'

He nodded. 'Indeed, we were. My lady,' he gave me a bow.

'Please come and take refreshment.' I gestured to my steward who busied himself with giving orders to look to the needs of my guests and their mounts. The horses' sides and mouths frothed with the sweat of extreme exertion.

'We have suffered a defeat, Nest!' Alice exclaimed before we had got far past the threshold.

I suppressed my urge to scream questions concerning my kin at them and, instead, led them to the trestle on the dais where my servants provided fresh water and towels to wash their hands, a beaker of strong wine and a hunk of new baked bread. 'I would know what has happened to all my kin,' I said to Miles in as sedate a voice as I could find.

'Your brother, my lady, has driven a Norman army from the battlefield at Crug Mawr.'

I tried to keep the joy from my face at his words, yet my joy also did war with my anxiety. 'This news had not yet reached us here,' I said slowly, as if my own slow speech might fend off hearing who had died.

'Ceredigion was invaded by the Princes of Gwynedd—Owain and Cadwaladr—and by your brother Gruffudd ap Rhys,' Gloucester reported. 'They took five castles including Aberystwyth and attacked Cardigan Castle, where I rescued this lady.'

'The Welsh warriors yell, "vengeance for Gwenllian!" as they run at the walls,' Alice told me, her eyes wide. 'Oh it was so terrible, Nest! The town has been burnt to cinders. We had to wade the river because the bridge collapsed with the weight of so many fleeing. The bodies of horses and men clogged the Teifi that ran red with gore. I saw skulls cleft with battle axes. Heads kicked and thrown, as if in a game of Shrovetide ball!' She turned white with nausea at her own description.

'Please, sir,' I begged, despairing that I would get much sense from Alice, 'I have many loved ones on either side of this conflict. Will you tell me what you know and quickly.'

He nodded. 'I understand. I am very sorry to tell you that your husband, Stephen de Marais, died in the conflict. He fought most bravely.'

'And my son Robert FitzStephen who was with my husband?'

'He's fine,' Alice burst out. 'The boy is safe inside the castle. Your husband would not allow him to go outside the walls. Don't worry. I saw him quite safe, Nest.'

But left him there, I thought. I tightly smiled my thanks to her. 'Can you tell me more, of the others?' I tried to keep my voice level as I addressed Miles of Gloucester.

'The Norman forces were led by Baldwin de Clare and Robert FitzHarold of Ewas. I arrived too late for the battle but rescued Lady de Clare instead and will take her to safety in England.'

'My sons?' I whispered.

'They were all there, Nest! You would have been proud to see them sallying against those Welsh savages.'

Gloucester was eyeing Alice, astonished that she showed no awareness that I was myself a Welsh savage. 'They all live,' he told me quickly. 'Henry de Normandy, William and Maurice FitzGerald? These are your sons, I believe?'

'Yes.'

'They fought bravely at the battle and have retired to Carew. I believe William took a small wound on his arm but it did not look serious.'

I swallowed. I could hardly believe it. 'Thank you. I am grateful for your information. And my brother and nephews?'

'This Gruffudd, the leader of the attackers, is her brother you know,' Alice inserted, giving Gloucester needless information. 'We can hardly be expected to give you news of the enemy, Nest! You are not safe here. You must flee with us.'

I looked at her with exasperation. I needed to have speech with Gloucester alone. 'Countess, you look in need of the attentions of a maid. Might I arrange that for you?'

She looked down at her dress and reddened. 'I had to get up in the middle of the night, in the dark. My maid was nowhere to be found.'

'Was she Welsh?' I asked quietly and I noticed that Gloucester smirked on the side of his face that was not visible to her.

'Yes, she was,' Alice said, knitting her brow.

I gestured to one of my maids and whispered in her ear in Welsh. 'Take Lady Alice to the *back* chamber,' I said with emphasis, not wanting my visitors anywhere near Maredudd and Rhys. She nodded her understanding to me. 'Susanna will assist you, Alice.' Susanna dipped a curtsey and led Alice from the hall. We watched them go and Gloucester turned back to me. I had deduced that he was a man of intelligence who had the measure of the situation and realised, therefore, that I could not be entirely trusted.

'Your brother and his two sons were not injured in the battle or the assault on Cardigan Castle. To my knowledge they are well.'

I breathed a deep sigh of relief and made no attempt to conceal it from Gloucester. 'I thank you for this information.'

'You have a hard job of it, my lady, with warriors ranged on either side. I cannot envy you that.'

I nodded my agreement with his words. 'Has the castle fallen?' I felt anxiety again for FitzStephen.

'No, my lady. Robert FitzMartin defended the castle and it has held against the … against the Welsh army.'

'Will you and Lady Alice stay overnight and rest before you journey on?'

'You are kind and I thank you, but no. I will get the lady to safety and have no way of knowing what is upon my heels. Do you wish to accompany us?'

'No.' I did not bother to elaborate on or soften my refusal and he accepted it in the same vein.

'This castle is Norman garrisoned, I believe.'

'Yes. My son, Maurice, commands here.'

'He will, no doubt, return soon.'

I nodded my agreement. 'I have one more question I would ask you, sir.'

He raised his eyebrows.

'The sheriff of Pembroke is a good friend of mine, Haith de Bruges. Do you know if he fought? How he fares?'

'There were no forces from Pembroke in the fighting. The sheriff is still safely inside Pembroke, to my knowledge. Won't you come with us, Lady Nest? There is likely to be more fighting in this vicinity.'

I shook my head. 'This is my land and my place.'

37

The Princes of Deheubarth

December 1136, Dinefwr Castle, Wales

Haith's hands were freezing, despite his gloves. His toes too. His hair was stiffened with ice. It was a freezing winter and he had been in the saddle for six hours on the journey from Pembroke. It was a long ride for a man in his sixties, but he had not wanted to stop anywhere on the way and explain his excursion to a curious host. His old battle wounds ached with the cold, especially his shoulder where he had taken an arrow on the road from Cardiff, close to the Tywi. Nest had saved his life that day. Snow lay heavy on the trees and fields and dripped cold onto his shoulders whenever it got the chance. Snow in sunshine could be a fine sight, but it was a darkening, grey day, and Haith felt oppressed by the weather and by the uncertainty of what he was riding towards.

Dinefwr was visible now. The rough wooden ringfenced compound stood high on the ridge above the expanses of the Towy valley floodplains that he rode through. Three smoke trails rose from hearths inside the compound. Gruffudd ap Rhys and his family had taken up residence here but it looked, as yet, to be a hasty, ephemeral structure. Haith's horse laboured up the steep incline towards the gates and, as he neared, he could see that the place was heavily guarded. Nest had written to invite him to spend Christmas here with her, and with his sister and son. It was an olive branch from her and one that he was not going to spurn. But, as a Norman sheriff, Haith had good cause to feel anxious anticipation at passing under the lintel of this Welsh enclave.

He had a gift of a fine knife in his saddlebag for the boy, for his son. There were small, jewelled and filigreed brooches for Amelina and Ida, and a shimmering girdle decorated with gold and gems for Nest. He had more small gifts for the family of his host and Lady Isabel had gifted him four bottles of good wine that were also filling out his saddlebags.

'This should earn you some kind of welcome, Haith,' she smiled. 'I'm sorry you won't be with us for the Christmas feast at Pembroke.' She had frowned at him, perplexed at his journey.

It had been difficult to explain the invitation, since he could name neither Ida nor his son as reason. He was forced to lie and give an unlikely excuse about previously unheard of Flemish relatives and the king's orders, when everyone knew that King Stephen's writ was running rather thin in Wales now. Isabel looked at him askance, but asked no further questions. Her husband was away attending on the king, but she would be safe enough in Haith's absence behind the impregnable walls of Pembroke Castle. Few Welsh tenants had paid their taxes on the last collection day and they were very likely paying tribute instead to Nest's brother. The returns that Haith could send on to King Stephen's coffers had been thin pickings. Haith continued to undertake his duties as sheriff as best he could but the machinery of Henry's administration was grinding to a halt. That part of Haith's life would soon be done with, buried with Henry and he did not know what came next.

Once past the guards at the gateway who had been surly but expected him, he found the courtyard deserted. The inclement weather must be keeping everyone inside. Haith grimaced again at his aches and pains as he dismounted and limped his way towards the stables, leading his exhausted horse. Here, at last, he found signs of life. There was a boy seated on a haystack and Haith commanded him to see to the horse. The boy told him in Welsh that he was a fewterer, not a groom and Haith would have to make shift for the horse himself. Haith resisted the urge to clout the boy. It would not do to raise any hackles here. So he made shift, finding a haynet and water and relieving his stallion of his heavy accoutrements. He rubbed him down, checked his hooves, unrolled a blanket, and slung it over the horse's back. 'Where is everyone?' he asked the boy in his poor Welsh and had to repeat the question three times before the boy decided to understand him and give him an answer.

'In front of the fire.'

'And you?' Haith asked. 'Why aren't you there?'

The boy indicated a box at his feet and Haith peered inside at a litter of six mastiff puppies. 'Looking after these,' the boy stated, shivering.

'Ah, I see.' Haith took the thick bearskin cloak from his shoulders and held it out to the boy, who widened his eyes in disbelief and did not take it at first. 'Take it,' Haith shook it towards the boy, 'but I want it back, mind, for my return journey.'

The boy, grateful at last, pointed out the door to the hall—one of the least ramshackle, wooden buildings in the compound. 'In there, Master. Those big doors.'

Haith pushed at one side of the door with his shoulder. It opened complaining on unoiled hinges and just enough to allow him to squeeze in. To Haith's surprise the hall was full. He shouldered the door closed again behind him. Ten trestles ran the length of the space, all fully occupied with men, women, and children squeezed close together. At the far end, on the raised dais, Nest lifted a hand to him. With his loaded saddlebags in hand, he started down the hall but an enormous Welshman stepped in front of him, speaking angrily in Welsh and pointing at Haith's sword. Haith gestured apologetically and transferred both saddlebags to one hand, to slowly draw his sword from its scabbard and lay it to one side of the door. All eyes were fixed upon him as he did so. He noticed that there were no other weapons set at the threshold and that other men seated at the trestles were wearing their armoury at their hips.

Nest's brother, Gruffudd ap Rhys, rose to greet him and Nest smiled warmly in welcome. 'I'm so glad that you decided to come, Haith,' she said. 'Be welcome.' Haith exchanged a kiss on both cheeks with Ida. Gruffudd introduced him to his sons, naming them proudly as 'the princes of Deheubarth'. Anarawd and Cadell, the two eldest sons, were young men in their mid-twenties, one with the fair colouring of their Cambro-Danish mother; and then, there were Gwenllian's surviving sons: Maredudd and Rhys. Rhys was four and had his mother's red hair, while Anarawd and Maredudd had their father's (and Nest's) black hair and blue eyes. When the greetings were over and Haith was seated, he took the opportunity to look around the hall and find his own son, Robert, at one of the lower trestles, sitting next to Amelina's husband Dyfnwal. Haith felt a pang that Robert had no knowledge that he was his father. Dyfnwal threw Haith a friendly glance. Robert was seventeen and filling out. He had the look of Haith, with thick, yellow hair, broad shoulders, and long arms. Haith wondered if anyone else would remark the similarity between them.

Nest was seated on the other side of her brother and asked, 'So, Henry has an heir, Haith, after all? His grandson, Empress Maud and Count Geoffrey's son. I hear he is known as Henry FitzEmpress?'

'Yes, he is a healthy child, three years old. He has a shock of red hair and is full of energy. The empress has two more sons now, Geoffrey and William. That would have pleased King Henry: a whole clutch of grandsons, but they are all still babies though.'

'I thought the empress was separated from her husband,'

Gruffudd remarked in perfect Norman French.

'That was so for a while, sire,' Haith responded, careful to give Gruffudd his honours as king, 'but she did, eventually, return to her husband despite their differences. Empress Maud was very ill after the births of her second and third sons and there were fears that she would die, but she has made a slow recovery.'

'If Empress Maud dies,' Nest speculated, 'Henry FitzEmpress will be a three-year-old contender for the crown of England and the duchy of Normandy with the Count of Anjou as regent?'

Haith noticed that Gruffudd was listening intently to this conversation, but everything they spoke of was common knowledge in England. It just took a while to travel this distance. 'The empress has regained her strength. She will take on the role of regent for her son herself.'

'And King Stephen will be displaced in due course?' Gruffudd asked. 'I hear the Norman lords are grumbling mightily that Stephen has not settled matters in Normandy yet, that the Angevins threaten to take control there.'

'King Stephen intended to cross to Normandy this year to claim the Duchy,' Haith answered, 'but he was delayed by events in England. He has appointed Waleran de Meulan as his lieutenant in Normandy and Walter de Clare fights alongside him. Geoffrey d'Anjou invaded Normandy and Empress Maud rose from childbed and came to his support but he was wounded with a javelin in the foot. The Angevin army had dysentery and had to withdraw, so there is still a stalemate in Normandy.'

'Stephen's wife is a descendent of the English royal family,' Nest told her brother. 'Her mother was the sister of King Henry's first wife, Matilda of Scotland. And she brings King Stephen control of a major Norman port and gateway to the English shores from Normandy.'

Haith smiled at her, but felt uncomfortable at the discussion. The official Norman line was that Stephen was the anointed king and that was an end to it, but many remembered that they had sworn an oath to Henry and his daughter the empress, and certainly she and her husband contended with Stephen for control of Normandy and might turn their claims to England itself in time. Strife between King Stephen and Empress Maud could only be to the advantage of Gruffudd and the other Welsh kings. The Norman hold on Wales was loosed more and more every day as many of the Norman lords were summoned to England to support Stephen against the rebels there and in Normandy. Haith decided it might be best to turn the conversation to another topic. 'I stay out of court matters nowadays, with King Henry gone,' he said.

He tried some of his rough Welsh as a courtesy on Gruffudd, admiring his sons, but his host answered him in French. From the corner of his eye, Haith saw Nest suppress a smile, but, perhaps, he thought, it was a smile in his favour rather than mockery of him. Ida was seated to his other side and took his attention. There was a great deal that she wanted to say, to catch up with what was happening in his life and hers.

At last the sumptuous feasting was done with and they rose from the table to the loud scrape of benches as all went about their business and servants began to clear the trestles. Haith counted a good hundred men. How was Nest's brother managing to feed so many? There must be some truth in the rumours that Nest had assisted Gruffudd to run a secret goldmining operation. As the only Norman-allied man here and as a sheriff responsible in the eyes of these Welsh for past harsh taxes, he felt resentment pressing on him as he moved through the courtyard to check back on his horse and the fewterer with the puppies. Dyfnwal and Robert were standing near the well with a group of men. 'May I take Robert to see the puppies in the stable?' Haith asked, pointing.

'Of course,' Dyfnwal replied. 'Go with Haith, Robert, he is a great friend of your Aunt Ida and of Lady Nest.' The young man nodded shyly and followed Haith. He was soon deep in discussion on the various merits of the puppies with the fewterer. Robert carefully helped the boy to tip milk into the puppies' mouths.

'Their mother won't give 'em milk, you see.' The fewterer had suddenly become the most loquacious person Haith had ever encountered.

'You are good with the dogs, Robert,' Haith told him. Little by little Haith got Robert to tell him something about himself, when he could get a word in edgeways past the fewterer's gabble. 'Brilliant with the bow, he is,' the fewterer told Haith, pointing at Robert.

'We should return to the hall now, sir, for supper,' Robert said and Haith nodded his agreement. 'I'll bring you something out,' Robert told the boy who was all smiles at that news.

Haith resumed his seat between Gruffudd and Ida. He looked around again at the Welsh soldiers he was seated amongst and then back to Gruffudd and the young princes seated with him on the high table. He was in the midst of a fierce enemy. Nest's family was steeped in blood and vengeance. Cadwallon, brother to Gruffudd's wife Gwenllian, had ruled in Gwynedd and killed three of his uncles, and then been killed himself in revenge by his wife's brother, the son of one of the slain uncles. Gwenllian had famously ridden out at the head of an army against Maurice de Londres and been beheaded, dying with two of her sons. Her other brother Owain was king of Gwynedd and her sister Susann was married to Madog, king of Powys. Nest's brother and his sons were never going to be living out their lives as peaceable farmers. There was no use hoping for that.

The conversation was stilted and Nest cast anxious glances in Haith's direction. This was a Christmas feast and antagonism could not breach the bounds of hospitality. And yet, there had been occasions on both sides when exactly that had happened, when someone was invited to a feast and then been betrayed to murder or imprisonment.

Carrying a guttering candle, Amelina led Haith down a very long passage, to a small, comfortable room at the end with a view out over the darkening moat.

'Am I in exile here?' Haith asked, making a joking reference to how far away from the rest of the household he seemed to be.

'Best place for noise,' Amelina announced in a deliberately mysterious tone.

'Noise?' Haith felt a little concerned. Was there a plot to murder him in his bed. He fondled the hilt of his sword.

Amelina tapped her nose. 'You'll see.'

The fire was lit in the hearth and the bed was comfortable. Haith looked at the door, worry knitting his brow. Noise? He wasn't sure that he could disrobe and climb into bed with some threat hanging over him. But Amelina had smiled and seemed happy about whatever it was she hinted at. She wouldn't be happy to see him murdered. Perhaps it was something to do with the children—singing Christmas carols or hanging stockings on doorknobs or the like. What would be the point in murdering *him*? There would only be a meagre symbolic value in assaulting the sheriff of Pembroke. And whatever the degree of estrangement between them, Nest would surely not conspire at his death.

He bent and slowly untied his boots, padded across the cold tiles in his stockinged feet and placed his boots neatly near the door. He unbuckled his sword belt and lent it against the bed, close to the pillow. He looked at the door for a few more minutes, swirling the wine in his mouth and swallowing it. There was no sound. Only an owl outside, beyond the moat.

Feeling foolish, he looked under the bed. Nothing there of course, except clumps of dust. He removed his breeches. He was bone-tired from his long ride, from the wine, from the heat of the fire, and the strain of being polite in the midst of tense hostility. Yet he was reluctant to close his eyes in sleep. He removed his shirt and lay on the bed naked, one hand on his sword. He turned his head to look at the candle on the table next to him that Amelina had lit from her own. There wasn't much of it left. The fire, too, was starting to burn low and the room would soon grow chilled without it. He could see no more wood in the room. No servant would hear him call down the length of the dim passageway beyond the door. He watched the candle burn down into a misshapen lump of pooled and cooling wax. It spluttered for a while and then died, plunging him into near-darkness, but there was still a dim, red glow from the fire. He thought he heard a sound in the passageway beyond the door. The doorlatch scraped as it lifted. Haith lay on the bed as if asleep and gripped the handle of his sword. If there were many of them he would not stand much chance.

'Ow, God's bollocks!' She stumbled over his boots at the door.

'Nest?' He released his grip on the sword and raised himself on one elbow.

'Haith? I can't see a thing.'

'Me neither.'

In the gloom he glimpsed a long, white chemise as she lifted it over her head and dropped it to the floor. She moved onto the bed and slid the silk of her naked skin against his, saying nothing more. The warmth of her body seared his flesh, hardened his cock. 'I'm sorry, Haith,' she whispered. 'About the king. It was always you that I loved. He … he needed comfort and I gave it to him as an old friend. Can you forgive me?'

'It doesn't matter now,' he said. 'We're too old for jealousies, I reckon. I always loved you too, through everything.'

'Are we too old for this?' Nest asked, sliding her hand down his stomach.

'I reckon not.' They made love in silence, with only groans and panting. He stroked her hair and swept his hand along the curve of her body, down her flank, returning it to the perfect round of one buttock. 'I would you were my wife, Nest. Is that presumption, given your rank? Perhaps your brother thinks to give you to one of the Welsh lords?'

'My brother may think all he likes but he will do no such thing. I have had enough of being given and will only give myself, if at all. May I think on it, Haith? I do not want to embroil you in the dangers and rigours of the Welsh resistance here against the Normans. You have standing amongst the Norman community that you should retain.'

'I care less for all that, Nest, with Henry gone. My loyalty was to him. Please do think on it, my sweet Nest. Or will you send me packing when you have had your fill of me, as you did de Marais?'

'I will never have my fill of you and don't compare yourself to him.' He could not see her face, but he could hear her smile. She gripped her fingers deep into his hair and he hugged her fiercely to him. 'We live. We flare. We do our best. We make mistakes. We die.' Nest's mouth murmured against the skin of his neck. 'We must keep trying to flare until we are dust. I had to take the chance that you still cared for me.'

Haith sat his horse in the courtyard preparing to say his good-byes to Nest and her family who were arrayed before the hall door. He wore the bearskin that he had reclaimed from the few-terer, and Robert was sitting astride a horse beside him with one of the mastiff puppies snuggled inside his jerkin. Haith and Nest had gently told Robert of his parentage. 'I knew it wasn't Amelina and Dyfnwal,' he said stoically. 'They've always been kind and loved me, yet I knew I wasn't theirs. I had a vague idea of something but I didn't know what. I have always loved you, Mother,' he had reached a shy hand to Nest's, 'and Ida, and now, I have found you too, Father.' Haith enjoyed the sound of the word 'father' in Robert's mouth. Haith had told Nest that Henry's will gifted him a small fort with a little land and tithes at Saint Clair's. The fort was close to Llansteffan and he had lately taken possession of it. Nest and Robert had agreed to Haith's proposal to give his son a home and office as his deputy there.

Haith opened his mouth to speak the formal words of farewell that would sever him once again from Nest but his speech was prevented by the sight and sound of Amelina pursuing a squawking brown hen across the courtyard.

'If persons knew how good a hen is in January none would be left on the roost!' she shouted in riposte to the laughter raised by her pursuit. Rhys made a lucky feint for the hen and caught her, pinioning her wings before handing her over to a puffing and red-faced Amelina. She took the hen and looked at Haith and Robert with tears in her eyes. 'Do not take your coats off before Ascension Day,' she admonished them, 'and remember that it is more wholesome to smell warm bread than to eat it.'

'We will heed your wise advice, dear Amelina,' Haith said and he and Robert turned their horses towards the barbican.

38

The Norman Exodus

March 1137, Pembroke Castle, Wales

I had not seen Haith since Christmas and clung to my horse's mane as she trotted across the drawbridge into Pembroke Castle feeling queasy at the thought of how I would encounter him. I smiled at myself. I was too old a woman to be bashful about bedding a man or to worry about what he would think of me in daylight as opposed to the pitch-black room at Dinefwr. 'Smiling, mother?' asked Maurice, beside me. 'Are you remembering when you lived here with Father?'

'Yes,' I lied. 'So I am.' I rarely thought of Gerald these days, except of course when I looked at Maurice or William.

In the aftermath of Crug Mawr and King Stephen's failures in Normandy the landscape of power in Deheubarth reformed around me. Many Normans had vacated Ceredigion and Dyfed after the Welsh victory, leaving only the garrisons at Cardigan, Pembroke, and Carmarthen holding out. My brother and the princes of Gwynedd were wasting no time in stepping into the voids. Gilbert FitzRichard de Clare had inherited the lordship of Cardigan after his father was killed and his mother, Alice of Chester, had fled with Miles of Gloucester, but he was with the king in England or on his estates in Kent and unlikely to return to Wales for a long time. Robert FitzMartin commanded at Cardigan on Gilbert's behalf and my son Robert FitzStephen was with FitzMartin. I was in hopes that I would see him here today, for the wedding, which had been relocated, away from the battle-bruised Cardigan Castle to Pembroke.

Haith was the first person I saw in the crowded courtyard. He handed me down from my horse and I looked around at a confusion of arriving and packing readying to depart. Carts stood loaded with goods, and servants were bringing out a mattress wrestled between them to throw on top of the pile. There was unrest and rebellion in England and many of the Cambro-Norman lords were being summoned to aid the king and abandon their footholds in Wales.

'Yes,' Haith told me. 'It *is* both arriving and leaving that you see. The guests are arriving for Lady Alice's marriage feast at the same time as her uncle and aunt are preparing to leave. Lord Gilbert de Clare has also been summoned to attend King Stephen.'

'And Isabel goes with him.'

'Yes, the whole household.'

'Come on,' said Haith, taking my hand, 'I will steer you through the melee to a beaker of wine.' My body thrilled at his touch. Maurice followed us into the hall, unaware of the invisible frisson between Haith and me.

My son FitzStephen broke from a group of men standing before the hearth to greet us. 'Mother!' He stepped back from his first effusive embrace, mindful that he was a man now and his peers stood watching him. I beamed at him. 'I am so glad to see you.' FitzStephen turned to greet Maurice. Haith nodded to me, leaving me in my sons' care and returned to his duties supervising the chaos in the courtyard. It had not been so awkward after all, encountering him. FitzStephen led me to the group of men and made introductions to some I already knew, and others I did not. My other son, William, was there, and would be in charge of

Pembroke when Gilbert de Clare and Isabel de Beaumont left for England. There was an informal truce between my brother and his 'Norman' nephews, my son Henry at Arberth, William at Carew, and Maurice at Llansteffan. They agreed to give him no trouble and he gave none to them. I was delighted that my kin had found their own way to accord.

'Robert FitzMartin, steward at Cardigan,' FitzStephen introduced me. 'Maurice de Londres, steward at Kidwelly and Ogmore.' Suddenly encountering de Londres like this, I looked down at my boots and did not wish to return his greeting. He had given the order to behead Gwenllian and her sons and I could find no way to navigate my anger at that. 'Lady Nest,' I heard him say and he moved tactfully away to another group of guests, mindful of my feelings.

Isabel came and took my hand. 'Nest, I would be grateful if you might come and talk with the bride, my niece, with me?'

'Of course.' She led me up the stairwell to a top chamber that had once been a bedroom occupied by myself and Gerald in the days of my first marriage. As we pushed through the chamber door, a young girl, sixteen or so, turned to us, her face streaked with tears, her maids tutting and fussing, trying to dress her in wedding finery. 'Aunt! How can you do this to me? And mother and father! I won't marry him! He is a Welsh brute!'

Isabel glanced at me embarrassed. 'Now, Alice. He is nothing of the sort. This is Lady Nest of Llansteffan. Robert FitzStephen's mother.'

Alice looked at me with a frankly unimpressed gaze. 'Lady,' she muttered.

Isabel took a soft cloth from one of the maids and wiped the tears from Alice's face. 'Prince Cadwaladr is the brother of a king, Alice. His blood is royal.'

'A *Welsh* king,' the girl said sullenly.

'Prince Cadwaladr is an ally of your uncle, Ranulf, earl of Chester. This is a splendid marriage for you.'

Alice stared at us, unmoved by Isabel's argument. Isabel looked in despair at me but I had few words of comfort to offer, knowing what it was like to be foist into a marriage that was none of your choosing. The girl was already a widow. She had been married first at thirteen to a minor English Norman and now at sixteen she was the peace offering from the de Clares to the royal family of Gwynedd that had bettered them in battle at Crug Mawr. Cadwaladr's elderly father, Gruffudd ap Cynan had died earlier in the year, formalising Owain's succession to the throne of Gwynedd that he and his brothers had occupied in all but name for the last ten years. Owain had decided that his formal crowning as king of Gwynedd was a fitting time to also make a show with this Norman marriage alliance for his brother Cadwaladr.

'Your children will be royalty,' Isabel stated.

'*Welsh* royalty,' Alice rejoined with distaste.

What I knew of her bridegroom, Cadwaladr, was not to his advantage. I knew that he was a traitor to my brother and was working to take Gruffudd's lands in Ceredigion. King Owain had recently pronounced that Ceredigion would be divided between Cadwaladr and Owain's son Hywel. My brother would contest it, but they had, as we expected all along, reneged on their alliance with him. I suspected that Cadwaladr was in league with Breri who had very likely caused Ida's arrest, the attempted poisoning of Haith, and the murder of Einon. Still it was my job to steel this girl to *her* job.

'Your husband is a great man,' I said with conviction. 'Cadwaladr ap Gruffudd ap Cynan, son of King Gruffudd of Gwynedd, brother of King Owain of Gwynedd, the great kingdom of the north of Wales. His deeds and the deeds of your sons will resound with glory in the chronicles.'

'*Welsh* chronicles?' asked Alice, sarcastically.

'Welsh and Norman.'

'Lady Nest is right, Alice,' said Isabel. 'Come, do not show your husband a face washed with tears.'

Alice swallowed. 'Very well,' she said, and drew herself up.

'It is our lot, Alice, to be brave in the hall, in our marriages, and in birthing our children. You must be proud and strong for your family's sake,' I said.

She nodded to me.

When Isabel and I returned to the hall with Alice between us, the Welsh contingent had arrived. Breri was standing at the hearth in close conference with Cadwaladr. Prince Cadwaladr was wearing fine Norman dress, which would, I hoped, make his bride feel a little better about joining her life to his. Cadwaladr was slender and of average height, with dark orange hair and a freckle-splattered face. His intelligent, black eyes surveyed us.

Noticing our entrance, Breri stepped away from the bridegroom and picked up his lute. He came towards us singing. It was hard to believe that this man, with this sonorous voice and beautiful words had murdered Einon when he carried the message in his beard, had exposed my brother to charges of treason, and worked to do the same to me. He was undoubtedly conspiring with Cadwaladr against my brother. I had no doubt that he was behind the poisoning of Haith, and here he came strutting with his lute. 'Month of March—severe is the cold wind upon the headlands, Every bird wings to its mate, Every thing springs through the earth.'

39

Exoneration

April 1137, Llansteffan Castle

Nest had sent a messenger to Haith, asking him to attend her at Llansteffan and prepare for a journey if he might be willing. Her message said nothing more and was mysterious. She and Ida were waiting for him in the hall. 'A letter came for Ida addressed to Benedicta,' Nest explained. Ida handed the letter to Haith to read for himself.

> *Count Amaury de Montfort at Evreux, to Benedicta. I hope my informants speak true of your whereabouts and that this letter finds you. I am very ill and ask that you might come to me. I remember how you aided King Henry in his time of illness. It would be a kindness to me.*

Haith looked up at the expectant faces of the two women. 'It's a very long journey, again, Ida, into Normandy. We grow old, you and I.'

'Yes, but he would not write and ask me for a trivial reason. He has need of me and I must go. Will you accompany me, Haith?'

Great walls made with the neat rows of small stones, created in the *petit-appareil* masonry style, rose to either side of them as they entered the city of Evreux, which had been the scene of so much fighting in recent times during the rebellion against King Henry. The palace was quiet and seemed abandoned. 'Where is the count?' Ida asked the first servant she could locate.

'Upstairs in bed, mistress, and not like to rise from it, I fear.'

'And the countess?'

'She does not reside here.'

Ida and Haith walked up the uneven stone steps to the solar. Entering the room, Ida controlled her shock at first sight of Amaury. He was wasted away to his very skeleton. Even so close to death, his bones showed the beautiful structure of his face, and his blond hair was paler but luxuriant still. Quietly, she sat on a low stool next to the bed and watched him sleep. A maid came and went with water and medicines and gave Ida a shy smile. He stirred and groaned at the return of consciousness and pain with it. 'Benedicta,' he whispered, widening his eyes on her in surprise. 'I did not think you would come.'

There was no point in correcting him with regard to her name. She stroked his hair gently from his cold forehead. 'Of course I came, Amaury. Of course.'

He struggled through pain to be able to speak again. She waited.

'I never forgot you. I have known many women, but you struck a special chord with me.'

'As did you with me.' She was leaning in close, looking with love into his eyes. His voice was low. Each word an effort.

'I wish I could fully embrace you, Amaury.'

'Don't be afraid. I won't break.' Haith drew back into the dark edge of the room to give them privacy and Amaury seemed unaware of his presence.

Ida moved carefully onto the bed and nestled her body against the bones of his. 'May I ask you something, Amaury? To give me peace of mind and also my brother.'

'Of course.' It was easier for him to speak—though that was difficult enough—than to nod his head.

'My brother has been enquiring for a long time now into the tragedy of *The White Ship*. He believes there was foul play.'

She had Amaury's attention. He listened in silence but his intelligent, brown eyes followed her words closely. 'He discovered that Gisulf the royal clerk was murdered onboard.'

He raised his eyebrows.

'I … I am sorry to ask this, to even think it, but I must know if you were involved in any way, Amaury.'

His mouth curved and his eyes lit up with amusement. He did not have the energy to laugh. 'Gisulf! Why would I … ah! Yes.' Memory dawned. 'He was troubling you and I said I would deal with it when we met in Reims. Is that it?'

'Yes.' She raised herself on one elbow to look earnestly at him. 'I beg you to tell me the truth of it.'

'Gladly. I had nothing to do with Gisulf's murder on the ship. I planned to take action against him but then heard that he had drowned before I had the chance to do so.'

'You were in no wise involved, then?'

'No.'

'That is a great relief to me, Amaury. I knew it. In my heart, I knew it, but I had to ask. You gave me no answer when I asked you in Fontevraud.'

'We had other things on our minds then, as I recall.' He closed his eyes, exhausted by the conversation and Ida too allowed herself to drift into sleep.

When he was sure that they were both asleep, Haith reached for the letter lodged in the inside pocket of his jerkin. He drew it out and turned the folded letter over a few times in his hands, contemplating the faded ink addressed to '*Henricus Rex*' and the broken red wax seal. It was the letter from de Bellême, which had suggested to Haith that Amaury and, by association, Ida, might have had some role in the sinking of *The White Ship*. He would not read it again. There was no need. Haith held the parchment out to the flames of the fire and when it caught alight he let it slip from his fingers and watched it collapse to ash. He breathed in deeply as the wax melted and released its odour to the room. Haith glanced at Ida and Amaury but they did not stir.

Some hours later Haith was woken by Ida moving from the bed to pull the curtains aside a little and look for fuel for the fire. The room had grown chilled. In the light from the window, they looked back at Amaury on the bed and saw that he was gone.

Haith accompanied Ida to the gates at Llansteffan, wearily declined her offer to enter, and rode on the short distance to Saint Clair's where Robert handed him a letter as his feet touched the cobbles of the bailey. 'The messenger came from England, Father. Perhaps it's urgent.'

'Nothing is urgent these days except the need for a bath and a quart of beer.'

Haith divested himself of his travelling gear, washed his face and hands and caught up with the news with Robert over a beaker. The letter sat on the trestle between them. 'Aren't you going to open it?'

Haith turned it over. There was a red wax seal but Haith did not recognise its provenance. 'I will. I will. Can you look to my horse, then?'

His son smiled his assent and left him. Haith slid his knife through the wax seal and unfolded the letter.

To Haith de Bruges. Greetings, Morin du Pin, Canon of St Peter's Priory, Dunstable. We are old battle companions and you will perhaps struggle to envisage me in a monk's habit with a shaven pate. Yet, all is changed with me, I assure you. I am entered a holy

order and am not long for this world. I beg that you might receive
my confession.

Haith sat up in his seat. Waleran had urged King Stephen to
give a pardon to du Pin and he had been allowed to return from
exile. Haith thought of him, as he instructed, clad in a monk's
habit at Saint Peter's in Dunstable, which Henry had established
years before. Yet Haith found it hard to credit the idea that du
Pin would not be wearing mail beneath that drab, brown robe
and its simple rope girdle. The letter continued:

I have made confession many times to my priests, but it is not
enough. I need to relieve myself of my burden and ask that it be to
your eye, by way of this letter. It is up to you to decide what you do
with this information but I beg you not to harm my lord Waleran
with it. It was never his conscious doing. It was all mine.
I heard from de Pirou that you sought information on The White
Ship *and particularly on Gisulf. I believe that you learnt that the*
clerk was an infamous blackmailer and held the bright future of
my lord Waleran in his grubby hands from a youthful error on
the count's part. He should never have committed his devotion to
William Clito *to paper of course, but he did and Gisulf laid his*
hands on that paper and made a noose with it for my young lord's
neck. I could not allow him to suffer the burden of that necklace.
I commissioned the murder of Gisulf on the ship, together with
Ranulf de Gernon, who was suffering the same blackmail at the
clerk's hands and would have it cease. It was the doing of those
idiots de Pirou and the fat butcher that what should have been
one death led to so many and one so particularly grievous to King
Henry. You know all this, I understand. But you do not know
that my lord Waleran had nothing to do with it. I swear it on my
immortal soul and hope that I will find some forgiveness in time.

*Perhaps, for the sake of an old battlefield comrade, you will light
candles for me. Many candles, Haith.*

A thousand candelabras each in a thousand cathedrals could
not cleanse Morin du Pin's soul. Haith caressed his brow with
one hand, trying not to think too much about how it must feel
to be responsible for the death of the king's son and 300 more
souls besides. Haith could not have lived with that degree of
guilt himself. No doubt du Pin had murdered de Pirou when
Haith came close to getting the truth out of him, and had
commissioned the assassin who attacked Haith at Westminster.

Haith could imagine du Pin, that hoary warrior, bringing
the same grim stubbornness to living with the burden of such
enormous guilt as he had brought to bloody castle sieges and
screaming, headlong charges into battle. And here, at last, was
the proof positive that de Gernon had also had a hand in the
murder and the sinking. This confession, this knowledge was of
no use now to anyone. Henry was gone and as Nest and Ida
had told Haith long ago, the facts did not bring back William
Adelin. Haith had given up his townhouse in London since he
was no longer required at court and was growing too old for such
travels. His possessions from London, including Gisulf's chest,
were stowed in the castle strongroom. Haith resolved to add
this letter to the chest. When Robert returned from the stables,
Haith was still staring at the folded letter. 'From a monk,' he said,
in response to Robert's curious gaze. 'A very bad monk.'

40

The Last Bastion

June 1137, Llansteffan Castle, Wales

From the casement window I watched the sun rise behind the copse at the top of the hill. Long tree shadows fingered their way down the green slope in the gold-red morning light. The ground was spongy and verdant after rain. Flowers were budding and trees were tentatively blossoming pink and white. In the hedgerows, new roses showed blood red amidst dark green foliage. Amelina ruptured my thoughts, banging through the door with a tray of delicious-smelling bread. 'There's a note come from FitzStephen.' He often wrote me cheerful letters, humorously titled 'From the last bastion'. Cardigan was not quite the last Norman bastion. Pembroke still had its Norman garrison and there were other Norman-held pockets here and there. In name, Carew, Llansteffan, and Arberth were Norman held—by my sons—but they had come to a peaceable agreement for it with my brother. I opened the note and was surprised to see that it was just one line. After one first read, I read it aloud to Amelina.

Mother, will you and Amelina come to Cardigan as fast as you may. We have need of your assistance here.

'It must be something medical, Amelina. Bring your potions and tell Maurice to instruct two men at arms to accompany us.'

'Who do you think is hurt?' Amelina asked as we hurried towards the stables.

'I don't know. Not FitzStephen since he wrote to ask for aid.'

'They must have wise women there they could call on,' Amelina said.

'I know. There is no use guessing why he asks for us.' I screwed my eyes shut for a moment. It was not one of my sons. Please do not let it be one of my sons. I thought I knew where they all were and that they were safe. I had heard from Angharad recently from Manorbier and she was well.

I tried to take my own advice and focus on the scenery around me as we galloped towards Cardigan. It was a four-hour ride and a long time for speculation. FitzStephen and FitzMartin were waiting for us in the courtyard and I saw from their faces that there was bad news, very bad news. 'Do not keep me in suspense, I beg you,' I said to FitzMartin, as he handed me down from my horse. 'What is it?'

'Your brother.'

'Gruffudd? What is he doing here?' I was bewildered. They bustled us into the hall as we spoke. There were two men lying on skins on the floor near the hearth. I ran to my brother. 'Oh, Gruffudd!' He could not hear me. His face was white, translucent almost. I looked up at the people surrounding him, and gripped the hands of my nephews Anarawd and Cadell who were weeping. Amelina knelt and gently unwrapped Gruffudd's coverings to find what ailed him. Bloodied bandages were wrapped around his torso and seeped red still. The life was draining from him.

I looked across at the other injured man and saw that it was the bard, Breri. 'What happened?' I asked Cadell.

'There was another attack on the castle,' FitzStephen told me in a low voice, seeing that his cousins were unable to speak.

'An attack?' I asked Anarawd. 'I thought there was peace with the marriage of Cadwaladr and Alice de Clare.'

Anarawd shook his head. 'My father, Owain, and Cadwaladr judged that they would take back all of Ceredigion.' He glanced at FitzMartin. 'We were aided by Danish mercenaries, but we did not succeed.'

'Your father was injured in the fighting?' I asked.

'No!' It was Cadell who had spoken in a forceful, certain tone.

'He's right,' Amelina said, her eyes on her patient. 'This is not a battle wound. Your brother has been stabbed,' she said to me. 'In the back. Under cover of the battle perhaps, but he has been given this death wound through treachery.'

'Death wound?'

She shook her head. 'I can make him comfortable. I cannot save him. He has lost too much blood.'

'It was this man, this bard, who stabbed him,' Cadell told me, gesturing at Breri's prostrate form. 'Anarawd felled him straight after. When we saw how serious the wound was that Father had received, we asked succour from our cousin and the commander of the castle here, FitzMartin. We knew we would never gain our own hall with Father.'

'I don't doubt that Cadwaladr ordered this slaying,' Anarawd said. 'He stands to gain. He wanted our father out of his way to take lordship fully of Ceredigion.'

'Where is Cadwaladr now?' I asked.

'Long gone. To the court of the earl of Chester, probably, to de Gernon. They are confederates,' Cadell told me.

I moved to look down on Breri. His eyes flickered open. 'Water, lady!' he gasped. I filled a beaker from a jug on the table and crouched to hold it to his mouth. When I made to move away, he grabbed my arm, but feebly. 'Lady,' he groaned. 'Will you send a priest to me?'

I nodded and gave orders to a servant to fetch a priest. Breri's breathing was laboured and he looked at me with haunted eyes. 'The priest will be too late,' he said.

Again, I made to move away and back to my brother's side.

'Will you hear me?' he groaned. 'Lady Nest, please.'

'Breri, you have given my brother his death wound. Why should I grace you with anything?'

'Please, from your gentle mercy.'

'The priest will be here soon.'

'He will be too late. I do not have long,' he gasped.

I sat on a bench and regarded him. His lips were turning blue and he was evidently in great pain with every breath he took.

'No one can forgive me for the things that I have done,' he said. 'It was the nature of my life. To lie, to betray, to kill. And sometimes,' he smiled through his pain, a tear trickling from one eye down his cheek and to his ear, 'to sing.'

I said nothing.

'One thing led to another. It started out as a lucrative jape. The occasional love letter purloined. The occasional nugget of overheard secrets. But I got in too deep and there was no way back.'

Still there was nothing I could say to him. I looked across towards the unmoving form of my brother.

'For a long time, I had a nice little business going with Gisulf where I was spying for Countess Adela de Blois and spotting any material that could serve two functions—answer to her need for information, *and* provide evidence for blackmail. But then Gisulf was greedy and turned on me. He had a letter evidencing a murder that I had enacted and held it over my head. It was in his chest of secrets he said. If du Pin and de Gernon had not done the job themselves of dispatching him on *The White Ship*, I would have done it myself and not botched it as they did.'

I look at him in disgust. Accidentally killing three hundred young people was a little more than a botch. He was oblivious to my response and I suspected that he could no longer see my face. His gaze was directed at nothing in particular, or perhaps he only saw his own sordid history in his mind's eye. His voice came in gasps and reluctantly I leant closer to hear.

'Your friend, Sheriff Haith, would not let go the thread would he? I knew the sheriff had Gisulf's box and I could not allow him to use that letter against me. His stubborn tenacity nearly cost him his life.'

'Were you involved in the murder of de Pirou?'

'No, that was all de Gernon, covering his tracks.'

'And Einon, at Llansteffan?'

'The beard message? That was ingenious. I enjoyed that, and used it myself a few times afterwards.'

I swallowed down my bile. 'And the poisoned gloves?' I asked.

He smiled and coughed on a gout of blood that leaked from the side of his mouth. 'Nearly as good as the beard, no?'

I did not respond and he could not see how his words painted horror on my face.

He began to cough more blood and Amelina came over. 'I'll not give him aid,' she said. 'What is he saying to you? Don't listen to it. Your brother is going, Nest. You had best go to him.'

I moved across and knelt beside my brother. Looking back over my shoulder I saw a young priest arrive too late, and Amelina sweep her hand down over Breri's dead eyelids.

My brother died an hour after his murderer. The men of his *teulu* acclaimed Anarawd as the new king of Deheubarth, their cries in honour of him subdued by their grief at the loss of Gruffudd, who had been a valiant opponent against the Normans when so many had capitulated and considered the kingdom lost. I kissed my nephew's cheeks with my own still wet with tears for my brother who had ruled his land for a mere year after a whole lifetime of struggle, after the terrible losses of his wife and sons. 'Take care of yourself, Anarawd.'

'We will be avenged upon Cadwaladr for father's death,' Anarawd said.

My heart sank. There had been so many generations of blood feuds amongst the royal families of Wales, and now my nephews were taking on vengeance against Prince Cadwaladr. I remembered how I had carried my own curse for vengeance for so many years on behalf of my father and brothers murdered by Normans. 'No. Take care of *yourself.* You must *live* and rule Deheubarth to honour your father and mother. *That* is what you must do.'

Anarawd said nothing in response. I looked at them, Anarawd and Cadell, my nephews, no longer boys, shouldering the weight of their responsibilities. 'I will take care of him, Aunt,' Cadell reassured me. I knew he would do his best but imagined how the weight of centuries of murder and treachery would oppose him.

41

Landing

September 1139, Llansteffan Castle, Wales

The tide was out at Llansteffan and I thrilled as always at the sight of the broad sandflats of the Twyi estuary. On the far bank a number of dark figures rendered miniature by the distance, moved around the ferry boat that they had hauled out onto the sands and overturned. The boat plied back and forth across the river when the tide was up. Now, they must be performing essential maintenance work on its planks.

I dipped my stylus to add the momentous news to the pages of my book.

September 1139 Empress Maud and Robert, earl of Gloucester have landed at Arundel and mean to contend with King Stephen for the throne that should rightly belong to Maud. The empress has been admitted to the castle by Queen Adelisa and they are under siege from King Stephen. My foster-sister, Mabel, countess of Gloucester, is also within the castle.

Mabel's husband, Robert had declared for his half-sister, the empress, the previous year, which had come as no surprise since relations between the earl and King Stephen had been growing worse with each day.

Stephen had led a disastrous campaign in Normandy attempting to lay claim to Henry's duchy. His ambitions ended in fiasco when fighting broke out between his Norman soldiers and the Flemish mercenaries in his pay. The king compounded his problems by alienating Earl Robert. Stephen was forced to an expensive truce with King Louis of France and left Waleran de Meulan in charge of defending Normandy against Geoffrey d'Anjou's annual incursions on behalf of the empress. There was little doubt that d'Anjou would take Normandy in due course. The Norman barons were displeased at these failures, which threatened their own interests, and the initial glamour of Stephen's crown dimmed with each wrong step and each loss and defection.

Since Earl Robert had declared for Maud, all England, Mabel wrote to me, waited for Henry's daughter to arrive, ravage the forces of the usurper, and take her throne. Henry would be smiling, lying in his tomb at Reading Abbey. Rumours had run everywhere that Mabel's husband was planning to invade on the empress's behalf and frantic preparations had been made to defend King Stephen's strongholds. The expectation of Maud's imminent arrival seemed to go on and on, until all began to fear that she would never, in fact, come, but those voices had been proved wrong. The empress was, at last, in England and she wanted her crown, first for herself, and then for her small son, Henry FitzEmpress. Rebels had been rising in her support all around England for the past year, which kept the Normans busy and out of Wales, and left us to make further inroads on our own gains.

Henry's administrative machine ground to a halt and Stephen's treasury struggled without the regular income wrung through the tax system by the sheriffs. More and more Normans withdrew from Wales where they no longer had the promise of protection from Stephen's court. Robert FitzMartin withdrew from Cardigan to Totnes and supported the empress. Miles of Gloucester declared for the empress and Brian FitzCount and most of south west England were won to her side before she ever set foot on the pier at Arundel. Now that the empress had, at last, landed with Earl Robert in England, war would ensue against her cousin, and they would fight to take back the crown that Henry had willed to her.

I rode to visit Haith and Robert at Saint Clair's. After our greetings, Robert left to go about his duties in the bailey. I placed my hand on top of Haith's. 'Do you continue your duties as sheriff of Pembroke, Haith?'

'No. I've ceded the office to one of King Stephen's cronies but there's not much sheriffing to do around here these days.' The last vestiges of Norman administration in Deheubarth had collapsed, and it was this collapse that had spurred me to visit Haith.

'I wondered if you might like to come and live with me, Haith,' I said to him boldly. There was no point in beating coyly about the bush. We were too old for all that. Either he wanted to spend his days with me or he did not. I knew my own mind. His eyes were warm and liquid and there I had my answer. He and I prepared to make a landing of our own—at Llansteffan.

I am lulled to sleep by the sea and I do not hear the church bells under the water anymore. I am loath to stop writing but I must. And I must place you, dear book, where no one will find you. I give you as an offering to this place where my harshest and my dearest memories have lived. Haith will be arriving in a few hours with his household and belongings and will move into my solar. Amelina has cleared some space for his possessions and now I must take care of things I do not want him or anyone else to ever see.

I can bring myself now to look out from the window of my chamber over this estuary and the beach where my brother Goronwy died. You never know how the past will turn out. Life does not really divide down those easy lines that everyone talks about, such as Norman and Welsh. It is so much more complicated than that. Blood is mixed in all of us, one way or another. Can we try to imagine a time in the future when our differences are dissolved forever in the rocking cradle of the sea? In my life I tried to hate, but in the end I had to love, several times over, and I am glad of that. I will hide this book that Henry gave me long ago. It has served its purpose. Its once smooth, blank pages are criss-crossed with lines, like my face. I closed the book, carefully keeping the stiff, loose leaves of Gerald's chronicle and my drawn genealogies straight between its pages. I turned the book over and over several times in my hands. I hugged it to my chest conjuring the faces in turn of everyone I had lost: my father, my brother Goronwy, then Gerald, Henry when I loved him, Queen Matilda, Faricius, Gwenllian, and, finally, Gruffudd. I took an undyed length of woollen cloth from my embroidery basket and wrapped it around and around my book, until it was muffled and mummied.

I left my room and emerged from the shelter of the tower to cross the bailey, heading towards the gatehouse. The weather was changing and I watched the rain approaching. Clouds blackened the sky like a pall of smoke. There was no wind and needles of rain fell straight down soaking me, making me shiver. I paused at the great stone barbican to catch my breath and lifted my face upward towards where the portcullis mechanism winds up its heavy weight. There are bees buzzing there that have made a home in the masonry. Bees make a place, instead of destroying it like locusts. I do not want the people I know to read my journal when I die, to find it among my papers. There was a pole leaning against the wall, and I used it to poke my wrapped book deep into the hole, up there with the beehive. One day, someone will find it and read it, but not yet.

Epilogue: The Bees' Book

The book lay waiting in a deep crevice in the crumbling castle wall after she had pushed it down with a long pole, where nobody would ever find it. On the pages of the book, her life whispered like wind in leaves, speaking the grammar of love, the vocabulary of resistance. Masonry bees moved into the crevice pushing the book further down, expanding the hole in all directions to hold their seething golden corridors in the darkness. The book lay captive in the hive, bound in amber chains of honey, its fabric woven into the solidifying honeycomb. The filament touch of the wings and feet of bees brushed softly over it again and again like her eyelashes against her cheek as she closed her eyes to remember the scenes of her life, to write her story.

The book listened to the ceaseless zzzrs of the bees, the thick drip of honey, the wind caressing the old walls of the ruin, the sea far below lapping back and forth, over and over, the seabirds calling as they flung themselves recklessly at the air, grouped to be blown together upriver, riding the thermals. In the past, long ago, the book had listened to other sounds: the clatter of horses' feet on cobbles, the shouts and laughter of men, women and children, groans of rope, chains and timbers as the portcullis was raised or the sudden rush and thud when it was lowered like a guillotine, swords clashing, arrows fluttering, men screaming, calling out at the last for their mothers: 'Mam!'. Those sounds were all long gone. Those voices had spilled their brief vivid lives into the vivid emerald lozenge of the bailey, leaving only a faint echo on the breeze, some impressions in the grass, beneath the grass, words scratched on parchment.

The bees went back and forth, their thighs loaded with pollen. They walked over each other and over the book like more black words let loose from the page to wander and find new homes in new sentences. The laughing children who had played around the castle well, running up and down the stairways, through the kitchens and stables, grew up to die in battle, in childbed, in sickbed, or released at last from the pangs of old age, their wishes, regrets and tears seeping into the soil. As time passed and the voices were silenced, the wall partly collapsed, chunks of stone tumbled to the ground and the bees angrily rebuilt their ramparts. The bees' fine filigree wings turned to piles of fine dust. The long legs of spiders traversed the crevice adding balled-up, sticky web. Slugs slid across the stone. No rain penetrated here. Occasionally clumps of snow thawed but the icy drips were swallowed quickly by the thirsty stone and none seeped into the book sealed in its golden carapace. The book was wrapped more and more in layers of honeyed time and waited.

Genealogies

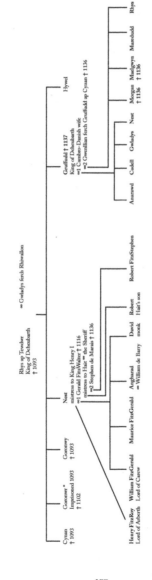

* Named Idwal in the Conquest series
∞∞ Named Haith in the Conquest series. That he was the lover of Nest and the father of a son with her is disputed by some historians
∞ Marriage
† Death year

Genealogy of the Gwynedd Royal Family

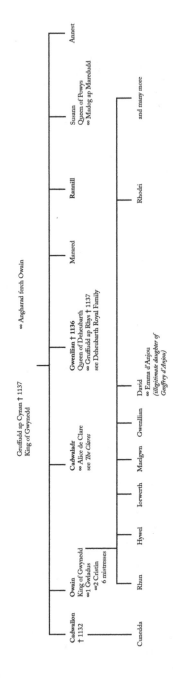

∞ Marriage
† Death year

Genealogy of the Kings of England and Dukes of Normandy

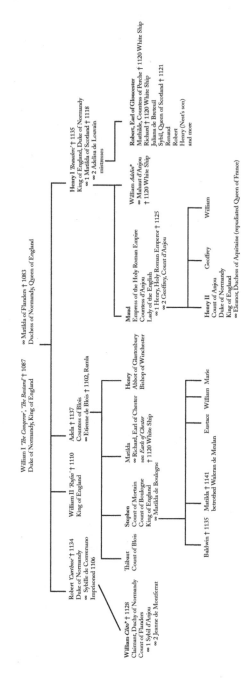

* *Clito* and *Adelin* are designations meaning heir apparent
∞ Marriage
† Death year

Genealogy of the Earls of Chester

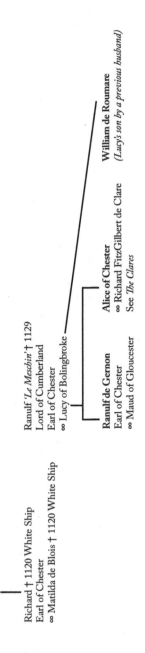

Hugh d'Avranches *'The Wolf'*, *'The Fat'* † 1101
Earl of Chester
∞ Ermentrude de Claremont

Richard † 1120 White Ship
Earl of Chester
∞ Matilda de Blois † 1120 White Ship

Ranulf *'Le Meschin'* † 1129
Lord of Cumberland
Earl of Chester
∞ Lucy of Bolingbroke

Ranulf de Gernon
Earl of Chester
∞ Maud of Gloucester

Alice of Chester
∞ Richard FitzGilbert de Clare
See *The Clares*

William de Roumare
(Lucy's son by a previous husband)

∞ Marriage
† Death year

Genealogy of the Beaumonts

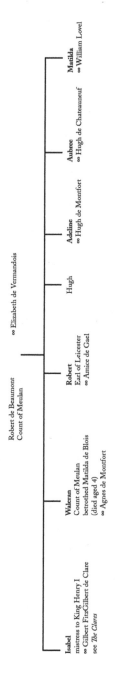

Robert de Beaumont
Count of Meulan
∞ Elizabeth de Vermandois

Isabel
mistress to King Henry I
∞ Gilbert FitzGilbert de Clare
see *The Clares*

Waleran
Count of Meulan
betrothed Matilda de Blois
(died aged 4)
∞ Agnes de Montfort

Robert
Earl of Leicester
∞ Amice de Gael

Hugh

Adeline
∞ Hugh de Montfort

Aubree
∞ Hugh de Chateauneuf

Matilda
∞ William Lovel

Genealogy of the Clares

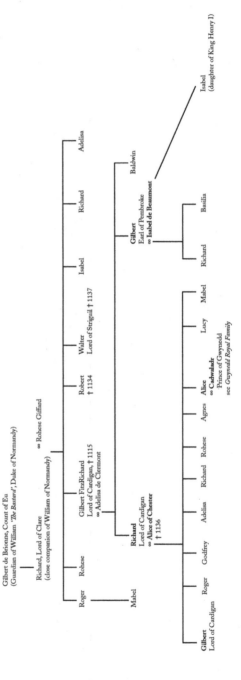

∞ Marriage
† Death year

Historical Note

The fictional characters Nest ferch Rhys and Haith de Bruges in this book are based on real historical people who lived in the eleventh and twelfth centuries. The *Conquest* trilogy draws on the known historical facts concerning the life of Nest. She was the daughter of Rhys ap Tewdwr, king of Deheubarth in south west Wales. Rhys was killed in battle by the Norman, Bernard de Neufmarché, in 1087. Nest was the mistress of the Norman king Henry I and had a son with him. She was married to Gerald FitzWalter, the Norman steward of Pembroke Castle. The Welsh prince, Owain of Powys, abducted her from Gerald for a while. After Gerald died, she was married to Stephen de Marais, the Norman constable of Cardigan Castle. The presentation in *Conquest* of how this sequence of events happened and how Nest coped with them is my imagining. Haith is based on Hait who is documented as the sheriff of Pembroke in the 1130 pipe roll (Green, 1986). Hait is presumed, from his name, to have been Flemish. It is my invention to make him a close friend of King Henry. According to Nest's grandson, Gerald of Wales, Hait was the father of one of Nest's sons (named by him as William). Haith's sister, Ida, and Nest's maid, Amelina, are my inventions. It is not certain when Nest or Hait died. I like to think that Nest lived to see her foster-sons and nephews Cadell, Maredudd, and Rhys take Llansteffan Castle in 1146 and each, in turn, become king of Deheubarth.

It took the Normans over two hundred years to conquer Wales, unlike the one day in which they conquered England in the Battle of Hastings. Huw Pryce has discussed the notion of

'Welsh' as either ethnically or geographically defined (2008). He has considered the idea of a post-national identity, the eventual merging of Welsh and Norman through intermarriage, and the beneficial role of the Norman and Flemish immigrants in twelfth century Wales. In the *Conquest* series, I looked at the coming of the Normans to Wales from Nest's Welsh point of view.

Gerda Lerner has pointed out that 'men have defined their experience of history and left women out' (cited in Richards, 2009, p. 158). In recent years, a number of historians (including Gwyneth Richards, Susan Johns, and Kari Maund) have set about the task of rescuing Welsh noblewomen from the footnotes of history (as Richards puts it) and to do more than simply 'add women and stir' (Erler & Kowalski, 2003, p. 9). Richards has argued that historiography has had a male bias 'which has hitherto rendered women more invisible than is warranted by the available sources' (2009, p. 24). These relatively invisible women in the early Middle Ages are the territory of my historical fiction.

Some of the major events referred to in this novel, such as the sinking of *The White Ship* and the drowning of King Henry I's heir, Prince William *Adelin*, are based on real events. The main contemporaneous accounts of the wreck of *The White Ship* were written by Orderic Vitalis and William of Malmesbury. Historians have been circumspect concerning the possibility of foul play in the wreck, as they must be, but I have taken fictional license and employed the suspicious circumstances surrounding the wreck in my story. Stephen de Blois (who later became king of England) did disembark from the ship in the company of William de Roumare. Two Tironian monks also disembarked. A butcher named Bertold of Rouen was the only recorded survivor. William de Pirou was listed on the list of victims of the wreck but, subsequently, appeared twice at court before disappearing under mysterious circumstances. Beyond that, the 'evidence' discovered by Haith in this novel is my invention and Breri is a figure of my imagination.

After the loss of his son and heir, King Henry's initial solution for the problem of the succession was that he and Queen Adelisa would have a son and, probably, that his illegitimate son Earl Robert of Gloucester would act as regent. When this hope faded, he focused on the aspiration that his daughter Maud would give him a grandson. Although the king's nephew Stephen de Blois had extensive holdings in England and was married to a descendent of the English kings, there is no evidence that Henry considered him as a potential heir. Instead, iconoclastically, King Henry I attempted to put a woman, his daughter Maud, on the English throne. He did not get his barons in England, Wales, and Normandy to swear to support her as regent, but rather to support her as his heir. If Maud's protracted bid to contest her cousin Stephen's usurpation of the throne had been successful, she would have been the first woman to rule England, Wales, and Normandy in her own right.

It was very tempting to write about Maud herself, but, in this book I wanted to stay focused on Nest and the Welsh events. There are a number of good fictional accounts of the extraordinary empress (see, for example, Elizabeth Chadwick's *Lady of the English*).

The Dolaucothi Roman goldmine is a real place. Medieval people were well aware of the Romans and their occupation of Britain. This was even more acute in the case of the Welsh who were descendants of the Britons who encountered the Romans, whereas the Anglo-Saxons arrived after the Roman withdrawal. Nevertheless, they were all surrounded by Roman ruins and the evidence of the occupation (walled Roman cities, villas, forts, Hadrian's Wall, aqueducts, Roman baths, Roman roads). Saint Alban was a Roman soldier, and Saint Alban's Abbey was renovated in King Henry's time, using remnants of Roman building materials. The Anglo-Saxons and Welsh mostly built in timber and it was only with the arrival of William the Conqueror and his sons that stone began to be used again in

Norman buildings in England and Wales.

Early medieval sources including the Welsh Latin text *History of the Britons*, Bede's *Ecclesiastical History of the English People*, the *Anglo-Saxon Chronicle*, and Gildas's *De Excidio et Conquestu Britanniae* make extensive reference to the Romans. Geoffrey of Monmouth's *History of the Kings of Briton*, which described the fantastical 'history' of King Arthur and referred to the Romans, was written around 1136. This text undoubtedly drew on earlier, oral versions of the stories that were in circulation. Early medieval nobility and clerics in England and Wales spoke Latin and read the Roman classics. Whilst Gruffudd ap Rhys and Gwenllian as Welsh royals would have received a classical education, Gruffudd's sons, perhaps, did not have such an advantage due to their father's impoverished circumstances in exile in Caeo. Nevertheless, they would have had information relayed to them by their parents and bards, and everyone was aware, from the Bible, the stories of saints, and the teachings of the Church, of the role of the Romans in Jesus's crucifixion and the subsequent Christian martyrdoms at the hands of the Romans. There were a number of medieval Welsh folktales and legends referring to the Romans (sometimes implying that they were an extinct race of giants), including the *Dream of Macsen*, based on a real Roman commander in Britain who was cast, in the story, as a Roman emperor. This story is referred to by Geoffrey of Monmouth and in *The Mabinogion*.

The crow that Haith operates in Chapter 13 was a real medieval engine of war. Jim Bradbury describes its operation at the siege of Ludlow in 1139, where Prince Henry of Scotland had to be rescued from 'its clutches': 'This was an engine consisting of a sort of large fishing rod on a balance, with a hook on the end, which caught hold of the prince'. Bradbury's source is a description of the siege by Henry of Huntingdon (1996, p. 66). Judith Green's *Henry I* makes reference to it (p. 185), but in use by Waleran's forces at Vatteville against the king. There are drawings that show the crow with a double grappling hook on the end, being used to break down a castle wall. It may have derived from a Roman marine engine of war known as the *corvus*.

England and Wales experienced thirty-five years of peace and prosperity during the reign of King Henry I. The king had to deal with sporadic rebellions in Normandy, especially after the death of his heir and towards the end of his life. However, after his death, there was constant warfare in England, Wales, and Normandy during the reign of King Stephen as he struggled against his cousin, Empress Maud, and her supporters. Some historians have dubbed Stephen's reign 'The Anarchy', whilst others have argued that it was not as anarchic as other commentators have claimed. Certainly, Stephen lost significant parts of the kingdom that King Henry I had ruled including Normandy and large parts of Wales. The civil war between Stephen and Maud went on for nine years.

Gwenllian ferch Gruffudd ap Cynan, Nest's sister-in-law, did lead a Welsh contingent into battle against the Normans at Kidwelly in 1136 and was defeated and beheaded. Andrew Breeze has argued that Gwenllian was the author of the 'Four Branches of the Mabinogi'. The stories do appear to map loosely onto geographies and histories in Deheubarth. Other scholars have not agreed with Breeze's hypothesis. See Matthew Francis's *The Mabinogi* for a beautiful poetic interpretation of the stories that may have been written by Gwenllian.

There is no record of who murdered Gwenllian's husband and Nest's brother Gruffudd ap Rhys in 1137. In 1143, Gruffudd's son Anarawd was murdered by a band of Cadwaladr's men and Cadwaladr, who aspired to rule Ceredigion, was exiled by his brother, Owain.

Nest's nephews, Cadell, Maredudd, and Rhys, seized a number of castles from the Normans in 1146, including Llansteffan. In 1149 Cadwaladr was driven out of Ceredigion, but that was not the end of his trouble-making. In 1151 Cadell was ambushed near Tenby and left for dead. Cadwaladr may have been to blame again on this occasion. Cadell's injuries were so severe that his brothers Maredudd and Rhys had to assume rule of Deheubarth. In 1152 Cadwaladr was exiled to England by his brother Owain and moved to the court of Earl Ranulf de Gernon of Chester. Cadell, meanwhile, went on pilgrimage to Rome in 1153.

Amongst the real-life Normans who appear in this story, Waleran de Meulan went on pilgrimage to Compostella in 1144 and accompanied the king of France on crusade in 1146. Returning from crusade, Waleran was shipwrecked near the mouth of the Rhône, but survived. During the civil war between King Stephen and Empress Maud, Ranulf de Gernon changed sides on several occasions and was not trusted by either.

Geoffrey d'Anjou was recognised as duke of Normandy in 1144. He succeeded in gaining papal favour (no doubt through substantial bribes) for his son's bid for the English throne in 1147. In 1148 Maud gave up the struggle for England to her son, Henry FitzEmpress, and returned to Normandy permanently.

King Louis and his queen, Eleanor of Aquitaine, returned from crusade in 1149 when Eleanor made an unsuccessful attempt to have her marriage to the French king annulled. Geoffrey d'Anjou and Henry FitzEmpress were in Paris successfully lobbying Louis to accept Henry as duke of Normandy and Henry met Eleanor, for the first time, during this visit. In 1150 Henry FitzEmpress became duke of Normandy at the age of seventeen, and soon after, Geoffrey d'Anjou died and Henry also became count of Anjou. On 21 March 1152 Eleanor's marriage to Louis, which had produced no male heirs, was finally annulled, and on the 18 May Henry FitzEmpress and Eleanor of Aquitaine were married in Poitiers Cathedral. Eleanor was ten years older than Henry. The marriage enabled Henry to add the rich domain of Aquitaine to his extensive territory.

Civil war between the forces of King Stephen and Henry FitzEmpress continued in a desultory fashion. In 1152 the archbishop of Canterbury refused Stephen's request to anoint his son Eustace as junior king. His queen, Matilda of Boulougne, died in that year. 1153 was a bad year for King Stephen. He was fifty-seven years old and was wounded three times; his son Eustace died suddenly and his other son, William, broke his thigh in a riding accident. Many parts of England had been devasted by years of civil war and even the hyper-aggressive Norman barons wearied of the conflict. In November 1153, at Winchester, King Stephen and Henry FitzEmpress agreed that Henry would become king on Stephen's death and this was ratified in a charter that Stephen issued at Westminster in December.

In 1153, whilst Ranulf de Gernon was a guest at the house of William Peverel the Younger, his host attempted to kill him with poisoned wine. Three of his men, who had drunk the wine, died, while Ranulf suffered agonising pain. Ranulf succumbed to the poison on 16 December 1153. Some historians have speculated that Peverel and Ranulf's wife Matilda (the daughter of Nest's foster-sister Mabel in this novel) were lovers and that she was also implicated in the murder.

King Stephen died on 25 October 1154 and Henry and Eleanor were crowned king and queen of England on 19 December 1154. Henry's mother, Empress Maud, continued to give him advice throughout her long life and died in Normandy in 1167. Despite the lack of male heirs resulting from Eleanor's previous marriage to the French king, she and King Henry II had five sons and three daughters.

Nest's youngest nephew, Rhys ap Gruffudd regained most of the kingdom of Deheubarth and Ceredigion from the Normans and was one of the most successful and powerful Welsh princes in the late twelfth century. Cadwaladr was reinstated as a Prince of Wales in Gwynedd in 1157 by King Henry II. In 1158 Rhys had to do homage to King Henry II and when Henry invaded Deheubarth in 1163 Rhys was stripped of his lands and briefly imprisoned. In 1165, Rhys made an alliance with King Owain of Gwynedd. King Henry II's second invasion of Wales failed and Rhys was able to take back his kingdom. He made a major assault on Cardigan and captured the castellan who was Nest's son Robert FitzStephen, the son of Stephen de Marais, and Rhys's cousin. After the death of King Owain of Gwynedd in 1170, Rhys was the dominant power in Wales. Rhys took a lesson from Cadwaladr and adopted Norman clothes and integrated with his Norman neighbours. Several of his children were married to Normans. Cadwaladr died in 1172. After a very long illness, Cadell died in 1175 at Strata Florida Abbey, which was established by his brother Rhys. Rhys made peace with King Henry II and ruled Deheubarth until his death in 1197. He was buried at Saint Davids Cathedral.

Today, you can visit many of the castle sites that featured in Nest's story including Pembroke, Carew, Cilgerran, Carmarthen, Cardigan, Kidwelly, Dinefwr, and Cardiff. It is not known where Nest ferch Rhys is buried but the spectacular ruin of Llansteffan Castle on a headland overlooking the triple river estuary of Carmarthen Bay, which first inspired me to write the *Conquest* novels, seems a fitting memorial to her extraordinary life.

Selected Bibliography

The epigraph for Part One is an extract from Dafydd ap Gwilym's poem, 'Yr Wylan' ('To the Seagull'), which was written in the mid-fourteenth century and is, therefore, anachronistic in this story of the twelfth century. The translation is by Robert Gurney (1969, p. 130).

Gwenllian's tale in Chapter 10 is a paraphrase of 'The First Branch of the Mabinogi' from *The Mabinogion* (2007).

The epigraph for Part Two is from Saint Augustine's *Sermons on New Testament Lessons* (Sermon 1, verse 23).

Haith's poet who writes that 'a jewel grows pale on you and a crown does not shine' in Chapter 18 is Henry of Huntingdon, cited in Weir, 2011, p. 188.

The translated extract of a poem by Hermann of Reichenau in Chapter 22 is from Peter Dronke's book on the medieval lyric (1996, p. 45).

The image of a renegade nun kissing the defleshed skeleton of her lover in Chapter 25 is a quotation from a letter written by Anselm, archbishop of Canterbury to Gunhild of Wessex, the daughter of King Harold, who left Wilton Abbey to live out of wedlock with Alan Rufus, Lord of Richmond (Southern, 1963, cited in Weir, 2017, p. 111).

The epigraph for Part Three, lamenting the loss of King Henry I, is from Henry of Huntingdon's *Historia Anglorum* and is available in the *Medieval Sourcebook*.

Several phrases here and there have been lifted from Matilda of Scotland's lively correspondence with Archbishop Anselm, quoted in Weir, 2017.

Some of Amelina's adages come from *The Physicians of Myddvai*. Breri's songs are extracts from the Welsh poetry of the Fairly Early Poets (as they are known), translated by the Celtic Literature Collective and derived from *The Black Book of Carmarthen*, *The Book of Taliesin*, *The Red Book of Hergest* and the *Hendregadredd Manuscript*, which are digitised and available online through the National Library of Wales and the Bodleian Library, Oxford and available in translation in the *Celtic Literature Collective*.

Primary Sources

Medieval manuscripts including *The Black Book of Carmarthen*, *The Book of Taliesin*, and the *Hendregadredd Manuscript*, National Library of Wales, https://www.library.wales/discover/digital-gallery/manuscripts/the-middle-ages/.

The Anglo-Saxon Chronicle. Written ninth–twelfth century. Michael Swanton transl. (2000) London: Phoenix Press.

Brut y Tywysogion (Chronicle of the Princes). Written 681–1282. Thomas Jones transl. (1953) Caerdydd: Gwasg Prifysgol Cymru.

Celtic Literature Collective, http://www.maryjones.us/ctexts/clyweid.html

Epistolae: Medieval Women's Latin Letters. Joan Ferrante transl. (2014). Available online: https://epistolae.ctl.columbia.edu.

The Mabinogion. Written c. 1060–1120. Davies, Sioned, transl. (2007) Oxford: Oxford University Press. (And see Matthew Francis below.)

Medieval Sourcebook, https://sourcebooks.fordham.edu/sbook.asp

The Physicians of Myddvai, medical advice dating from the thirteenth century, some of which appeared in the MS *The Red*

Book of Hergest. Collected and published by John Pughe in 1861.

The Red Book of Hergest, https://digital.bodleian.ox.ac.uk.

FitzStephen, William, *Norman London.* Written around 1183. Essay by Sir Frank Stenton & Introduction by F. Donald Logan (1990) New York: Italica Press.

Gerald of Wales, *The Itinerary Through Wales and the Description of Wales.* Written 1191 and 1194. Lewis Thorpe, transl. (1978), Harmondsworth: Penguin.

Henry of Huntingdon, *Historia Anglorum*, c. 1154. Diana Greenway, ed. & transl. (1996) *A History of the English People 1000-1154*, Oxford Medieval Texts, Oxford: Clarendon Press.

Henry of Huntingdon, *The Chronicle of Henry of Huntingdon.* Thomas Forester, transl. (1853/1876) London: Henry G. Bohn; London: George Bell and Sons, 1876, pp. 400-409; reprinted in Archibald R. Lewis, ed. (1970) *The High Middle Ages, 814-1300*, Englewood Cliffs; NJ: Prentice-Hall. Available online: *Medieval Sourcebook*, https://sourcebooks.fordham.edu/source/henry-hunt1.asp.

Orderic Vitalis, *Historia Ecclesiastica.* Written 1123–1141. Marjorie Chibnall, ed. & transl. (1969–1980) *The Ecclesiastical History of Orderic Vitalis*, Oxford Medieval Texts, 6 vol. Oxford: Clarendon Press.

William of Malmesbury, *Gesta Regum Anglorum.* Written 1125–1142. R.A.B. Mynors, R.M. Thomson, M. Winterbottom, eds. & transl. (1998–1999) *The History of the English Kings*, Oxford Medieval Texts, 2 vols., Oxford: Clarendon Press.

Secondary Sources

Dictionary of Welsh Biography, https://biography.wales.

Bradbury, Jim (1996) *Stephen and Matilda: The Civil War of 1139–53*, Stroud: Sutton.

Breeze, Andrew (2009) *The Origins of the Four Branches of the Mabinogi*, Leominster: Gracewing.

Cawley, Charles (2014) *Medieval Lands*, http://fmg.ac/Projects/MedLands/Search.htm.

Chibnall, Marjorie (1993) *The Empress Matilda: Queen Consort, Queen Mother and the Lady of the English*. London: Wiley-Blackwell.

Crouch, David (2008) *The Beaumont Twins: The Roots and Branches of Power in the Twelfth Century*, Cambridge: Cambridge University Press.

Dronke, Peter (1996) *The Medieval Lyric*, Woodbridge: D.S. Brewer.

Erler, Mary & Kowaleski, Maryanne, eds. (2003) *Gendering the Master Narrative: Women and Power in the Middle Ages*, London: Cornell Press.

Francis, Matthew (2017) *The Mabinogi*, London: Faber & Faber.

Green, Judith A. (2009) *Henry I King of England and Duke of Normandy*, Cambridge: Cambridge University Press.

Green, Judith A. (1986) *The Government of England under Henry I*, Cambridge: Cambridge University Press.

Gurney, Robert, ed. (1969) *Bardic Heritage*, London: Chatto & Windus.

Hingst, Amanda Jane (2009) *The Written World: Past and Place in the Work of Orderic Vitalis*, Notre Dame, Indiana: University of Indiana Press.

Hollister, C. Warren (2001) *Henry I*, New Haven/London: Yale University Press.

John, Susan (1995) 'The wives and widows of the Earl of Chester 1100–1252', *Haskins Journal*, 7, pp. 117–132.

Kealey, Edward J. (1972) *Roger of Salisbury: Viceroy of England*, Berkeley: University of California Press.

Lacey, Robert (2003) *Great Tales from English History*, vol. 1, London: Little, Brown.

McDougall, Sara (2017) *Royal Bastards: The Birth of Illegitimacy*, Oxford: Oxford University Press.

Pryce, Huw (2008) 'The Normans in Welsh History', *Anglo-Norman Studies*, vol. 30, pp. 1–18.

Richards, Gwyneth (2009) *Welsh Noblewomen in the 13th Century*, Lewiston, N.Y.: Edwin Mellen Press.

Truax, J. A. (2009) 'All roads lead to Chartres: The House of Blois, the Papacy, and the Anglo-Norman succession of 1135', *Anglo-Norman Studies*, vol. 30, pp. 118–134.

Turvey, Roger (2013) *Owain Gwynedd: Prince of the Welsh*, Talybont, Ceredigion: Y Lolfa.

Ward, J. C. (1988) 'Royal service and reward: The Clare family and the crown, 1066–1154', *Anglo-Norman Studies*, vol. 11, p. 261–278.

Weir, Alison (2017) *Queens of the Conquest: England's Medieval Queens 1066-1167*, London: Vintage.

See my website, traceywarrwriting.com, for posts and further information on my research.

Acknowledgements

I lived for several years in Pembrokeshire near many of the Welsh and Norman castles and places mentioned in the *Conquest* series. Walks around the Carmarthen Bay estuary with its triple river estuary and the ruins of Llansteffan Castle looming on the cliff-top were a major inspiration for these novels. I am very grateful to Literature Wales for awarding me a Writer's Bursary to work on the *Conquest* series.

Thanks to Bob Smillie, my muse who keeps me company through the ups and downs of writing and life in general. I am very grateful to my daughter Lola Rose for her work on my website and social media and for being wonderful her. She is an inspiration when writing about strong women. Countless thanks to all my supportive family and friends.

I am grateful to my writing buddies who have been such good critical friends, especially Jack Turley, Tim Smith, Ann Hebert, Denise Gibbs, Anita Goodfellow and Madeleine Hall. I am very grateful to Richard Willis, the founder of Impress Books, who was my first editor and encourager. Thank you also to Sophie Evans, who worked as an intern with me. I'm grateful to Jeff Collyer and the team at Impress Books and Untold Publishing.

And finally, immense thanks to the readers of my books. It is always a great pleasure to hear about other people's experiences of living through the world of a book.